BROTHER WOLF

BROTHER WOLF

a novel by
ELEANOR
BOURG
NICHOLSON

CHRISM
PRESS

This is a work of fiction. All characters and events portrayed in this novel are
either fictitious or used fictitiously.

BROTHER WOLF

Cover artwork by Matthew Alderman
Cover design by Rhonda Ortiz

Chrism Press, a division of WhiteFire Publishing
13607 Bedford Rd NE
Cumberland, MD 21502

ISBN:
978-1-941720-56-1 (print)
978-1-941720-57-8 (digital)

For my husband, who found my vampire theories wanting.

For my baby brother, who isn't a wolf but breeds howlers.

For my mother, who remains my first and most dedicated reader.

Chapter 1

O, wonder!
How many goodly creatures are there here!
How beauteous mankind is! O brave new world,
That has such people in't!

— William Shakespeare, *The Tempest*

"Isabel, for mercy's sake, let this awkwardness pass."

The man's voice, strong and exasperated, intruded into my consciousness, interrupting the soothing, arrhythmic break of waves against the side of the ship. I glanced up from where I had been gazing abstractedly into the ocean and looked around. At first it seemed that I was still alone on deck on a cold, clear morning. Perhaps I had imagined the voices. I dismissed the thought. The narrative force of my imagination, powerful though it was, did not often proclaim itself audibly, and I *had* heard the words. I looked again.

The brightness of the sky struck the front of the ship. I forced myself to peer into the light, and after a moment of blindness passed, I saw the man and the woman.

They were set against the scenic backdrop of a calm sea and morning sky with its stratified color, tinged in dusky red tones that made sailors mutter darkly under their breath. Little wonder that the pair caught my attention: a handsome couple framed in silhouette against the dawning light. The light played across their features, revealing the handsome, bronzed, smooth-shaved face of the man, with hints of red and gold dancing in his curly hair. His voice pronounced the richest variety of the King's English, but his appearance cried forth the Viking and the Celt. Beside him, the huge black eyes, ink-black hair, slender form, and dramatic features of the woman. A gypsy or a Jewess witch ripe for burning, I thought.

"I am sorry that you feel there is awkwardness," the woman—Isabel—replied. "To speak truthfully, I was not attending."

Her tone exploded my initial, rapid reading of the scene. I had imagined them tensely opposed, on the brink of either a passionate embrace or a bitter remonstrance, which in novels were equally indicative of romantic attachment. But, though the man still gazed at her in a manner readily explicable as expressing romantic intent, her voice expressed nothing more than that she *had* been thinking something different.

The man laughed—a deep, comforting sort of laugh. "Isabel, you truly have not changed."

She frowned, as if taking this comment under solemn consideration. "I rather trusted that I *had* changed. There are many things… These last ten years. It is sometimes difficult to know what of it was real."

"Is that what you were thinking of?"

"In part, yes. And I was, I fear, wasting energy in petty regret."

"Regret?" There was no mistaking the hopefulness in his voice.

Could it be that she deliberately misunderstood him? "Yes, regret. This situation should not have arisen. I know it is wrong of me, but I can't help wishing that I had done it myself, without entangling anyone else. Then I could have been sure we had done it rightly to begin with. No loose ends. Nothing left undone."

"From what I understand of it"—his voice was stern and, I thought, scandalized—"you did it quite thoroughly."

"Not thoroughly enough," Isabel insisted. "There must have been something wrong. Something to cause this new disquiet. Perhaps the dismemberment and scattering were improperly executed. We did not oversee that part. Jean-Claude felt it was somehow indelicate."

"Indeed," her companion said dryly.

"Jean-Claude has always had that squeamish strain."

"Perhaps not *always*. There have been times—"

"That was the mistake. I should have kept him well out of this. The removal of the head seems particularly to have—"

"Isabel, is this helpful?"

"True. Regret can serve no purpose now. A temptation—and one from a source we recognize. And yet…I wonder…"

The man waited, but she did not finish her statement. Without thinking, I inched closer. Dismembered heads certainly brought piquancy to this intriguing scene, elevating it beyond the merely romantic.

If I hoped to hear more, I was, for a moment, disappointed. They once again stood in silence. The woman must have been entertaining a sort of argument in her mind, for she tossed her head as if to dismiss some intrusive thought, like a horse might flick its tail to dissuade a fly.

The man marked it too. "Isabel, is there anything—anything you have not told me?"

"Told you?"

"Anything that leads you to think that this is more than I have supposed?"

"Oh, no," she said quickly—too quickly. I hoped he doubted her because I certainly did.

He watched her a moment. "By heaven, I wish you were well out of it."

"Perhaps you have forgotten, Sir Simon. It was you who came and fetched me."

"That is so," the man admitted, "but was it necessary?"

"It doesn't work that way. I could not have told you what had happened, but only that something like it had happened or was going to happen. The lot of Cassandra."

"You're a veritable sphynx, as usual." He shook his head. "I admit it freely—I cannot keep pace with you in riddles, nor can I match you in regrets."

She sighed and wrapped her cloak more tightly around her. "Probably not. But, my friend, it is far easier to dissect what has been than to look forward with dread to what is coming."

"Your choice of words!"

"There isn't much to be done except talk about it. Nothing to be done until… And what an impossible task is before us!"

"All will be well."

"That depends entirely on what you mean by 'all,' Simon Gwynne. Right now, I would settle for effective and lasting patricide and leave the rest to God."

Yet again, a thrilling note. Patricide! One of the foundational archetypes of every mythology.

Her noble companion was less thrilled. In fact, I thought he sounded rather irritated. "Isabel, sometimes I wonder if you recall why we are doing what we are doing."

If he were irritated, he seemed immediately to regret it. Heroic figures aren't prone to biting their tongues, but he might have done so.

She was silent for a moment. Then she said softly, "No. No, I haven't. And I am unlikely to forget."

"Isabel…"

"Do you know the history of that peculiar practice? Look at that man there—the boatswain, I think. What do you suppose he is doing?"

Instead of replying to this unusual declaration or attending to the boatswain, the man—who must have needed some outlet for his annoyance—turned, fixed his eyes on me, and addressed me with a curt: "Pardon me, madam. May we assist you in some way?"

I had become so fascinated by their bizarre exchange that I had forgotten myself and was standing but a few paces away, openly staring. Conscious of the flush rushing to my cheeks and across my nose, I gasped, "Oh…no. Thank you. I am quite well. Very well, in fact. Yes, thank you."

"I am delighted to hear it," replied my tormentor in a tone which expressed the opposite. "We will then bid you a good morning."

"Y-yes, of course. G-good evening. I mean, good morning."

My face still hot, I bowed and rushed up the deck. Behind my retreating back, the woman chastised him. "Was that imperious tone entirely necessary? You flustered that poor young woman."

"Isabel, I have no patience with frumpy, busybody old maids."

"You silly man, she's nearly a child! And probably quite charming!"

This was doubly unendurable! To be critiqued by an ill-natured, arrogant stranger and patronized with well-meant but manufactured compliments by his companion—it was too much! My indignation mounting, I stepped back to return and defend myself. The turn was ill-judged. I was rounding the bend to port, and the too-precipitate countermovement unsettled my balance. I stumbled and fell against the railing. Before I had a moment to hope that no one had witnessed this fresh display of grace and poise, I was lifted back to my feet by a pair of wiry, muscular arms.

I looked up to mutter my thanks and, to my surprise, beheld neither a passenger nor a member of the crew. My young rescuer had a strong air of the vagabond about him, from his swarthy face to his wiry frame attired in the tattered relics of what once must have been gentleman's dinner clothes. He raised a dirty black newspaper-boy cap from his head, liberating a wild mass of black curls. He grinned, displaying a wide, perfect array of shining white teeth. Pursing his lips, he emitted a slow, low, owl-like cry.

"Ooooooo-huu!"

I opened my mouth to speak, but he held one long-nailed finger to his lips in a universal signal for silence and disappeared back around the corner whence I had come.

Astonished, I stood frozen for several seconds then, belatedly, hurried after him. The deck was empty. My rescuer had vanished.

For some time, I leaned against the railing and considered all that had occurred. Then I felt a smile of delight dancing at the corners of my mouth.

"Really, Athene Howard," I said aloud to myself (a tiresome habit, my father has assured me more than once), "this ship is quite the most exciting and unusual place you have ever been."

Here was mystery! Here was the unknown! It was reminiscent of my father's work—how many mythologies were built upon a strange preoccupation with patricide!—but here was no dead text to be pored over by a scholarly recluse. They were not lunatics either; some of my father's close colleagues were inclined to spend their time studying such unpromising subjects. Attractive, dynamic, and interesting. It was as good as any play, and perhaps I could witness the second act.

Before I could pursue such a delight, or even determine how it should best be pursued, my glance fell on the reproachful face of my watch. My father's papers needed my attention. I reluctantly turned in response to duty's call.

As I made my way back to Father's cabin, I briefly entertained the idea of speaking to him of what I had seen and heard. Perhaps my dramatic description would shake him from his labors to assist me in analyzing this new cast of characters. After all, "Charles Howard knows many things." Even Doctor Hennessey admitted it at that celebrated debate on the spirituality of mythological dream theory, which had brought us to America in the first place. "It would be foolish for any," that red-faced, angrily virtuous scholar had said, "to question the extensive knowledge of my distinguished friend on many, many subjects."

Poor Doctor Hennessey. He had striven so hard to label my father an ineffectual pantologist, to no avail. My father's vast knowledgeability and cultivated, impersonal academic air had once again carried the day. My father's ability to speak at length without actually saying anything had always fascinated me. I refused to investigate this peculiar talent of his, however, for to do so would be to shatter the delicate illusion which he and I peacefully inhabited together.

We were returning on the steamship *Corinthian* after a stay of five weeks in various American cities where Father had delivered a series of lectures about the symbolic nature of the selective unconscious. I had spent those weeks in happy wanderings. I had prepared his papers beforehand, collating his ever-wandering thoughts to support formal presentation before an audience and leaving the rest to the slow dominance of his manner. Let him win his wars of attrition. I, for a time, was free to explore.

My father had liberal notions of the restraint propriety should place upon his daughter. Perhaps if I had been blessed with a more striking physiognomy or a strong libertine inclination this would have been ill-fated, but such as it was, I had attained the respectable age of twenty-three without experience of harassment by either a chaperone or the lascivious attentions of strange men. The only men who paid me any notice were my father's middle-aged or elderly counterparts, and then only when they were in an advanced state of drunken academic reverie. On occasion my name conjured for some sodden scholar confused notions of lusty mythological entanglements, but I could easily extract myself from that sort of situation. Moreover, since my father was not inclined toward drunkenness or public misconduct, he did not frequently burden himself with that sort of company. My father preferred his vices private and perfunctory. An orgy would have been far too disruptive and far too humanly interesting.

On this trip, no one had bothered with me at all, and I had reciprocated by bothering with no one except myself. I attended a few academic dinners in Father's company. Three or four times he was invited to dine with colleagues while I was not, likely because his colleagues were as unaware of my existence as he often was. On these evenings I devoted myself to organizational labors until an advanced hour of the night, when I retreated to my private room and, ensconced in a large armchair before a self-indulgent fire, I devoured the novels I had found in the shops near our modest boarding house in Greenwich Village. Once I went in secret to the theater to see a tempestuous musical farce. I had convinced myself I could lie and tell my father it had been a performance of *Antigone*. I might have spared myself the bother of concocting this transparent falsehood, since my father did not ask me where I had been and might even have failed to notice that I had been away.

I explored every museum and even glanced into a few churches, considering their various forms of architecture and admiring the heavy darkness in one or two of them. A baroque Bavarian Gothic church in Manhattan was my favorite—a place haunted by somber-faced men in white. My father might have had greater empathy with me in this than he would have had he known of my lapses into popular fiction. As he graciously noted in a news interview in the *London Daily Chronicle* some years ago ("An Expert Reflects on *The Golden Bough*"), he bears no antipathy to his old religion, however far he has advanced from his early, blind belief in it. In fact, if I hadn't seen documents that attested to the fact, I never would have believed he had once been a Papist priest, albeit briefly.

"Charles Howard is an archetype of tolerance," as Doctor Hennessey put it sternly at the conclusion of that memorable debate. It was the one rude comment he permitted himself as he acknowledged defeat. He was admirably restrained, I thought, because everyone knew how much he resented the sponsorship my father's work had always received from the Lauritz Aldebrand Estate.

Now Father's lectures were finished, and we were aboard our steamship, one day of our transatlantic passage already complete. Our ship was snug and our places secured for a reasonable price—the income of the faculty of the Université de Paris, even for a member of the Académie des Sciences Réligieuses and with the additional generosity of the Estate, did not permit reckless squandering for the sake of traveling on one of the regal ocean liners. Though I have not the experience of a first-class cabin on the Cunard line, I thought our accommodation and our liberty of movement throughout the ship perfectly pleasing regardless of our second-class status. For the moment, my father had no opinion whatsoever. He spent most of his time in his cabin poring over notes or reading one of the many books procured throughout his tour of New England universities.

That was how I found him. I knocked at his cabin door, recited to myself the opening lines of Horace's *Odes* by way of measuring a self-prescribed length of time, and knocked again. Then I entered, permitting the door to close loudly behind me.

He contracted his brow into a mild frown, but the noise provoked no further recognition.

My father was probably a well-looking man in his youth. He was tall and slender, but the stately bearing that I am sure he once possessed had become cramped and wizened from long hours bent over his books. His mane of white hair he wore longer than was fashionable and swept to the side, with an air of bygone romance in its wisps and more than a hint of absentmindedness. When his attention focused, his features—the long, thin nose, the pointy chin, and the deep set of his light-gray eyes—became striking. The only thing that roused him was when he had an academic opponent at his mercy. Then my father became gleeful, energetic, and singularly cruel. He had delighted in the obliteration of poor, old-fashioned Doctor Hennessey.

Such moments were rare. His habitual attitude was that of universal blindness save for the one precise point on which his attention was at that moment fixed. This morning was no exception. I cleared my throat four times before he looked up, blinking.

"Athene," he said, probably identifying me for his own benefit.

I acknowledged that I was indeed the child of his bosom.

He sighed. My levity of mind was something over which my father pretended to grieve. "What is it, girl? I'm in the middle of a complex problem."

"If it is the footnote issue we discussed this morning, I already corrected it. My notes are on that page right there at your elbow, Father."

After this uncharacteristically direct attack, I launched without preamble into a recitation of the morning's adventures, describing the man and the woman I had seen, though not mentioning the strange boy on deck. I had no desire to betray the presence of a stowaway, though I little feared my father would be roused to mention it to anyone.

"And *I* think," I said as I finished my tale, "there is some sort of thrilling mystery to explore."

He murmured a mild, "Indeed, Athene?" Then he returned his wandering attention back to his work.

I well recognized this impasse. My childhood was built upon it. In my youth, while brooding over one such frustrating paternal interview, I overcame years of disappointment and wounded childish affection when I realized that my father probably could not help this lack of enthusiasm. It was something wrong in his glands or some such irreversible decree of heredity. Thus freed of the burden of resentment, I came to consider these opportunities of rousing him from his work as filial duty. Disruption by "The Interruption"—the pet name with which I am sure he christened me in his mind—was, on most days, his only source of exercise. Consequently, I knew when the siege must be temporarily lifted.

I settled myself at a table by the tiny porthole and began correcting his papers. Usually, my critical editing and organization of his notes proved absorbing enough. He made such a lamentable mess of his notes that making sense of them was like unraveling a complicated mystery. That day, however, my attention was soon distracted by other matters.

I thought of my father's mercifully short-lived marriage. For a few moments I watched his head bob and sway with the movements of his pen and wondered if he had ever entertained high visions of romance in his youth. The selection of my name seemed an indication of some such jejune enthusiasm. He sought profound spiritual experience in ancient myth and perhaps tacitly hoped that this search would beget Wisdom personified—thus he named his daughter for the goddess Athene. When he found that I did not spring fully formed from his head into precocious cognition, he had retreated further into a labyrinthine cave of ancient texts and neophilosophical lampooning of them, and, to the best of his considerable abilities, forgot about me. Even when I, through assiduous study and practice, had trained myself into usefulness as a stenographer and secretary, he was inclined to sigh, comment on the unintelligibility of my shorthand, look fretfully at "The Interruption," and descend once more beneath the piles of his disheveled papers.

Thus, in addition to shorthand and other useful skills, I had learned strategy. I knew I must await some outside prompt or assistance in prizing my father from his papers. To pass the time, I rifled through my bag, left in an unobtrusive corner, and produced a stack of notebooks. I selected a fresh one and delighted for a moment in its pristine pages. Then I set myself to making a rapid, shorthand account of the scene I had witnessed.

My meager notes completed, I tried my hand next at a sketch of the intriguing pair I had met on the deck. I half dreamed that, given a sudden and unexpected inspiration of genius, my sketch might capture my father's attention and draw him into fascinated consideration of the mystery I felt sure lingered somewhere aboard ship. But even as my pencil assaulted the page, I was forced to chuckle over my childish ambition. For this drawing to capture my father's attention, it would require a supernatural endowment of the talent I utterly lacked. I added a few disembodied heads floating above them and sat back to evaluate the result. Finding that the addition looked more like balloons than like heads, I erased the figures and abandoned my artistic endeavors.

The noise of my eraser provoked an irritated "hush!" from my father. I took advantage of this near attention to demand, apropos of nothing, "Why do you carry Gosse with you? He has nothing to do with mythology and dream."

He looked up from his notes and blinked away his deep analysis of Smith's work on the Chaldaean Account. "The myth of origin,

Athene. The desire for purpose rooted in the imagined creative power of the gods." His gaze returned like a homing pigeon to his page.

"Is there a connection," I persisted, "between that myth of origin and Christian liturgical observances in springtime?"

That did it. The day before, as we hurried to reach the dock and board our ship, we had been delayed because of an Easter-related procession taking place in front of St. Patrick's Cathedral. My father had held forth on this particular point for three quarters of an hour, ceasing only when the logistics of transferring his innumerable trunks and bags of books and notes flustered him out of the harangue.

"The universality of myth," Father now began in his most sonorous tones, "has long been stifled by the attempts of Christianity to consecrate what is primal in man and claim it as an expression of divinizing significance. Thus, throughout history we may see incessant papal efforts to suppress and appropriate the feasts of the gods."

I wished I had thought to procure an apple or some other sustaining snack to support me through this scholarly siege. The day was advancing, and we must be overdue for a meal. "I wonder what happens when the gods want their feasts back."

My father looked at me over his glasses, grunted, and returned to concentrated silence.

Before I could formulate a new attack, a loud bell rang in the distance.

"That's the dinner bell," I said. "Did you hear it, Father? *Father!*"

"I know how hungry you are, Athene," he said without looking up, pretending to fatherly authority. "I wouldn't keep you from your supper."

Resolve battled against base appetite. Resolve won. Hoping he could not hear the contradictory noises generating from my disgruntled stomach, I declared, "I shall wait for you, Father."

"Really, Athene. There's no need. I would not have you wait on my account."

"I don't mind." I smiled and crossed my arms to demonstrate that I was determined to outwait him. He eyed me over his glasses, irritation beginning to hint at the corners of his eyes. It was enough attention to go on with. "So," I persisted, "what *do* you think of those people, sir? Do you suppose them to be a tragic romantic pair thrust together yet kept apart by cruel Fate? All that wonderfully Greek material of dismemberment too. Rather piquant, don't you think?"

That was too much, even for my father. "Come, girl. We will go to our meal."

I rose, but hunger had stirred up a war of frustrations within me. I bore with ill grace but without surprise the fact that my father would dismiss this interesting new topic. All the best and most exciting myths were the ones he cared least about. While I thrilled to the dramatic narrative style of the Greeks, he plodded through the preachy, uninspiring passages of more ancient texts. That he had appetites, I knew. All men did, I told myself with worldly wisdom. These he satisfied routinely and unemotionally far from my eyes. There would be no wicked stepmothers in my future. Nothing so interesting would ever happen to me.

At the same time, I *was* hungry.

Further, a new thought had emerged—one to banish any hint of sullenness. Those fascinating and hopefully mysterious people must require food too.

"Athene," sighed my long-suffering father, "do hurry up."

"Yes, Father," I said cheerfully and without even the appearance of meekness.

CHAPTER 2

The land circled by the sea, where once the great king of the gods
showered upon the city snowflakes of gold; in the day when the
skilled hand of Hephaistos wrought with his craft the axe, bronze-
bladed, whence from the cleft summit of her father's brow Athene
sprang aloft, and pealed the broad sky her clarion cry of war. And
Ouranos trembled to hear, and Mother Gaia.

— Pindar, Olympian Ode 7

MY FATHER, WHO IS NOT AT ALL A SOCIAL CREATURE EXCEPT AMONG
the fourteen other men in the world who care about his theories,
accepted the guidance of the head steward (a black-haired man of
French descent, pomade, and Swedish scent) to a small and isolated
table. He proceeded to eat a hearty supper of corn and crab soup,
over-salted biscuits, greasy halibut, and a salad of bitter greens, all
accompanied by several glasses of what he condescended to identify
as a fine white wine.

I ate my food quickly and without much attention. I was too
focused on finding my quarry. For some time, it seemed that I would
be disappointed. I was so disgruntled at this that I was on the verge of
saying something for the sole purpose of aggravating my father when
the tall, disapproving man and his dark-haired companion entered.

I began to eat more slowly.

This change in speed was marked enough to capture even my
father's attention. "I still have work to do this evening, Athene."

"Do you, Father?" I responded brightly, determined to mistake
his meaning. "How glum for you. I'm sure you would like my help.
I'll come and attend to things while you study."

That silenced him, as I knew it would. He turned to stare off into wounded unconsciousness—imagining, I have no doubt, what infinitesimal point of study would next bear the brunt of his suffocating contemplation—and I watched the progress of that fascinating couple across the dining room. I was not accustomed to prayer but had a superstitious investment in the power of will cribbed from cursory readings of some books and papers Father cherished. If spontaneous incantation could do aught, I would make the attempt.

"Come over here," I commanded under my breath. "Come over here. Come over…"

My father looked up. "Athene? What *are* you doing, girl?"

"Nothing, Father. Nothing." I continued to stare at the man and woman. The steward was persuading them across the room, and they appeared to be moving in our direction.

My father adopted a sad, tired note in his voice. "That little point of Norton's. It will take me some time to settle."

I refused to take the hint. "How exhausting for you." I watched the couple threading their way across the room in the steward's wake.

"Well, Athene, I know you're tired…"

I turned to him, widening my eyes and smiling my most innocent smile. "Why, no, Father. I'm not tired at all."

For a fraction of a second, he narrowed his own eyes at me. I relented. He was an awful bore and had never treated me with anything like affection, but, I reminded myself, it must be a lonely existence among so many books, especially when burdened with a tedious, ill-matched daughter. (In later years I would reconsider this point and come to a different conclusion. Father was completely contented in his well-crafted but dusty tower of solitude.) In any case, he *was* my father, and most myths and traditions recommended a degree of solicitude and deference to such a personage.

"I am sorry it has taken me so long with my fish and salad, Father. Why don't you go back to your cabin? I know you have a lot of work, and you shouldn't be held up on my account."

"Yes." He sighed. "I know I am tedious company for such a young person. I know I am only fit for old tomes. I do hate to abandon you thus, my child…"

He was continuing in this vein, rising from the table with a rapidity that belied his words, when something thrilling distracted me, and I ceased to maintain the pretense of dutiful attention. As my father had begun his movements toward departure, a shadow had fallen across our table. I looked up to see the steward, gracious and expectant.

"I see you are leaving us, Doctor Howard. I do hope you enjoyed your meal. Yes, yes, let me help you. Is there anything else I can do for you this evening?"

Father, who was still persuading himself that he was the hero of an unsung tale of patriarchal self-sacrifice, broke off to mutter his satisfaction with the food, refused every offer of further service, and shuffled off to his shipboard sanctuary. Meanwhile, I simultaneously endeavored to look as if I would remain for some time and as if I could easily permit the addition of new persons to share the table.

The steward oozed so much graciousness that I wondered if his uniform would be greasy to the touch. As Miss could clearly see, the room was filled to capacity. Would Miss be so kind as to permit him to place two more people?

Miss *would* be so kind.

Thus, I found myself seated opposite the two people I felt sure were more interesting than anyone else I had ever met in my life.

That neither of them found me interesting was apparent.

They nodded their grateful recognition of my role as pseudo-hostess without any indication that they recalled me from our encounter on deck that morning. Then the young woman occupied herself with listening to the steward's menu monologue, while the man looked around the room with a frown—in every possible direction except at me.

I did not mind being thus ignored. It provided me with ample opportunity to study them so I could improve my sketches. The man was, as I had already noted, distinctly handsome. Broad-shouldered, barrel-chested, and square-jawed, he exhibited all the earmarks of English civility in the unlikely form of a warrior. He was decently attired in a dark gray suit, such as an English gentleman usually wears while traveling, but I thought the blood-stained armor, tunic, and cape of a British chieftain would have better become him. I should have liked him to be on my side in a battle.

I turned next to look at his companion. One glance at her in full light revealed why such a hero would be unconscious of me. She was the sort of woman that fairy tales and myths describe. "Hair black as ebony, skin white as snow, lips red as the rose..." That was not quite right, I told myself with some asperity. Those unnaturally large, luminous eyes and that pronounced nose had more complex potential. "What big eyes you have, Grandmother..."

Those eyes flickered full upon me, bringing my impertinent imaginings to an abrupt halt. I had just begun to feel quite uncomfortable when, without revealing the thoughts that lay behind that glance, the woman returned her attention to the steward. Finally, commissioned to bear simple fare to both parties, that tedious individual retired to the wings, leaving the three of us closely together on the stage.

The man continued to look around the room. The woman gazed at the tablecloth.

At this moment I became aware of the challenging nature of my situation. My narrative exploration of plots and personalities had ever been textual or vicarious. Here I was faced with two strangers whom I believed to be windows into a fascinating, tortured new world, and I had not the foggiest idea how to beguile them into revelatory conversation. One cannot ask real, live strangers to give up their secrets as easily as one may extract them from an inanimate book. This required finesse—something I lacked. Never had I so grieved my father's failure to ensure my instruction in the rules of etiquette.

I grasped at triteness. "It's been an easy voyage so far."

The man seemed not to have heard me.

The woman raised her eyes for a moment, once again fixing me in that vast, impenetrable look. She nodded politely then returned to her untroubled perusal of the tablecloth.

People who talked airily about dismemberment and parricide had no business being this inscrutable.

"Is this your first crossing?" I persisted.

Once more she raised her eyes. "No."

Such an interesting accent. I wondered what her nationality was. I hoped she would continue speaking, but she did not. When I saw those long, dark lashes begin to drop down toward the table once more, desperation took hold of me.

"It is mine. Well, my second, really, if you count the trip over, though that's only if you don't count the trip when I was a baby. I don't remember it, and it was only to see my grandmother, who didn't care for babies much, so Father was stuck with me, and I don't know what the passage was like then because I was an infant. I imagine it was dreadful, or perhaps it was dreadful because Father has never spoken of it, and I am not really sure how I know about it except someone must have said something and that's how I know."

I broke off, pained by self-loathing. As I had rattled on, the woman had listened without speaking or displaying any emotion whatsoever. The man, after several moments of stolid resistance, had finally turned to me with the horrified look of an outraged Englishman confronted with a halfwit female. He probably even suspected me of being an American.

For a moment, their eyes were fully upon me: hers impassive, his revolted. "Indeed," said the woman softly.

Then they resumed their previous occupations. He gazed away, and she transferred her attention from the linen to a small candle in the middle of the table.

I could have stamped my foot with frustration.

The steward returned with a lanky, adenoidal adolescent of a waiter who bore a teetering tray of food for my companions. By the time the scarcely ordered cascade of plates and utensils had subsided, and the steward and his nasal retainer had again departed from the scene, I had built back up my courage and began once more with cheerful determination.

"I'm Athene Howard," I said. "My father—that was my father who just left us—he is Charles Howard."

Neither batted an eyelash.

"Charles Howard of the Université de Paris."

They remained unimpressed.

"His theories on the universality of mythological archetypes are well known," I said, aping a pride I had never really felt about his achievements. "The archetypes are pregnant with significance in the development of the individual psyche." That was a quote, though I pretended it wasn't. "Sculpts nations, not only people. Scholars in Vienna and Budapest and London and Paris all look to him. The United States too." The last was an afterthought but one that provided me with a bridge to a less burdensome topic. "We've come from the United States. I mean, I am sure you know we have. And you have too. How interesting. We were mostly in New York. But not entirely. Were you mostly in New York too?"

The woman endured this speech with watchful patience. I paused for breath, silently begging her for a response. I don't know if it was mercy on her part, but she deigned to give me what I so desperately desired.

"No." She returned to her perusal of the tablecloth.

I was about to begin again—recklessly embracing whatever topic might pop into my head—when an unexpected comment forestalled me.

"Athene." The man frowned. "Sprung from the head of Zeus."

"That's right. Only I didn't, of course. It's…it's just a name."

"Indubitably." He turned to his meal and began to eat with an unassailable focus.

Thwarted, unhappy, and torn between embarrassment and annoyance, I stood up. "I…I must return to my father. It was…

lovely to have met you. Goodbye. Or, as the French say, *au revoir?*" I hoped my voice did not sound embarrassingly wistful.

As I threaded my way back through the tables, I heard the man's deep stage whisper. "Can she be human?"

"Oh yes," said the woman, without a hint of irony. "Quite."

I hoped my ears were not as scarlet as my face surely was. Just because he was an intriguing hero didn't mean he had carte blanche to be loathsome.

I made my way slowly back to my father's cabin. The ship was so large that it absorbed within itself most of the motion of the sea, but I found my legs unsteady.

It was my father's fault. If he had not been so careless of propriety, so dismissive of common convention, I should have had social instruction sufficient to have weathered that strange encounter with greater success. Instead, I was left maudlin with disappointment.

If my mother hadn't died, perhaps I should have been happy or at least capable of carrying on a civil conversation. This last was a promising thought, since I was abandoning myself to self-pity. Unfortunately, my mother had never been of interest to me in my imaginings except as a mysterious facet of my father's personality. I wasn't certain how the logistics of childhood maldevelopment operated, either on a universal mythological or a personal scale, but one day, when I was twelve years old and had committed some mistake that had incurred my father's supreme irritation, he had opined at length on the probable cause of my endless failures as a daughter. "If your mother had lived!" he concluded tragically. I think he had forgotten such a creature ever existed, but she was a useful point in his unhappy tirade against me.

I was a great deal older than twelve, and my attitude toward my father had increasingly become dispassionate, but the disapproving look on the face of that curmudgeonly hero rankled. If ever I had provocation for moody self-reflection and bitter indictment of my father, the mortifying dismissiveness of the Englishman and his strange companion was it.

"What more is there to say?" I quoted to myself in strident tones. "I must die, a parricide, I am an anathema."

It was an ill-chosen moment for Greek theatricals, though my father had spent a great deal of his time (and subjected me to a great deal) in consideration of the Theban plays. Someone entered the corridor at its far end, stopped, stared at me as I made this dramatic pronouncement, and scurried away before I could see who it was.

Anathema indeed. This fresh cause for embarrassment counteracted my mood. I was beset, struggling not to erupt into a fit of giggling. Why not carry it off in proper theatrical style? I sighed with overdramatic emphasis that might have become a Hamlet and opened the door to my father's cabin. Unfortunately, in the enthusiasm of the moment, I performed this simple action more aggressively than usual. The door slammed into some unseen obstacle. The obstacle cried out in acute pain and anger.

"Athene! You clumsy girl! Look what you've done now!"

My father flung open the door, where he had been standing with a book in one hand and a small penknife in the other. With the blow from the door, the knife had leapt as if by its own volition to stab deeply into his arm. The wound was alarming and disproportionate, like something out of a cheap, ghoulish piece of carnival entertainment. I glimpsed exposed bone before crimson blood, dramatically spurting and splattering like spilled paint, poured over my father, over me, over everything, even to the point of staining the toes of my shoes as they peeped out from under my dress. The matter-of-fact voice of that strange woman echoed in my ear. *I think I would settle for effective and lasting patricide, and leave the rest to God.*

"Father," I said, "let me help you."

"Stupid child, out of my way. You've done enough!"

"Father, please! Let me help!"

"Girl! Get away! Steward!" He shouted the command past me, still angry but also hoarse, with a trembling hand clutched to the wound in his arm.

"I am so sorry, Father!"

"Silence, you stupid girl!"

I fell back, grieved. Another Oedipal line leapt to my mind and came, unbidden, in a whisper from my lips: "O woe is me! Methinks unwittingly, I laid but now a dread curse on myself."

"Athene!" He spoke my name in a new tone, staring not at me but at the blood as it spread (with unnecessary enthusiasm), dripping from his hands upon the floor.

"And who'd have thought the old man had so much blood in him." This whispered misquotation I could not place. I was too busy looking at my father, whose face had a ghostly pallor. One, two, three staggering steps brought him past me and into the corridor.

At that moment, a strange figure turned the corner and came into view. My father collapsed to the ground, a stained, mangled heap of beard, dust, and tweeds before the newcomer.

I froze in shock. The person standing on the other side of my father's prone body stared back at me, taking stock of my grotesquely discolored clothing. I stared back, my horror eclipsed only by my bewilderment at this strange and unexpected figure.

My father had fallen in a heap at the feet of a tall, big-boned woman with severe French brows, small eyes, and a dark crescent-shaped birthmark that stretched down across her right cheek and chin. No other detail of her face or person could be descried, for she was, in fact, a nun, bedecked in the ascetical, oppressive white regalia and black veil of her order.

CHAPTER 3

18 APRIL–21 APRIL 1906: YET IN THE ATLANTIC OCEAN, WITH LITTLE PROGRESS

> Relentless walls! whose darksome round contains
> Repentant sighs, and voluntary pains:
> Ye rugged rocks! which holy knees have worn;
> Ye grots and caverns shagg'd with horrid thorn!
>
> — Alexander Pope, "Eloisa to Abelard"

I WOULD PROBABLY HAVE CONTINUED TO STAND THERE, TURNED TO stone as punishment for my inadvertent assault upon my father, but the nun intervened. In a moment, she knelt before him, feeling for his pulse.

"He is not dead," she said in rapid French. "Don't snivel, girl."

I had no intention of sniveling, but I did not dare say so. There was something in the quality of the nun's voice which made anything less than immediate obedience impossible.

"We will need help in moving him. Go fetch someone—the doctor if you can find him, but the steward will do."

I nodded and ran off.

As I rounded the corner, I almost collided with the couple I had left in the dining room. If the man named Simon had not caught me, I would have fallen to the floor.

"Good God!" he cried.

"Sir Simon," snapped the nun, "there is no justification for lapses into blasphemy. Control your temper."

To my astonishment, he accepted this rebuke with a meek, "Of course, Sister Agatha. I beg your pardon," in more than passable French.

She rattled out yet another command. "You will do. Take his legs and here, Sister Magdalene, you take one arm."

I stared at Isabel, thus improbably addressed as a fellow nun.

"Girl, can you bear his head? Don't turn faint. You'll drop him."

I was not remotely inclined to faint, especially after such a brisk, pragmatic caution. We struggled with the deadweight of my father back into his cabin and placed him upon his bed, among the dust and books and blood. Robbed of consciousness, even his thin, wiry frame became so oppressively heavy that, had it not been for the strength of the Viking Briton and the towering Frenchwoman, we could not have moved him. Despite my better efforts, I ill-managed his head and knocked it twice against the doorframe, incurring a sharp reprimand from Sister Agatha.

He was upon the bed, and I stood, uncertain, lapsing into a childish habit of shifting my weight from one foot to the other. Something in the movement must have recalled him to life. His eyes, still closed, squinted with the contraction of reawakened pain. "Stupid girl!" he hissed through gritted teeth. "Stupid, clumsy, curse of a girl!" He opened his eyes, and I braced for the impact of well-vented paternal spleen upon my unfortunate head. Then his eyes widened, and every strained muscle of his bloody body relaxed with the force of his astonishment.

"Father, I..." The words froze on my lips. He was staring not at me but above my guilty head. His gaze fixed upon the face of that grim, solid, imposing figure in white.

I turned to look and saw the color drain from the old nun's face. When she spoke, it was without a tremor, though without looking at me. "Well, child? Don't dawdle. Hurry along for the doctor."

I sped away. When I returned a few moments later with the steward and a doctor in tow, my father was once again unconscious.

The doctor dismissed us all. Sir Simon and the two women, seeming to have forgotten me, walked silently down the corridor and disappeared. I was left alone, standing over grotesque blood stains that peppered the floor in an irregular pattern matched by similar discolorations upon my dress. The stains were an indictment, not of my accidental attempt at assassination but of my flippant and unaffectionate attitude toward my father. At another time, I could have viewed it placidly, but there was something about the pallor of his face and the crude, garish hue of the blood…

I turned at a soft touch upon my elbow.

The younger woman—Isabel or Sister Magdalene, whatever she was called—spoke quietly, in her gently accented English, "Sister Agatha bade me tell you not to worry yourself."

I could only nod my thanks. She received this matter-of-factly and departed.

I wandered toward my own cabin, contemplating the cast of characters that had come together for this strange little scene and still unable to read the mystery they represented. That night my dreams were vivid and, in episodic fashion, chronicled the doom imposed upon reckless, clumsy, parricidal girls.

The next morning when I presented myself in my father's cabin, prepared to suffer his ire in humble silence, I was astonished to find him sitting up in his bed, his wound bound, and his eyes glittering with some unknown enjoyment. I knew that light well, and it boded ill.

"Athene!" For once he sounded pleased. "You're just who I needed. Sit down here beside me."

This was an even more alarming development. Perhaps he was febrile, and his mind was beginning to give way.

I took the proffered seat.

"Now, Athene. I did not attend yesterday when you told me of those people. Tell me again. Don't ramble but tell me everything."

It was a curious invitation—one certainly unprecedented in the whole of my young life. The novelty so discomposed me that my performance as narrator was uninspiring. Nevertheless, my recital seemed to satisfy my father. He drummed his fingertips together for a few moments, sucking in air and holding it in his mouth then exhaling it in an audible aspiration. He used this tactic in debates: demonstrating thoughtfulness while dismissing all enemy theories.

I shifted in the uncomfortable wooden chair.

The noise reminded him of my presence. "There you are, Athene. Hurry along now. Go and fetch that old French battle axe."

"Father?" I faltered.

"You know, the nun. Agatha. My sisterly savior! Go! Tell her I want to see her."

I was aghast. Even with my limited knowledge, such a task sounded like a sin against the most basic rules of etiquette.

My father looked at me over his glasses. This look at least I recognized. "Don't gape at me, girl. Do as you're told. Don't worry"—he was smiling, and I didn't like it—"she won't argue. She'll be ready to come as I bid. You'll see."

Had I gazed upon the feared face of the Medusa, I could not have been more completely petrified. Given the choice, I would have likely opted for the gorgon, since my studies would have guided me to a fitting mode of self-defense.

Trembling at the thought of the deserved set down I was to receive, I left the room and searched the corridors for the sister—or, at least, for a steward to tell me where the sister was to be found. I kept hoping against hope that she had somehow left the ship mid-ocean, perhaps called away by spiritual business or kidnapped by pirates or anything that might have spared me from the mortifying task of delivering my father's request.

I found Sir Simon first. He was standing on deck alone, his hands behind his back, looking out to sea. As I made my way over to him, a childish timidity crept over me. Indeed, my heart was pounding in my breast so tumultuously I wondered he could not hear it.

"Par-pardon me, sir," I said—or, rather, squeaked.

He turned and looked down on me.

"I…I do beg your pardon." I hoped my face was not as flushed as it felt. "My father…my father wishes to speak with Sister Agatha. He sent me to tell—to ask her if she would please come to him. He's still weak, you know. But of course you don't know, and I'm sorry to be of trouble, but—"

To my disgust, my voice broke at this point, making me sound perilously close to tears befitting a hyperemotional female.

His creased brow softened, and his hands dropped to his sides. "I shall take you to her at once, Miss Howard. And…er…dry your eyes, do." This last was almost a plea and solidified his standing as an Englishman. The man clearly possessed that nationally imbued horror of awkward hysterics.

Gesturing for me to follow, Sir Simon led me down several corridors. At the door of a small cabin, he knocked. The younger woman opened the door and appraised us with her unemotional glance.

"Isabel," said Sir Simon, "here is Miss Howard. She has a message for Sister Agatha."

Isabel fell back in silence, and I saw the older French nun sitting perfectly upright in a chair, a large book with black and red lettering poised upon her lap. She raised her eyes from the page and looked at me for several moments. Embarrassment paralyzed me. I could not speak, could not deliver any sort of message, and could not think quickly enough to manufacture civil euphemisms. But she must have had some means of understanding my errand. With a sigh and a mournful shake of her head, she closed her book. "I shall go."

She stood and glided silently from the cabin. At the threshold, she paused and looked down on me. I could not read her expression, but I felt some strange sense of shame. I hoped she might say something of moment, but she merely commanded, "Lead on, child."

When I delivered Sister Agatha to my father's cabin, I hoped he might be asleep or occupied with the doctor or somehow have changed his mind. My hopes were dashed. He was sitting bolt upright in bed, his eyes still glittering with that strange and indecorous excitement.

He greeted her with ostentatious politeness. "I do beg your pardon, Sister, for my unsightly appearance and the impropriety of inviting you into this, my personal cabin. I do hope you will forgive me—an invalid and a sorry wretch! Do sit down and make yourself comfortable. Athene!" His voice changed. "What are you about? I wished you to bring the good sister's companions as well. I have so many thanks to deliver, after all. Go and fetch them. Now, girl."

I looked at Sister Agatha, waiting to see if she would argue with this obvious dismissal of me. She said nothing. She simply sat, looking at my father.

"Athene!" my father snapped. "Hurry along!"

I removed myself once again.

"Now, Sister," I heard my father say as the door closed behind me, "let us have our little chat."

I fairly ran until I found Sir Simon, once again alone on the deck, and breathlessly recited the request. This time I had little energy for embarrassment; I was too troubled by some intangible thought, some strange sense that leaving the nun alone with my wiry, near-sighted father, with his irreverent notions and uncertain manners, would be both inappropriate and dangerous.

Sir Simon seemed perplexed but willing enough. "I shall fetch Isabel," he said gruffly.

"Do hurry."

After finding Isabel, which took much longer than I would have liked, we returned to my father's cabin. I opened the door without knocking, and we walked in.

"You will come and visit me sometimes," he was saying to Sister Agatha in a petulant, pleading voice. "You see how trapped I am by misfortune! I feel certain your society would bring delight to my sorry, lonely hours. And—who knows! Perhaps your virtuous demeanor will inspire a sad sinner to return to the Church of his fathers."

He turned to his newest visitors and delivered his few trite, rapid expressions of gratitude. They received this silently—Sir Simon with frowning courtesy and Isabel without looking away from Sister Agatha's face, which she had been watching since we first entered the room.

My father sighed. "I find I am tired. Athene, fetch me another blanket. I believe I shall sleep. Thank you—" He yawned as he spoke, almost rendering the words inaudible. "Thank you, Eloise."

The sister stiffened. "That is not my name."

"Oh, dear!" cried my father, wide-eyed, the picture of innocent confusion. "I wonder why I thought it was."

Simon stared at each of them in turn, his face puzzled and even mildly alarmed. Isabel had looked away and was examining a small book lying open on the floor beside the bed. With her toe, she nudged the book so that it flipped closed, relieving the pressure to its spine and revealing its title. I made a mental note to inspect the book myself as soon as I could. Anything that could capture her cool attention was worth the effort.

"Good day, Miss Howard." Sister Agatha swept from the room, taking Sir Simon and Isabel away in her wake.

Left alone with my father, I saw a side of him that I had rarely witnessed—a gleeful, smug degree of enjoyment. Usually, this was reserved for moments when he triumphed over his academic adversaries. This time, the closest he came to revealing the source of this private delight was an impromptu harangue about hypocrisy.

"Hypocrisy," quoth he, "is one of the most monumental sources of weakness on the part of certain sorts of people. They have so far repressed an honest, realistic assessment of themselves that the suffocated truth begins to fester and creates myriad tormented, grossly entangled desires and emotional contortions. Such things metamorphize the self into the most monstrous shapes. This is the breeding place of nightmare and mysticism."

I escaped as soon as I could.

In the corridor, I stood for some time looking down on the bloodstains of the previous day. Dismemberment and parricide were the stuff of myths, but this slowly changing color was real. Isabel's past—the dismemberment and the scattering—that must have been real too. She could have executed both without emotion, I felt certain. Would not that make her some sort of monster?

I shook my head and reminded myself that she and Jean-Claude—whoever he might be—had not overseen that business. If I didn't watch out, I would start to develop nerves. To dispel such instability, I nudged the blood stains with my toe. I wondered what their final shade would be. Perhaps the entire corridor would require new carpet.

"Miss! Miss Howard!"

Turning, I beheld the harried form of the head steward. Several tufts of his black hair had broken free of pomaded restraint and stood forth as rebellious standards. "My dear Miss Howard! Your father! Such a tragedy! And now this! Endless apologies. It will be fixed as soon as possible and we will be on our way."

I tried not to stare at the bobbing, waving tufts. "What do you mean?"

"Something in the engine—so tiresome, but they're working away on it diligently, and we should be back on our course soon enough. Soon enough. Can I interest you in a tidy supper? Do come to the dining room, my dear Miss Howard…"

"Back on our course," I repeated blankly. "Are we off our course?"

"Not at all! Merely at a slight standstill, but soon enough, my dear Miss Howard, soon enough, and with a lovely chicken to offer you this evening…"

The delay was in fact three days in length.

My father bemoaned the news, though I did not know why it mattered. We were merely returning to our uninteresting everyday existence in Paris. However, it afforded me small but ever deeper glimpses into the mystery that so occupied my thoughts. We were constantly in the company of those three travelers. I could not determine why my father insisted upon it, and why Sister Agatha submitted to it, but it permitted me to observe even more closely that fascinating pair, Sir Simon Gwynne and Isabel. Isabel's surname was part of the mystery. She was always and ever Isabel, except when Sister Agatha called her Sister Magdalene. Some time passed before I had the courage to inquire, and then Simon, who was reading quietly and probably wishing I would mysteriously vanish, spoke to me so gruffly that I wished I had not.

He relented almost immediately. "Don't look so crestfallen, Miss Howard. Isabel has been in a convent for the last ten years. There she goes by that other name. She is not yet vowed to that life—and whether she will return is unknown. For now she is to be addressed by her given name."

"But Sister Agatha..." My question lingered on the air.

"You may conclude that Sister Agatha disagrees."

"But with which part?"

"For that," said Sir Simon, returning to the book in his hand, "Sister Agatha keeps her own counsel, and I suggest you and I do the same."

Since there was little else for me to do, I followed his advice. In my little notebook, right below some notes about ritual dismemberment in classical myth, I recorded the information about Isabel.

On the second mystery—the mystery of my father and Sister Agatha—I expended little paper but a great deal of curiosity. Every morning I found my father and Sister Agatha waging war over the coffee cups. Even the language was a point of contention. My father danced between English and French while Sister Agatha, with regal Breton pride, persisted in the latter. He reveled in tormenting her, but why she accepted his invitation day after day I could not imagine. Civility had never before been expressed with such sharp, merciless teeth. Nature revealed in blood, tooth, and claw.

The analogy is unsound; the viciousness was all one sided. Further, it could not be explained as the result of a natural impulse or instinct. I had never seen my father so determined in his pursuit. It exceeded even his complete annihilation of that meek *professeur des universités*, Georges Guillet. Professor Guillet had foolishly attempted to question my father's dismissal of the flood myth. The blighted, drowned thousands had fared better than that hapless academic.

I came to an absolute certainty that my father had known the nun years before—and perhaps had known her intimately when he was a priest. I tried to imagine the most likely scenario—to my mind, one of age-old passion and burning resentment. But as I looked at Sister Agatha, sometimes catching her in a moment of unveiled emotion, I found this hypothesis doubtful. Something other than love stood between these two strange creatures—some fearful bond, more akin to hate, which gave my father power over the woman or at least persuaded her to this inexplicable docility in the face of constant, petty provocation.

"One thing I've always wondered about," my father said one morning with an air of innocent musing. "The Battle of Rephidim. These stories leave so much of the real to our imagination, don't you think? If the prophet had a head cold and mucus began to flow grossly down his face, would it have been better to give attention to decorum or to serve the arbitrary requirements of Providence and remain, arms outstretched, to ensure victory? Drop his arms and give up the day? Leave him—your prophet—besmeared? Give in to mercy and decorum? Or be steadfast in your undignified zeal?"

Sister Agatha did not respond. The only indication that she had heard him came from a slight flush in the large birthmark upon her face.

She quitted the room a short time after, but she was permitted only two hours' respite. By the midday meal, my father declared himself recovered enough to stagger down to the dining room, bringing misery and me in his wake. Only a few days before he had been so occupied in his studies that nothing short of an earthquake would have roused him to consider his surroundings. Now, aside from frenzied searches through his books for passages that seemed to confirm his private thoughts and frustrated cries for notes that he had left at home, he was forever engaged upon summoning or hunting down his habited victim.

He strode across the dining room, ignoring the cooing ministrations of the steward and merely grunting at the doctor, who was either attempting to pay his respects or express his disapproval of this behavior on the part of a convalescent. Following him, I wondered, not for the first time, if his mind had been permanently affected by the injury.

"Ah!" he cried, presenting himself at the table where Sister Agatha, Sir Simon, and Isabel were sitting over their modest meal. "You see? Lazarus is restored! It is enough to give one faith, is it not?"

"Good afternoon, Doctor Howard," said Sister Agatha calmly. "We shall give you our table. We are finished."

"Oh, dear me, no!" said my father with mock distress. "It cannot be. When I had so set my heart on such companionship as I make this first, timid attempt at restored health. No, no, my dear Sister Agatha, I really do insist. You couldn't be so cruel as to leave me alone."

Sister Agatha glanced in my direction.

"Oh, Athene," my father chuckled. "I suppose you're hungry as usual." He added, in a stage whisper which was even more mortifying, "She's small but has the appetite of a pack of boys."

"Miss Howard." Sir Simon rose suddenly. "Please, sit."

Head ducked, I slid into the proffered seat.

I did not attend to most of the conversation over that meal. My father applied himself to his food with gusto. I could not say what we ate—something with the flavor of ash and despair. My mind, which was occupied in introspection of the most painful and least productive nature, arose back to the surface in time to hear a strange exchange between my father and the Frenchwoman.

"But then," he was saying, "we all know what frustrations and desires lurk behind those high walls. Really, I say we all know. I should say, Sister, that you know best."

I did not know of what he spoke yet felt the deliberate barb he aimed at the flesh of that imposing woman with the moon-like discoloration on her face. I looked up to see if the birthmark would once again change color.

It did not. Sister Agatha instead drew herself to her full height. "I have never felt the need or the desire to covet the questionable consolations of the state of life of others."

My father chuckled loudly at this. "Bravo, Eloise! A hit! A veritable hit!"

She flushed, throwing the birthmark into sharp relief as anger got the better of her self-control. "My name, sir, is Sister Agatha."

"Indeed," he said with the air of a man soothing an irrational woman. "Indeed, I can't think why I keep forgetting it! Yet it *is* so!"

Sir Simon, who had been standing beside the table, leaning against the wall with one shoulder and attending to all that was said, looked from one to the other, his forehead creased. Isabel gazed at the ground, a picture of beautiful abstraction.

"Ladies and gentlemen." A courteous, triumphant voice spoke from the front of the room. We all looked up at the head steward, his pomaded black hair shining forth like a dark beacon. "I am delighted to inform you that our mechanical issue has been repaired, and we are once again on our way towards Calais. We will arrive there by tomorrow morning—delayed, indeed, but in good order."

He then began expressing his gratitude for our continued patronage of the company, but a few young men applauded with lusty American vigor, drowning him out. A happy melee broke out, dispensing the charade of civility. Most of the people in the room ceased listening altogether and left their tables to return to their cabins. No one in our party moved. My companions were staring at my father. At the sight of his face, the relief that had risen in my stomach now quavered.

"My dear Athene," said my father in a dangerously affectionate tone as he helped himself to more buttered bread, "I do believe we will accompany these good people in their quest. How fierce you look, good Sir Simon Gwynne! You quite alarm me, my good sir! Perhaps I shall take this bread knife with me to bed tonight. It would not do to suffer yet another attack. Have no fear, dear fellow. I mean you no harm. In fact, it may be that you will have cause to be grateful for my sustaining aid."

"I thought we were going to Paris," I said, startled.

To accompany this strange group on their adventures was a tantalizing prospect. Yet there was something in my father's expression and in the rictus of courtesy upon Sister Agatha's face that sent a creeping sense of shame and horror of this proposed change through me.

"In time, girl." My father watched me with something like an indulgent eye. "In time. For now, I have decided to assist these good people in their quest. Is that not so, Sister Agatha?"

We all looked to the Frenchwoman. Even Isabel raised her eyes and gazed with fixed attention on my father's victim.

Sister Agatha blanched but for the lurid line of that mark upon her cheek and chin. She sat there, a woman transformed to marble, or perhaps a pillar of salt.

The bustle of happy passengers had not abated, and the large clock on the wall continued its slow progress around, marking the passage of time, which seemed to have slowed as we waited to hear what Sister Agatha might say.

Finally, she sighed, and, looking at Sir Simon and Isabel, said with quiet finality, "Yes, Doctor Howard will accompany us." Then she turned a severe look upon my father and added, "For the sake of your soul, sir, not for the sake of your theories."

My father rolled his eyes heavenward. "Your pious platitudes are doomed to disappointment, Sister, but you will be grateful for my assistance in this quest ere long!"

"But...but..." I stammered, desperate for clarification. "What is this quest?"

This time there was no mistaking the glee in my father's smile. "Why, don't you know yet, girl? We're fierce hunters on the trail of *le croquet-mitaine*. Or—" He bowed toward Sir Simon, whose brow was bent thunderously over his infuriated eyes. "Master Bogeyman."

I stuttered out, "But...but that's nonsense."

"Yes," said my father with palpable delight. "What larks, Athene! What larks!"

Chapter 4

22 April 1906: Calais to Zagreb

With a rope's end round the man, handy and brave—
He was pitched to his death at a blow,
For all his dreadnought breast and braids of thew:
They could tell him for hours, dandled the to and fro
Through the cobbled foam-fleece, what could he do
With the burl of the fountains of air, buck and the flood of the wave?

— Gerald Manley Hopkins, "The Wreck of the Deutschland"

THE NEXT TWELVE HOURS HAD THAT BEWILDERING QUALITY ONE experiences in certain dreams in which everyone is embarked on an enterprise that consists of complicated rules and mysterious motivations—and you, the dreamer, are the only one who has not the foggiest notion what is going on. My father and our new companions appeared to be well informed of our mission, yet none of them bothered to explain. I hardly saw Sister Agatha, Isabel, or Sir Simon during that time, though even if I had seen them, I doubt I would have been able to bring myself to ask any direct questions. Would they not turn, like the phantoms of a nightmare, and wreak destruction upon me as fitting judgment for my presumption?

So there I was, hurried and bustled and chastened and directed by my father into packing his scattered things into some semblance of order. I began to long for the return of our established routine. Better to be dubbed "The Interruption" and duly ignored than to receive such constant, nagging attention.

"Don't crush those papers, Athene!" "Girl! Have you no sense?" "Where are my trousers? Not those ones! The tweeds!" And, with a tragic sigh, "You fret me out of patience, girl."

I was not a passive martyr to his mood. At every free moment I added to my notes, determined to dispel the clouds of theatrical mystery. All I required was a framework of understanding, a point or theory on which to build my scholarly reading. As I packed my father's scattered books, I came across the volume that Isabel had touched with her foot and covertly examined. It was a small book with a promisingly lurid title: *The Book of Were-Wolves.* I wondered that I had not noticed this among my father's library before. While he was not looking, I slipped the book into my pocket and later hid it among my own belongings so that I might delve into it in private. They might exclude me from their counsel, but they could not stop me from conducting my own inquiry into the mystery. Bogeymen indeed.

I slept the sleep of the just that night and remembered nothing of my dreams.

We arrived in port so early in the morning it could easily have been considered the middle of the night. The early morning is a strange time, full of fancies and fears. My father would have said that fancies and fears were the mark of the unsophisticated or unstable mind, bound up with superstition—yet I thought to myself, if there really were such a thing as witches, their eponymous hour would be well chosen.

I awoke at three to the sound of bells, whistles, cries, and the grinding, whirring, rushing noise of maritime industry. The crew moved with increased urgency, which at first I attributed to frustration from our long delay on the waves.

Then I heard the scream.

It was long and lasting, a clear issuance of terror. I could not have said whose voice uttered it, or even whether it were a man or a woman. Only later did I learn that a third mate, half drunk, had stumbled in the darkness and rose to find himself soaked in sea water and something red, thick, and sticky. He had picked up the strange object that had brought him flat on his back on the wet deck—something round, like a ball dropped by a young boy. It had been lodged for some time among the rigging, but rolled free with the leisured rocking of the ship. But this was not a ball. When the inebriated mate inspected his discovery, he found instead the wide, staring eyes of a human face fronting a decapitated head, frozen with the shock of sudden death.

"He must have fallen from one of the upper decks," Simon told us after an unappetizing breakfast. We were all gathered in Sister Agatha's room, our luggage and ourselves duly prepared for departure. "He had apparently sneaked up to the crow's nest. He fell and became entangled in a cable. The force was enough to…" He paused, looking first at Isabel, who, as usual, looked unmoved, and then at me. "…to detach his head. Death must have been instantaneous."

"Was it one of the crew?" I asked, horrified. Did disembodied heads follow these people about?

"No, it was a stowaway, they think. A young man who hid himself down below deck. The crew had been watching for him. He had committed some pranks or theft. The search was, I gather, very thorough last night. That is perhaps why he risked coming above deck."

A chill crept around my heart as I recalled the strange, dark-faced boy I had encountered days before.

"What omens!" I could not read my father's tone. "Such things are to be expected in the hunt, Athene. Spirits roused provoke strange and wonderful occurrences, do they not, Sister Agatha?"

"Death is a tragedy, Doctor Howard," she replied with studied somberness. "And violent death bears a particular degree of horror. But death has no sting…"

"Yes, yes." My father nodded indulgently. "Do find consolation even for mysterious assassinations, dear Sister!"

Sir Simon's shoulders stiffened. "It was an accident."

My father shrugged and turned again to Sister Agatha to deliver a businesslike description of our plan of travel. Calais to Paris. Paris to Zurich. There my knowledge ended.

I had obediently sketched out our plan the previous evening. My father had no sense of travel timetables. As he tacitly claimed my organizational clarity as his own, I only half attended, my mind still fixed on that strange tragedy. I tried not to imagine those final moments—the dance of the entangled victim, like a fly enmeshed in the snare of a spider and, in its struggle to escape, hastening its own death. Perhaps he was desperate. Perhaps he was frightened. He had been a startling apparition that day when I saw him—for I was convinced it was the same boy—but had not seemed threatening. Perhaps he had been in pursuit of Isabel. I looked up at her then hurriedly looked away. It must be coincidence. Grotesque but unconnected. In any case, the boy did not deserve this ignominious, violent death. Even if he had been a villainous creature, he must have had a mother.

Faced with the melodramatic and unlikely vision of that strange boy as an infant coddled in the arms of an imaginary but doting and now tragically grieving mother, I brushed away a tear and tried not to notice Sir Simon's watchful—and, I felt certain, critical—eye upon me.

As we began the slow, stilted movements of formal departure, Sir Simon moved beside me. "It happened quickly, Miss Howard," he said gently. "He probably didn't even know it was happening. He would have had little time to fear—or even to suffer."

I didn't believe him but tried to pretend I did.

"Do hurry, Athene," my father complained. He never liked early morning travel. "We've been held up long enough on this wretched ship."

However, he allowed time, as we departed, to express to the head steward how much the experience had been lacking in every comfort and basic necessity. The steward bowed his pomaded head and bore the rebuke in mournful silence. I imagine he had heard it innumerable times already.

We had walked down the gangplank and were on our way to a waiting cab when Isabel spoke again. "There isn't any wind."

Sir Simon and I looked at her.

Her eyes remained unwaveringly upon our faces. "There hasn't been much in the way of wind for days, and last night was placid."

"What do you mean?" I asked.

"I mean that your father is correct. This is much of what you are to expect, Miss Howard. You are embarking on a journey of blood, darkness, and strangeness. To deceive you into expecting less would be cruel. Imagination is not an asset in work such as this."

"Nor human feeling?" I asked before I could stop myself.

"I suppose that would depend on the feeling." Then she climbed into the cab and proceeded to stare out the window without speaking, her expression indicative of either complete serenity or paralyzing boredom.

Travel from the pier to the train station was quick. Calais, though it must have its own rich personality, has too long been defined as a major point of arrival and departure to be known for anything else. Our desired train would depart in only two hours. We would not need lodgings for the night. Our journey could proceed apace.

Somehow, I could not passively accept the prospect of those two hours. I had no illusions about my companions. For many days ahead, I would be trapped in uncomfortable silence. The two women settled themselves on long, hard benches further along the platform. They closed their eyes, probably in prayer. Sir Simon began to walk purposefully from one end of the platform to the other. My father settled himself a little way off, produced a small notebook, and began scribbling into it.

While I could, I would embrace a moment of freedom. I set down my bag and, unmarked by Sir Simon and the two women, turned to walk to the entrance of the station.

My father's voice checked me. "Where are you going, girl?"

"For a walk."

"You'll be late," he predicted and turned back to his book.

I did not argue the point but walked to the door and out into the inviting sunshine and air.

The road from the station wound in one direction back down toward the edge of the water, into the busy heart of Calais. I gazed back at the sparkling horizon and would have spent time in meditation on the strange events I had thus far witnessed, but an attractive cacophony of rich bustle and tinny music behind me turned my attention. Further down the trim road were the unmistakable signs of a traveling carnival. Without hesitation, I bent my steps toward the fair. If anything were calculated to be utterly different from the dour, uncommunicative group on the station platform, surely it was a dirty little place of revelry filled with local peasantry and gawking tourists.

As is commonly the case, the reality of the carnival was much dirtier and more sordid than childhood visions would lead one to expect. I was not fond of circuses, finding the contortionists particularly unnerving and dreading the manufactured tension of the high-wire act, but the earthy joviality of sword-eaters, fire-swallowers, and strange creatures was like a rich field study in anthropology.

A diminutive figure waddling personally through the crowd bumped against me. "Pardon, mademoiselle."

I smiled at the swarthy dwarf, who, with his unkempt beard and motley attire, looked a deliberate conflation of the fairy tale of Snow White and the heritage of the medieval jester. Even as I nodded acceptance of the apology, I felt with one hand for my little purse.

The quick eyes of the dwarf caught the movement. "Thieves come in all forms, mademoiselle."

I flushed and produced a coin, pretending that this had been my intention.

The dwarf accepted the tribute with a wide grin and strolled away, calling over his shoulder, "Beware of deceivers and vagabonds, mademoiselle!"

I was frowning thoughtfully after him when a long, bony hand gripped my arm. I jumped and turned to see the dark, grimacing face of an old gypsy woman leering invitingly at me from the fortune teller's tent.

"Come, sweet English lady!" she cried. "Come! Come for your fortune, dearie! I will see your many lovers!"

"That I doubt," I said, my humor restored. "I'll happily let you ply your trade, Mother."

I ducked my head to enter the shrouded tent and took note of each detail. The woman's head and shoulders were adorned with worn, fringed shawls, and her neck strained from the weight of stained, heavy-looking jewelry. Aged tapestries made the tent suffocatingly close, and the strong smell of stale tobacco turned my stomach. A little oil lamp upon a table would, I thought, work well with the shadows and insufficient light to intensify the performance.

She gestured me into a chair, which creaked threateningly as I sat on it. She must have only solicited visits from females of small stature. One generously-formed farmer and the wicker seat would collapse in despair.

She sat opposite me, cackling and crooning a ditty I wished I could hear more clearly. There was a strange intonation in her French. I wondered if one might procure a book of Romany dialects as easily as one might acquire instructional manuals in more respectable languages.

"Give me your hand, pretty dearie!" The old dame leaned over my palm to inspect it, clicking her tongue over the lines. "Ah, dearie lady! This is good! Ah! Good fortune! A noble lover, full of passion! But first, oh, many dangers! Many, many dangers. Then happiness!"

"That's agreeable enough."

"And many, many children…"

"A natural consequence of the lover full of passion."

"Great good fortune attends you! But first…"

"Oh, the dangers. Yes, tell me, Mother, about the dangers."

The dame pulled the lamp closer and inspected my palm. I could feel wiry hairs from her nose tickling my skin.

"Yes, the dangers. Lady, I…"

The old woman's pause, which I had assumed was for dramatic emphasis, lingered oddly. She tightened her grip, and I looked up. Her face had turned pale, and her breath came in quick, heavy gasps.

"Mother, you are unwell. Let me get you some water. Let me…"

"No, no!" She cried in a strange, unearthly voice that was almost a moan and began babbling in her native tongue. I started from my seat but was forced back down by her unshakable hold upon my hand. "No, no! Listen! You have no time! You must not go! The children of darkness are cursed, and doom follows upon their heels!"

I tried to pull my hand away, but she clasped it in both of her own with a strength of which I would not have believed her capable.

"Please! Let me go, Mother. You are not well. Let me go!"

"Isabel!"

The name, uttered in desolation, struck me to stone.

"What…?" I gasped out finally, "What? Who…?"

The old woman, racked with deep sobs, rocked back and forth in her chair. "Isabel! Isabel! Oh, mercy! Isabel!"

"What of Isabel? How do you know her?"

"The children of darkness are cursed! Doom follows upon their heels! He—he will come! The blood cries out from the ground! The blood of a father! The severed corpse will be whole!"

I started back from her, once again attempting to wrench my hand from hers, but her long, sharp nails dug into the flesh of my hand.

"He will come! Vengeance! Oh, vengeance! We must fly!"

"Who is he?" I demanded. "What are you talking about?"

She let go of my hand and moved to hurry away from me, but, as if we had changed places, I arrested her in my arms and repeated my urgent questions. "Who is he? What are you talking about? Tell me!"

Her eyes, dilated and wild, fixed on me. She hissed out a single, terrified word that was like a pronouncement of death:

"Marcus."

With a final moan, she stumbled forward and pushed past me, oversetting her table in her agitation, and vanished through the folds of the tent and into the sunshine.

Breathless, my heart racing, I stood there staring after her. Her words echoed in my ears. "The children of darkness…the children of darkness…the severed corpse made whole…Isabel…" And that last name, so chillingly uttered: "Marcus."

A feeling of sick, inchoate apprehension washed over me, and I ran out of the tent. As I rushed into the sunlight, I collided with the solid form and frowning face of Sir Simon Gwynne.

"Oh!" I cried, torn between relief and inexplicable guilt. "Oh! Sir Simon! You're here?"

It was perhaps not the most intelligent observation. He looked a bit startled and more than a little irritable. "The train will come soon, Miss Howard. You mustn't wander off… What is it? What has happened?"

"Nothing." I involuntarily looked back over my shoulder. "I… nothing. The tent was rather close. I am better now. Thank you. I am coming."

"You would be advised, Miss Howard, to remain close at hand. This is not a pleasure tour."

He glared at me, but I was too shaken and too relieved at his powerful presence to resent the rebuke. We walked in silence, and I struggled to regain my breath and my composure. Before I could do so, a piercing whistle announced the present departure of our train, and we were forced to run the last length of our way back.

The train was beginning to move away from the platform.

I hesitated for one instant—leaping onto a moving train was something outside my experience—but Sir Simon was less timid. Grabbing me about the waist, without seeming to notice my racing heartbeat, he hoisted me up onto the moving steps and jumped up after me, nearly knocking me into the arms of the amused porter.

Chapter 5

22 April–7 May 1906: Calais to Zagreb

A mountain never meets a mountain, but a man meets a man.

— Romany Proverb

I dreaded meeting Isabel's eye when we reappeared, but she seemed as occupied as ever with her own thoughts. Sister Agatha's eyes were closed. Beyond a grunt that signaled that I had fulfilled his every low expectation, my father made no comment on my breathless reappearance. Having restored me to the company, Sir Simon appeared to forget my existence. I could regain my composure without fear of being observed.

We took our places, assuming what would prove to be our recurrent positions for some time. Whether in a cab or on a train or for the endless hours we spent in waiting rooms at various stations, it was always the same. Isabel would stare out the window. My father would settle himself into a corner and go to sleep, awakening to complain fretfully about the ordeal of travel but mostly permitting his mind to wander into myriad abstract arguments with invisible opponents. Sister Agatha would sit with her eyes closed but with her lips moving—not in deliberate counterargument to my father, I thought, but in prayer. Sir Simon, the only one of the group who, in other circumstances, might have been inclined to carry on a conversation, was preoccupied with other things. When forced to sit, he would do so with furrowed brow, glaring at every passerby and tapping one well-tailored knee with annoyed fingertips. When he was not thus restrained, he would prowl back and forth on platforms or pavements like a belligerent dog protecting his turf.

My travel plan, though crafted with the minimum of information, was a sound one. Unfortunately, our journey seemed doomed to an endless series of unexpected delays.

Between Brest and Nantes, flooding on the tracks. We were left to spend the night in Orléans and departed one day behind schedule.

Between Nantes and Lyon, as we passed Clermont-Ferrand, the engineer suffered a heart attack, and we were marooned for six hours. We arrived in Lyon to learn that the next available train had departed a few minutes before. After another unexpected stay overnight, we were now three days behind schedule.

Between Lyon and Turin, engine trouble. Another day's delay.

When we departed Turin, we found that we had become separated from Sister Agatha. We all got off at the next station and awaited her. At the sight of her three hours later, my father, who had taken to pacing the platform muttering to himself or to that ubiquitous imaginary opponent, suddenly broke off with, "Ah! Eloise!"—spoken in what really seemed to be a tone of relief.

Thus reunited, we began again.

Between Turin and Milan, a massive herd of wild goats took up immovable residence on the track. The engineer's attempts to avoid them only intensified the bloody carnage of the impact.

Between Milan and Venice, more flooding and three nights marooned among the canals.

I make no mention of passports, of dour, suspicious inspectors, and of official interrogations at each border. These mundane details of travel were there in abundance too. Every time Isabel handed her passport to the officials, I tried to discover the secret of her identity: a surname, a country, anything to connect her to the gypsy woman's raving about the children of darkness. But her documents were bound in black leather that, alas, my vision could not penetrate.

One day, after the latest of the freak accidents—I believe it was the sudden death of the engineer—Sister Agatha said, half to herself: "The ways of God…"

"Are mysterious indeed," my father ended glibly and, for once, without sarcasm.

She looked up at him. He smiled somewhat ruefully. "You see, Sister, I do not forget. I simply have gone beyond."

Her thoughtful silence was heavier after that.

At the Venezia-Mestre, I tripped on the platform and fell with an inglorious clatter upon the ground. My father sighed loudly and said to no one in particular, "It is a mercy we are on the mainland or she would have launched straight into the canal."

Sir Simon helped me to my feet without commenting on my blush. I was too mortified to thank him and hurried into the waiting room to pass the weary hours until it was time to depart once more for our final destination: Zagreb.

It should not be thought that, after my strange encounter with the gypsy fortuneteller, I was peacefully unconcerned through all of this. Indeed, keeping my father in line and ensuring he did not leave his passport in at least a dozen places along the way was occupation enough for six daughters, but my mind ran swiftly and persistently along the unsatisfactory details I had thus far gleaned of our adventures. More than once I considered speaking to Isabel or Sir Simon of what the old dame had said to me, but Isabel remained distant in her manner, and Sir Simon frowned too frequently to be approachable.

After the goat bloodbath near Vercelli, when my companions were sleeping or otherwise occupied, I slipped my hand into my purse and retrieved the volume by Sabine Baring-Gould, which I had appropriated from my father's belongings. I had taken the precaution of covering the book with a piece of leather cut from one of my bags. I had no desire to attract the attention and the rebuke of my father or of any member of our party.

I do not know what I expected in that little book, but after the promising beginning of the introduction, I was disappointed. It was merely a collection of myths and legends related to human-to-animal metamorphosis, neither as comprehensive nor as entertaining as it ought to have been. "WHAT is Lycanthropy?" asked Baring-Gould. "The change of man or woman into the form of a wolf, either through magical means, so as to enable him or her to gratify the taste for human flesh, or through judgment of the gods in punishment for some great offense." Straightforward enough but hardly new information. I was no closer to knowing why the book had been among my father's belongings. Father had spoken of bogeymen, and the old woman of the "children of darkness." Cannibalism and violence against peasant females seemed a grotesque new development yet one suited to the dismemberment theme. But where did werewolves fit in?

The object of the author I could readily identify, as it was one with which my father would have been sympathetic. All these fascinating stories, which were familiar to me from my father's work, were merely the background for the eventual articulation of a thesis that these strange occurrences were the result of madness and animal appetites harbored behind the façade of human rationality. The relationship between supposed manifestations of lycanthropy and outbreaks of violence, rape, and cannibalism seemed a pedantic business. My father, a dabbler in anthropology in support of his own theories, could readily have identified which races might show this tendency most strongly. Yet another body of myth cruelly reduced to a mundane human mental state. No wolf-men, merely cannibals and lunatics. I sighed.

Once again, I sensed Sir Simon's critical eyes boring into the back of my head. I looked up to see him craning his neck to see the page open before me. I closed the book and affected an air of nonchalance, but it was too late. He was gazing at me with that familiar look of suspicion and moral outrage. He must have recognized the book—though why he would read a book about werewolves I could not imagine. I determined to continue my studies in privacy at some future date. Meanwhile, I was forced to rely on limited knowledge and my own wit to decipher the truth about this quest. I gave full license to my imagination, concocting a host of weird and wonderful explanations.

We were seeking the gypsy love child of a deposed king.

We were working to free Isabel from sinister chains that precluded her blissful marriage to Sir Simon.

We were traveling to uncover the true source of Sister Agatha's birthmark, which was something to do with the priestesses of the goddess Diana.

We were searching for a mysterious potion that would transform my father into an Arthurian hero and resurrect the form of his beloved queen so they could rule over some as-yet-undisclosed kingdom. I even threw in a few lycanthropic details to make sense of the presence of the Baring-Gould book.

None of these scenarios fit the circumstances, and none of them addressed the gypsy woman's haunting words, but the scenes wherein lovers were tragically parted or heroically reunited, mothers restored upon their deathbeds to their long-lost children, and villains routed by the desperate efforts of a few brave souls entertained me as we wound our slow, uncomfortable way across Europe.

On the last leg of that journey, I drifted off to sleep in my corner of the carriage, lulled by the sound of the wheels on the tracks, which drowned out the noise of my father's snoring. My dreams were confused but had a recurring a theme of "traveling forever without a destination."

"Very well, Isabel. The Romany know of our journey."

The words pushed me into the antechamber between sleep and wakefulness. My eyes were closed—indeed, I could not seem to open them—but my ears drank in the soft speech of my companions.

"I am sure the news has gone before us." There was Isabel's voice, placid as ever.

"They are not friendly to you." That was Sir Simon.

"Can you blame them?"

"Yes, I can. And do. And I shall not treat them with any ill-timed compassion."

"As to that, I recommend you defend yourself fully. They will not spare you if you fall into their path, Sir Simon."

"Nor you?"

"They would certainly not spare me. They would be fools to do so. And the Romany are not fools."

"Fools to have tangled themselves in the affairs of the children of darkness, perhaps."

"Thus they have learned to avoid lapses into ill-timed compassion."

"But now, when the children of darkness are the children of light…"

"The children of light? Jean-Claude and I?" Isabel did not sound convinced…or concerned. "We are still the children of Marcus, Sir Simon. You would be best served not to forget that fact."

Before Sir Simon could reply, the train slowed and lurched as the engineer put on the brakes. The train wheels shrieked their protest, jarring me fully into wakefulness. I opened my eyes and saw Sir Simon standing at the door of the carriage. My father snorted and sputtered, rubbing away the last vestiges of sleep from his eyes.

Sir Simon met my eyes. "Zagreb."

In the lull before we departed the train carriage, I slipped my notebook from my bag and circled three times around a scribbled hypothesis: "Jean-Claude—brother."

Our five-days' journey had more than doubled, so there was some justification for the general attitude of bedraggled exhaustion as we departed the train and were driven through the city. We wound past the Sava River, weaving through streets of noble buildings with a strong European flavor and Mediterranean tile roofs. Beyond the dwarfing height of the Gothic cathedral, we arrived at a large though simple ecclesial structure in dusky stucco.

We waited in the cab while Sir Simon went to the door to make inquiries. Through the window I watched the door open to a barefoot man dressed in a brown robe and with his head shaved in the fashion of a tonsure. Their conversation was not long. Sir Simon returned to us, frowning.

"I do not know what has happened. They must have been delayed." He glanced at Isabel, but she said nothing.

Sister Agatha nodded. "We will wait." She turned to the driver. "We will need accommodation." Our ordeal of traveling discomfort was not yet finished. We attempted six small inns before we could find rooms.

"Madam Sister," said the endlessly bowing proprietor of the small, cramped place that finally took us in, "Apologies! We are overwhelmed. We are tragically full up. We are…"

We were forced to share: we three ladies squeezed into one room, and my father and Sir Simon were imprisoned together in another. To this day I consider it miraculous that my father did not meet his death at the hands of that towering, long-suffering hero during this time.

For several days we waited, trapped, an echo of that eerie delay upon the water. Every day we would visit the Sveti Franjo— the Monastery of St. Francis. Every day we would return to the inn dissatisfied. Restlessness descended. Isabel remained quiet and detached from her surroundings. Sir Simon paced the streets, his face grim. My father spent his time reading, taking notes, and pursuing Sister Agatha's company. She continued to be resigned to his companionship and would sit, weary and frowning, as he delivered some passionate harangue against a minute point or scholarly quibble. More than once I entered our shared room and saw her kneeling on the ground, her face clasped in her hands. What she might have felt inclined to pray, I could well have imagined, but since her way of life probably discouraged prayers of destruction against her enemies, perhaps my imagination misled me.

Meanwhile, I explored this new city. After three days of wandering, I flattered myself that I had a passing mastery of the local streets and could have negotiated them even in the dark. I soon had the opportunity to put this mental boast to the test.

One night, when the moon was full, sleep eluded me. I lay for a long time listening to the quiet breathing of my companions and watching the tricks of light that made the room nearly as bright as day. I could have read without straining my eyes. Finally, when I had given up all hope of resting ever again in the entirety of my life, I drifted into a few hours of fitful sleep.

The change in the stentorian breathing of Sister Agatha first awakened me. After a moment of bewilderment in the imperfect darkness, I could see the restless, irritated movement of the older woman in her bed. Suddenly she sat up. I turned to see what had aroused her patent annoyance.

Isabel was muttering something in her sleep—something rhythmic, like a prayer—but either her voice was addled by sleep, or she spoke in a language unfamiliar to me.

"Sister Magdalene!" Sister Agatha's voice was sharp. "Wake up!"

Isabel turned, continuing her garbled argument more loudly, but she did not awaken. Suddenly she screamed, startling me so that I sat up. I had never witnessed someone else's nightmare. As I stared, Isabel moaned and began to thrash about the bed, still bound in some twisted limbo between sleep and waking.

Sister Agatha rose rapidly from her bed and crossed the small room. "Wake!" She shook the young woman. "Sister Magdalene! Isabel!"

The sleeping woman, shaken from the dark grip of what must have been a particularly unpleasant dream, sat bolt upright in bed, hissed what sounded like a curse in a tongue unknown to me, and pushed Sister Agatha away from her so violently that the older woman stumbled backward across the room.

For a moment they remained in this theatrical pose: Isabel, her white face a mixture of terror and defiance staring into the darkness, and the majestic form of the Breton nun cowering against the stolid wooden framework of her bed.

Isabel was the first to speak. "Forgive me, Sister," she said in her usual cold, emotionless voice. "For a moment, I did not know you. I do not know what I have been saying."

"I should hope not," wheezed her victim, on whose face the birthmark stood out in a lurid hue visible even in the imperfect darkness. "You—you know what Mother said—and know better than anyone—what—what was said when we left. Remember what you have been. You must… Girl, you must not give in to those dark dreams."

Isabel stared at her, a marble statue of unreadability.

"To lash out like one possessed. Isabel, what does it mean? Is there something—something you haven't told me? What ails you, child?"

Still there was no response. I wondered that the deafening beating of my own heart did not force her to speak.

Sister Agatha remained upon the bed and tightly clasped both knees. The moon-shaped scar upon her face continued to throb. She spoke on, more to herself than to the younger woman. "We can't be rid of that uncertainty. Is your character suitable to our life? I don't know. I just don't know. God only knows. Sister Catherine, she is not one to pose behind false courtesies. No, she never liked you and made that clear, but much of her concern had validity. Recklessness, irresponsibility—that is what she called this quest we are on. If she has told Mother once, she has told her a thousand times…. Well. Enough has been said of that. It is not her place to consider the question of your vocation. But this journey…this enterprise…may it not be of a greater risk even than Mother considered?" She shook her head, dropped to her knees, and began to murmur something—some prayer—that I could not hear.

Meanwhile, Isabel had risen silently and begun to dress. She had donned a dark cloak over her simple black dress when Sister Agatha suddenly became aware of these preparations and interrupted herself midsentence to rise to her feet.

"What *are* you doing now, girl?"

"I need some air," was the quiet response.

Before the older woman could protest, Isabel opened the door and slipped away. Sister Agatha remained on her bed, closing her eyes in what I assumed was an even more desperate plea toward heaven.

I would not wait for heaven. I too rose, dressed, wrapped a dark shawl about my head and shoulders, and ventured out into the city. Sister Agatha, absorbed in that silent converse with eternity, seemed not to notice me. I do not know what I sought or how I thought I might give comfort to Isabel. My one thought was so simple it could have been a command from a good genii: go out and see.

There was no sign of Isabel in the moonlit street, but that did not stop me. I knew where I wanted to go. Using the dominating peaks of the cathedral spires as my guide, I soon stood in the street before the simpler façade of the monastery church. My curiosity, heightened and never satisfied, had led me thither. Always when we visited, I was left alone outside on the street or in a cab. I was not permitted to join in their secret meetings. Even my father, cynical critic though he was, had somehow wormed his way into their confidence. I harbored deep resentment on this point.

On the side of the church was a large crucifixion scene. I looked for some time at the two women at the feet of the crucified. One looked weary, the other euphoric. I wondered who they were supposed to be. My education in the Christian tradition was much less robust than in other mythologies.

Isabel must be here. This was the only place they had visited during our stay, the only place that seemed to hold any interest for her. I made my way around the back to the large wooden doors, and, after a moment of hesitation, I pulled one with a firm hand. To my surprise, it opened, and I scurried inside. As it closed behind me, I thought I heard the rhythmic, bored hooting of an owl. An omen, I thought to myself. Or a benediction.

The darkness was heavier here, sprinkled with a wild array of color from the shafts of moonlight streaming through a long succession of stained glass windows. Ranks of candles throughout the building bore dancing, flickering flames. I could sense the presence of neo-Gothic beauty and imagined, rather than saw, the deep blue of the ceiling. The gold stars painted upon it twinkled even in that surreal nocturnal blending of darkness and light. I felt secure in this strange place, even in the darkness. Grotesque scenes depicting the torture of saints notwithstanding, it exuded a strong feeling of sanctuary. No gypsy curses or disembodied heads here—not in our modern day and not in my prosaic little life.

I wandered about for some time, peeking down dark aisles and into corners.

"Isabel?" I hissed.

There was no answer and no sign of her.

Finally I sat down upon a bench, feeling the strangeness of the hour. Without considering much the propriety of my actions, I lay down and almost immediately fell into a deep sleep.

It was still night when a noise nearby startled me, and I sat up, wide awake and confused as to the time and place. Looking up, I saw a man standing a few feet away, perched upon a side altar, his body oddly twisted and his arms reaching toward the empty darkness.

Several moments passed before I could calm the beating of my heart and permit my mind to work—a statue. He was merely a statue. The poor man St. Francis, in his ragged brown robes and with bloodied, outstretched palms. His face, which gazed so fixedly upward into nothingness, wore an unnerving look of ecstasy. The face of a mystic or a madman. I knew which hypothesis my father would have advocated.

So striking was this figure that at first I did not notice his companion. An errant shaft of that extraordinary moonlight burst out for one dramatic moment then died with a silent whimper. In that moment, something new caught my eye. I realized that at the side of the saint stood an enormous, gaunt brown wolf with unblinking red eyes that shone bright in the darkness. I wondered if the artist had used stone or paint to capture that eerie, fiery hue. The color of the fire of the underworld or the Christian hell.

A chill came over me, and I shuddered. I was cold and cramped, unnerved from my unmaidenly resting place. What would my father have said, I thought, smiling to myself.

Just as I was about to rise and return to the inn, my eyes fell once again upon the saint's companion. What I saw froze the marrow of my bones. As I sat, immobile in terror, the figure of the wolf changed before my eyes. Each shifting feature changed so swiftly that it dazzled my eyes—illusory, intangible, like the patterns of light through a spinning, multifaceted prism, or the spectacle of a carnival entertainer. A wonder, a trick.

The snout smaller. The eyes narrower, gentler, and with the light of a very human agony in them. The hair falling away, revealing taut cheekbones and a scraggly beard, as one sees on men in the streets who have been drunk for days.

There before me, crouched and cowering before the unconsciously ecstatic saint, was a man, his brown robes tattered and stretched, his body long, thin, twisted, and taut from the ordeal of metamorphosis. Still shaking under the influence of some strong, overwhelming emotion, the creature raised his eyes and looked at me. For one breathless, dreadful moment, our eyes met. Then the broken figure, racked with sobs, half-stumbled and half-loped off through the side door. As it closed behind him, a rush of air extinguished several of the candles beside me.

I do not know how long I sat there, staring transfixed at the spot where the strange creature had stood beside his carved patron. Suddenly, out of the darkness, I thought I saw the grinning dark face of the stowaway boy—that decapitated face from the ship. I blinked, and the face had disappeared.

This new vision brought me back to myself, and my fingers began to tremble, a movement that spread until every limb shook and my teeth chattered with icy shock. I stood, wrapping my shawl more tightly around my shoulders and shaking myself to be rid of that overwhelming, bewildering feeling. A dream. A vision. A hallucination—complete with werewolves and disembodied heads. I took a few unsteady steps before I froze once again in terror.

There at my feet was a tattered remnant of brown fabric. I cringed as if it were some talisman of evil, yet curiosity still pulsed strong within me. I extended one timid foot and nudged the fabric. It unfolded before me and disclosed a large tuft of coarse, matted fur.

I ran through the church, tears of abject terror streaming down my face, and burst out of the doors into the light of the dawn—into the startled arms of Sir Simon Gwynne.

CHAPTER 6

8 MAY 1906: ZAGREB

"Mein Vater, mein Vater, und hörest du nicht,
Was Erlkönig mir leise verspricht?"
"Sei ruhig, bleibe ruhig, mein Kind;
In dürren Blättern säuselt der Wind."

— Johann Wolfgang von Goethe, "Erlkönig"

AWARE ONLY OF MY TERROR AND THE OVERWHELMING CONSOLATION I had discovered in the broad chest and muscular arms of the astonished Sir Simon, I at first had little consciousness of the impact of my dithered hysteria upon him. Nevertheless, it soon dawned on me that my frantic, tearful repetitions of "A man!" "Teeth!" "Not a statue!" "The hair!" "Burning eyes!" "That face!" and "The horror!" seemed oddly comprehensible to my bronzed and, I felt sure, unwilling hero. He did not push me away but held me tighter.

I raised my face, blotchy and sodden as it must have been, to look up at him. "It was dreadful." I sniffed. "I was so...so frightened."

"You were dreaming," was all Sir Simon said, but he lacked both conviction and facility in lying.

I pushed myself away and, punching his chest with my fists in childish emphasis, permitted the tears to continue to stream down my face. "I wasn't dreaming! I wasn't! I know what I saw, and you know it too! No one will tell me! Everyone leaves me on the side! You want to keep it all from me, as if I were a child or a halfwit, and you could not care less what I have seen and heard on my own! Pompous ignorance and neglect! It's unjust! Unjust! Unjust!"

At about this time, I became dimly aware that we were observed. Nearby, a thin, wiry grocer with an Asiatic flavor in his bearing was preparing his stall for the morning market. He stared at us, frowning with increasing hostility and suspicion at my companion.

Perhaps provoked by this surveillance, the English side of Sir Simon's character became more pronounced.

"Miss Howard, you are overcome. Do control yourself."

My flow of tears continued unchecked.

"Miss Howard, you really must…"

Catching the grocer's eye, Sir Simon said something rapidly in a language with which I was not familiar—neither Italian nor French.

The cloud on the grocer's face cleared. He beamed at me and gave a rapid-fire series of instructions to Sir Simon. Judging from the many and varied gesticulations in every direction, it seemed as if we were being told to take turns that negated each other. I was about to say so (perhaps with some foolish thought of proclaiming my own mastery of the streets), but Sir Simon thanked him, tucked my arm in his, and stalked off with me in tow at a speed that relieved me of breath—and, without breath, one cannot continue to deliver a highly emotional scene. This too struck me as unjust. After that terrifying ordeal, I had earned the right to that performance.

I expected to be restored in disgrace to my father, my perfidy exposed to all, and my person condemned to some ignominious confinement. Sir Simon was likely of the school of thought which believed that emotionally unstable females ought to be plied with smelling salts and locked in their bedrooms. I was surprised, therefore, to find myself seated in the early morning at a small riverside café.

Sir Simon ordered a robust breakfast for me. I started, without much conviction, to argue.

"Goblin chasing," he said dryly after dismissing the waiter, "is for overwrought and undernourished children. You will eat as you are told or"—he held up his hand to block my impulsive interruption—"or I shall continue to tell you nothing."

That was enough of a threat to persuade me to eat as instructed. He was right. I found my appetite and, discovering that midnight marauding and "goblin chasing" left me ravenous, relished the eggs, polenta, and cornbread with paprika, dry meats, and two cups of strong coffee. I would have enjoyed another cup, but Sir Simon intervened.

"You're already skittish. One more cup and you'll be talking even less sense than usual." He smiled as he said it, belying the criticism of his words. "You really are the most exasperating child, Miss Howard."

"I'm not a child. I'm quite a woman, for all you are treating me like some irresponsible infant. I'll have you know," I added, "that you have no idea of the breadth and depth of my scholarly knowledge. My father would never admit it, but his career would likely be in shambles without me. And anyway, I wish you'd all call me Athene. Then I really will feel certain you are going to let me into your confidence at last."

"It's not a fit story for your ears, and if I had my way, you would be well out of it."

I bristled. "As I just told you, I'm quite grown up, Sir Simon Gwynne, as you can plainly see if you care to attend to me at all. I've found myself bizarrely enmeshed in this business, and I don't know how I am to weather it if I am not granted basic information. It isn't fair or reasonable. It is this sort of silliness that leads to all sorts of perfectly likeable characters dying horribly in stories when a little bit of a warning might have saved them."

He burst out laughing. "Come to think of it, why on earth *should* I take you into my confidence? Goddess of wisdom? More the spirit of reckless mischief! The impertinence of it! Telling you anything will only encourage you."

"I *did* eat my breakfast," I said primly. "And you said you would tell me all about it."

While this was not strictly true, he appeared to take it in good humor. I hoped this mood would continue. His handsome face was warm and reassuring when he smiled. "I am not a storyteller," he warned. "I'm a practical man, and I've no time for flights of imagination."

"Luckily, I've a surfeit of it. Be as practical as you wish and I will fill in what's missing."

He tried to look stern, but I leaned my elbows onto the table and propped my chin onto my two hands and waited.

He sighed and, with a resigned but not unkindly air, began. "You were not dreaming, Miss—Athene. There are some poor souls beset by darkness—part men, part beast. Your father would call it a sickness or a delusion. Something to be cured by doctors of the mind. We would call it an evil oppression. A crippling wound that, though they strive to overcome it, can only be relieved by God's mercy."

"It is a fiend," I quoted, "a worse than fiend, a man-fiend—a worse than man-fiend, a man-wolf-fiend."

"Yes. I thought I saw you reading Baring-Gould. Thoroughly inappropriate reading material for—"

"I didn't expect it," I admitted, interrupting him. "That fortune-teller spoke of darkness and the children of darkness, but she didn't say anything about wolves."

He frowned. "What *did* she tell you?"

"Oh," I replied as lightly as I could, for I did not mean to distract him from his tale by a tale of my own, "she became hysterical. Babbling dreadfully about darkness and danger. Nothing concrete. She was clearly terrified, poor creature. But never mind that. The creature I saw last night, was he one of these wolfmen?"

"Yes." Every trace of levity vanished from his countenance. I saw grief and something else unfamiliar to me—a sort of manly compassion for weak, broken creatures. "I am sure that he was. One poor man in the grip of the madness, seeking sanctuary again that his soul might be restored."

"How can he be restored? Isn't it a business of drugs or enchantment? Is that something that can be healed, like a sickness?"

"It is not so simple. Through prayer, discipline, and penance, often they can be relieved from the worst of their malady and spared those dark episodes where the man is transformed to the beast. The poor man you saw last night will today be in despair and terror from the nightmare of whatever he has done in the night in that other form."

"Why, then, are we here? Have we come to see these creatures? Why? What can we do? Are you here to help them somehow? Is it…is it Isabel's brother?" The questions poured out of me, though prudence decreed caution in pressing Sir Simon too eagerly. The well of his confidences was all too likely to dry up.

He paused. "Isabel's brother is one such poor soul. For nearly ten years he has been in the care of religious brothers like those we visit here. He has been safe and, as best he can be, well. He's kept in a small, secluded place in the countryside nearby here. Some weeks ago, however, I received word that he was in great distress and had begged to see his sister. I journeyed to New York, where Isabel has lived since the time of their separation. Isabel, accompanied by Sister Agatha, has come with me to see Jean-Claude. We were to meet here, in Zagreb. Even now we await his arrival."

"What will you do?"

"That I cannot tell you. I do not know what has troubled the boy, though he must now be fully a man. And I cannot say what Isabel will deem best."

"She is not like him."

There was no question about this in my mind, yet some cloud passed over Sir Simon's face. "She is not beset as he is with the mark of the beast, if that is what you mean."

"The children of darkness," I murmured. Then I ventured, "The children of…Marcus?"

Sir Simon sat forward. His face darkened. "Where did you hear that name?"

"The gypsy used it. And…" I took a deep breath. "And I heard Isabel say it once. I didn't mean to listen—she spoke it when I was half asleep. Is…" I hesitated, for a forbidding look was on his face. "Is he dead?"

"Yes," he said shortly. "Do not speak of him to Isabel. Miss Howard—"

"Athene!"

"Athene, you must promise not to speak his name to Isabel."

I solemnly agreed. Anxiety still creased his forehead, so I attempted a new approach. "What have you to do with it?"

The shaft was ill-judged. The shadow upon his face deepened— the shadow of a wall between me and his private thoughts.

"I am their friend," he said.

He offered no further details, but I could readily supply them myself. In a moment I envisioned a younger Isabel riding bareback on a monstrous, wolf-like steed, galloping across English moors, her long black hair wild in the moonlight. And there was Sir Simon, barrel-breasted and impassioned, sweeping her into his arms and declaring with deep, possessive throbbing in his voice, "You are mine!"

"No," cried she, resisting his embrace and turning away her face, "it cannot be, because..."

Here my imagination faltered a bit. Would she consider herself unworthy? Would it be more that she had singled herself out for some cruel sacrifice—like a suttee, where Indian wives were immolated on their husbands' funeral pyres, except in this case it would be for a brother? Or perhaps she had made a pact to free her brother of the werewolf curse by self-imprisonment in a nunnery? Perhaps...

I realized that Sir Simon's satirical eye was upon me. I banished this narrative puzzle and tried not to look as self-conscious and guilty as I felt.

"There is one thing more you must promise me, Athene Howard," he said. "You must promise me you will not gallivant about at night."

"You must have been out at night too," I pointed out, "or at least in early morning."

"I am not an unprotected female. I know the dangers, and I am prepared for them."

"Are you armed?" I asked breathlessly.

Rather than responding, Sir Simon glared before sighing and removing an aged but well-tended gold watch from his breast pocket. On its back was a strange, etched design—some heraldic symbol with a bee at its center—but he replaced it in his pocket before I could see anything more.

"It's time we went." His voice brooked no opposition. "They will be on their way to the monastery by now."

I followed meekly, grateful for the little glimpse I had been granted into the inner life and logic of this daring enterprise and not wishing to endanger my precarious new position in his estimation. I felt sure that he was motivated by pity and pragmatism, and that he feared the impact of my continued uninformed recklessness. It was not flattering, but it had brought about an improvement in circumstances nonetheless. My notes would develop considerably that evening.

I was mildly self-conscious when we arrived back at the monastery. The others were descending from a cab when I walked up alongside Sir Simon. I did not know what to expect—what sort of censure or suspicion for my midnight disappearance or the fact that I was now in company with Sir Simon. Isabel too concerned me. What might be her behavior toward me after I had witnessed that bizarre outbreak of passion she had displayed in the night?

I need not have bothered with either concern. As usual, my comings and goings were completely lacking in interest to my father. The others continued to consider me of little consequence—not out of incivility but simply because all things paled in comparison to their pressing object.

Sir Simon knocked at the door. A short man wearing spectacles and that increasingly familiar brown robe opened it, and the others passed through the portal into the sanctum beyond. Sir Simon still stood back and, as I hesitated on the threshold, beckoned for me to follow.

The other three started, as if noticing me for the first time. "Athene," said my father with clear annoyance, "wait outside."

Sir Simon stood between me and the door. "It is best and safest for all of us to be informed henceforth."

This was the first but not the last time that I wondered who precisely was the leader of this adventure. Sister Agatha had seemed dominant upon the ship. Then we had witnessed my father's strange power over her. On the other hand, from what Sir Simon had told me, the real object and motivation of their journey was the delivery of Isabel to her brother's side, giving her preeminence of will in what would follow. Yet for all his courtesy to the two women and his acceptance of Sister Agatha's inexplicable decision to admit my father to their company, there was a way in which Sir Simon towered above them as the man of action. I could not untangle it.

Whatever the hierarchy might be, the others recognized—or at least acquiesced—to Sir Simon's mandate. My father shrugged and walked down the hall behind the young man who had opened the door. Sister Agatha, who seemed the least troubled of the three, gave a slight but stately bow in acceptance and followed. I glanced at Isabel. She was looking directly at me, her dark eyes searching. She stood thus for a full minute, leaving me to squirm as if I had been subjected to a penetrating inquisition. Then, as she was about to speak, we were interrupted by a loud, angry knocking at the front door, punctuated by some choice words in a coarse Italian dialect.

A second brother in brown, with a thin, anxious face and wisps of fading flaxen hair—the fading blood relation of that same race scattered throughout the city—materialized beside us and hurried toward the door. He opened it to disclose the florid, sweaty form of a nearly apoplectic farmer. His stringy black hair was matted and unkempt, and his heavy features seemed borne down by the weight of gross, self-indulgent habits. He was in high and unrestrained temper. The force of his verbal assault nearly knocked down his victim.

"Again! Again!" He shrieked in his native tones. "Again! Six cows! Six! My best cows! I shall have the law on you all! You will pay! You will pay for all! I, Giovanni, shall make it so! You mewling monks with your vicious beasts! They should be slaughtered all! I shall tell! I shall tell! You will pay!"

The young man in brown, who seemed ill-equipped to handle the onslaught, had made a few attempts at conciliatory noises but in vain. He could not slow the tide of the farmer's fury.

Then an icy-cold voice broke through the tirade.

"Be silent," said Isabel.

Startled by this uncompromising command, the farmer stopped abruptly, his mouth agape and his face swiftly turning a lurid purple hue.

She fixed him with a stern, unblinking look, her black eyes revealing a basilisk-like quality. I recoiled from her, as if I and not this petty man were her unhappy object.

"When you say six," Isabel continued in the same hard tone, "you mean one—and that one was aged and already dying of neglect. You lack mercy as well as discretion and abandoned that poor, dumb animal to the wild. You could not be bothered even to put her out of her slow misery. You were not there to tend to the animals you feed—irregularly, for your habits are as coarse as your manners. You were, in fact, paying your secret addresses to the wife of the butcher. He will soon become aware of this sordid affair, and you would be best advised to reform your life and embrace penance and temperance."

At the mention of the butcher's wife, the face of the gaping farmer blanched. He seemed to be on the verge of impotent protest when Isabel dismissed him.

"You will leave now, and you will not return to this monastery again, else I shall hear of it."

A few moments later he stood outside the closed door. I waited to hear if he would renew his frenzied knocking. I thought I heard his voice muttering in hushed tones, "*Stregheria.*" *Witchcraft.*

I felt there was a great deal of sense in such an accusation. Isabel was not like her brother. But, then, what *was* she?

"Isabel…" began Sir Simon.

She looked at him coolly. "Yes?'

He sighed and shook his head. "Nothing."

She nodded as if in approval of his change of mind. "Let us follow the friar," she said and walked rapidly down the hall. Sir Simon followed with a firm step, and I hurried along in their wake.

We joined the others in a small parlor devoid of decoration where three tonsured men in brown robes waited. They were standing when we entered and beckoned us, bowing with gentle civility, into simple wooden chairs. Then one of them—the eldest and, by his manner, the master—sat as well and looked at us.

The unexpected stillness unnerved me. Silence was the custom of the place, and that slowness and quietness of expression, which I'd attributed to some underlying sense of caution was, I came to believe, a product of their way of life. Silence, discipline, and prayer. A life of simplicity and perhaps of peace as well.

Isabel, rather than the master of the friars, spoke first. "He will not come. You do not know where he is."

Slowly, soberly, the friar shook his head. "He will not come," he repeated in a soft, slow, droning voice. "We do not know where he is."

"He has been gone from your care for how long?"

He smiled a weary, sad smile, still in that slow, ponderous way. "Why do you ask what you already know, my child?"

She merely looked at him, patiently waiting.

"Ten days." He sighed. "The small house in which he has lived for so long is far withdrawn from the city, but it should not have taken more than a few days for them to arrive. As we have told you, thus far we have thought perhaps they were delayed somehow in travel, as you were. We learned this morning that they were delayed by the search. For he…"

The silence lingered for an intolerably long time before he gently shook his head. "I begin wrongly. Here are Brother Leopold and Brother Sebastian. They were his companions and will tell their own tale."

The two brothers thus identified had been standing in respectful silence with docile hands hanging straight at their sides. Their serene immobility had fascinated me for some moments—I was myself prone to attacks of fidgeting and when forced into waiting for something fell into that habit ("singularly unladylike" my father said) of shifting my weight from one foot to the other.

"He has long been with us in silence and solitude." Brother Leopold spoke in the same quiet, measured tone as his superior. "Of late, he has spoken of you often, Sister, and was fitful and anxious. Dark dreams had come upon him. His prayers were sometimes frantic, and he looked about him constantly, as if some new darkness were nigh."

"And before," said Isabel. "This is not a sudden change. You have seen the signs."

"Not so well as you might expect," said the second brother with a sorrowful shake of the head. "Inattentiveness at prayer we cannot always see, for it can be concealed. We did not at first notice his absences. And his temper had returned. It was sudden and quick. One day for some slight or injury he struck at one of the brothers and dealt him a blow upon the head. It brought blood. The sight of that blood put him into a frenzy, and he would do penance so severe that his elders stopped him, lest he do to himself even more grievous injury."

"Measures were indeed taken," said Brother Leopold, "and to all disciplines and cautions he responded with a great show of mortification and grief. Yet such scenes became more and more frequent."

"The madness was descending," said Isabel, "and I am sure there were other low habits that permitted its final mastery."

Neither of the friars spoke. I could not imagine they would argue with Isabel. She spoke with frank certainty.

"The other," continued Isabel. "The third who was with you. I would speak with him."

There was a pause. Brother Leopold and Brother Sebastian exchanged swift, troubled glances before looking toward their seated master.

He met her face unwaveringly, again pausing for a long time before speaking. "He is unwell."

"I know it," she replied. "Yet I will see him."

For several minutes—which felt to my impatient mind like an hour—they stared in silence at each other. Finally, the master nodded. Brother Leopold departed from the room. We remained there in grim silence.

What of the others during this strange interview? No one else had spoken, and no one seemed to expect anyone else to speak. My father had a small notebook open upon his knee and had been assiduously scribbling minute notes throughout. They would be largely useless to him until I had unraveled them. Sister Agatha sat with her hands folded in her lap, her eyes nearly closed and her lips moving in the wordless aspiration of silent prayer. Sir Simon had been uncharacteristically still, like a Viking hero transformed into a bronze statue.

This last thought brought back the memory of my nighttime adventure, and I shivered. I wondered where that strange creature was now, and in which state—beast or man. My superficial investigation into the realm of werewolves led me to believe that there was a powerful relationship to the phases of the moon. On the other hand, the representations of anthrobestial metamorphosis that riddled folklore and nursery tales were not always moon-bound. Perhaps he was even now a wolf, chained in some dark dungeon beneath this place with its silent, serene friars and sterile, unadorned walls. I found it hard to imagine this quiet man in brown, with his furrowed brow and slow, measured speech as concealing dark, violent secrets. But was that not, in essence, the case? Were they not the keepers of monsters?

This was a grim stream of thought and prepared me ill for what soon would follow. Just when I had said to myself that, more than anything in life, I hoped never again to see the man-wolf whom I had seen transformed the night before, the door opened, readmitting Brother Leopold and another friar. As I gazed in anxious horror, he who had been a wolf stood before us, his head bowed and his face red and swollen, as if from hours of passionate weeping.

Chapter 7

8 May 1906: Zagreb

Ah, how the poor little sister did lament when she had to fetch the water, and how her tears did flow down her cheeks! "Dear God, do help us," she cried. "If the wild beasts in the forest had but devoured us, we should at any rate have died together." "Just keep your noise to yourself," said the old woman, "it won't help you at all."

— Brothers Grimm, *Hansel and Gretel*

The newcomer stood upon the threshold for a moment without speaking or even making eye contact with any of those within. In the light of day, I could see him clearly. He was younger than I would have thought from my nightmare encounter. His eyebrows and beard seemed to retain some mark of the beast, for they were the first and most prominent characteristic in that shattered, strained face. His eyes, which remained lowered, were concealed beneath puffy, exhausted eyelids. I noticed that he had exchanged his ragged robe for another, this one worn yet intact. His feet were bare, and dark black hair curled across the tops of them.

"Brother Luke," said the eldest friar in a firm voice. "Sit."

One of the others drew a chair to the center of the room. The wolf-friar wearily obeyed.

"Speak of what you know," was the next command.

This time he did not immediately obey. I wondered if his recent transformation had robbed him of speech or if he were merely recalcitrant. Would the others be startled if he began to howl? Perhaps he was still teetering between the sane and the feral. I wondered if anyone had thought to bring a weapon or some other means of defense to this strange meeting. I was glad for the presence of Sir

Simon. He had not admitted to carrying a gun, but I was certain that he could deal with any assault.

"Brother Luke." Isabel spoke this time, her voice clear and much louder than I expected it to be in that hushed place and with that clearly unstable young man present. "Tell me of your friend. Tell me of Jean-Claude."

Small, dark eyes flashed with anger and flew to her face. When he did speak, I half expected him to growl. His accent was faint, but I thought I heard strains of Spain or perhaps Portugal. "Brother Jean-Claude was kind to me."

"I am sure he was. Jean-Claude has a genius for empathy." Something in her tone made this sound less than praise.

With startling rapidity, his face registered a spectrum of intense feeling. "He is a good man. He has a weakness. What man does not? Who is to judge these weak, broken men? Can you see into the hearts of men? Can you see into your own hearts? You do not know what it is to be shackled to madness! You do not know how you can battle ceaselessly against the draw of the moon only to find yourself in the toils of that evil spirit once more. One misstep! Only one! And all the years of upright, forthright behavior come to naught! You cannot know—"

"Brother Luke, I am not here to discuss the morality of your plight. I am here to learn what you know of Jean-Claude."

I thought her sternness uncalled for, but it had its impact.

"Why should I tell you?" He fell back into his chair, his eyes lowered and his posture completely uncooperative. "You won't understand."

"You will tell me because I may yet help him."

"What can you do that others could not?"

"That is my business. Yours is to tell me what you know."

"He is a good man," returned the brother.

"He has had a capacity for goodness, but his actions will have their due consequence, as well you know. As he embraces the viciousness, he will descend, destroying all goodness and giving evil full reign."

The brother was now breathing heavily, his eyes red with renewed tears. "How can you speak in this way! Do you not know how he loves you? How he speaks of you! And you—have you no heart? You think *he* is the monster?"

The other brown-robed men moved to intervene, but Isabel checked them firmly with a gesture of her hand. "How does Jean-Claude speak of me?"

"He loves you. He would give his life for you. He would kill anyone who threatened you. And you—you're his sister. You speak of him so…"

"I speak of him this way *because* I am his sister. You cannot pluck him from this madness. You cannot stop him. Though he is like a brother to you, and your friendship is deep and lasting, you cannot stand between him and the darkness when he embraces it. You cannot save him."

"Can you?" he snapped, a jealous flush in his angry eyes.

"No."

"Then why have you come?"

"Because he asked for me. And that is a sign that his descent is not yet complete, and there may yet be hope. I know him, and I know the madness. I know too the darkness. Like Jean-Claude, I was begotten of it. We are forged together—shackled, perhaps—against the darkness. And if the darkness consumes one of us it may well consume the other. I do not bear the mark of the beast. The darkness in me is quite different. I can yet fight it ably and perhaps give Jean-Claude a chance—a moment—to escape from this new hell he forges for himself. But there may also be a long course of blood and horror before us, no matter the outcome."

"How can you be so unfeeling?" the man cried, once again speaking the question in my own heart, which was rent by the distress of this strange, wounded creature and his despair over his friend.

"What purpose could be served by tears?" Though I thought she spoke gently, she retained that matter-of-fact coolness that made it seem she was incapable of compassion. "Now," she commanded, "tell me all you know."

Brother Luke's eyes fell again, and he twisted his hand in the rope tied around his waist so tightly that impressions stood out white and painful upon the skin. "I came to these brothers seven years ago. I was desperate. Near death—or hoped I was. They restrained me for some weeks. When I awoke from that hell, I found a life, a peace I had never known and…and a companion unlike any other I have known. You say he was like a brother to me. I do not know, for I have had none. But there was a friendship so deep in our shared suffering that it was better than a brotherhood." He shook his head. "No one knew that Brother Jean-Claude was in any danger. He was cheerful. Ever smiling. Praying and serving. Obedient. Clever. Loved by all the community."

I feared his fingers might be severed, which made me think once again of dismembered corpses.

"There were some who said envious, spiteful things, but it was clear why they would calumniate someone we knew to be affectionate and kind. They said his friendships were indiscreet, but his motives were always pure. Always loving. There was no proof of their vicious hints. None at all.

"At first when he was absent from prayer, there were ready excuses. He was busy serving the poor. And once he was caught in a rainstorm and could not return in time. That made malicious tongues wag, but he was soaked through and truly penitent and submitted to every discipline. We only began to be truly concerned eight weeks ago. There were other incidents. I am sure you have already heard of them. Sudden violence and the horror that followed."

He paused and wetted his lips with his tongue before going on. "One night he did not return to the cloister at all. It was late on the following day when he came back to us. He was not himself. I do not know what account he gave, but the discipline was severe that time.

I saw him and tried to speak to him, and he was restless and...not himself." Once again he looked up, with renewed defensiveness in his eyes. "It was not like him to be unkind or vicious to his brothers. It was a sign for greater concern even than his mysterious absence."

Once again, his eyes fell, and the relentless, tortuous contortions of the rope continued. "A few weeks passed without incident. Then another nighttime absence. This time he was found in the morning cowering in a heap before the altar. His habit was torn almost into shreds, and there was...blood...upon his face and hands. Once again I do not know what he said, but I do know that he asked for you. It was agreed that he would journey here to meet you, but—but there were strange portents in the night. Owls shrieking and a moon like fire in the sky. Even the strongest of us must have struggled alone in our cells. The next day we awoke, and he was gone." He shrugged. "He bade no one farewell. The rest you know."

"Were there any visitors?" Isabel asked. "Any letters or messages? Anything that you saw? Any other person who might have roused the wolf?"

"No, I tell you. There was no one. No one." He looked at her with the first spark of something like curiosity I had seen in him. "Who do you think would have come?"

"No one," agreed Isabel quietly. "No one. Now, what happened on the journey here?"

He did not respond and began mulishly tracing figures on the floor with one sandaled foot.

"You were not sent with them," she said even more quietly. "You followed."

He looked up at her, sullen again. "Why do you ask questions when you know the answer?"

She did not reply.

After a moment, he shrugged. "Yes, I followed. I sneaked from the monastery in the early morning and followed. We traveled quickly, though our means were modest. Even from a distance I could see that Brother Jean-Claude was fitful and anxious. That delayed their progress. He seemed reluctant and even resisted as they drew near to our journey's end. One night…nine days ago…ten…I do not know. I was sleeping in the woods some distance from the others so they would not see me. We were near to Zagreb. And he was to be restored to you, whatever his reason might be.

"In the night I was roused by some sense of danger. We children of the night, even when we resist the call of darkness, we retain many of those other senses. I had not been in wolf form for many years—not since I was brought to the brothers for safekeeping. I needed no constraint. I could hear our fellow creatures of darkness—the bats flitting above the trees. Larger creatures prowling for a meal—the clever lynx and the lumbering bear. The ceaseless, dull call of the owl, harbinger of destruction. A scene so familiar, yet I was not part of it. It did not threaten me or interest me. Then, once again I heard the owl, and a strange feeling crept over me. A chill over my heart. I looked up and I saw him."

His eyes widened, and he gazed out into the middle distance, as if the vision and its horror were fresh upon him. "There upon a large rock, striking harshly against the moonlight. He twisted with the pain of transformation, struggling against it, but as it gained mastery, he embraced the violence. The creature rose, massive and majestic, his head bowed as sweet, cruel liberty washed over him. The greatest among us and the mightiest. A legend rising before my eyes. That howl… It was not of pain but of strange triumph. The freedom of the beast who had regained his ascendency."

The passion ebbed from him in one fierce tide, and he sat, deflated and in despair, a sorry object before this attendant audience. "Then I thought there must be no mercy for such as we are." He began to weep. "How can we not fear that we are beyond hope? How can we not fear that all of this"—he gestured about him—"must be a lie?"

I wondered no one stopped him. It seemed discordant in that place, and I assumed that his fellows were duly horrified. They did not *look* horrified or even surprised. Perhaps they were used to these sorts of soul-wrenched theatrics. I wondered how many in the monastery were like this bizarre wolfman. It must have made for unpleasant supper conversations, with men who might explode into bestial violence at any moment, and would thereafter collapse like hysterical females.

"Last night," said Isabel, calm but relentless, "last night you went to find him."

"Do you not understand at all?" He pleaded, the tears continuing to stream down his face. "How could I not attempt to find him—to save him—even if it cost me my soul? Yes! I would give that! I would bear the fires of hell—and do it gladly!—if it gave him a chance at salvation!"

I was impressed in spite of myself, but Isabel merely said, "Do not barter with God. It avails nothing. But—" she shook her head "—I do understand. A little. Now. You have told me everything?"

He nodded.

"Go with these men. Give yourself to their care. You may yet be restored."

"And Brother Jean-Claude?"

"What of him?"

He wetted his lips again. "Can I… May I not come with you? I could help!"

"No, you could not. And you will not come with us. Do not expect to see him again in this life. Pray that you may in the next." With this uncertain consolation, she dismissed him.

"Go with Brother Leopold," said the superior, not without kindness. "You know what must follow."

Brother Luke rose, trembling, nodded his obedience as if he were too weary or too grieved to care what became of him, and slowly stumbled out of the room.

"What *will* happen to him?" I blurted out as the door closed behind them.

This earned me an annoyed glare from my father and a cautioning glance from Sir Simon.

"He will be constrained for some time," said the superior, "and given such tasks and such discipline as to restore his self-mastery. It will be a long time before he is restored. For now, he will be close to the beast, capable of another collapse without warning. The blood of the wolf is roused, and it will take much time to calm and contain it." He turned to Isabel. "Do not judge Brother Luke by this."

She shook her head. "Do not grieve yourself. Did I not say I know the madness? How could I judge his torment? Keep him safe as best you can. I pray he regains his peace. But you must ensure his restraint is quite fast, for he would brook any danger to escape while he still believes he could follow our trail. Do not be imprudent in your gentleness. Mere locks will not check him. Prepare for him as you would one at the height of his nighttime powers. In the madness of his affection, he may yet prove more dangerous."

The old friar bowed his head. "It shall be as you say."

I would have asked more questions, but the renewed warning look from Sir Simon was inescapably clear, and I submitted to it in hope of soliciting further information from him later. Indeed, I could not risk endangering his newfound openness, limited though it was.

"Have you a map?" asked Isabel. "Show me precisely where these things took place."

From a small table by the window, Brother Leopold produced a map, and we crowded around it to see.

The superior pointed to a small, unremarkable point close to the city. "There is a village nearby. And we have heard some reports, subsequent to your brother's disappearance, of violence to cattle. Nothing yet of a more serious nature."

"No man's blood," noted Isabel coolly. "That is well. It will not be long."

"What is it that awakened him?" asked Sir Simon.

Isabel did not look up from the map, but the superior shook his head. "We cannot say. Brother Luke is right that some of the brethren suggested that he had fallen into other sins, paving the way for this return of the wolf. But beyond his disappearances, there was no sign of any other viciousness."

"No woman," said Sir Simon grimly.

"No woman," the other agreed.

My father made a sotto voce comment—something about David and Jonathan—that, by its tone, was meant to be pejorative.

Isabel stopped and turned to him, her eyes full upon his face and her eyebrows raised. "Doctor Howard, do not let your obsession limit your understanding. And do not be misled by the puppy-like devotion of that unfortunate brother."

I thought my father would make a spiteful rejoinder, but he took this rebuke in stride and fell silent.

Isabel returned to the map. "You may not have known of a woman, but there may well have been one. I would be astonished if there were not. It matters little now—blood and vice have awakened the beast. This cannot be ignored or erased. Only repented, if there is still time."

"There is only one thing that I can imagine might have roused our poor brother," the superior said slowly.

Isabel looked up.

"There has been some talk and some fear of the rise of a new darkness in our midst. I have seen nothing here, but there have been hints of evil spirits, newly awakened. You asked if anyone had spoken with him. You of all people know well that the spirits of darkness can deliver messages invisible to even the most anxious eyes."

Something in this made Sir Simon's eyes narrow, and he looked at Isabel, but her gaze was unwavering and uncommunicative.

"The gypsies are restless," the friar continued. "Perhaps there you will find answers."

"You know the dangers that lie there. If Jean-Claude has fallen among them, they will not spare him." Then she repeated those words I had overheard upon the train: "They are not such fools."

"Fools, Sister?" Sister Agatha had not spoken through this entire strange exchange, so this soft question made me jump. My father too looked startled and curious.

Isabel nodded. "Pardon, Sister Agatha."

"Some power?" mused Sir Simon. "What would have put Jean-Claude under the sway of that power? I should have thought…" He stopped, looked at Isabel, shook his head, and said nothing more.

The superior turned once again to Isabel. "What will you do?"

"We will go to the place where he was last seen. I do not expect to find much, for the trail has gone cold, but perhaps we will find some clue that will lead us on."

"What do you require of us?'

"Nothing. We have all that we need. We must travel swiftly. If we have a need of you, we will send word. But you must not expect it."

The friar nodded. "Go with God, Sister. And may he have mercy on your enterprise." He raised his hand in blessing. My father, arrested in the act of scribbling furiously in his notebook, hesitated. Then he shrugged and continued to write.

A few minutes later we stood together outside the monastery. I was considering how different the façade looked in the daylight and not attending to the conversation when my father's petulant voice drew me back to the present.

"All I said was that there are developments in psychiatric medicine that may prove beneficial. Such medieval practices as I am sure are daily witnessed here are—"

"If you're suggesting the electrostatic machine again," began Sir Simon with visible anger, "let me tell you, sir, that I consider your comments as unhelpful as they are inappropriate. Pray recall that you are our companion and guest on sufferance, and your purported expertise is useless in the face of an earnestly real problem."

My father's face turned a purple hue, and he launched into what promised to be a lengthy treatise on the backwardness of medieval superstition, the limitations of unsophisticated intellects, and the incomparable developments in modern scientific theories.

"Owls," said Isabel quietly.

My father stopped mid-sentence and stared at her.

I had heard the hooting as well and wondered what had prompted the nocturnal bird to awaken betimes—so passing a thought about an almost insignificant noise that I was startled to hear Isabel call attention to it. I looked at her suspiciously, though of what precisely I could not say.

To my astonishment, she was smiling. "A tribute to our goddess of wisdom, perhaps? Come. We must prepare to depart as soon as possible."

At the inn, as I collected my things, I tried not to pay too close or too obvious attention to my two companions. But my mind was full of those two women. Sister Agatha had spoken so little that day, and I was curious to know what went on in her regal Breton mind. Isabel remained an impenetrable enigma, and she also seemed to sense what I was thinking, so that inquiry must remain impossible. Who could question anything when met with that coolly evaluating gaze? Nevertheless, I hoped that my progress with Sir Simon would be matched by a growing understanding with at least one of the other members of our company.

Sister Agatha, intent on packing her simple belongings, did not appear conscious of my presence. I thought I saw her look once or twice toward Isabel with something like concern in her eyes, but such glances were so brief that I always doubted myself a moment later.

I finished my meager packing and sought out my father.

Most of his belongings we had sent on to our house in Paris as we passed through, but he had still managed to reduce his part of the small room to complete chaos. There was no sign of Sir Simon, so I quietly entered and began to assist in gathering and organizing my father's scattered effects.

"Well, there you are, Athene," said my father with heavy, wounded sarcasm. "I wonder you have time to assist me in my painful efforts. So busy and involved you seem to have become."

I said nothing, continuing to collect sundry garments, three notebooks left upon the floor, a fourth wedged between the bed and the wall, and five abused texts discarded into a heap beside his traveling trunk—the smallest he possessed but three times larger than my own.

"Are we to continue on with them, Father? Or are we to return to Paris?"

"Why, girl! Now that you are so intimate with these good people, could I deprive you of their company? I am not so selfish!"

There was nothing to be gained by continuing to attempt to speak to him while he was in this mood, so I finished my efforts in silence. He was willing enough to sit down and watch, finding no small relief for his frustrated feelings through constant, petulant criticism.

I did not complete my work too soon. Within minutes of our arrival downstairs, Sir Simon reappeared to announce that he had procured a private carriage for our use. The driver, a lean figure in black with a low, sweeping hat, quickly stowed our luggage and beckoned for all passengers to take their places.

Squeezed between my father and the side of the carriage, I finally found that my nighttime adventures had caught up with me. We were on our way to face untold dangers, but the bulk of Sir Simon was opposite me, and that was security enough. After a few half-hearted attempts to keep awake, I fell deeply and dreamlessly asleep with my head against the cold upholstery.

Chapter 8

> ...Now he invented something new
> And sly. He raised the illusion of dust on the Nemean
> Plain. The generals gazed astounded at the fog overhead.
> He added tumultuous noise, a clamour that seemed like
> Weapons clashing, galloping cavalry, fearsome shouts
> On the wandering breeze. The leaders' hearts pounded,
> The men murmured, confused...
> To the fearful nothing is false.
>
> — Statius, *Thebaid*

Some hours later, I awoke with a jolt and found myself in imperfect darkness and pronounced discomfort. After a moment, the racket of unsteady wheels on an uneven road helped me recognize my surroundings. We were still in the carriage, and night was beginning to settle upon us.

Just as my mind adjusted, the carriage suddenly stopped.

"We have arrived," said Sir Simon, and I thought his voice sounded grim.

"Thank God," said my father with impious inflection.

"Doctor Howard, please," replied Sister Agatha.

It appeared to have been arranged between Sir Simon and Isabel that he should disembark from the carriage upon our arrival. As he left us to execute his part in this delicate business, I wondered how he would go about the inquiry. Would he walk to the tiny inn in the village? My initial, fleeting impressions, which were gained via my limited view of the window, identified this place as small and practically uninhabited, but surely there must be an inn of some sort. Would he enter, stunning the local inhabitants into suspicious silence with his distinctive, foreign manner, and, with untroubled mien, engage the fat proprietor in conversation and demand, "Pardon me, good sir, we are looking for a werewolf. Have you seen aught of one?"

This seemed unlikely even for so resolute and fearless a campaigner as Sir Simon Gwynne. (I had developed quite a heroic narrative for him already—an incoherent collection of dramatic, tense, thrilling scenes, from which he always emerged victorious.) He would, I supposed, choose a much less exciting and more subtle approach. Reality always would disappoint, even when one was embarked on mysterious lycanthropic ventures.

We waited for a long time in the waxing darkness. There was a strange quietness in that place. Even at this evening hour and in this small, inactive village, there should have been some noise and bustle. I wondered if it were a holy day.

Someone—I could not see who—came and lit a streetlamp outside a large building. It was obscured from my sight, though I imagined it might be the church.

Still we waited. The silence was becoming increasingly disquieting. I was tempted to tap the windowsill—anything to break up that monotony—but I feared the inevitable rebuke. Several more minutes passed. I developed a mild itch in my right foot and began to squirm, both to dismiss the unpleasant sensation and to find some outlet for my growing nervous excitement.

This provided my father with an outlet for his own, more peevish, apprehension. "Athene! Can you possibly contrive not to make the entire carriage uncomfortable by your fidgeting?"

I was about to make my insincere apology when a new sound— even stranger than the silence it shattered—interrupted the eerie quiet. It was the sound of music. A jovial twanging, plucking sound, as could be heard from a lute or a mandolin, and a low but cheerful voice singing some song, the melody of which was unfamiliar.

Sir Simon's face appeared at the window. "The village is deserted."

"Not entirely deserted." I nodded in the direction from which came this new sound.

"Indeed not," agreed Sir Simon.

"We will come," said Isabel quietly.

"What is it?" Sister Agatha sounded uneasy. "Shall we not go on?" I imagined her crescent-shaped birthmark pulsing in the darkness.

"No." Isabel's quiet voice rang with certainty. "I do not know what it is, but it *is* something, and we must go and see." Without further discussion, she stepped down from the carriage.

Sister Agatha offered no further opposition or question and accepted Sir Simon's assistance in climbing down. Father followed.

I was, of course, last. I was about to brazen it out, following them whether they permitted it or not, when Sir Simon beckoned to me, extending his hand to assist me and even granting me the hint of a reassuring smile.

"Wait for us," Sir Simon called to the driver—unnecessarily, I thought, for our darkly cloaked and heavily hatted coachman could hardly have been so cruel or so heedless of his payment as to abandon us in that empty place.

Now my eyes cleared. It was indeed a tiny village, the bulk of which was still obscured from our view. I suspected the existence of a small square or marketplace—not teeming with stalls and farmers and their wares at this time of night but at least giving some indication of life. We walked along the uneven stones of the streets, a motley crew of visitors. With every step, I felt less and less welcome and increasingly exposed to some intangible danger. But from whom? We were horribly alone. The only sound or sign that the ghostly town had ever known living men before was that hauntingly merry melody plucked by an unseen hand.

Perhaps, I thought, the hand is unseen because it cannot be seen. Perhaps there is a ghostly musician or a demon minstrel wandering the empty streets—streets that are empty because he has murdered and consumed the inhabitants of the village and now lies in wait to lure us into some dark alley and dismember us too. I recalled the painful painted grimaces of the clowns of the Cirque Medrano. Those hideous creatures, with cruel laughter artificially frozen upon their faces, would suit this scene—unexpected and terrible, and hungry for the blood of innocents.

Just as this disturbing fantasy sank in, and I began to consider a precipitate return to the carriage, we turned a corner and reality dispelled the dawning nightmare.

There, under the guttering light of another streetlamp, sat the long, lank form of the musician. His legs stretched out in what looked to be long, light, wide pants, and the bulk of his body was encompassed in a thick, vast black cloak. He wore a wide hat arched low over his face and appeared focused upon the long tamburica in his hands. He seemed unconscious or uncaring about our presence. He did not even look up. He merely continued to pluck at the strings and to sing in that same low voice. The melody remained unfamiliar to me, though I thought I heard stray words in French. I even imagined I heard the word *loup-garou* but dismissed the thought. I could not see him clearly in all of his robes and under that hat, but no clown's grin peeked out from the shadows.

At his side stood a small cup declaring his occupation as that of a minstrel beggar. There must be other people in the town, for I could see the glint of coins in the streetlight. Unless, of course, he had placed them there himself.

Sir Simon stepped forward as if to approach the mendicant then stopped. If he had been a cat—a disrespectful comparison for so tall, manly, and stalwart a figure—I would have said his ears pricked up.

"What's that noise?" asked Sister Agatha.

As we stood there, the faint murmur that I had attributed to my imagination steadily grew into a rumble, as if it were portentously announcing the approach of an earthquake. It was a bizarre cacophony of sound, as you might hear when many disparate voices, blending with the tramp of many feet, crush together into a disturbing, incoherent whole.

They came together out of the darkness, lit by the burning torches held by many hands. A surging sea of faces—each separate and distinct in the light but united as faces of fury, fear, and bloodlust—like a crowd of the same man over and over, multiplied into a mob. And with the torches were borne pitchforks, sickles, and other implements of the harvest. A bloody harvest and a ferocious force to execute it. There might have been as few as fifty men among them, but it seemed many hundred.

A hand touched my shoulder, and I looked up. I had stepped close to Sir Simon, unconsciously seeking reassurance. He did not look at me but absently patted my shoulder before moving so that he stood as a giant defense between the approaching crowd and my father, me, and the two other women.

The peasant mob stopped all at once, their eyes keen upon us. Mild surprise seemed, for a moment, to distract them from fury. If that were the case, the moment passed quickly. Eyes swept over us, ignoring the musician at our feet, who paid the mob the same courtesy by continuing to pluck at his instrument without looking up. The murmur resumed, and the mob moved on.

The men were tending toward a new section of the village—that center of its life, which had eluded us so far. As the crowd brushed against us, drawing us stumbling along with it, trailing unevenly along its periphery, I thought I saw in its midst some strange, dark bulk, drawn by ropes and many hands, with grunting, angry noises shouted over it.

For a moment, the bustle was so overwhelming that, terrified, I turned and thought I had been lost from the others. I looked around wildly, seeking a friendly face but only seeing the brutal sameness of those angry men.

A strong hand reached out and pulled me free. Too fearful to smile, I cowered against my savior instead—perhaps a more comprehensive expression of my gratitude.

"Be watchful," murmured Sir Simon in a low voice, his eyes still trained upon this strange crowd of men.

I nodded and joined the others, who had kept together by his side. My father did not notice me. I thought he looked pale, blinking bewilderedly in this strange and nonacademic setting. No one here would care about his theories. None of his weighty thoughts could protect or spare us. My heart was twisted with pity or some remnant of proper filial piety. I breathed something like a prayer that no harm would come to him.

We turned a corner, and I saw in an instant what the crowd had pulled along with it. I could not miss seeing it—six men were preparing this prominent prop in a new scene of that macabre theater. There was a large stone cross that marked the central point of the village. Upon it, freshly suspended by a rope about his neck, was the body of a man. The six executioners had climbed down and stood gazing up at their handiwork. The lifeless face shone white and blue in the vicious light, and large purple bruises blended with smeared blood across its features. One of those closed eyes was almost indistinguishable, crushed beneath dry, crusted blood. The clothes were ragged, torn, and bloodstained, though whether this brutality had been visited upon the man before death or in the moments when the corpse was dragged against the cobblestones, who could say?

"Is it... Is it..." I whispered the question so softly that I doubted any could hear.

Sir Simon, not ceasing his vigilant watch, shook his head.

"Then...who..."

No answer.

The crowd, its vengeance realized in murder yet its fury still whetted and keen, encircled the cross and murmured in uncertainty and impotence.

Isabel called out something—something I could not understand but clearly a command—in a cold, clear tone.

Her voice struck the crowd into silence. After a moment's hesitation, the men fell back, still clutching their fiery brands and their weapons, and a thin path threaded between us and the cross-bound corpse as Isabel walked forward, her eyes fixed on the dead man.

Sir Simon moved to follow her one moment too late. The crowd swallowed the path in her wake, and we were left helpless spectators.

"No," he said under his breath. "No, Isabel. No!"

The center with the cross must have been on higher ground, for now we could see Isabel clearly. The mob, torn between eagerness and uncertainty, hung back, intensifying the semblance of a stage, with Isabel and the cross with its corpse displayed before us all.

She had made her way to the front and stood below the dead man. Two of the six at the front—the champions of vengeance, beloved in their bloodiness by their fellows—were still on ladders, precariously balanced from their work in stringing up their victim. They stared down at her, mirroring the anger and strange dismay that swept the crowd.

Isabel looked up at them. She lifted a hand and repeated her command so clearly that I imagined I could understand the words.

"Cut him down."

Like adolescent boys caught in some stupid prank and trapped midway between bravado and sullen shame, the two ladder-bound men hesitated, frowned, then quietly, begrudgingly obeyed. The taut rope, unevenly hacked, gave way, and the lifeless body collapsed to the ground beside Isabel.

"*Borsorka!*"

The word was shrieked so shrilly that for a moment I could not clearly discern it. The voice was like what I might imagine in the Furies or some other half-woman, half-animal monster, possessed of insane, vicious passion.

"*Borsorka! Borsorka! Borsorka!*"

On the far side of the crowd, opposite us, a new and distinct host stood. These men brandished knives and spears. Their dark skin and colorful dress proclaimed them to be of the Romany gypsies. At their head stood a wizened old hag, so aged and decrepit she was almost simian, dressed in even more colorful garments than the men about her, her ugly face a rapidly constricting and changing network of wrinkles. She extended one bony, crooked finger, its long nail pointing damningly at Isabel.

"*Borsorka!*" she shrieked again.

Isabel looked at her coldly. She was disheveled from our struggle against the crowd, and her hair had loosened from its constraints, falling in long, dark locks about her face. A mischievous gust of wind took up that hair and danced with it. The unfeeling beauty of Isabel stood stark against the moonlight.

I recognized the word the gypsy crone shrieked at this strange, unearthly woman. Even had I not, I could well imagine what her denouncement meant. *Borsorka*. Witch.

Isabel certainly looked the part. In that moment I thought I knew what the face of the moon herself must be like. The catalogue of names—names I knew as well as my own—came unbidden to my mind. Diana, Artemis, Selene, Hecate, Luna. Moon goddesses or the moon herself, each in her way a deity of darkness, cruelty, and sorcery. Cold and exquisite, in a scene of violence that was of her heartless making. Would the priestess of the moon rouse her hounds and bid them tear us all to pieces?

I shook my head to rid myself of the thought.

The old woman began to shriek an incomprehensible litany, and as I watched, the crowd wavered, looking from the denouncer to the silent, beautiful, accused woman, so unconcerned in the face of danger. Not the witch—the unstained virgin saint, unthreatened by danger and death. A placid Joan of Arc standing upon the pile of wood as the flames began to lick her heels. Would nothing provoke in her a human feeling?

Nothing, I thought, answering my own question, except perhaps the body of that murdered man.

The murdered man. I had struggled with every thin nerve, every unsteady insistence of my will, not to look at the grotesque carcass hanging above the heads of the angry crowd. That man deprived of life. Better to think of him as something that had never lived. A horrible but soulless object. Now it lay upon the ground. A body, once human, now unmoving and unfeeling. I had never seen a dead man before, and here was one that captured with dreadful earnestness the completeness of that final darkness. The victim of the brutal mob, lying in a heap at the feet of Isabel as she stared back at the rage-filled gypsy. I would not look. I could not look. Not now, when so vital a scene was unfolding before me.

Yet a stronger power than I possessed urged otherwise. The moon, that cruel huntress, hungry for her own prey, demanded my attention, illuminating the corpse with her cruel shafts of light and drawing my gaze inexorably back to the thing I so abhorred.

The tricks and surreal conjuring of the circus came again into my troubled, disjointed thoughts. I remembered the words of a thin Frenchman who sat near me so many years before as I watched the transformation of the contortionist into strange, wonderful, dreadful shapes.

"It is not what it seems. It is a trick—remember!" whispered the man to his son, a chubby schoolboy whose wide eyes and fascinated gaze must have mirrored my own. I too could not look away, though my stomach and my mind rebelled against the display of human bodies twisting and turning so painfully.

It is not what it seems. Even as I stared so unwillingly at the body of the dead man, it seemed I could detect a subtle change—a change so slow and creeping that I told myself that I must have imagined it. No…no…the hair upon the face was materially altered. The hints of a fledgling beard were masked now by thicker, more insistent hair. The blood was matted against it. The skin disappeared, swallowed up by the thick, harsh growth of hair. No, not hair—fur.

Sir Simon was gazing with a furrowed, frustrated brow at Isabel and the gypsy. I gripped his arm. "Look!" I whispered hoarsely, pointing at the newly metamorphosed body.

Frowning, he followed my finger. Then his body tensed, and he moved as if he would push his way through the crowd to Isabel.

Before the thought could turn to action, the eyes of the wolf flew open, burning fire raging in their depths.

This was no imagination. From snout to tail, the body—not dead but grossly alive—was no longer a man, but a furious creature, born of moonlight, madness, and blood. The rope still bound about its neck, the roused beast leapt, teeth and claws sharp and vicious in the gleam of that eerie light, and, striking Isabel, thrust her to the ground.

Sister Agatha screamed. The crowd, swayed from blood lust to surprised horror, recoiled from the bloody slaughter.

Someone shouted something I could not clearly hear, three shots rang out, and the creature collapsed upon his prey, a lifeless pelt.

Silence descended, shattered almost instantly by the harsh, angry cackle of laughter that erupted from the gypsy woman. As the shocked crowd hung back, Isabel thrust the corpse from her and rose, blood staining her face and dress, her skin providing an almost translucently white contrast.

Sir Simon was at her side in a moment and grabbed her, dragging her back through the crowd toward us. Then the gypsy, still laughing, shrieked again—a bloody command, clear even though her language continued to elude me.

Isabel stumbled, but Sir Simon picked her up and slung her indecorously over one shoulder. Now he was beside me, grabbing my hand, and dragging me along in a run. My father was at my side, scurrying frantically. He stopped, hesitated, and reached back to grab the arm of Sister Agatha, who struggled to keep up, her long robes entangling her legs and impeding her progress.

Another figure materialized at her side—the tall figure of the minstrel, his face still hidden by his outlandish hat. He took Sister Agatha's other arm and hurried her along. As he ran, the cloak parted. White robes disclosed beneath that concealment shone out, blending against the white gown of the panting Breton nun.

We twisted and turned down the streets, the noise of the mob heavy upon us. The gypsy hag still screamed, goading the crowd after us, irrational in its heated desire for more blood. For *our* blood.

"No! Turn here!" cried the minstrel in the clear tones of the King's English. "Sir Simon! All of you! Come!"

We instinctively followed his command and found ourselves near the carriage. As we ran toward it, the figure of our coachman appeared from the darkness and swung into his place, a smoking rifle in his hand. The horses, stamping and plunging with frantic energy, responded to his ruthless restraint, and stood with the pretense of patience and obedience, though I could sense twitching nerves across their tense, sweaty bodies.

The pounding feet of our pursuers thundered in my ears.

Sir Simon threw Isabel into the carriage then lifted me in place beside her. Next, Sister Agatha, though whether Sir Simon or my father lifted her I could not have said. My father followed, then Sir Simon, nearly crushing me in his haste to be aboard.

Our new companion slammed the door behind Sir Simon. The lowered window beside me framed the face of the unknown musician. He smiled (a smile that might have been infectious, were we not running for our lives) and thrust an unwieldy object into my arms—an object that uttered its own twanging protest.

"Thank you, miss," said the stranger cheerfully. Then he disappeared from my view. The carriage swayed and rattled as he climbed aboard the driver's seat. I was still staring after him when another face—the face of our coachman—appeared in that same window.

I screamed.

It was the dark face of the stowaway gypsy boy—the boy whom I imagined decapitated at sea. Without appearing in the least bit dead, his face split in that memorable smile. Chuckling at my astonishment, he arched his eyebrows at me and hooted his same deep, owl's cry—"Ooooooo-huu!"—in my face.

The shrieks of the crowd were upon us, and the first rude hands grasped at the carriage—too late to wreak their vengeance.

"Ride, boy!" cried the minstrel to the coachman at his side. "Ride!"

The next instant, the carriage was careening through the darkness.

The shriek of the aged gypsy echoed with a ferocity that outpaced its faintness as it fell farther and farther behind us: "*Borsorka*! Death, Isabel! Death!"

CHAPTER 9

9 MAY 1906: A CROATIAN HILLOCK AND, THEREAFTER, PARIS, *LA VILLE LUMIÈRE*

Though far I roam, that thought shall be
My hope, my comfort, everywhere;
While such a home remains to me,
My heart shall never know despair!

— Acton Bell (nom de plume of Anne Brontë)

UNLIKELY THOUGH IT WAS, I MUST HAVE FALLEN ASLEEP. ONE moment I was jolting about in the darkness, the ungainly instrument in my arms thudding relentlessly against my head with each lurch of the carriage. The baying of hounds and the cries of bloodthirsty men came in ruthless pursuit, the threat of vicious dismemberment barking at our spinning wheels. In the next moment, it seemed as if I were blinking in the shafts—not of moonlight but of broad day. The dew-dripped, rosy-tipped fingers of Eos, lifted from the immortal, divine Oceanus, had already dispelled the dark mastery of the moon goddess. Now the morning sun blazed with a greater intensity even than our pursuers had raged.

I was still blinking, trapped between nighttime visions and the relief of morning disillusionment, when a loud twanging noise assaulted my ears.

My father grumbled from his place curled up in one corner of the carriage but offered no further remonstrance.

I retrieved the minstrel's tamburica from the floor where I had dropped it, but Sir Simon gently took it from me without speaking. I wondered if he had slept at all.

Isabel leaned back in the corner, her head turned so I could not see her face. Perhaps she was asleep. I could not imagine resting peacefully if I had been the target of so much malice, but Isabel, in her strange inhumanity, might well have been able to do so after any assault. I wondered about her mysterious nightmares. Would they intensify now that danger was enfleshed in Romany hordes?

Sister Agatha was sitting straight, her eyes fixed upon the uninspiring view outside the window. Her crescent-shaped blemish looked dull and uncommunicative—no hope of reading her thoughts through that expressive birthmark. I wondered if she were still frightened or disturbed by the unsettling events we had witnessed. Perhaps she was praying. Her mouth was pursed in a way that seemed to render dialogue, even with a divinity, unlikely—but I had little experience of prayer and could not say what it should have looked like.

"We will stop soon," she said suddenly and matter-of-factly in French. "They are far behind us, and we must speak."

As if her words were a command, the carriage clattered roughly to a stop. Sir Simon descended first, quickly. My father followed him, grumbling, as if he were suddenly desperate to stretch his cramped body. Sister Agatha and Isabel—who was not, it seemed, asleep—followed.

I stepped out upon the grass and looked about me. We were on a hillside, with one forest line far behind us and another far ahead. A few stocky trees dotted the landscape, and a small herd of cattle meandered aimlessly nearby. One lumbering, pregnant cow with black and white spots and a stupid expression affixed one lazy eye upon us. After a few seconds, she dismissed us with bovine acuity. There was no other sign of life. We were alone and unremarkable in a lonely and unremarkable world. The contrast to the drama of the night before seemed so stark that, like a child whose emotions have been worked to the point of frenzy, I found myself feeling deflated.

My rapid though morbid survey of the environment concluded in time for me to witness the lanky, dark-skinned boy gazing at Isabel with the most remarkable expression on his face. I was still trying to identify the emotion behind that look when, before she could stop him, he swept his hat from his head, fell to his knees, and moved as if he might kiss the hem of her dress.

"No, Mihai," she said coldly in French. Then, as he bowed his head in submission, she added with a hint of something that might have been kindness, "You've grown, boy."

"Princess." His voice was a strange mixture of eastern dialect, the French language, and a lilt that I assumed was part of a gypsy heritage. "I promised I would serve you. I promised, though you said nay. I knew! I knew the new darkness—the darkness which is old. The anger of the Machvaya is roused, princess. I rushed to aid you. They are angry. They wish to destroy all. No one enemy—all are enemies. No friends. You are not forgiven, princess. The past is fresh as if new. And only blood will satisfy."

"You have watched many nights."

"I came upon the seas, princess."

"There was a death, Mihai."

I shivered, either from the exhaustion and chill or from the memory of that unwitnessed but too-clearly imagined seaborne episode of midnight dismemberment.

"The darkness too came upon the seas, princess. There are many who watch for you. I am pledged to serve you, and I shall protect you from the evil upon your heels."

"The blood debt will continue, Mihai."

He shrugged. "It was only the half-wit Erich. No one will punish."

"What of God, Mihai?"

He shrugged again, though with less dismissiveness. "Erich willed you harm, princess. I am pledged to serve."

Isabel lapsed into silence and looked upon the ground. The strange boy named Mihai, bowing his head again in submission, backed away from her presence as if ceding his place to higher personages.

Now the strange minstrel spoke, addressing the old Breton nun, who had silently watched this exchange between her charge and the boy.

"Sister Agatha," he said in tones that did the hallowed halls of Eton proud, "I am Brother Philip. I am sent to you from Brussels. I have a letter from Father Pierre Jarvais."

Sister Agatha received the letter, broke through the wax seal, and read its contents without any change of expression upon her face.

The introduction of this new, unknown figure was certainly mysterious to me, but I could not discern whether the name had been any more familiar to her ear.

As she read, I glanced at the boy called Mihai and found he was grinning at me. He settled unceremoniously upon the grass, reached into his pocket, pulled out something, and tossed it to me. Something round and hard—an apple.

Relieved and grateful, I found myself grinning back and, following his example, settled myself upon the grass like a careless peasant girl and abandoned myself to blissful, juicy enjoyment. I felt as if I hadn't eaten in years—and violence, werewolves, and gypsies made me frightfully hungry. Had it only been a day since I had boasted to Sir Simon of my organizational brilliance and capacity for academic synthesis? For now I was happy to play the part of the undesired, overgrown child of the enterprise. Let the rest of the company quarrel among themselves about the next step. I had an apple to eat. As I focused upon this critical task of consumption, I mused upon the varied appearances of apples in mythology. The tantalizing golden apples of the Greeks—the race of Atalanta, the ill-fated judgment of Paris, and the labor of Heracles in the Hesperides. The immortality and eternal youth of the Norse gods. The silver branch of Irish myth, signifying the coming of death. And was not the forbidden fruit relished by Adam and Eve popularly conceived as an apple? So much wagered and lost on this juicy but small harvest morsel—too small, I thought sadly. My hunger was sharper than before.

I finished my fruit before Sister Agatha finished her perusal of the letter. So focused was I in relishing every sharp, tangy bite that I paid her little notice beyond commenting to myself that it must be a very long letter indeed.

Then she lifted her eyes from the page and slowly dropped her hand and the letter down at her side. There was mud on her white robes and another stain that might have been blood. I tried to recall how or when she had thus soiled the fabric, but the events of the previous evening were yet too muddled in my recollection to be of any help. I wondered if the stains could ever be removed. I didn't think it likely.

"We are recalled," announced Sister Agatha in a voice as devoid of emotion as Isabel's might have been.

"Where?" Isabel asked.

"Kain." Sister Agatha frowned.

"Near Tournai," Brother Philip clarified.

Perhaps the apple had rejuvenated me, or perhaps I was sufficiently awake to register this declaration with stark, awful clarity. *Tournai. Dornick.* The dual names of the city had struck a chord of memory, visible in my mind's eye in the form of a map. A location somewhere near Brussels.

"On whose authority?" Sir Simon frowned, displeasure gathering like clouds across his large brows.

It was a valid question, I thought. My own supposition regarding authority in this ramshackle enterprise had undergone many alterations and adjustments over the weeks we had spent together. Here was another player upon the stage.

My apple exhausted, I tossed its meager remains off into the long grass, surreptitiously wiped my sticky hands on one of the few unsoiled spots on my skirt, and ungracefully pulled my legs up so I could rest my chin against my knees. I hoped this authority question would take them some time to discuss. I had a strong feeling that the conclusion of the argument would bring some bleak new reality to play, possibly dispersing the deep clouds of adventure altogether. I would happily embrace any impasse to postpone the inevitable.

"There is some…" the brother was saying.

"Disagreement?" Sir Simon supplied the word, still frowning.

The young brother smiled. "There is some *discussion* of the best proceeding at this time. There is also the question of due authority since there is an overlap of concerns with our Franciscan brothers."

"If they are not able to take care of the business, it must yet be dealt with by those who can."

"Perhaps. Nevertheless, this question of authority must also be dealt with."

"It was not last time," said Isabel without raising her eyes from the ground.

"No," said the brother, looking at her. "It was not."

If he hoped by that look to encourage her to say more, he clearly didn't know Isabel. She lapsed back into silent distraction.

"The trail is here." Sir Simon's broad jaw jutted out in stubborn emphasis. "We were sent to follow the...him. To track him before he goes to ground."

"That is beyond my knowledge," replied the minstrel brother. "Sister Agatha is to come with her companions to Le Saulchoir and await further instructions there. Such is my errand—that and the command to give you aid if I found you in any danger." He smiled. "It is a time for prudence, is it not? And careful thought?"

"Not rash action," supplied Sir Simon, arms crossed with defensive annoyance.

Brother Philip was graciousness itself. "That too is beyond my knowledge and my authority." He looked to the two women. "Will you come?"

"Of course she will," snapped Sister Agatha, though with a nervous glance at Isabel.

Isabel was still looking down at the grass, as if she were lost in some deep thought. For a long, awkward moment, she did not reply. Now everyone was watching her—everyone except my father, who had appeared not to hear anything that was said.

I began to squirm with vicarious discomfort. Finally, when I was on the verge of saying something to break the silence, she tossed her head—that odd movement of hers, like a horse flicking its tail to be rid of a pesky fly—and looked up.

"I will come," she said.

Father had been sitting upon the steps of the carriage in silence, staring off fixedly at something intangible. He suddenly looked gray and old—so much so that I almost regretted not sharing my apple with him. He might have been listening, but I suspected his attention was far away. His lips sometimes moved, but if he were in conversation with his invisible opponent, this for once seemed more of a commiseration than an argument.

Now he shook himself with a frown, as if awakening from a daydream, and said in the tone one often hears from small children and academic experts, "I have important work to do."

Then he turned and caught sight of me. His frown deepened. "Athene, I've sacrificed enough time…"

Indulging you. The words were unspoken, but I could guess the narrative he had constructed for himself. This entire enterprise was to be laid at my door, justifying him, the selfless, long-suffering *paterfamilias*, in dismissing my needs and desires for a considerable time to come.

"But I have work to do," he insisted with waxing, tragic pettishness. "I have tarried too long."

I looked at that mysterious bunch of adventurers, with their shared knowledge and their secret rules. That alliance of truly interesting people. They would go to Brussels, and we would go to Paris. Was this then to be the end of my share in their adventures? I had visited Belgium in the past, but the land in which they sojourned would be unlike any I might explore by myself. They would be in churches and convents, with moldy rituals and chanted secrets, chasing down preternatural monsters. We would be in libraries, lecture halls, and, if I were lucky, one or two dusty sites of ruthlessly disenchanted antiquity.

If I were lucky.

I was not lucky. I would not be in Brussels. My heart sank into my stomach, mixing ill with the remains of that apple.

"We must go home, girl," my father said in a grieved, insistent voice as if I had argued aloud with him.

Home. Horrible word. How could I go back to that dull, uneventful world after this thrilling adventure? I glanced at Sir Simon, half pleading, half glaring. He wasn't looking at me. He was looking at that killjoy minstrel in black and white, and occasionally at Isabel from under that eternally furrowed brow.

I turned to her and found her watching me.

For a long, pregnant moment she gazed at me with her expressionless face. Then she turned and moved as if she would return to her place in the carriage. At the door she paused and looked at me once more. I felt sure she would say something, give me some consolation or reassurance or invitation. But she did not. She merely looked, took her seat, and transferred all her attention to one corner of the trim around the carriage window.

The others followed her in silence. There was nothing for me to do other than to follow too, unless I wanted to cast my lot in with the cows. Soon we were bustling away—not in chase or terrified escape but on our pedantic and uninteresting way toward boredom.

Unlike our travel in the weeks previous, the return to Paris was rapid and uncomplicated. No delays, no drama. Our parting from the others was achieved so quickly and uneventfully that I was not even permitted a moment to breathe, much less grieve. One glance in a crowd, across a train platform, as we hurried aboard the railcar that would carry us so swiftly and ruthlessly to Paris—one last glimpse. Sister Agatha, restored fully to her stately bearing, nobly enwrapped in a black cloak. The erstwhile minstrel, Brother Philip, at her side— thin, discreet, and unremarkable, save for the large black instrument case strapped to his back. Isabel, hair orderly, cloaked in black as well, and with a simple black hat shading her striking profile.

I wondered how my father could so effortlessly cast off this group, which had seemed to electrify his interests. Something in that midnight violence had disrupted the flow of his obsession. I would never know its origin. All my suppositions of his relationship with Sister Agatha had gone up in smoke, along with my hopes, dreams, and newfound enthusiasms.

I have not mentioned Sir Simon Gwynne. That was perhaps the cruelest wrench of all. Isabel and Sister Agatha had, in their ways, largely ignored my existence, yet it had not seemed heartless in them to do so but rather the result of their distinct natures. Sir Simon had seemed to be different—a human connection in a crowd of strange, inhuman or superhuman creatures. I had begun to wonder if some fellowship had been struck between us. On the dividing platform, that wonder evaporated with the rest of the fairy tale. Sir Simon left without saying farewell and without a backward glance, seeming only occupied in the proper disposal of passengers and luggage in their own train.

The whistle sounded. We began to move forward slowly, and, with increasing speed, to lurch powerfully into a hurtling, rapidly changing countryside. At the last instant, I looked back, craning my head around the window in the most unladylike fashion, hoping to catch a face gazing toward me. There was no one—unless I was to count the pimply, red face of the leering porter, who jumped at my stare, dropped a bag, and, as he bore the infuriated reprimand of the bag's owner, fell away from my departing view.

I settled back miserably into my seat and listened to my exhausted father snore contentedly in his own place.

In what felt like the merest moment, the dramatic country and thrilling, romantic world had vanished, like the change of scenes upon the stage, and the orderly stolidity of Parisian streets stood in their place. I tried to imagine the blood and drama and viciousness of bygone days in those very streets, but that day I could dream up no exhilarating image of sobbing innocents, strapped upon a tumbrel, dragged toward *Madame la Guillotine* amid the shrieking, bloodthirsty crowd. Had this been the site of vigilante tribunals? Firing squads? What of the mass execution of priests and nuns? It seemed impossible. No barricades could I imagine, no foolhardy young idealists, screaming of revolution and reformation, recklessly rushing toward annihilation. No triumphant parades of Napoleonic might. Such clean, petty, bustling streets. Even the license and depravity I knew (through popular reputation, not through personal experience) lurked among the lights in other districts seemed boring. There was our house at the end of the row, hideous and stately with its clean, tall lines and light-yellow paint faintly peeling.

The door creaked as it opened.

"Good day, Doctor Howard," said tall, thin, elderly Georges. "Welcome home." Then he added, "Good day, miss," with the same pretense of respect he always afforded me.

As I gazed through the doorway into the dark hall with its overladen furniture that seemed, even when meticulously cleaned, to be stifled by weighty dust, the helplessness, hopelessness, and pointlessness of my life rushed over me. That I might not mistake the depths of my despair, Fate intervened. I tripped on the doorstep and nearly fell, stumbling in, twisting my knee, and, in my effort to regain my balance, knocking into one of the many small tables in the hall. This hideous object, with an ornately painted ceramic top depicting the unsightly efforts of a faun with regard to the virtue of a doughy-faced nymph, clattered to the floor with unnecessary violence, scattering a silver dish, several envelopes, a small parcel, an unpolished bronze candlestick which broke upon impact, and a small bowl of vague, unimpressive *objets d'art*, which scattered to the corners of the hall, much to the blinking consternation of Georges.

My father turned to glare at me from under arched brows. Then his eyes fell on the package that I had inadvertently thrown to the floor. Part of the paper had fallen away, revealing enough of the contents to distract his attention. He picked up whatever it was with a grunt and tore off the rest of the wrapping. It was a book—a small, dark-covered, tightly bound volume. That much I could see, though the title was concealed from my view. A missive was contained with the book, and I could make out the familiar lines of the coat of arms of the Lauritz Aldebrand Estate at the top of the page.

As my father perused the letter, a scowl spread across his face. With a low grumble, he stuffed the package and letter under his arm, stalked off through the right-hand door that admitted from the hall into his private study, and slammed the door behind him.

I was left alone in the invisible dust and emptiness, with Georges ineffectually attempting to tidy the wreckage I had caused and a thin, slatternly maid (unknown to me and one in a long, nameless line of unsatisfactory staff) who leaned against the staircase watching and without bothering to assist.

It was too much for flesh and blood to bear. Without offering even an apology to poor Georges, I ran up the stairs to my own room. I imitated my father in the unfeeling and loud closing of the door behind me and threw myself upon my tidy little white bed with every intention of gazing at nothing in particular as I contemplated the hopelessness of my own eternally dull future.

Unfortunately, laudable though this intention was, the questionable comfort of that familiar space and the exhausting time we had spent for many, many days previous proved too much for me. Within a few minutes of commencing that session of maudlin self-pity, I fell deeply and peacefully asleep.

CHAPTER 10

10–16 MAY 1906: PARIS, *LA VILLE LUMIÈRE*

It does not follow that a deep, intricate character is
more or less estimable than such a one as yours.

— Jane Austen, *Pride and Prejudice*

I AWOKE REFRESHED AND RENEWED THE FOLLOWING MORNING. THE
dirt of travel became instantly unbearable and, to the irritation of the
maid (who, I learned, bore the unlikely name "Desirée"), I ordered a
bath. Impervious to the satirical gaze of my ill-tempered attendant,
I indulged myself with vigorous ablutions until her sullen facial
expressions intruded too insufferably upon my peace, and I dismissed
her from the room. As I mused in the filthy water, I considered my
life from a different aspect.

As a heroine, I was not entirely lacking in qualities. My education,
though disorganized and primarily autodidactic, was advanced. I had
not ventured to imagine an existence requiring a plan for self-support
but was certain that I would be equipped for something or other. For
now, the security and shelter of my father's home would permit me
to engage my most developed skills in addressing a new and exciting
course of study. This was not only an indulgence of heartfelt desire.
It was a question of practical prudence. I had no relations and few
friendships, none of them intimate. I would inherit my father's estate
in the event of his death, but I knew even more than he did how
little that comprised. I had no intention of marrying a stolid, dull
academic of my father's acquaintance—a wearisome, eventual sort
of alliance to ensure I did not end my life a downtrodden wretch in
the gutter.

No! I splashed the water to emphasize my decision. My ambitions were higher than such a sorry denouement. I would stand proudly on my own two feet as Athene Howard, adventuress and lycanthropic-researcher—or whatever the official title might be. I doubted I could manage anything more vigorous. The brute force displayed by that vicious creature as it leapt upon Isabel… I shivered as the memory came back. Well, I thought, if I am not to do the battle myself, perhaps I could provide some sort of scholarly support. After all, there must be *some* advantage to my unconventional upbringing.

But how to pursue this thrilling avenue of self-improvement? I ruminated for some time on this point. The Baring-Gould book was one resource but was insufficient. In addition to the werewolves, I needed further information about the gypsies. I would commence that very evening in acquiring more, combing through my father's extensive library for possible texts applicable to the question of man-to-wolf metamorphosis or regarding the practices and beliefs of the Romany.

For the day, I had a secondary object to pursue. It required additional pondering, thus I pondered while swirling the unappealing murkiness of the bath with my fingers.

The index finger of one hand swirling in the water here—that was Brussels.

The thumb of the other hand swirling there—that was Paris.

"And never the twain shall meet," I sighed.

This was true. Brussels and Paris, though intimately linked in many ways, are not physically convergent.

"Well," I said, "if I cannot reasonably bring the mountain to Mohomet or Mohomet to the mountain, I can at least pursue some local foothills! I *shall* seek out these robed Papists and, through a radical or mystical or magical super-endowment of diplomatic savvy, persuade them to admit me to the ranks of some sort of junior apprenticeship."

Nodding with renewed confidence, I rose from my chilly bath— not quite like Aphrodite from the foam, but with a more coherent sense of purpose and a great deal less carnality than that self-absorbed goddess. Within minutes, I was respectably attired for my pursuit of adventure and dashed down the stairs to demand and partake of breakfast.

"Is my father still asleep?" I asked of Georges. This was not merely a polite query. I wanted to calculate if my evening assault on the library would be impeded.

"Professor Howard left early this morning, miss."

That did surprise me, and I arched an eyebrow to indicate it. Georges had, however, lapsed back into his consideration of things absent.

"Georges, I shall want my bicycle."

He departed to fulfill my express desire, and I meditated upon the information with which he had provided me. It was odd. I would have expected my father either to have been out late, seeking what impersonal, masculine relief he required after our long travels (I considered my attitude pragmatic on this sordid point of my father's private life), or to have stayed awake in his study, finding comfort in the familiar depths of his research. Either way, I fully expected him to have been in his boudoir, secluded and unapproachable, until the long, painful hours of morning had passed. Energetic early ventures of any kind were not typical of the man. I wondered what that provoking package had contained. The Lauritz Aldebrand Estate had always appeared to be an uncomplicated source of benevolence. If the letter and parcel were concerned with business, my father's lawyer would handle it. If they were concerned with scholarship, I would be burdened with it all too soon.

Perhaps, I considered, my father's mood was precisely the same as my own. Perhaps he too found this return to the familiar disconcerting after our thrilling and ultimately dissatisfying adventures, and was driven, like me, to seek out this elusive new world that we had lost.

The idea of my father eagerly pursuing apprenticeship among the werewolf-chasing Papists made me choke upon a small piece of baguette. I attempted to resolve my coughing contortions with tea, which turned out to be scalding, and thus, when I departed from the house a few minutes later, still coughing, I felt somewhat less possessed and refreshed than I had after my bath.

I decided that the library could wait. My mood was not attuned to passive scholarship. I fixed my hat upon my head at a slightly jaunty angle to demonstrate to the observing world my new persona as an adventuress. All this effort produced was a stare from an impertinent robin from a nearby tree. Undeterred, I clipped up my skirts to avoid the gears, climbed aboard my metal steed, and set out on my campaign.

Most great leaders who have taken upon themselves the task of assaulting European capitals have at least set aside some time to work out a clear plan, taking into consideration terrain, if nothing else. Not I. I prided myself that I had a pseudo-native's knowledge of those Parisian streets and knew that those streets were practically riddled with ecclesial-looking buildings that must be associated somehow with that mysterious band.

Within a few hours, I permitted myself to purchase a small map. Anything larger would have labeled me eternally as a wide-eyed tourist.

My pride survived through several days of fruitless wandering before I descended to the somewhat-mortified investment in a copy of *Bradshaw's*. Though the latter promised to guide me to "ALL THAT CAN BE SEEN and HOW TO SEE IT WITH THE LEAST FATIGUE, TIME, AND EXPENSE," the edition proved slightly outdated, with unhelpful results.

Unfortunately, I had never paid much heed to Parisian ecclesial history. Thus, over seven days of dedicated quest and exhaustive exploration, I found myself piecing together the limited, fragmented knowledge I had unconsciously carried about with the rest of the scattered information housed in my brain. Suddenly, phrases to which I had never fully attended carried with them a deep and distressing new meaning—especially *la séparation des Églises et de l'État* and *laïcité*. It seemed that I had set out on my ambitious crusade at a moment when the Papists were under strong governmental constraints. It dawned on me that, while I associated this country of my birth with candles, processions, priests, and ugly Madonnas, I had witnessed such displays only in my childhood and thus remembered them imperfectly and dimly.

I had never spent so much time in the dull emptiness of churches in my life. This was a cold, silent, unfamiliar realm. Sometimes I sat inside, resting my feet and considering the architecture. I saw little activity, and such as there was seemed surreptitious but not in the way I could have hoped. There were no conspirators or warriors against demons here—just elderly peasants, wide-eyed children, and tearful females. There were few priests—that surprised me—and those who did appear seemed focused upon whatever petty business their day's schedule demanded of them.

On the fourth day, which happened to be a Sunday, I had tangled the edge of my skirt in the gears of the bicycle, set it aside in disgust, and stalked into the nearest church, thereby stumbling into one of their Masses. Since my knowledge of Latin equipped me for consideration of passages in Virgil, Ovid, and others, I could follow the language of the ritual when I could make it out—most of it was whispered or raced through in the most incoherent manner. The substance of it eluded me. I was disappointed, in fact. Inasmuch as I had expected anything, my imaginings would have tended more toward gorgeous, intoxicating ritual with deep, resonant chanting and clouds of incense. This particular specimen of worship appeared to be presided over by a discontented cleric, perhaps anxious for his aperitif and his luncheon and definitely rushed for time. The only part of the proceeding over which he labored with slow consideration was his sermon. This consisted of a confusing consideration of the Jonah myth and went on for so long that I fell asleep through part of it. This lapse in manners and attention neither increased nor decreased the comprehensibility of his ponderous consideration of the text. I stood for a long time at the end of the dull ritual, staring down at a large glass sarcophagus with the wizened, leathery body of one of their saints. Then I left the little church without much respect for the entire business. Something more unfit to associate with the brilliant, fascinating company of werewolf-chasing heroes even I could not concoct.

As the days passed, my disappointment became ever keener. My evening endeavors were as unsuccessful as those of the day. I had revisited innumerable texts, classical and modern, exploring every possible angle. Mythology and *transformisscience*, folklore and anthropology, the writings of Charles Darwin—as dull as ever. Through the night I worked, reading, noting, and collating my notes. Petronius and Ovid, Reginald Scot and Gervase of Tilbury. I spent a great deal of time delving into Barrow's *Lavengro* and *The Romany Rye*, but since the author seemed more philosophically than mystically inclined, there was little to assist me in understanding the gypsy connection to this adventure. Nevertheless, I noted details of Romany religious practices, especially regarding blood debts and sacrifices. Again and again I returned to the Baring-Gould book and found no further consolation, no further clue. I did not require the author to testify to me the existence of such beasts. What I sought was an avenue into the mysterious world of Isabel and Sir Simon Gwynne, an excuse to return to that thrilling company. Memory brought their faces before me as I worked—dancing, taunting phantoms.

Lost, lost, lost, Athene…all lost…

The little chime of a Rococo clock awoke me. I lifted my head from the page where it had fallen in slumber and gazed at the rebuking timepiece. Three o'clock. The witching hour again. Time for the goblins and ghouls to appear. I looked around, almost hopeful of hearing some growl, some sign of an unnatural foe.

No creatures were there to trouble my rest. I gazed at my unfinished page and saw it was smudged. That would mean ink upon my cheek. With an uncharacteristic feeling of defeat and several pointed comments about the slatternliness and perfidy of the Muses, I retired to bed.

I awoke with a new, startling resolve. I would seek information of my father.

I had hardly seen him since our return to Paris. Passing many days without speaking to each other was not unusual but spending so much time in my own scholarly pursuits, ignoring and neglecting the organizational disasters he was concocting downstairs in his lair, was quite irregular. I would require weeks, if not months, to restore his work to some semblance of cohesion, but for the moment I did not care. From our limited contact, I could tell that some deep problem occupied him. I spared little thought for what that might be—probably some petty squabble with his colleagues or a new theory advanced by an upstart scholar that required a vicious set-down in an academic journal. I still assumed it had something to do with the mysterious package that had awaited him upon our return. A steady stream of correspondence had continued to issue from and return to the house. I diagnosed this as the result of one of those singularly trivial academic quarrels in which he was so frequently embroiled, and thus I found it an unintriguing prospect, especially when I had something much more fascinating to occupy my thoughts.

But I was waxing desperate. I had tramped throughout the city for days and days on end. My body ached from inordinate exercise and insufficient sleep. My systematic approach had brought me nowhere. I would try an unsystematic one. "After all," I told myself, mimicking the voice of Doctor Hennessey, "Charles Howard knows many things."

Thus, one evening, at the end of the sixth day of unhappy, unproductive exploration throughout the city, I ventured to the door of my father's study. The door was slightly ajar. I nudged once, twice, and a third time—enough to view the scene before determining the best way to provoke him to assist me.

His study was a large room, but it had always seemed oppressive, laden as it was with books and shelves in chronic disorder. Mountains of texts piled high about the walls and in little hillocks throughout the room. In the middle of the range stood a large, dark mahogany desk, always littered with disorganized papers. Considering the years I had spent introducing order into that chaos, I should have been dismayed, but upon witnessing the scene my exhausted, preoccupied mind contracted, and strange, long forgotten memories rose to the surface.

I remembered when, at a young age and full of imprudent enthusiasms, I sneaked into the room in my father's absence. I had thought to surprise and delight him with my consideration and unknown skills as a secretary. His martyr-like sulking had persisted for nearly three months.

That was the first time I had dared to enter this sanctum uninvited. Usually I stood outside the closed, locked door, shifting my weight from one foot to the other, considering how I might attract his attention and never finding the means to bring about this miracle.

Now I could see him sitting in the midst of the rubble of books, brooding over several open volumes and a tower of papers, all scribbled over in his recognizable and unintelligible scrawl. A dusty, near-sighted owl, or a misshapen, enchantment-bound dwarf in the bowels of his mining hoard.

Owl or dwarf, he would not want me there. This familiar recognition was upon me in a moment, and it transformed me back into the figure of the small, spindly-legged and unloved "Interruption" of childhood. This unpleasant remembrance staggered me for a moment, and I leaned against the doorknob for support.

The door creaked a protest.

My father looked up, blinking.

"Who is it?" He was still blinking, as if endeavoring to return from a far distance into the present moment.

"It is I, Father."

"Athene." He said my name meditatively, presumably because he was still far away.

"Yes, Father."

His brow creased with the effort of thought. "What is it, Athene?"

"I…" My words deserted me. "Nothing, Father. You are busy."

"Yes…yes, Athene," he replied still in a distant, uncertain voice. "I am busy."

I turned to go, but then, thinking I heard his voice again, turned back. "What is it, Father?"

He was looking at me, frowning as if considering something to himself. For several minutes we stood there in silence, looking at each other. I marked the lines on his aging face and the wisps of hair, now at their dustiest. I wondered, for the first time, if this business that now occupied him was one of those petty, everyday points on which he loved to waste so much of his time. Or was it something else?

Finally, he seemed to come to a decision. He shook his head and spoke with slow, ponderous precision, as if carefully weighing each syllable. "No, Athene. No. Go now."

I did not press the matter. I left him, returning to my books and my own endeavors.

The next morning I arose and threw myself with renewed vigor into the hunt. In addition to the unfortunate circumstance of the expulsion of the religious orders from France, my newfound hagio-vocabulary was of no assistance. All the information I had ferreted away from those weeks in the company of *religieuse* and Sir Simon availed me little. I could question timid old ladies in their lacy veils about monks and nuns, though I couldn't bring myself to speak of werewolves and other horrors to these pious, wrinkled women. But all my questions seemed to do was fill their eyes with tears and drive them, clinging more fiercely to their beads, to scurry away down the street or back into the safe darkness of the closest church.

In the afternoon of that seventh day as I, aching, dusty, and discouraged, finished my fruitless exploration of the Romanesque Saint-Julien-le-Pauvre, I happened upon a triumphant plaque mounted under the Third French Republic, declaring the passage of the building into Melkite hands. I didn't quite understand what this connoted beyond the fact that it demonstrated, once again, the tragic futility of my efforts.

I leaned against the handlebars of my bicycle to consider the scene before me. The quiet simplicity of the churchyard caught my attention and, for a moment, distracted me from my considerable irritation with the political climate that had so unexpectedly frustrated my worthy efforts at heroic apprenticeship. For some minutes I read through the long list of names spread across the gravestones. Lefebvre, Desmarais, Bourg—this latter appeared so many times that I felt convinced the bearers of it were peasants. No one else would have been so indecently prolific.

An odd thought struck me. The graveyard should have been a place of thrilling suspense and dark mystery. Perhaps the contrast of those past events had robbed the atmosphere of its natural tension. Or perhaps my sensibilities were dulled. It was all so frightfully mundane. That new, thrilling enchantment I had discovered had indeed vanished from the world, and my enthusiastic efforts to recapture it had all ended in dull failure.

The street was quiet but for a group of dirty young boys who were playing some sort of game near the next corner. I wondered if these unsightly beggars were worth the attention of *les gendarmes*. More Romany vagrants perhaps, I thought. I hoped they wouldn't get into any trouble and thought it likely they would. I wondered if their lives were more exciting than mine—and I thought that likely too.

After watching the boys for a few moments, I attempted to focus my wandering thoughts upon my insurmountable problem. The sun beat down on me but not to the point of discomfort. From under my hat, a stray lock of hair had loosened from the unstylish, low knot in which I typically twisted it. Warmed by Helios' rays, I chewed on that liberated tress.

Perhaps this deity of the Papists required some sort of sacrifice. He appeared to be an uncommunicative sort, even with my limited experience of supernatural entities. If he desired blood, I was stymied.

I had no fatted bullocks to spare, alas. In fact, as I thought about it, I found I was ravenous and, even with my desire for adventure still keen, would have struggled to persuade myself to give up any fatted anything for anyone, even a deity. There was the Iphigenia route too, but I refused to be stretched out on an altar and have my throat slit so that the blood could run down and be lapped up by some grossly incarnate divinity.

All this thought of hunger and thirst was enough to convince me that I required sustenance of some sort ere I continued. I ceased to abuse the wisp of hair (which, as I considered it, was a poor replacement for actual food), straightened up, shook the dust from my clothes, and produced my small purse to itemize its contents.

"I don't suppose you listen to people like me," I muttered as I counted out sous and francs, "but if you do listen to anyone and have time to spare, and if you have any ideas to suggest, I'd rather appreciate it."

I was noting with satisfaction that my coinage was more than sufficient to meet my present needs and desires while wondering if my first attempt at prayer to the Papist god required the addition of "amen" or further precise address when realization of the full danger of my absentmindedness rushed upon me. In my peripheral vision I had seen that the dirty boys and their game had moved closer to the steps of the church. Now they were right beside me.

"Bonjour, mademoiselle!" shouted the first boy in my face, grabbing the handles of my bicycle.

Startled, I almost lost my balance, and was forced to grasp the bike firmly to right myself. As I stumbled, the second boy snatched my purse right from my hands.

"*Merci bien!*" cried the thief.

"*Merci infiniment!*" crowed a third.

"*Merci mille fois!*" They all cheered over their shoulders as they scattered with breathtaking speed in every direction.

My befuddled, bewildered pursuit brought me into the middle of the street, almost within the murderous scope of a bustling, dark red Renault automobile. The driver shouted a rebuke at me. Shaken, impoverished, and scarlet with embarrassment, I scurried back to the safety of the sidewalk and walked along, pushing my bicycle, until the scene of the theft and the rattling noise of the departing vehicle were far behind me.

Free from watching eyes, I stamped my foot with vexation. "If that's how you answer prayers, it's no wonder they've thrown so many of your silly priests out of France."

I made my way home, irritated and hangdog. Georges was there on the threshold. I surrendered the bicycle to his care and stepped into the hall.

There, before me, stood a veritable tower of trunks and packing cases.

"Athene!" It was my father's voice in its most exasperated tones. "What *are* you about? We shall be late for the train!"

"Train?"

"Are you not even ready, girl? We shall be late, I tell you!"

"Why? What is it?"

"Am I to explain everything over and over, Athene? The estate! We must go! Immediately!"

"But," I said, "where are we going?"

The martyr groaned. I half expected him to lapse into a performance of *King Lear*, but instead he merely looked his exasperation and responded clearly: "Brussels."

"*Brussels*? We are going to *Brussels*!"

"We..." With a visible effort, my father stopped himself from parroting back at me. "Yes, Athene," he said, taking refuge in sarcasm. "But not if you don't hurry up."

"Amen, amen, amen!" I crowed. "We are going to Brussels! I shall pack at once!"

I threw my hat into the arms of the Georges, who stood beaming at my lapse into complete insanity, and ran up the stairs, laughing. On the landing, I stopped and turned back.

"How long will we be there?" I bellowed down. "Never mind! I shall be ready in two minutes! Oh, Father! I *love* you!"

Before he could retrieve his jaw from the floor and restore his horrified face to its irritated expression, I ran into my bedroom and began throwing my possessions into the center of the room, all the while muttering a happy, "Thank you, oh thank you, oh thank you!" I assumed this was sufficient thanksgiving if the situation were, in fact, the doing of that illusive deity of the Papists.

A disapproving sniff hailed me from the door.

"Desirée," I said, "pack everything! I am going to Brussels! My bicycle too! I shall have everything!"

Her eyes swept across the room, taking in my pile of books and notes and the untidy mountain range of garments, shoes, and miscellaneous supplies I was still amassing in the middle of the carpet.

"Everything, mademoiselle?"

"*Everything*," I replied firmly "And, Desirée, do hurry. We are going to be late."

Chapter II

18 May 1906: Le Saulchoir in Kain

It is by willing obedience, therefore, that you show
mercy not only toward yourselves, but also toward
superiors, whose higher rank among you exposes
them all the more to greater peril.

— The Rule of St. Augustine

PERHAPS I SHOULD HAVE STOOD FOR A LONG TIME SURVEYING THE
exterior of Le Saulchoir before I approached. I was, however,
impatient to advance my purpose.

I had arisen early in our lodgings (a respectable rather than
resplendent house in the Woluwe Saint Pierre) and, in the cold, early
hours of dawn, had escaped my father's company and made my way
to the train station. He had been deeply occupied in business about
the estate and had not bothered to invite me into his confidence,
to my considerable relief. My heart was set on other matters and
would pursue those by means of the earliest train to Kain. As the
train hurried out of the wakening city and into the countryside, I
consulted a few discreet maps I carried in my small purse along with
a notebook well-packed with information gleaned from my careful
studies over the past weeks.

It was yet morning when I stood before the monastery. It was a
vast, aged expanse of a building, standing solemnly and silently in a
wide, flat landscape shaded with trees. I did not notice any willows
to justify the name of the place, but perhaps these listless, lithe trees
were kept in discreet seclusion. Perhaps they had been cut down by
order of a severely ascetical cleric. The front door looked neither

inviting nor threatening. If ever a building looked as if it were asleep and unconcerned with passersby, this was that building.

Having made these general observations to myself, I would waste no more time in launching my assault. I marched up to the door with a determined step and rang the bell. Its gentle clang echoed with a slow, almost lazy dullness before falling back into sleepy silence.

A minute passed. Then five minutes. Then a quarter of an hour, though it felt closer to an eternity. I rang the bell again, more timidly this time. No one came.

No, that is not true. A little noise from the ground prompted me to glance down at my feet and I saw there a small white mouse, frozen mid-scurry, gazing up at me with bright curiosity and, I suspected, a touch of incredulity.

"And what do you think *you* are doing here?" its black, snapping eyes seemed to say.

A valid question, even from a furry inquisitor. I began to fidget and even to wonder what on earth I would say when—*if*—someone ever came to that ponderous, implacable door to open it and grant me an audience. I might even have suspected the place to be deserted, a haunted ruin, the stuff of Gothic fiction, with a rodent Torquemada who at any moment could transform from a mouse into a snarling, man-eating beast, vengeful claws outstretched and harsh teeth gnashing wildly toward me...

I looked down again. The creature was still there, and if mice have such facial details, its eyebrows were raised satirically. After three scornful sniffs, the mouse shrugged and scurried away.

Its departure extinguished the flames of lurid imagination. This place was not dead and perhaps was not even asleep. The grounds gave testament to living, methodical care. More likely, the inhabitants were busy communing with their deity and couldn't be bothered about silly things like visitors at the gate.

The door opened upon me and my thoughts with a slow, yawning creak. A blinking elderly face peeked out, housed above that memorable white hooded habit.

"Good day, *Père*." I hoped I did not look as absurd as I felt.

"Good day, mademoiselle," he replied, still blinking, with a courteous little bow.

"I am here to…to…"

As he continued to blink, panic seized me. I truly had no excuse to be there, and if I could not persuade this probably kind and perhaps mentally deficient old man to admit me, he would close the door, showering blessings on my head like ashes, leaving me without even the questionable company of his furry forerunner. I could not state my true object—to track down my lost companions and finagle a place for me among their company.

"I am here to see Father Pierre Jarvais," I blurted out, retrieving this name of authority from the store of my memory.

To my astonishment, he bowed again and slowly, ever slowly, pulled the creaking door wide open before me. Following the example of the mouse, I scurried over the threshold before the man in white could change his mind.

We stood in an open hall, flanked by two sets of closed doors, with a hallway before us and large double doors ahead. A large Dominican stood immobile on a pedestal in one corner. My escort gestured with slow graciousness toward the left and with his gradual, creaking lack of haste opened the door. I entered the small parlor thus disclosed to me and took a seat upon a well-worn chair.

"Please…" he began.

I must have anticipated him by sitting before he had instructed me to do so. I began to rise, but he beckoned me back into my seat.

I sat a second time, feeling quite foolish.

"I shall fetch the prior," he murmured, nodding to himself as he closed the door behind him.

I glanced uneasily around the room. It was simply furnished, with a small divan displaying faded but well-kept upholstery and the chair, with an alarmingly straight back, on which I sat. A small, unornamented clock hung on the wall. Though it correctly marked the time—I had checked it against the delicate gold watch I wore upon my wrist—I felt it was moving at a fraction of a normal pace. In fact, I was sure that it slowed into an irregular *tick tick…tick… …tick…* My watch, consulted again, indicated that this was not the case. I did wonder, though, if my timepiece had fallen under the influence of that place and was itself moving more slowly than before.

I looked away from the clock before it could drive me mad. A number of prints that I assumed depicted spiritual topics caught my eye next, and I rose to inspect them.

The crucifixion scene I recognized, but this differed in one critical point from the one outside the Franciscan monastery in Zagreb. Two additional figures were in the scene, attired in white. Clearly anachronistic but an interesting addition. Was it vanity, I wondered, that led their imagination to place haloed friars at the foot of the cross? One figure had an extra allotment of illumination—a star sparkled over his forehead. The other had, I was certain, an axe in his skull.

A curious place to carry one's weaponry.

The next picture I could not as easily place. Two brown-robed men, half-reclined upon what looked like the Italian countryside, either newly roused from sleeping or staring in stunned ecstasy at a red-tailed angel. Nothing in my vast store of knowledge equipped me for interpreting the image.

I had more than enough time to contemplate the works. I finally surrendered to the overwhelming urge to look once again at my watch and at the clock. They mocked me in unison. Half an hour had passed.

What *would* I say to this priest when he appeared? I knew nothing of him beyond the title of prior and that he was somehow the cause of the end of all those thrilling adventures in Zagreb. What sort of authority would he have? What interest could he have in speaking with an unschooled heathen?

This last question caused me to consider the terms pagan and heathen and to wonder which classification suited me. I did not come to any conclusion.

"The least they could do," I said aloud, "is provide their long-neglected visitors with some sort of reading material! Anything would do! Even pious platitudes!"

At this inopportune moment, the door swung open and an extraordinarily tall, thin man in white, armed with a profile singularly lacking in consolation, glided into the room.

"Bonjour, mademoiselle," he said in a deep, emphatic voice. "I am Father Pierre Jarvais."

This seemed undeniable. I gaped at him, dismayed.

He awaited me patiently for some moments then prompted, "You wished to see me?"

I stood up, opened my mouth to respond, and discovered that spontaneity would give me no aid in this dreadful scene.

"I…"

I do not say that Father Pierre Jarvais was an unkind man, but there was something in that aquiline nose, aesthetic frame, and well-postured height that obliterated my self-assurance and ability to formulate sentences.

"Please," he said, "be seated."

I settled back into my chair awkwardly and endeavored in vain to collect my scattered thoughts. This was not a person likely to be sympathetic with my heroic ambitions. He might think I was insane—or, worse, impertinent.

He watched me with every conceivable indication of perfect patience.

Still I could think of nothing to say. "I…"

I once again stopped. Never in my life had I been so reduced to inarticulate misery as I was with those steady eyes and unquavering eyebrows deployed against me.

The prior seated himself opposite me. If he meant to put me at my ease by sitting too, he failed. "You wished to speak with me, mademoiselle?"

"Y— Yes…" I managed to stammer.

He waited for several moments. I said nothing more.

"Do not be afraid, child. Take your time."

If this was the reassuring tone he took with young women who found themselves in the family way and came for counsel and forgiveness for their errant romancing, I was sure they would leave a groveling mess of penitence and never sin again.

"I…I am Athene Howard."

He nodded with an air of unshakable patience. "Yes, Miss Howard? What can I do for you today?"

"I…I met some…that is…I was traveling with my father and…and…"

My situation was becoming steadily worse. I would—I must!—stem the tide of disaster. Desperation overtook me. I took a deep breath and launched into the most ill-constructed and inarticulate monologue imaginable.

"We were returning from New York, you see, and that's when we met Sister Agatha…" Was it my imagination or did his already still eyebrows freeze with an even more intense immobility? "Because she found us after my father stabbed himself, which was really my fault, but it was an accident, and they knew each other from before, I think, when my father was a priest. That was before, well, before me… But that doesn't really matter because then we traveled with them, and no one explained things to me, and I saw that werewolf in Zagreb, so Sir Simon explained but only partially, and we went to find the werewolf—but not the first one because he is still there unless he has escaped—and we were almost killed by the gypsies, and Brother Philip came, and I think he saved us or that strange boy, I forgot his name. He said we should come back—Brother Philip, not Mihai—that's his name!—and he said you said we must, so everyone came, and we returned to Paris. I prayed, but I don't usually—not at all, actually—so when I heard we were to travel to Brussels I felt sure I…well, I came here…"

I trailed off, wondering if Father Pierre Jarvais had the authority to have me burned at the stake.

He looked at me with what was probably an expression of quiet pity but felt like contempt.

"Miss Howard," he said gently, "you are perhaps slightly mistaken as to our purpose here. We are a mendicant order, dedicated to the preaching of the Gospel. There are many opportunities for young women to grow in understanding of our dear Lord. It may be that, given time and reflection, you will come to understand the call in your heart. For now, I think, the most prudent step for you is to return to your home. You are English? This may be of interest to you."

From a hidden pocket he produced a small pamphlet entitled *Simple Prayer-book* and handed it to me.

I took it, desolated. "Thank you."

He nodded kindly and rose. "I shall see you to the door, my dear."

I stood up, trying to formulate one last reason why I should be permitted to stay, some way to extend the interview until I could think of something to the purpose. I was opening my mouth to frame my excuse—or my plea—when a thunderous crash outside the parlor door forestalled me.

This disruption to the silent serenity of the place even startled my stern host. He actually jumped. Then, after staring for half a second as if in shock toward the sound, he moved with a swiftness I had not expected of him to grasp the door handle and fling it open.

There before us was a red-faced, red-haired young man, a soiled black smock protecting the white of his robes, hurriedly gathering up a mountain of books scattered across the hall. He looked up at Father Pierre, and the blush on his cheeks attained an even deeper hue. Even as he continued to collect his scattered library, he gathered one corner of the front piece of his habit and raised it to his lips, his eyes raised in mute apology to the prior.

Before that worthy could speak, a strange noise—like the clucking of a hen but from the throat of a man—came from behind the large statue. A second friar was there, likewise armed with a soiled smock and bent over in recovery of the lost texts.

"Now, now, Brother," said a kindly and irrepressibly English voice, "it's no use sighing after spilled milk, even when it happens to be books—a dreadful abuse of metaphors."

The second friar stood up, and I saw a round, bespectacled face beaming down upon us over a pile of massive, red-stained, ancient books with gilt Latin titles upon their bindings.

When he saw the prior, whose sternness had not abated, this new figure also raised a corner—not of his white robe but of the filthy smock—to his smiling lips. "Pardon, Father Pierre, for this volume-inous interruption."

The emphasis was clear, and the unexpected pun brought a chortle into my throat. I stifled it as best I could and tried to pretend to have coughed, but I knew Father Pierre was not deceived.

"Such a mess!" said the cheerful English friar. "But we shall have it in order swiftly, shall we not, Brother William?"

Brother William, crimson to his ears, nodded, only half looking up from his task.

Setting down the retrieved pile upon the table in the side parlor, the smock-wearing friar turned his smiling face to me next. "I do apologize to you too, my dear."

My heart swelled in response to that sympathetic face. "I am Athene Howard," I blurted.

"Indeed!" he said, smiling even more broadly. "How splendid. Which branch of the Howards?"

I almost responded, "The unimportant one," but instead gasped out, "The…the…my father is Charles Howard."

"Ah, not the Norfolk branch." He had begun to stack the books back into Brother William's waiting arms. "Lovely family. There used to be a priory at the foot of Arundel Castle, but of course—" He stopped, as if struck by a wondrous new insight, and dropped a particularly massive volume into the arms of the young friar. "Charles Howard! Of course! Charles Howard! And so you are, Miss Howard! How perfectly delightful!" He dropped another book onto the pile.

"Delightful!" He added two more. "I am Father Thomas Edmund Gilroy, my dear. I am delighted to meet you."

"Father Thomas Edmund," declared Father Pierre in a deep, disapproving voice, "is assisting with our library. I believe," continued the prior with austere politeness, "that Miss Howard was preparing to return to Brussels."

"Not before a cup of tea!" cried Father Thomas Edmund. "And then I shall escort her home. It is the least I can do, given our rude interruption. Ah, yes, Brother William!" That red-haired friar was beginning to look as if he might collapse from the weight of the tower of tomes. "I have not forgotten our task. Unlike Father William, you will not stand on your head but balance these books with agility!"

"*Alice in Wonderland*." I sounded dazed, as if I were in a dream.

The round-faced priest beamed at me and ushered me back into my chair. "Miss Howard, please be seated once more! Brother William and I shall restore this precious cargo to its rightful place and I shall return to you with tea before, as you might say, you could dot another i—Bob Cratchet!"

Chuckling at this unseasonable reference to Charles Dickens, which delighted me anew, he departed.

For a moment, the prior narrowed his eyes at me. He was probably determining how best to have me cast from the premises. In the end, however, Father Pierre merely excused himself and left me in solitude in that little parlor. But, oh! With what changed feelings I considered the walls of my confinement! Hope, liberated from Pandora's box, had momentarily taken flight before returning to take up residence in my breast. I could have danced, but I restrained myself, for fear that Father Pierre might reappear and take advantage of the lapse to warn me off the grounds.

In what felt like mere moments—a comical contrast to the tedium of the passage of time just an hour or so before—I found myself seated across a tea service, partaking happily of that comforting brew, with Father Thomas Edmund Gilroy presiding over the cups.

The smiling cheerfulness of this new character on the stage of my life was like a ray of sunshine—or an overheated stage light on the brink of explosion. It might combust at any minute, showering me with microscopic glass, but for now, like the most innocent and credulous audience member, I basked in the renewed illumination.

He was very cheerful indeed.

"I am here in Kain on an errand of mercy," he said. "I am assisting in the rehabilitation of our library. The intermittent tolerance of the French government has exacerbated our itinerancy, and the state of the library sadly reflects this. You could say it has...willowed away."

It took me the merest moment to recognize this as a play of words on the title of the abbey (Le Saulchoir or "the grove of willows"). I chuckled. "Are you a connoisseur of puns?"

"Alas! It is one of my worst characteristics. In my youth, I suffered rebuke by many for similar lapses into wit. 'Cleverness is not the same as wisdom,' said my elders. Even so, I persisted. Then one day we heard a tale that vindicated me on every point."

"Indeed?"

"Once upon a time," he said in a low, confiding sort of voice suitable to the telling of fairy tales in the nursery, "a pious member of our community journeyed into the depths of the darkest jungle to preach to a tribe of cannibals. As they were less than receptive to the Gospel, they determined not to waste such a fine piece of meat. At the moment when they were about to submerge their victim into a cauldron of boiling water, he protested, 'I cannot be boiled! I am a friar!'"

I collapsed into appreciative hilarity, but he continued in a somber voice. "Thus he was saved from martyrdom and went on to evangelize unharmed for many years." His voice changed back into merry kindness. "Let me refill your cup, my dear, and you can tell me all about it."

Thus comfortably established, I began my story. Perhaps I was too naïve, but unlike Father Pierre, the round-faced, bespectacled man conveyed an immediate sense of trustworthiness. I unburdened myself of the saga without hesitation. With Father Thomas Edmund, I was concise, orderly, and coherent. He listened attentively, interrupting once or twice only to offer me more tea.

When I concluded, he looked at me for a few moments in silence. I met his gaze, wondering—but not fearing—what he might be thinking.

"Miss Howard," he said, "what do you wish to do?"

"I…I want to help," I said.

"Help with what?"

"With…whatever it really is. To find Jean-Claude. Or to do whatever I can."

"Why?" Like the interrogation by the mouse, this was a valid question.

"Because it fascinates me, and I think I may be of use." I explained the research I had undertaken and even produced, somewhat timidly, my little notebook.

He looked this over carefully, smiling, but not in a patronizing way. When he concluded his perusal of my notes—and, indeed, he looked at every page—he nodded, more to himself than to me.

"Well, Miss Howard, we will think and pray and consult." Then he smiled—such a sweet, kind smile upon his round face. "Come, my dear. I shall accompany you home."

That journey back to Tournai, from carriage to train, then from train to carriage, and finally a walk through many streets back into Woluwe Saint Pierre, remains so dear and so memorable to me, though I can scarcely recall the content of our conversation. I have a sense that we spoke of everything and of nothing. We did not speak of quests for werewolves or the threat of gypsies, yet it never seemed as if the priest were avoiding the topic. It simply did not arise. I felt the weight of obsession lifting from my brain. Such is the relief born of renewed hope.

When finally we walked up to the door of the house where my father and I had taken up our temporary lodging, I realized with a start that I was hungry from the exercise. For some reason, this made me chuckle.

The priest looked at me with smiling inquiry.

"I'm quite ravenous," I said. "This is my greatest heroic weakness, I fear. I cannot persist in any endeavor without regular meals."

Before my fingers could close upon the ugly Gothic brass knocker to summon the maid and announce my return, the door flew open. There stood my father wearing his hat, with a large black dispatch case under his arm. He looked from me to my companion, and at the sight of that amiable, bespectacled face he positively goggled.

"*Good...God!*" His cry mingled alarm and horror to an almost comical degree.

"He is indeed," said Father Thomas Edmund Gilroy, a gentle rebuke in his voice. "It is good to see you, Charles. It has been a long time."

CHAPTER 12

> We cannot tell the precise moment when friendship is
> formed. As in filling a vessel drop by drop, there is at last a
> drop which makes it run over; so in a series of kindnesses
> there is at last one which makes the heart run over.
>
> — James Boswell, *Life of Johnson*

SHORTLY AFTER THIS DRAMATIC ENCOUNTER, I WAS SITTING AT A
small round table at a nearby café, feasting upon baguette,
cheese, jam, and strong coffee, with the two men seated opposite
me. Their comportment could not have differed more widely
had they deliberately determined to represent ill-temper and
serenity respectively.

While Father Thomas Edmund seemed delighted by the flavor
of his own beverage—and as delighted in my own enjoyment of the
repast—my father neither ate and drank, alternately looking out the
window, his lips moving in the midst of some tempestuous argument
with an absent adversary, or glaring at the table in bored irritability.
He avoided looking at Father Thomas Edmund.

"Charles," said the priest with that same sweet smile, "Doctor
Thornfield's new book is worthy of your challenge, but not, I think,
your contempt."

That made my father raise his eyes toward Father Thomas
Edmund, but he didn't speak. This was likely because his mind was
still occupied in that argument with the absent.

"How did you know what he was thinking?" I breathed, thrilled.

Father Thomas Edmund chuckled. "It was a childish trick, my
dear, and I really ought to apologize. Like the performances of Dupin

and the good Sherlock. I did not, however, analytically follow the train of your father's thoughts." He gestured to the edge of the table. A book perched there, and I could just discern the author's name on its newly minted binding.

My father was glaring at it with redoubled irritability, probably as an outlet for his impotent annoyance at the situation. "Thornfield," he rattled out in a harsh, almost metallic voice, "has dived too deeply into Viennese theory without grasping its true significance. The reality of the subconscious is a critical, long-neglected field, and it illuminates our appreciation for the vast, universal experience of repressed desires. He wishes to reduce this experience to a vagary of an unstable mind or a hallucination, instead of the point where desire permeates and transforms, revealing the deep lusts and furies of primitive man. He is just as limited in his understanding as that *other school,* which insists upon viewing all through the lens of dogmatic fantasy. And"—he looked sternly at Father Thomas Edmund over his glasses as he concluded—"you know this all too well, sir."

The priest merely chuckled. "You have not changed, Charles. Still as fierce as ever." Then he turned to me. "Do you like Tournai, Miss Howard?"

"Yes, I suppose I do. I think there may be more…" I was about to say "more excitement" but, at the last minute, transitioned into: "…more to…see."

"Ah, yes. The history of the city is quite remarkable, quite remarkable. What have you seen so far?"

"Not very much," I admitted.

"He avoids the real point in hand, you see, Athene," interrupted my father in his most combative tone. "You forget, Gilroy—I know you of old. I'm not to be put off by indulgent smiles and deliberate obtuseness. I should have known you were at the bottom of this."

While I could never have accused him of indulgence or recklessness in smiling, it did flash across my mind that my father's entire life had been a study in deliberate obtuseness, but I said nothing and simply looked to his new adversary. The offensiveness in my father's tone echoed, yet surpassed, his combativeness toward Sister Agatha in earlier days. I wondered, not for the last time, what on earth these men had been to each other in the past.

Father Thomas Edmund Gilroy appeared unruffled. "I am sorry for your frustration, Charles. I am happy to discuss any point with you."

"Discussion is hardly possible with one so determined to be deluded. Man advances, man's knowledge expands, and you still gaze backward. Blind, Gilroy. Blind."

Father Gilroy merely smiled.

"You take the inner yearnings and torments of man and seek to disguise the reality with thick layers of moralizing, antiquated nonsense."

"Ah, yes. You would have the beast justified rather than conquered or redeemed, would you not?"

"What is your connection with this anyway?" demanded my father, ignoring the question. "It's not your area of expertise, is it? Or have you widened your attention to things bestial?"

"Are they redeemable?" I interjected eagerly.

Father Thomas Edmund nodded pleasantly. "In many cases, yes."

"How do you do it?"

He looked slightly surprised. "Oh, my dear. I don't!"

"Don't you battle werewolves?"

"Oh no."

I was dumbfounded. "You are not a werewolf hunter? What... are you?"

"Oh," he said, still in that pleasant, conversational way, "I am an historian."

I was crestfallen and must have looked it.

He smiled. "Dear mademoiselle, did you expect something different?"

I felt the warmth of blood rushing to my cheeks. "I suppose I did."

"No, my attention is otherwise focused, but there are some important points of shared purpose. It's the business of my Minorite brothers. The followers of Holy Father Francis. We who follow the path of our Holy Father Dominic, on the other hand, why, our attention, when it is given to such matters, focuses upon the blood-drinking undead, not the feral lycanthrope."

I could have crowed with delight. "You battle vampires?!"

My father positively snorted.

Father Thomas Edmund smiled. I wondered if he ever *didn't* smile and decided it would be a tragic day if so. "It is one of the commissions given to the Dominicans by papal edict, yes."

"Delusions decreed by delusions," my father pronounced in a voice dripping with academic snobbery, "and ratified by delusions!"

"*What the deuce!*"

This unexpected exclamation came from not from the priest but from behind my head. I jumped and wheeled around to see the unmistakable form of Sir Simon Gwynne in silhouette in the doorway, with the sun shining behind him. As he came out of the light and settled into greater visibility, I could see that his sandy Viking brow was contracted, and the look he directed at the table was positively thunderous.

"Do sit, Simon," said Father Thomas Edmund mildly. "I am in the most delightful company. You know Doctor Howard and his daughter, Athene, do you not?"

Sir Simon collapsed into a chair next to me, and that burdened piece of furniture groaned its protest. For a few moments, he looked from one man to the other—glaring at my father from under those heavy brows and looking with perplexity toward the priest, who continued to sip his little cup of tea.

"I beg your pardon, Father," Sir Simon said with a surprising note of humility. Belatedly, he glanced toward me. I was relieved to see there was no anger in that gaze. "You are not in Paris."

"No." I felt the inadequacy of the reply. "We are not."

"I thought you were in Paris."

For the first time I felt guilty for thrusting myself once more into this business. I opened my mouth to apologize—though I could scarcely have said for what I would have apologized—but a thought struck me.

"Dominicans!" I said aloud. "Do you know that there is a bit of cleverness here too? The Latin for dog is…"

Sir Simon groaned, but Father Thomas Edmund Gilroy looked pleased. "Yes. Thus, the followers of St. Dominic are the *Domini canes*—'The Dogs of the Lord.' You are not the first to question the papal delegatory allocations on this precise point. It is a lovely little bit of cleverness, but there is actually a deeper meaning."

I nodded encouragingly, like a good little pupil.

"While with child, the mother of our holy father, St. Dominic, dreamed a strange and wonderful dream wherein she gave birth to a small dog—a dog with a flaming torch in his mouth. With that torch, he set fire to the world."

I took a deep breath, delighted.

"A wonderful, beautiful tale," continued Father Thomas Edmund. "Returning to the subject of revenants and lycanthropes, however, we—"

"The practice has its roots in primitive rituals," interrupted my father. "Originally, they used monkeys in their worship. Concluding in ritualistic sacrifice, as described in Gilgamesh."

"They?" I asked. "Who did?"

"The Papists, of course, Athene."

My brow creased with concentration while I mentally explored the catalogue of careful scholarship I had amassed on the subject. "I don't remember that part in Gilgamesh. But what does that have to do with these wolfmen?"

"You never can keep up, even when it is clearly explained, Athene. The monkey god was a forerunner for the obsession with this primitive metamorphosis and the regression of man into a bestial form."

"Where did the monkeys come from?" That seemed to me to be the most bewildering part of the business. Monkeys had played no part whatsoever in any of the texts I had explored.

"Sea-bound Aztecs first introduced them," my father replied in his loftiest tones. "We can discern these details in Lemprière, of course."

Since I associated that name with a classical dictionary, I could not quite follow the connection. I looked at my father in perplexity. Perhaps his mind was truly and finally going. Or perhaps—I was fair enough to consider this a possibility—he had stumbled upon information that had thus far eluded me. "I have not found that," I said cautiously. "You will have to show me the reference."

For a moment, my father regarded me silently over his glasses. Then he turned to Father Thomas Edmund Gilroy and arched one eyebrow.

A small frown creased the priest's forehead. "You always did speak nonsense tolerably well, Charles."

My father was clearly amused and pleased with himself. "It does demonstrate the degree of credulity in play, does it not?"

"Hardly. Notice that she demanded your chapter and verse, Charles. She has good sense, my friend. I cannot imagine her easily seduced by heterodox notions."

He spoke lightly, but my father flushed with sudden anger.

"I have cultivated her intellect well," he snapped, "so she would be far beyond your powers of persuasion, I can assure you."

"I am sure she would be!" Father Thomas Edmund laughed. "I have never been called persuasive! Cheerfully bombastic, perhaps."

"I require no persuasion," I said, a trifle hotly. "I have the evidence of my own senses to bring to bear. I saw one of those poor creatures in that church, Father. And again—as you well know—in that village. If it were not real, why would we flee for our lives?"

"Athene, you use words without proper reference. Sometimes I really do think—"

I interrupted my father in turn. "Are these creatures everywhere?" I asked Father Thomas Edmund. "These creatures or the ones with which you are associated?"

"Associated." He chuckled over the word for a moment. "Yes, my dear, evil spirits and fallen creatures are all around us. They are not, however, usually to be seen in daily life."

"Why not?"

He cocked his head to one side. "You can discern the answer to that question readily, Miss Howard. Why do the gods of the myths usually approach mortals in mortal form?"

"Semele and Zeus. The gods are less alarming in the guise of men. Mere mortals cannot withstand the glory of Mount Olympus."

"Let us consider a counterpoint then. If men went about seeing their fellows transformed into beasts or witnessed the onslaught of preternatural terrors in the night—"

"Your churches would be full," I said with a chuckle.

"At least initially," he acknowledged. "Therefore if, as I and those like me believe, these creatures operate with an opposite goal in view, would they not be likely to avoid undue visibility?"

"Yes." I sat for a few moments in silence, digesting this. It was not remotely as exciting as I could have hoped. I was sorry for it. And yet...and yet...there were *some* consolations, and this was perhaps my only opportunity to plead to remain attached to that fascinating company.

When I looked up again, I was surprised to find Sir Simon gazing at me. Surprised in that scrutiny, he did not look away, but continued to watch me with furrowed brow for a moment more. Then he uttered something that might have been a curmudgeonly sigh and returned his attention to Father Thomas Edmund. The priest was observing my father, who was himself looking angrily at the table once again.

"What..." I stopped with a mild uncertainty. It would not do—I *would* go on, though I felt increasingly sure I was presumptuous. "What can I do to help?"

"With what?" barked my father.

Sir Simon, who appeared to be on the brink of an irritable reply himself, changed his tactics to say, "You are most kind, Miss Howard, but we have nothing that could—"

"Thank you," said Father Thomas Edmund at the same instant and with gracious solemnity. "We are honored to accept your assistance." Then he smiled.

Sir Simon looked aghast. My father, disgusted.

"Of all the absurd posturing—" my father began.

"At the moment," the white-robed, bespectacled priest continued, "you have found your friends at an impasse. Permission and authority are critical to the sort of enterprise in which they are engaged. In addition, many of them have taken a vow of obedience. Thus, they must obey."

"Can't someone waive or undo the vow?"

"One's vows are to God himself. It would not be a comfortable thing to imagine them dispensed." He blinked meditatively. "One could, you see, be quite wrong, and then where would one be?"

I did not entirely follow, but felt I was making headway and meant to pursue my advantage. "How are you involved?"

"I am not much involved, but I am what you might call an interested party. I have known the twins for many years. For now, as Isabel is in this period of waiting, I am sure she will be delighted to have your company."

I was less certain but did not say so.

"I will bring you to see her tomorrow, if I may."

To this suggestion I readily assented.

At this, my father rose from his chair. "I have business to which I should be attending. Come, Athene." He nodded curtly at the two men and would have left, had Father Thomas Edmund not extended a hand in his path.

"It is good to see you, Charles," he said. "I am glad you are well."

My father grumbled something, put on his hat, and scurried out the door.

"I shall see you tomorrow." I hoped I did not sound too eager.

"You won't...forget?"

"Indeed not, Miss Howard. We are delighted to have you with us. Are we not, Simon?"

Sir Simon, his face flushed as he bent over the broken lace of his boot, did not reply. I smiled at the priest and hurried after my father.

That evening, when we returned to our lodgings in a highly reputable street, presided over by an eminently respectable proprietress—a widow by the name of Madame Deshalle—I climbed into my bed without the satisfaction of having received answers to my many questions but with a real sense of comfort in the reunion with the band of strange, wonderful Papists. That sweet, pleasant new priest. Sir Simon. And tomorrow, Isabel! Who knew what sort of exciting new scenes would unfold before me! Perhaps I would even witness the romantic denouement of that puzzling pair. I wondered if Isabel appreciated Sir Simon. All things considered, he was a marvelous hero.

As I drifted away into sleep, my last conscious thought was a perplexed one. There was a strange sensation at the back of my eyes, as if a creature were lurking there. The sensation intensified as sleep came upon me. It slithered across my subconscious so that, though sleeping, I am sure I began to toss uncomfortably—nervously—among the bedsheets. My dream, if dream it was, never gained full articulation as a narrative, but even in its primordial form, the strangeness of the dawning vision nurtured the sensation of discomfort so that my skin began to tingle.

Dancing, slithering forms wafted about me. Thin, lizard-like forms without faces waltzing to a Viennese melody. Long tendrils trailed behind them. Ribbons or gauzy scarves. Swirling, twirling, creeping, crawling up onto my bed and...

With an effort, I reached down from sleep, grabbed at my drifting mind, and dragged myself up into wakefulness.

The dark room echoed with the sound of my labored, frantic breathing. I looked around, half in and half out of sleep. It was my bedroom, yet not my bedroom. Tournai. We were in Tournai.

I reached for the candle on the little bedside table—a quaint bit of old-fashioned practicality that I alone appreciated. My hands were shaky, so it took me more than a few seconds to light the match.

In the sudden blaze of light, I saw the thin, serpentine face looking in a considering sort of way at me. For a moment I froze, staring and blinking to verify for myself that I was indeed seeing what I thought I was seeing.

My midnight guest cocked his head to one side as if he were quizzically evaluating me.

I squeaked and dropped the match. I felt about for another and hurriedly—and even more ineffectually—endeavored to light my candle.

Another blaze of light.

He was still there and seemed irritated by my erratic proceedings. Still with his head cocked to one side, the snake rose to an alarming height of several feet from its coil upon the carpet, hissing and rising, hissing and rising.

Clinging to the candle, I leapt to my feet and let out a piercing shriek. Without thinking, I made one desperate leap from the bed toward the door. Alas, I missed my footing, knocking against the bedside table and falling to the ground with a thunderous crash. Without pausing to test the excruciating pain of my bruised body or to determine how close this clumsiness had brought me to my serpentine adversary, I scaled the chest of drawers. There I sat, my aching legs curling around me, shrieking and shrieking while the snake continued to rise and hiss at me.

The door swung open, revealing the form of my father, his face contracted in a frown.

He looked first to the bed. Then to me. Then to the inordinate length of snake. When he saw the creature, he staggered back against the wall and stood there, frozen, his mouth agape and his eyes wide, gazing in horror as if he could not bear to look away.

How long this drama would have continued, I cannot say, but we were interrupted. Another actor appeared at the door—the young son of the proprietress. He paused for a fraction of a second, uttered some sort of blasphemous exclamation (I could not recognize the dialect, but I could readily guess at the meaning). Then he lunged across the room and grabbed the neck of the snake with his bare hand. The tail of the creature flailed upward as it struggled to strike the face or hands or any part of the body of this fearless adolescent hero. Untroubled by these efforts, the boy caught the tail in his other hand, cursed lustily back at the serpent, and carried it off in triumph and, I assumed, to a dark and unequivocal demise.

Meanwhile my father and I remained where we were—he paralyzed against the wall and I perched atop the chest of drawers in my nightdress, looking as if I were the inhabitant of an asylum. It was as if we had been caught in the performance of a thirty-year-old sensation novel and had been robbed of the drama even as we were rescued from the snake.

The proprietress herself now appeared fully dressed in the doorway. Either she slept thus attired for action or had taken the time to dress before venturing to investigate the noise from her upper rooms. "It is most unfortunate," said Madame Deshalle in her gentle voice. "Most unfortunate. The mademoiselle, she is most distressed. Alas! It will all now be well. Quite well. We go to sleep again, yes?"

"We go to sleep again? *No.* In fact, we will never sleep again."

"Alas! The creature is gone. There is no reason, good mademoiselle, to fear."

"There is every reason. Do you usually have serpents in here?"

She looked grieved that I would suggest such a thing. "*Certainement pas!* Mademoiselle!"

"By no means is it certain, Madame! A giant serpent has just emerged in my bedroom. How am I to know if it is not an infestation?" My voice shrilled, which can be explained and, I think, excused by the circumstances.

Madame looked at me with an eye that would have served a stern governess well. It certainly would have quelled a rebellious young person (and perhaps was the source of the unnatural fearlessness of her offspring). I, as I was made of a resolute fiber, was not intimidated. Arming myself for battle, I perched, ready to maintain my position until the end of time if necessary—or at least until dawn's early light illuminated the world and gave me the opportunity to seek other lodgings free of snakes.

At this precise moment of strong resolution, my father, who had remained in silent petrifaction through the preceding acts of the play, made a faint whimpering noise and crumpled into an unconscious heap upon the floor.

I scrambled down beside him and endeavored to restore him to his senses. Madame scurried away and reappeared with a small blue bottle of *sal volatile*. Uncorking it, she wafted liberal amounts of the foul stuff into both our faces. My father awoke, choking and sputtering, even as I fell back from the suffocating odor, hitting my head against the wall.

Father erupted at our landlady in a torrent of French abuse but halted after a moment to moan tragically, holding first his head then his stomach. Before he could regain his tongue, I assisted Madame in raising my father and half-guiding, half-carrying him back to his boudoir. We deposited him on the bed just as the boy returned, whistling a folk tune and carrying a little cardboard box.

"See! See!" He held out the open box. Within nestled the decapitated head of the serpent, its mouth open, frozen in the vengeful, impotent fury of violent death. One glance was enough.

"Go!" I propelled him with my hand toward the door. As an afterthought, lest he fail to appear the next time creatures of slithering scales and poisonous fangs threatened us, I added, "Thank you."

He shrugged and skipped off with his treasure.

"Your father is well, mademoiselle," said Madame with the air of one who is patient with a hysterical child. "You must sleep."

"I will not sleep. I will stay with him. We should see the doctor."

"In the morning, in the morning." She waved her hand airily. "You must have your rest, mademoiselle."

"I shall never sleep in this house again."

She shrugged with Gallic indifference and walked to the door.

"Wait!" I barked. "Stay here!"

She looked startled and deeply offended as I dashed out of the room.

Moving as quickly as I could, looking frantically into every corner of the passageway as I endeavored not to acknowledge the petrified feeling at the pit of my stomach, I hurried back into the snake pit that had formerly served me as a place of rest. In an instant, I snatched up a large red Indian shawl I had left draped across a chair, pausing only to make sure that no serpents were attached to it, and raced from the room to return to my father.

I was rather breathless as I crossed the threshold. I caught my breath, nodded satisfaction, threw the shawl unceremoniously into a chair, and set about collecting candles.

I heard but did not heed a few muttered comments about "expense," "danger," "setting the house alight," "these English!" I diligently continued my task of recklessly lighting every available candle and bedecking the furniture throughout the room with enthusiastically blazing wicks and melting wax.

Eventually, Madame shrugged again and left the room.

Left alone with my father, I pulled a chair close to the bedside and leaned over him. His breathing was regular and healthy. I considered waking him to assess whether he really were in any danger but dismissed the thought. Better to leave him to his sleep. Morning would come soon enough.

I leaned back in my chair and wrapped the red shawl about me, settling myself to ponder deeply the nature of serpentine evil.

The daylight was making timid headway about the corners of the windowpanes, and the candles had long dwindled into unobtrusiveness before, huddled in my chair, the weight of my eyelids overcame me, and I finally slept.

Chapter 13

19 May 1906: Yet in Tournai

Hominem unius libri timeo. (I fear the man of a single book.)
— Erroneously attributed to St. Thomas Aquinas

I awoke cramped and uncomfortable in my chair, with a strong feeling that I had dreamed vivid and unpleasant things. All I could recall involved dusting each card in an interminable card catalogue in a labyrinthine library. I think I had reached the letter G and was studiously brushing the silt of ages from the misfiled citation for Ptolemy's *Geographia Cosmographia* when the pain in my left knee, which was wedged against the wooden edge of the chair, interrupted my sleep.

Groaning, I opened my eyes. For a moment I couldn't place my surroundings. Then I remembered the snake. At that thought, I sat up straight to examine my father's room.

No serpents could I espy. The room had that unnatural, rumpled, blurry look one associates with first awakening. The furniture was faded, as if it had been aroused from fitful sleep and had not yet undergone the necessary ablutions to be seen in public. I could readily empathize.

I glanced at the bed. With a start, I realized my father, though still half reclined and with the bedclothes up to his neck, was fully awake—had been for some time, by the look of him—and was watching me with keen, focused attention. He did not look away or pretend not to have been observing me, as he usually would have done, but continued in this watchful, meditative mode, with eyes glued upon my reddening face.

"Good morning, sir," I said, feeling like an awkward, gawky adolescent discovered in some foolish posture.

"Good morning," he replied.

Several seconds of silence followed.

"I trust you slept well."

"Better than you, I think."

I grimaced. "It wasn't pleasant, but"—a gentle lie, but a polite one—"better than I expected after such a night."

"Hmm." His brow still furrowed at me.

Several more awkward seconds passed.

"Well…"

"Athene," my father said, as if about to pronounce something of profound import.

"Yes?"

"Remember…"

"Yes?"

My father looked annoyed, but he finished his sentence without a change in tone, "You have an appointment this morning."

I recalled the promised visit to Isabel and scurried out of my chair to go and change. "You don't mind me visiting them, do you, Father?"

"Not at all," he said with pointed lack of interest. "Seek and find. Knock and it shall be opened to you. Follow the men of one book!"

"One book?"

"Indeed, my child. Do not be dismayed at the lack of development or variety or sophistication in their ideas. Embrace the simplicity and take comfort in the rituals. I have a great deal of work to do."

I accepted the dismissal quietly, ruminating over his censorious comment. My scholarly heart was roused—if not to alarm then at least to mild concern. At the door, I once again recollected the serpentine disruption of the previous night and skidded to a stop to look back. "Father, we can't stay—"

My father frowned. "Do go, Athene. You will be late."

I went.

A short time later I emerged, decently and tidily attired, to hurry along the street in time to meet my promised escort.

Despite my father's assertion to the contrary, I had so much time at my disposal that, instead of lingering at the chosen meeting spot in front of the massive Romanesque front of Tournai Cathedral, I walked a little to the side and surveyed a construction project then in hand. It was large and sprawling but still in that indistinct early phase where a sewage system might easily be mistaken for a palace.

"What is it to be?" I asked a passing laborer who was struggling with a large wheelbarrow.

He stopped, set down his heavy load, removed the piece of straw he had been chewing, and spat away the dross. Then he shrugged. "Bah. I don't know. It is for the king. Or the church. Legrand!"

A petite, weasel-like worker, who looked like he was going to expire under his own load of rubble, stopped beside his colleague. For a moment he stood panting and, lounging against his discarded burden, lit a soggy-looking cigarette. "More room," he said, after several fortifying puffs of the cheap-smelling tobacco. "For *la cathédrale*."

"When will it be finished?" I asked.

The men chuckled and shrugged but offered no estimate. I was about to press them further, for my curiosity was aroused, when they straightened, doffed their dirty, coarse caps, and began nodding and bowing toward some approaching figure.

I turned, expecting to see an angry foreman, but instead saw the smiling face of Father Thomas Edmund Gilroy, Homburg hat upon his head and black cloak gently flowing. He greeted the two men in French with a strong English accent. They bowed again before they returned to their work, chuckling as if at some secret joke.

"It is beautiful, is not it?" asked the priest, gesturing toward the site.

Beautiful was not the word that had leapt to my mind, but I did not wish to be uncivil. "There is a great deal of potential there, certainly."

"Yes. A great deal."

"I was just thinking," I ventured, eager to outline the thesis I had been formulating, "it could be anything. It could be something beautiful or something hideous. Something practical or something artistic. It really could go either way."

The priest considered the point. "It seems so, yet the elements of the plan of the architect are all there."

"It could be badly built. Some obsessive, drink-addled lunatic could step in and destroy the architect's original conception."

"Yes, of course." After a pause, he said, "It is rather the same with men."

We stood without speaking, looking down at the unearthed foundation of the future basilica.

"Come," said Father Thomas Edmund, "let us go on our visit."

The little row house where Isabel and Sister Agatha were staying was in a modest street, a residential haven in the midst of the bustle of a pleasant little metropolis. As we walked, the priest regaled me with the complex history of the place, particularly the many changes of fortune it had withstood in the course of time. French, English, Dutch, Austrian, Belgian—all had held sway here. "In fact," he chuckled, "it seems a fitting refuge for our motley band of misfits and outcasts. We all can claim sonship with so confused a patrimony."

"Why are the sisters here and not in a convent?"

"It has been deemed advisable for them to remain here, close to our own house in Kain, as we await clear instructions regarding their errand."

"Who has deemed it?"

He appeared not to have heard me. "Here we are. I do believe we are expected."

His belief was somewhat challenged by what followed. A trim, respectful-looking young woman in maid's attire welcomed us at the door and ushered us into a tiny parlor. As the door opened, the voice of Father Pierre greeted us.

"All due consideration will be given to the pertinent points, Sir Simon," that lofty personage was saying with painful patience. "In such matters, pastoral care, prudence, and proper authority must be carefully weighed."

The Viking-Celt hero was standing, arms akimbo, frowning. Anger and annoyance seemed to be battling for control, but Sir Simon struggled against both and said with only a slight degree of heat, "I tell you there is an occult danger rising that could consume nations. This is not the time for slow contemplation. This is the time for aggressive and immediate action."

Father Pierre answered with the same unwavering courtesy, to Sir Simon's obvious frustration. "I can understand how you could come to that belief, Sir Simon. We will inform you if and as soon as we have any decision pertinent to your own scope of labor. Now I must return."

Father Jarvais looked to Father Thomas Edmund.

"Good morning, Father Prior," said that worthy cheerfully. "You anticipated even our early efforts. Did he not, Miss Howard?"

"Good day, Miss Howard," said Father Pierre Jarvais with his gracious smile.

I mumbled a greeting, wondering how so courteous a man could convey even in a greeting his complete dislike of me. If I saw much more of him, I told myself, I'd develop the sort of complex in which my father's colleagues so delighted.

At the door, the voice of Sir Simon arrested the friar. "I beg your pardon, Father," he said, though he sounded more self-controlled than penitent, "for my heatedness."

"Granted, Sir Simon. I understand your passion and your personal feeling in this matter."

"I also beg," Sir Simon continued with increased volume and a deepening frown indenting his heavy eyebrows, "that you will consider what I have said and be moved to a greater sense of urgency."

Father Pierre bowed his head, though not, I thought, as any sort of concession, and left us.

As the door closed behind him, Sir Simon began pacing the room like a caged animal—not a wolf or a wildcat, I thought, but a well-meaning bear—as if endeavoring to dissipate the anger and distress that introduced such ill grace into the forms and mannerisms of due courtesy and respect.

"All will be well, my son," said Father Thomas Edmund Gilroy.

"That is as may be," responded the other tartly as he continued that exhaustingly brisk exercise. "If so, it will not be through the assistance of that—of Father Pierre."

Before the priest could respond, the door opened again, and Sister Agatha, with Isabel following her, joined us.

"Good morning, Father." Sister Agatha bowed her head. "Good morning, Sir Simon. Good morning, Miss Howard." She encompassed me in welcome with another bow and sat down on the edge of a worn wooden chair with a back almost as high as her own figure was straight.

I looked to Isabel next and found, to my astonishment, that she was smiling, her own small but undeniable gesture of welcome. "Hello, Miss Howard. Welcome."

"Th-thank you."

"Do you know, we rather hoped you would be restored to us."

I looked from her to that regal, moon-scarred nun and found the gentle smile of the younger woman reflected in the face of the older one. It was one of the most joy-filled moments of my entire life.

THE NEXT FEW WEEKS THAT FOLLOWED STAND OUT IN MY MEMORY AS something strange and dreamlike, though they were the most ordinary and quiet of all that dramatic time. Even Isabel appeared calm and untroubled. I visited her every day and our conversations— for such, indeed, they must be called—spanned many topics. There was nothing dramatic in those days.

Once, when I ventured what was perhaps a silly opinion about religion, Isabel remarked coolly, "You're very young, Athene."

And sometimes you're a sanctimonious prig, I thought rebelliously. For the first time in my knowledge of her, Isabel burst out laughing. "Yes. I suppose I am."

I colored scarlet to the roots of my hair and took refuge in sulky accusation. "So you *do* listen to thoughts."

"I don't. But some people's countenances express too much to avoid it."

She and Sister Agatha had taken up temporary residence in the home of an elderly French woman in a small, rural neighborhood. It was a small home in a row of small homes, modestly but adequately outfitted in two floors and over-furnished in a strongly Victorian manner. The lady, Madame de Lontaire, was so aged and, to my mind, so dotty that she might have been an ancient forbearer of Sister Agatha or a complete stranger to everyone, a kindhearted simpleton of an old woman presumed upon for the convenience of these ecclesial personages. Sister Agatha and Isabel *must* live somewhere and, though the precise logic for the rule escaped me, they could not reside among the cloistered men. Why not live in the home of a sweet woman who blinked and smiled and cooed over her tea and never left the little pink sitting room where her dedicated maid doted so tyrannically over her?

This maid, Hortense, could have been the terror of my life, but she somehow assumed I was as sweet and as simple as her mistress and developed the habit of providing me with little gifts of cookies and sweets to carry as I went about my self-imposed scholarly tasks. These became less Gothic but, to my surprise, not one whit the less satisfying. This remained a time of singular happiness in my life. I had happened into an arena of playful scholarly investigation and unexpected fellowship. Days followed days, all on that same, frictionless plane, without consequence, without the reality of life and death intruding upon me. When I think of that period of life, it is all cheerfulness, little sweets, long walks, and friendly conversations.

There were a few momentous occasions. One came after a quiet dinner at the lodgings of Sister Agatha and Isabel. I wondered if it were the presence of the former that persuaded my father to attend as well. He spent most of his time in Brussels at the university, which greatly contributed to my freedom and ease of living. He returned to interrupt the happy flow of existence only once or twice a fortnight. More than once I had tried to imagine what the acquaintance had been between my father, the nun, and the priest in their heady youth, before my father had decamped from their fold. It seemed at times that they had been intimates. At other times, it seemed that they had hardly known each other. This evening, I wondered why my father had bothered to inflict himself on the company. He was brooding and annoyed and hardly spoke.

As we labored through our modest meal, the conversation ventured into the realm of religious practices. I ventured an opinion about the cruelty of the convent, comparing it to the vicious practices of suttee and other sacrificial offerings of unprotected females. (By this it may be seen that I had ventured into a degree of easy familiarity with the company that was far beyond expectation.)

"The daughter of heresy is not likely to understand," said Sister Agatha with unwonted severity.

"I'm not a heretic," I cried indignantly. "I'm a heathen!"

"I think you're probably a pagan," responded Sir Simon dryly.

"No, really. I looked them all up, and I am quite sure. Father's a heretic. I'm a heathen."

"Or a pagan."

"No, you're not either." Isabel had been so quiet that I had assumed her thoughts were far away. "Heathens and pagans are unbaptized."

"Is this a fruitful conversation?" asked Sister Agatha.

"I'm unbaptized," I said proudly.

"No, you're not," Isabel replied without looking up from her meal. "Your old nurse did it secretly."

This time everyone turned to stare at her, which did not seem to worry her at all.

My father recovered himself first. "The old busybody!"

"Can she do that?" I demanded of Father Thomas Edmund.

"She *should* not," he said, "but she *could*..."

Isabel nodded at him.

"Well then, it seems you are an unconscious Papist, Athene."

I suppose the revelation of my belonging to their world should have thrilled me to my core. As it was, I felt deflated and disappointed. It all seemed so unremarkable. So ordinary.

From behind his spectacles, the eyes of Father Thomas Edmund twinkled at me.

"I suppose she was fond of me..." I said, in gently tragic tones, imagining a pathetic scene, my nurse weeping over my infant curls and blessing my uncherished head with sanctified tears.

"She was a morbid, illiterate old fool," my father spat out, "with a frantic notion that you'd be dragged off to the fires of hell if she didn't."

"What was her name?" I asked, determined not to be done out of every consolation.

"Do you think I recall the names of every ignorant female in my household for twenty years?"

"What was her name?" I asked again, this time looking to Isabel.

She shook her head and softly, almost compassionately, said, "It does not work like that, Athene."

The topic passed, as did the evening, leaving me to ponder where my place might be in this complicated cosmos.

Meanwhile, I was not idle. My father's sarcastic comments provoked me to strong and deliberate action. I was determined to delve into this question of the "one book." I was timid of broaching the point with the white-robed friars. Inquiring of the more regal among them would have been unthinkable impertinence, and I feared even an unintentional offense to the sweet kindness of Father Thomas Edmund. Better first to investigate so that my inquiry might at least be intelligent.

My forays into research at the Library of Tournai were much more complex than I had anticipated. The "one book" was a several-volume affair with the promising title of *Summa*. A key to everything, a rival proposition to the unlocking of mythologies proposed by my father. I selected the most modern from the various available editions—an 1894 six-volume imprint—requested the first volume, and prepared to assay it.

My Latin was strong from years of supporting my father, though his interests did not often require me to use my knowledge of the language. After reading several pages, my fluency returned, and I made good progress in understanding the words of the text. Its voice was more challenging. It was more philosophical and abstract than the works my father would have considered. The text was also decidedly lacking in narrative.

I was, however, well-trained and could delve with scholarly precision into any text, no matter how dry. Over the course of that day and two days following, I progressed through overarching claims about sacred doctrine, the dismissal of polytheism, the seemingly contradictory Trinitarian theory, creation (which disappointed me with its lack of reference to various myths), the existence of spirits (which interested me greatly, as it appeared connected in various ways with the preternatural occupations of our present enterprise), an exhaustive exploration of the relationship of spirit and matter and the existence and nature of the soul, and an interesting logistical study of the government of creatures (which did not, as I expected it to, attack theories of civil government but addressed the subject at a much more elemental level). The passages on demonic assault were particularly pertinent.

The next volume, which I tackled in a single day, was much more entertaining. In addition to discussing death and theories of happiness, it dived deeply into consideration of morality—human action, the passions, habits, vice and sin (my notes on these were positively thrilling), law, and grace (the least interesting, I feared). So fascinated was I with elements of the degrees and divisions of sin that I sketched for myself what I considered to be a rather excellent chart, complete with a few illustrations drawn from a host of sources, especially Greek and Norse mythology.

I was particularly proud of this effort and admired the results on a beautiful, quiet evening. My father was in Brussels, and I had the house to myself. I had almost persuaded myself to forget the incident of the snake—almost, but not quite. I did check the room thoroughly before bed each night—opening the small closet and inspecting each shelf to the point of removing all my belongings systematically and shaking out every article of clothing, pulling back and shaking each of the garishly floral bedclothes one at a time, shining a little electric torch into the corners under the bed, and moving each piece of furniture aside to inspect its nooks and crannies. Before turning out the light, I would take a thin green towel, roll it up, and shove it under the door to seal the room entirely.

This evening, my defensive measures adequately undertaken, I nestled under the well-aired bedclothes, recklessly munching on a piece of moist gingerbread from the latest packet from Hortense, and gloated over my excellently executed notebook.

"Yes," I remarked to myself as I closed my book. "I have done well."

It was a happy time indeed.

CHAPTER 14

15 JUNE 1906: TOURNAI

It is a wise father who knows his own child.

— William Shakespeare, *The Merchant of Venice*

I WAS CLEARLY ASLEEP. I WAS IN THAT RARE STATE OF DREAM WHERE one understands that one is but a passive viewer on a strange but impersonal dreamscape. I swept past swelling, gauchely colorful houses of the nouveau riche, assailed by an unseasonably chill air.

My progress, which seemed more in the nature of floating than of walking, ceased before a particularly prosperous-looking rowhouse. It rose before me, new and bright and self-satisfied yet oddly distended, as an image in a carnival house of mirrors might be. The streetlamp beside me blazed into light, throwing an unnatural glow against the façade of the house. The bland pale yellow of the paint appeared a lurid red-gold in color, like an ancient hoard of treasure bathed in blood.

The inside of the house was in darkness, save for two lighted windows—one from a room on a lower level, the other—a fainter light—from a room upstairs. This disturbed me. My forehead creased in a frown. By all rights, the lighted windows should have been side by side so that the house would appear as a face possessed of two infernally lit eyes. Instead, I felt as if I were being glared at sideways, a mocking angle, even for ghouls. I began to wish I might wake up.

"I don't want to see anything more," I declared aloud.

It being a dream, however, there was little choice in the matter. Up, up, up I floated, past the lower window (where I descried a shadow passing by the light), and up, up, up toward that dim, uncertain, flickering light in the upstairs room.

I passed through the walls without injury and found myself in a large, silk-encumbered boudoir. A place of stale air and immobility bound by the enchantment of sleep.

My mind began to rush. Scenes raced past and swirled around me so quickly that my stomach turned with panic. Meanwhile, a large clock with a disapproving face tsked the seconds loudly, like a dowager sniffing contemptuously over the unsophisticated fragility of human existence.

There was a woman on the bed. Sleeping, I thought. She lurched upward, emitting a piercing cry of agony. The vision accelerated. The room was full, the bed surrounded by cold, clinical women who labored unsmilingly over the tormented one. Sweat, blood, and that piercing, primitive cry of unadorned pain over and over again.

The room was empty once more. The woman lay sleeping—or perhaps dead—upon the bed. And there, in a lace-suffocated bassinet, were two small creatures bound in stark white muslin.

I had turned my head in my dream to attempt to look more closely at the swaddled figures, but the room revolved before my eyes, and I saw the woman once more.

She rose from the bed, her face still marked with the delirium of labor, and began a slow, unsteady yet purposeful passage across the room, moving as if in time with the disdainful sniffs of the dowager clock. Each step brought pain, marked in a twitch that crossed her face, from her forehead to her eyes and down into the firm, desperate determination of the mouth.

For a long moment, the woman stood beside the bassinet gazing down, a strange, unreadable look in her eyes. Then, from a hidden pocket of her nightgown, still grossly stained from birth, she drew forth a tiny vial. Uncorking it, she leaned over and poured out its contents—slowly—chanting something quietly in Latin. The words escaped me, though I struggled, in this paralyzed state of dreaming, to hear.

Twice she pronounced her little private ritual. I thought I could see her sigh. Then, a fit of shivering overcame her, and she grasped the sides of the bassinet.

"I'm sorry," she whispered in French. In one swift motion, she produced from beside the bassinet a large white pillow, festooned with ribbons, and pushed the pillow down, crushing it against the sleeping infant faces.

Before the cry of horror that rose in my throat could do more than choke me, the woman wrenched the pillow away, staggering and falling awkwardly at the side of the bed, her hands and fingers desperately palpating her throat as if to free it from some unseen restraint. Her face, transfixed with horror, turned a lurid shade of purple as her wide, wild eyes fixed upon the open doorway.

The room revolved again to display a tall, nonchalant figure leaning against the frame of the door. A man in a scarlet smoking jacket fancifully embroidered in gold. As I watched, sensing rather than seeing the writhing torments of the woman beside the bed, the man played with his many rings—twisting a flashing circle of emeralds, tapping at the stolid face of a massive sapphire, moving the ruby from one finger to the next and back again, toying with a coy amethyst. Not a finger was bare. Now the rings appeared to bounce and dance like light, brilliant balls in the hands of an adept carnival entertainer.

"Marcus!" A croaking, desperate plea that turned my sleeping stomach and made my soul cry out with desperation to awaken and be free of this dreadful scene—that plea didn't disturb him in his juggling performance. "Marcus! Please!"

He waited until her eyes, still fixed upon him, stared out unseeing, and her body ceased to move. Then he stepped from the doorframe and sauntered over to the crib.

I could see the contents of the bassinet now. Two infants. A boy—an unnaturally hairy, hideous little brute with bristly black hairs all over his face and his tiny earlobes—snored loudly on the left side. And on the right, a diminutive girl, a little cocooned insect, pinioned by infant incapacity and expert swaddling. The little knitted cap imperfectly concealed her raven curls—a few peeked out on her tiny white forehead. And beneath this fringe were a pair of wide, open, and eerily alert black eyes.

For some moments, the man and the newborn stared at each other, unblinking. He still maintained his posture of indolent unconcern, but he ceased to play with the rings on his hand. She looked up at him with her strange, feline watchfulness—patient, unmoved, and comprehending.

As if testing her attention, he waved an airy hand and caused the amethyst to materialize from the air, disappear into nothingness, and reappear once more upon his finger.

The infant girl watched without blinking.

Minutes passed, broken only by the metronomic precision of the dowager clock and the heavy, doglike snoring of the infant boy.

Finally the man spoke in a deep voice with a charming note to it that would benefit a stage performer: "Tricks are for the bemusement of fools. Sleep, Isabel."

For a moment, she hesitated.

"My will is inevitable, Isabel. Sleep."

Then the newborn girl's large black eyes closed.

A smile played about the man's lips, a shadowed mockery of affection. "Good night, my children," he said and walked from the room without pausing to glance at the unmoving form on the floor. I could almost feel the last wisps of human warmth dissipating from the dead woman, giving way to the cold sterility of death.

"Honor thy father, Miss Howard."

The voice, coming from the door, wrenched my attention back to encounter the cold, amused stare of the man gazing directly at me.

"My will, Miss Howard, is inevitable."

He smiled widely then. As if prompted by this effort, his face cracked, separating from neck to crown in a crooked line. Then, most horrifying of all, it broke fully in two, decapitated from the stump of his neck, falling to the floor with a sickening thud.

With a shriek that nearly suffocated me, I sprang out of the dream so violently that I leapt out of my bed and ran across the room to throw open the window and lean out into the open air. The dream faded away, leaving a bewildering, disorienting feeling in its wake.

The dying woman's words echoed in my ears. *Marcus…please…*

As if in response, I heard the voice of the old gypsy woman: *The children of darkness are cursed, and doom follows upon their heels!… He is coming… Marcus is coming…*

I dressed myself and, without bothering to eat, retrieved my bicycle and ventured into the morning street.

I had passed down only one or two streets when I was startled by a sudden shower of rain. Ill-prepared for such perils, I parked my metallic steed, hurried into a small café, settled myself at a table, and began digging in my large, unwomanly bag. In my youth I had briefly assumed the affectation of a delicate, feminine, Victorian reticule—the sort of thing a maiden aunt of yesteryear might have carried. I soon found, however, that the practical limitations of such a handbag were too considerable to be endured. Now, when inhabiting an urban scene, I bore about with me a brown leather Gladstone bag that attracted a great deal of unflattering attention but suited my needs. Having assembled my notebook, pencil, and various reference tomes upon the table, I set the bag on a neighboring chair and attempted to recommence my honorable labors in the field of Christian mythology.

I found, however, that my exploration of the question of the nature of angels (with attendant illustrations depicting the winged messengers and their evil, horned counterparts) had lapsed into notes about the details of my dream. Why would the head be decapitated and split in half? That seemed inordinate. In that early conversation so many months ago, Isabel had insisted that she and Jean-Claude had nothing to do with the dismemberment of the body. Had the gypsies considered this an additional step in guaranteeing the death of their victim? Why were there no scholarly studies of gypsy practices which specifically addressed the dispatching of surpassingly evil but mysterious men? Perhaps I should…

No, no, no! These questions, I reminded myself sternly, were absurd. I was basing academic hypotheses on the content of a dream. It must be entirely my own imagination at work. I was attempting for the fifth time to refocus my attention on the realities of scholarship when a pleasant, familiar voice interrupted the steady beat of the rain and addressed me. "Ah! Well met, Miss Howard! May I join you?"

Even though I immediately recognized Father Thomas Edmund, I jumped so hard at the first sound of his voice that I knocked several books onto the floor.

Father Thomas Edmund slid into the seat opposite me, smilingly retrieved my scattered belongings, and gestured with his forehead and eyebrows toward the drizzling scene outside. "Such an unexpected shower. Alas! I have ill-represented my fatherland and have ventured out without my umbrella."

I was about to reply with a witticism at the expense of the English people, when another voice—a voice that made my companion start with surprise and look up—intervened.

"Padre! What the devil—I mean—blast it! Here you are!"

Our new companion was an astonishingly tall, slim youth with a shock of thick black hair, large eyes of an indecently bright blue, and a nervous, jerking manner. So spasmodic and skeletal was he in manner and appearance that, at first, despite his respectable black suit, gloves, hat, and cane, I thought he was an especially solvent street performer.

"William," said the priest. "Bless you, boy. What brings you here?"

"Oh, the good, dear pounds, shillings, and pence, Padre!" said the young man with overdone good will. "Business, you know."

"How remiss of me." Father Thomas Edmund looked to me. "My dear, this is Mr. William Cantor. William, this is Miss Howard."

"Greetings, Miss Howard," said the young man with what I supposed he meant for a flattering tone. I wondered if the palms of his hands were wet. His hair seemed unnaturally greasy—though perhaps that was from the rain.

Without invitation, he moved my bag to the floor and settled himself at the table. "No hope for it," he sighed, gesturing to the rain. "No umbrella. Blasted imprudent. Blasted imprudent. No cover, such a bother. Haw-haw!" The awkward joke—if such a thing might be called by such a name—delighted him, and he repeated it to himself, sotto voce.

"Yes," he said, in response to no one in particular. "Business is a challenging...well...business, I suppose. No time to be idle or get myself into trouble. You can set my mother's mind at rest on that point, Padre! I suppose..." He eyed the priest with a suddenly narrow look. "I suppose you've seen her recently and heard all her motherly concern?"

"I am sorry to say that I have not seen Mrs. Cantor for nearly a year, William," Father Thomas Edmund replied. "Not since the last time I saw *you*, in fact."

"Ah!" The young man brightened visibly. "Not for a year! That's sound. No...no letter either?"

"I have not heard from your mother. I do hope she is well?"

"Oh, well enough." The young man waved his hand to emphasize his dismissal of such a petty concern. "You know how she is—the mater. All nerves and anxieties and empty pieties. Oh, I say, that's rather good, isn't it? Anxieties and pieties. That's the mater to the life!"

He laughed for some time then subsided into an awkward silence.

"What is it that you do?" I asked politely.

"Oh, you know the sort of thing," he said vaguely. "Money and all that business. It's confounded difficult to make your way in the world without it. Money, I mean. Foul lucre. It's the governing force of the world."

"Do you work for a bank then?"

"Not exactly. I work for the government."

"The Belgian government?"

"No," he replied indignantly. "The British government!"

"What is the British government doing in Belgium?"

"The Empire spans the globe, don't you know?" said the lanky young man with a renewed air of self-importance. "I am here for a meeting of various personages discussing questions regarding trade and currency. One fellow in particular. Remarkable man. Positive genius for money. Name's Zoran. And it all comes down to money, after all. That's what happened in Morocco. In the end, the bankers had their say and the bankers hold sway." He seemed pleased with the poetic twist, so he repeated it. "The bankers had their say and the bankers hold sway. Every loan guaranteed by the bankers of those great nations of England, France, Spain…"

"And Germany?" I finished, questioning.

"And Germany."

"And who," mused Father Thomas Edmund, "is behind the bankers?"

For a moment, I assumed Mr. Cantor had not heard the priest, but, as Father Thomas Edmund sat, silent but expectant, the young man finally responded. "Oh, you know how these things are. Wheels within wheels and powers within powers. Well…" He stood abruptly. "It seems to be letting off—the rain, that is. It was well to see you, and my mother would be pleased, and if you see her you may tell her how well I am and how virtuous you find me." He grimaced, as if enjoying a private joke to himself. "I must return to my work now."

"Thank you for your time, William," said the priest. "I hope I may see you again soon."

"Oh, yes, I am sure. Ah, look. The rain is letting up, is it not? I must dash—must dash. Oh, yes, we will meet again. Certainly, certainly. I am busy, though, you know. Business. Pounds, shillings, and pence, you know! And you with your—books, was it? Of course. Stirring you out of your libraries. I'm surprised you are not more dusty—haw haw!" And with this awkward laugh at yet another unamusing joke, he loped off into the last drizzle of rain.

I watched his retreating figure for some time, meditating on the bizarreness of his gait and wondering if it were characteristic of his family or his own special talent. Whatever his business, he was probably less than successful in his profession. He seemed to me, in fact, to be a thoroughbred ass.

When my eyes returned to the priest, he was frowning into his teacup.

He looked up, trouble behind his eyes. Then they cleared and he smiled at me once more. "You will be on your way now, and I shall be on mine."

"Do you go to see Isabel?" I asked.

"Not this morning. There is something else into which I must inquire."

I yearned to ask him about it, to find out what that strange interview had portended, but I felt I was not at liberty to do so. My dream too still lingered on the fringes of my mind. I nearly spoke of it but backed away from the notion. He might, for the first time in my acquaintance with him, chide me for my Gothic imagination. So I bade him farewell, gathered my books into my bag, remounted my bicycle, and ventured on my way.

To my surprise, Isabel met me at the door of their lodgings dressed for pedestrian passage through the city streets.

"I was just coming to see you," I said.

"I am on my way to fetch a misdirected letter," she replied.

"What an odd errand."

"Perhaps so. Hortense was baffled about the instructions and seemed to think the letter was important. Thus, you see me here before you."

"May I accompany you?"

"I would enjoy your company, but are you not ill-laden to walk further?"

"It has become rather heavy," I admitted, looking down at my much-worn bag.

Isabel smiled. "Luckily, a solution is readily to hand. Leave it here and let us be off."

I stowed my overbearing handbag suitably in the little parlor, behind one of the chairs, left my redoubtable steed to rest against a tree, and we once again ventured forth.

We walked in contented silence. Isabel seemed at peace, and, relieved of my burden, I too was in good humor. Indeed, though I had previously thought myself much in need of a rest after my exhausting nighttime vision, now I felt reinvigorated.

The post office was not far, but when we turned down into what should have been a wide avenue, we were forestalled. A low barricade was in place, with police on our side. On the other we could see a large, bustling group of men—laboring men in rough tunics and aprons, shouting angrily but indistinctly. As I stared at this sudden encounter with violence, a leering man with dark hair and a patch over his left eye brandished a spade at me. I fell back a step in my surprise and alarm.

"Come!" cried a policeman with a weary face and a red, bulbous nose. "Young ladies, it is not safe here. You must go."

"But what is it?" I asked.

His answer was swallowed up in the noise of the angry crowd. "You must go!" He ushered us down a side street—quite in the wrong direction from our intended destination—then guided us two streets further before commanding: "Go that way!"

"Wait!" I cried, but he was already gone. For a moment we stood there in silence. "What shall we do?" I finally asked.

"We shall return home," Isabel replied. "If there is unsafety in these streets, we will return to Sister Agatha."

Then, without prelude, the sky darkened. Two wide, rough clouds, rushing together, collided with mob-like frenzy, erupting into an angry, suffocating, violent deluge. We struggled, immediately drenched through every layer of clothing.

"*Mesdemoiselles!* Young ladies! This way!"

We could hear the voice but could not see through the streaming gray-blue of the downpour.

"Come! This way!"

I grabbed Isabel's arm, and we struggled through the torrential rain toward the commanding voice until we nearly stumbled on the steps of what looked to be a vast, noble building made of austere white stone.

"Come in! Come in! Do come in, young ladies, before you are drowned!"

We obeyed and found ourselves dripping inelegantly onto a thick red carpet of oriental design in the midst of a large, formal entryway.

The elderly servant—for such I took him to be, from his posture and his livery with the ornamental crest emblazoned upon it—coaxed and clicked his tongue over us. "Poor mesdemoiselles! Do come! Come here! You must wait here! Do warm yourselves by the fire!"

He ushered us into a small side room with a blazing fire, still concernedly gesticulating. "Do wait! Do wait! Rest! Warm yourselves!"

I hurried to the hearth—a vast, stone-crafted business that displayed a roaring fire—and endeavored to warm myself. Drying myself seemed an impossibility.

"You will not be interrupted here," our kindly host pronounced before passing through the door and shutting it behind him.

"What an extraordinary thing!" My teeth chattered. "Sudden crowds and sudden rain. And that fellow. Do you suppose they are this hospitable to every passerby?" I looked around the dark, elegant room, ornately furnished in wood paneling, scarlet tapestries, sculpted mahogany chairs, and opulent curtains of green and purple. The atmosphere was stifling. "What is this place? Isabel, where have we come to?"

Before Isabel could reply, the door opened to reveal a tall and lanky young man with unnaturally blue eyes wandering into the room.

"Blast it!" He stood stock still at the sight of me. "Here you are again!"

Before I could make any sort of introduction—which would have proved difficult since I found I could not remember the young man's name—he loped off through the door and shut it behind him.

"Who was that?" asked Isabel without evincing much interest.

"Someone I met this morning," I said. "He's involved in banks... or money...something like that." I looked around. "Where is this place?" I repeated. "Do you suppose it is some sort of embassy?"

"I have no idea. Look, the rain is lessening. We will leave soon."

I looked out the window with her, but I saw the threatening edges of clouds that approached and did not retreat.

"There is something not right here. Where did the crowd come from? And why were they so angry?"

"It is all right. It is nothing to do with us. Come, Athene! Be calm! That imagination of yours is quite unruly sometimes." With that, Isabel graced me with one of her rare smiles.

"Good day, my child."

Isabel froze, and the smile faded from her lips, vanishing as if it had never been.

The words were spoken by a gentle voice, but something in that easy, untroubled lilt with an accent I could not place struck cold terror into my heart.

It was the voice of my dream.

I turned slowly toward the speaker and beheld a slight man of muscular but slim build, with white hair slicked flat and exuding the strong perfume of macassar. His white moustaches too were tastefully trimmed, a balance of sophisticated style and a gentle hint of military precision. His suit of black silk at first seemed indicative of asceticism, but there was something in the rich sheen of the material and the excellence of the cut, not to mention the antiquated ruffles of lace at his wrists, which bespoke the devout dandy. An elegant man. I could not have said with any assurance what his age might be. The whiteness of his hair and the straight black stick upon which he leaned at first gave me a sense of antiquity, but as I looked more closely, the vibrancy and vigor of youth seemed better to characterize his person. Much of this I considered later, for in the moment of first encounter the one detail that commanded my attention was the single, large scar spanning the front of his face, beginning on the right-hand side of his forehead, stretching down from the crown of his head, across his eyebrows, nose, and lips to crest his chin, dividing his head in two.

He was looking at Isabel with clear amusement and something like affection.

Isabel stood as still as a statue, gazing back at him with that old unemotional expression upon her face. I wondered that I had ever imagined her capable of smiling.

"Sir," she said finally, "how is this?"

"Isabel." His smile broadened. "Need I tell you?"

For a long, painful moment she did not reply. Reduced, as usual, to the role of spectator, I found my alarm mounting with each inexpressive pause. The use of her Christian name dawned on me secondarily, and by that time my terror was so acute that it could scarcely have intensified. The man looked at Isabel with narrowing—laughing—eyes.

"I thought you dead," she said quietly.

Now the man chuckled openly. "You certainly did your best to make it so. Fortunately—or perhaps you would say unfortunately, my dear one? So foolish of you!—your best, which was quite good, was not good enough."

She returned to her irritating air of unconcern. "It seems not."

His amusement seemed redoubled by her bored, disengaged manner. I bit my lip before I could burst out, "But they didn't handle the dismemberment! That was the gypsies!"

"My dear child!" continued the man to Isabel with mock astonishment, "you are not really surprised, are you? Have you not known for weeks? Or have you been so stifled and deluded as to imagine it all some dark, cruel dream?" He clicked his tongue. "Are your nightmares so dreadful, little one?"

Isabel said nothing.

Her lack of response did not seem to bother him in the slightest. "I am remiss," he cried. "I have not told you of the present business I have in hand. You do not even know my name! I did spend some time considering the name I ought to take—I truly did. I played with many names and many meanings, searching for the perfect capturing of my past and this glorious new present. In the end, I eschewed petty symbolism. My name, my dear, is Marcus Zoran. Why Zoran? You well may ask! There are so many names I could have taken, from alpha to omega. This was simply one I had not tried, and how musical it sounds. I retained Marcus. Perhaps it was sentimentality. If so, I confess to it. Perhaps I feared my dear children would not recognize me if I were too much changed. The marks of the knife were so crude, after all. Perhaps…no. Not my sweet, affectionate children! So much for my name. My work is quite as it has always been. And your work…let me see…your work…" He broke off and laughed. "Oh, my girl, look at those eyes. How you struggle to command your mind. To withstand every thought or feeling that might open the door to me. How long can you resist me? Not as long as you think, alas!"

"No?"

I jumped to hear her speak, thinking a trick of my own ears extracted sound from that statue of a woman. No, it was Isabel who spoke. Her voice was so low as to be almost a whisper, but the note of grim challenge was discernable.

"No," he replied—or agreed—shaking his aged head sadly. "Even now, you see, your battlement is breached. Why else would you be here?"

Silence renewed and redoubled. Deep waters, these.

"What?" He was all genteel astonishment now. "Did you think this a strange coincidence? Like the plot of some quaint novel? *Quel charmant!* I never thought to find lingering threads of romance in my sweet girl! I had no idea you had ever bothered to read such books. Or perhaps this is some secret, untapped fountain of your own. How long have you harbored this so-well-concealed capacity for imagination, Isabel? No, you are not here through the capricious machinations of Fate, my girl. You are here because I called you. You will always come when I call." He waved one hand airily to mark this fact. "And though you stand there arming your soul to resist beyond death, to withstand every torture, or even to take your own life and escape the call—you will always come. Do you know why, Isabel?" He laughed, as if catching himself in some error. "Of course you know, my child. But do you know that *I* know it? Oh, really, shall I be forced to tell you why? It is because I have something you seek. Have it even more surely than I have you. He was always a much more obedient a child, Isabel. And, after all, he struck first. Oh, yes. The plot was yours. Poor creature. He never could think much for himself." He sighed. "You could have been such an asset if you had only had some gentleness, Isabel."

Still she stood there, watching and listening, and I remained the painful, miserable, paralyzed spectator of this cruel, strange scene.

He cocked his head to one side, like a thoughtful bird—a bird of prey, perhaps, taking careful stock of its victim before tearing out its throat and devouring its flesh. "What shall I do with you, my princess?" A moment later he had found his answer and tapped his long stick against the ornate marble of the floor in a rhythm wordlessly expressive of self-satisfaction. "You have done penance, have you not? Ah, but penance self-imposed. Hardly the same bite as vengeance. In the words of the immortal bard, how sharper than a serpent's tooth it is to have a thankless child! You will find, my dear, that there are some things even sharper." He stopped tapping his stick and leaned heavily upon it, gazing at his daughter.

"Have you seen this one?" he asked, apropos of nothing. With a flourish of one jeweled hand, he produced a small red gem and held it out between his finger and his thumb. "Here it is, and now it is gone." With another flourish the gem vanished, and he displayed his empty hand. "And here it is again!" The gem materialized from nothing above his head.

"I shall plague your mind," he purred, continuing to conceal then reveal the gem—now between his fingers, now from behind his ear, now from the empty air—and I was powerless to withdraw my fascinated, terrified gaze from the dancing bauble. "I shall overrun the walls of your reason and release the floodtide of your hate. Yes, Isabel. Yes, I sense your hate. I feel it more keenly than you permit yourself to feel. Now—what a conundrum! You have pledged your life to mercy and love. Oh, and repentance. Let us not forget repentance! But of what do you repent now? I think I could answer that question, but I don't seek to shame you, child, or to continue to mortify you by telling you what you already know. Are you entertained yet, Isabel? Such paltry games—tricks for the bemusement of fools. Let me see…where was I?" He made a business of remembering. The stick tapped thoughtfully. "Ah, yes, yes. That was it! When the floodtide of your hate is released, and your soul is steeped in the desire for blood, then…" He reached out his hand with a long, crooked finger, and, in the instant that the flashing red of the gem once again disappeared, gently touched her pale cheek. She flinched as if struck with a whip.

"Why, then I shall crush you, my poppet." He chuckled at this dreadful conclusion, as if he had expected his audience to share with him in his delight.

A scream rose in my throat, and I, the captive nonentity, choked it back into futile silence.

"You will go now." He dismissed her with a slight gesture of the stick. "Go back to your little haven, Isabel. Avoid, I do entreat you, association with those filthy vagrants who assisted you in the past. They will not welcome you, Isabel, but I believe you know that. You are safe from them here. They will not venture too close to me, I think." He yawned. "The Romany have always been tiresome. They will be dealt with in turn."

Isabel did not move.

The man smiled. Then he turned toward the door and, without once looking in my direction, said in a mockingly portentous tone, "Remember, Miss Howard!"

My heart thudded riotously in my chest at the sound of my name on his lips.

"Be dutiful to your father. Always be dutiful. *Honour thy father so that you may live long in the land the Lord your God is giving you…*"

Still I stood there, petrified, enslaved by his voice.

"Do not worry about Jean-Claude," he added airily before the door closed behind him. "I have him well in hand. Oh, Isabel, how I have missed our little chats."

The moment the door clicked shut, Isabel, so long frozen into immobility, snapped back into living, frantic movement. She nearly ran from the room, and I, released of my own paralysis, stumbled along at her heels, glancing, terrified and confused, over my shoulder.

We were at the door. Some unseen hand opened it, and we burst forth into the open air. Before the door closed behind us, Isabel turned toward the bushes and began with unmaidenly energy to be sick.

Under other circumstances I would never have presumed to offer her support. But there I was, holding her up as she retched violently into the dirt. Even as we heaved together in this revolting enterprise, I noticed with a dull feeling that might have been shock, shorn of its power, that the streets were open and unassailed by men—angry or otherwise.

"Where have they all gone?" I whispered.

Isabel did not appear to hear me. Still she vomited against the foliage.

Finally her illness subsided and she stood, so pale her skin was almost tinged with blue. I handed her my handkerchief. She nodded, though her eyes were fixed on a distant and invisible point, wiped the corners of her mouth, and, after a few shaky steps, regained her composure sufficiently to walk with a firm stride down to the sidewalk and up the street. I hurried after her, sometimes looking behind me to see if we had been observed or if some dark figure were following us. The streets were clear of skulking predators. The clouds had vanished, revealing an unnaturally bright blue sky. Syrupy birds chirped somewhere, surely mocking us.

CHAPTER 15

15 JUNE 1906: LE SAULCHOIR

> But in the next moment I cursed myself for being so
> great a fool as to dream of hope at all.
>
> — Edgar Allan Poe, *A Descent into the Maelstrom*

WE HAD PROCEEDED ON OUR WAY FOR SOME TIME BEFORE I REALIZED
that we were traveling toward Le Saulchoir, not the house where
Isabel and Sister Agatha lodged. This was reassuring. I thought of
the smiling face of Father Thomas Edmund and felt certain of safety
and support. Then the face of Father Pierre Jarvais popped into my
head, unbidden.

This less consoling image made me pause for a moment on the
dirty pavement. If anyone could look into this baffling, dark business
of Isabel's father and derive from it a reason to abandon me forever
to a dark and dismal fate, it was probably Father Pierre. He would do
so with unwavering courtesy, of course.

"Isabel…"

The clattering of a farmer's cart interrupted my nervous
thoughts. I looked ahead and saw my companion, her arm extended
in a signal for the driver to stop. He did so, clicking his teeth at the
horses and eying Isabel with marked curiosity.

"Will you take us to Le Saulchoir?" she asked curtly.

"Oui, oui, mademoiselle," he said.

Isabel mounted into the cart, and I scurried up alongside her.
One look at her cold, unfeeling face and every question—every
word—died upon my lips.

We rode in silence. The farmer, perhaps having some intuition
that guided him to read the characters of his passengers, spoke only

to his horses, whom he coaxed and chided and to whom he promised a world of delights if ever they returned to their stalls to rest from such noble labors.

The farmer put us down at the gates of the monastery. Isabel stalked down the path to the front door. I threw a hasty word of thanks over my shoulder and hurried after her.

I imagined that the farmer watched us for a moment, shrugged, clicked his tongue against his teeth, and rumbled off with his ambling horses toward home and peaceful sleep.

Isabel had none of the hesitation I had displayed upon my first visit to Le Saulchoir. Now she moved with a rapidity that was positively brazen in comparison. At the door, she rang the bell forcefully three or four times.

We were met not by my ancient acquaintance from before but by the young, red-haired young man I remembered as assisting Father Thomas Edmund in his archival labors.

"I must see Father Thomas Edmund Gilroy," pronounced Isabel in cold tones of command. "The matter is urgent."

Habits of obedience must have been strong in him, for, without questioning, the young man reddened, nodded, and gestured us quickly along the path, through the front door, and into that self-same side parlor before leaving us to seek the other friar.

Isabel did not sit, nor did I. We stood there, she expectant and I increasingly awkward and inchoately fearful. I wished I could speak of what we had seen and of my own dream. How on earth had Marcus been able to breach the security of my mind? How could Isabel and Jean-Claude be protected? How could you kill someone who was already dead—and so thoroughly dead? In how much danger did I stand? But I could not dare to speak, not in the face of Isabel's own studious, unapproachable silence.

Though it felt even more tormentedly prolonged than that last time, the clock testified that we only waited for two and a half minutes before a hurried step announced the approach of Father Thomas Edmund.

"Good day, my dears," he said as he entered the room, Sir Simon close on his heels. "We were just speaking of…" He broke off and looked from me to Isabel, and his eyes, arrested by her face, had a mark of absolute attention I had never before noted in him. "Child, what has happened?"

"I have seen my father," said Isabel curtly.

I sat down heavily in the chair, overcome with exhaustion and a fit of uncontrollable trembling.

Father Thomas Edmund stood still, but he did not look shocked.

"You knew." Isabel spat out the words. "You must have known."

"I did not know," he said quietly. "But I feared as much."

"Why did you fear it? And why didn't you tell me?"

"Sit, Isabel. Sit down."

She did not obey but spoke with increasing violence. "You *will* answer me. You *knew*. Why didn't you tell me?"

"Isabel," his voice grew even more quiet, "sit down."

Still she stood, a picture of suppressed, suffocating passion. "Are you about to tell me that it is our fault? That we made this happen?"

"That is not what I am about to say."

"Well then," she said bitterly, "*I* shall say it. His rise to power, the consummation of that dark pact forged decades ago—it required blood. Sacrifice. And we—stupid, blind pawns—we poured it out. We conspired to do what he desired us to do. Everything we have done. All the hard work. It has all been his own doing. It is always his own doing. The children of darkness are doomed. The children of Marcus are doomed."

If she could have wept it would have been a relief. Instead, she continued in bitter, cold fury. "I could not see him coming. Some time ago I sensed him, but I thought it must be a lingering echo. A wound. The parroted mockery of a demon. *Isabel. Someone is coming. Someone is coming.* I thought it was my imagination. I heard it first in a storm—it could have been a trick of the storm. It could not have been my father—that is what I told myself. He was dead. Long dead. I made quite sure of it. I oversaw the division and the scattering of the corpse. Never mind the blood. I've done due penance for it. Again and again I have done penance."

"When did you first hear him again?" asked the priest.

"Months ago," she said. "It doesn't matter. I did not credit it. After that, the voice came intermittently. There were no real harbingers of doom yet. Tempest and gale, thunder and lightning, fire and darkness—all of his omens. Just the voice—that mocking voice. *You are not safe. Someone is coming. And coming for you.*"

Now she sat down, her eyes still roving about the room.

Sir Simon was standing just inside the door, immovable, watching Isabel with his soul in his eyes. The entire world had melted away and me with it, I thought—and the thought was strangely painful.

"I am not afraid of the darkness," said Isabel. "Wild, frenzied shadows—that is the stuff of petty nightmares. Not for me, who can instinctively divine a true spirit of evil from a mere phantasm. I know the order of such things. But my peace, my prayer was lost. All lost. Like a hollow incantation. He has robbed me—robbed me once again."

Now her eyes were upon me, as if I had spoken, though speech was impossible for me in the face of this torrential flow of words from one so long silent. "I am no credulous spiritualist, Athene. And I am not—I will not be—a practitioner. I resist this curse, but I can't escape it. A special sight, piercing the mundane, sensible world and bringing me into that other world—such a familiar place—where the creatures of evil are trapped between this world and eternity and dance their foul *rigaudon* of death. 'Isabel, I am talking to you. Listen. Someone is coming, Isabel. You are found out, Bella. You cannot hide any longer. Someone is coming. You always were my favorite, Bella. You know that. My little princess. So precious…cherished. And now I am warning you, as my favorite. Someone is coming.' Taunting my dreams, robbing me of my peace. First it was coaxing. Then would come the abuse. Always he turned to violence. Yes, he has been taunting me for months. I have tried to convince myself it was exhaustion speaking or my own imagination—if I possess such a power."

She licked her dry lips. "In the early months in the convent, the silence was oppressive. I had escaped the voice forever. I kept waiting for another one—the soothing tones of this new God. I rather expected him to boom mighty sayings down upon me each morning, guiding and guarding me in this new peace, this happy seclusion and safety. Yet all was silence. It was three years before I found peace in the silence. And then it returned. 'Silly little Cassandra. Always to see, never to be believed. Would you warn them, Isabel? Warn them that someone is coming? Someone is here, Isabel. It is too late. Now, Isabel. Now you will suffer for your sin. I…I am coming. And I will exact just vengeance. Blood cries for blood. Blood cries for blood. Blood cries…' Oh God, let me die!"

She looked up at Sir Simon, her face taut and agonized. "I knew before you came that Jean-Claude had returned to the darkness. Even so, I…I could not imagine that my father had arisen. And now, now…" She looked down at her hands and once again spoke with a stark, almost clinical lack of passion. "I am robbed of both peace and penitence. All I regret now is that my guilt is not absolute. I can only regret that we failed. The blood that has stained my hands—will it stain them again? Will I be crushed by him, as he says, or shall I thrust his soul into hell, with no mistake this time—his soul and mine with it?"

She sat in silence for several minutes, interrupted only by the steady, merciless ticking of the clock. Then she said, her cold, emotionless voice fully restored, "You knew from the beginning that he would return."

"From the beginning?" replied Father Thomas Edmund. "How absolute that sounds! No, my child, but, considering the unconventional and, I may say, unorthodox means you employed in dispatching him, I have expected that we would face some form of resurgence. The laws of folklore and myth are rooted in a sort of man-concocted half-logic, a brew of sacred ritual and straight superstition. The laws that govern the spiritual realm, however, and the earthly realm too are much simpler. You need the proper authority and the proper tools. And your father knows this too well—as does his mistress."

This was a new idea and I fixed upon it, trying to resist the memory of the brutally murdered woman of my dream.

"Who is his mistress?" I asked timidly, relieved to have something to clarify beyond the bewildering mess of Isabel's dark suffering. "Doesn't he just operate on behalf of Satan?" I recalled my notes of demonic activity, muddling them with the more recent diagrams I had constructed to illustrate angelic powers and classifications.

"All evil things are ruled by the Evil One. There are lesser degrees of mastery, though, and I believe that what we are dealing with here is something on a lower scale."

Father Thomas Edmund began gesturing in the air with his hands, like a professor might, chalk in hand, when sketching out tiers of a scientific pyramid.

"If we consider the degrees inherent in the demonic hierarchy, and place at the top—or, perhaps, more appropriately, at the bottom—the tyrannical viciousness of the Evil One, we will see dependent, subservient powers with increasing corporality. Thus we begin with—"

Holding his hand flat, he thrust it out and held it firmly in place: "The superstitious gypsy, the dupe, the dabbler in things magical and occult. Slaves without understanding and without special power. Above this we see—"

He elevated his hand by half an inch: "The werewolf, the man reduced to the brute, bound by disordered passion and slave to a higher, more corrupt intellect. Next—"

Once again, he elevated his flat hand by half an inch: "A creature such as Isabel, with strong intellectual powers or other preternatural abilities, a potential foil to the force that seeks to control her, yet all too easily herself a slave. Now—though this is an oversimplification, and there are other degrees we could identify here—" He elevated his hand once again. "We see the father."

"Thus far you imagine him only in terms of his power over those below. He can indeed have power over both of his children—you, Isabel, and Jean-Claude. He has advanced far in his own darkness. We might conceive of him as a master of the occult, or, as age-old superstition would put it, a dark priest or *wærloga*—the warlock, the Druid, the *zokor*. But you must once again remember—"

He thrust out his hand and held it flat then elevated it again to indicate a superior tier: "He is beholden to some stronger power for that which he claims to himself. There is some other being and he is subordinate to it."

"But what is that?" I demanded, "and how are we to catch it?"

"You must stop!" The cry was sharp, and the rebuke was clear. Isabel stood with her hands out, palms held upward, a gesture of despairing empty-handedness. "I am no use to you. Don't you see what this means? I know what he does and how he does it, and that much I can tell you. Hundreds of years ago he would have been put to death for sorcery. He wields gold and villainous magic, a peddler of wealth and power to great men with petty, gross desires. If a nation falls, his gold is beneath the wreckage. If rebellion springs up and governments collapse, his gold ignited the powder that brought such destruction. He delights in this collapse, this devastation. I could look, I could tell you—"

She broke off, closing her eyes and biting her lip so that a bead of blood appeared and stood starkly against the white of her teeth. After a deep breath, she opened her eyes and looked to Father Thomas Edmund, shaking her head. "The temptation is too keen for me to chance it. You must be prudent, Father. You must be more than prudent—you must be cautious. I am not a safe confidant in this."

"You would not betray us," Sir Simon exploded.

"I cannot say that," Isabel replied, still looking at the priest. "I do not wish to. On the contrary, I am fearful of doing so. But I do know that I could so easily expose you in one weak attempt to learn more."

"I don't understand," I said. "What sort of attempt?"

"If I attempt to see where my brother is. If I attempt to see what tangled plot Marcus weaves around him and around us. Don't you understand, Athene, that it is like opening a door, and I cannot ensure that he—that my father—cannot look back through it and see all that I know from you?"

"This is ridiculously complicated. How on earth are you supposed to be kept safe if you are not kept clearly informed? It sounds to me like an abysmal sort of proceeding, calculated to breed all sorts of unnecessary dangers. In fact, this sounds like precisely the sort of inane practice that is at the heart of silly novels."

"I have not read silly novels," said Isabel simply. "But I know that you must be careful what you say to me."

"Can't you look into our heads and see anyway?"

"No."

"Then how *does* it work, Isabel?"

She did not reply.

"I suppose you think me impertinent. Please don't look at me like that, Isabel. I'd rather you cast me from your sight with a rebuke than go into that...that..." I stopped. There was no polite way of saying it.

"You are incorrigible, Athene." She almost smiled. "It is a sensitivity. If I were to dedicate my attentions to it as I once did, I could cultivate it to a point of deep perception beyond thought."

"Reading minds, you mean? Like cheap mediums in a carnival. Are those real, by the way?"

"There is a dangerous mixture of charlatanerie and the diabolical. Many are indeed charlatans. I, alas, am not. I do not read minds. But I have knowledge, knowledge I would be spared."

"Can...can your father read our minds?"

"No." The firm answer came from Father Thomas Edmund, not from Isabel. "He cannot. Nor can any evil spirit. He can but read your actions. The only one who possesses perfect knowledge is God himself."

This made no sense to me whatsoever, but I was too timid to inquire further.

Once again, silence fell. It was broken by the priest's practical voice. "Come, my dears. You must eat."

"I am not well," replied Isabel. "I must be alone. I shall go to the chapel."

I thought Father Thomas Edmund would try to stop her, but he nodded and accompanied her from the room.

I looked to Sir Simon, who was watching their retreating backs. I looked away again quickly, mortified to see the emotions writ so plainly on his honest features.

We sat together in silence.

A few minutes later the priest returned to us. "I have told Father Pierre you are to stay and speak with me," he said, "and as it is late, he has granted permission for me to serve you a meal in the larger parlor."

He gestured us into a nearby room of a much larger scale, where several friars were even then arranging a table and chairs. Within a few moments, we were set to enjoy the simple fare of the friars. Even in his absence, I imagined I could feel the piercing eyes of Father Pierre upon me when I entered the room, and this basilisk-like intensity for some time overwhelmed my thoughts. I could hardly take stock of my surroundings until Father Thomas Edmund had pronounced Latin in benediction, and we commenced the meal.

We were not alone. I was seated across from Father Thomas Edmund. Beside me was an impish-looking young novice named Brother Ephrem. On my other side was a young French friar with dark curly hair, a brooding countenance, and an air of attempting to look older and more thoughtful than perhaps he was. His name was Brother Vincent, and, after nodding his greeting, he ate his meal in morose silence.

I discovered I was completely ravenous. With a modest plate of bread, cheese, and roughly cut greens before me, I began my inquiry. "I don't understand the whole business. That man, Isabel's father. He doesn't seem that powerful. Evil and villainous, yes, but he's an elderly man. Possibly infirm. Why can't we simply capture him and compel him to submit or to pass off into death or whatever it is he needs to do?"

Father Thomas Edmund shook his head, but before he could speak I demanded, "Who was he? Who is he? I understand that they must have conspired to kill him and that it didn't work."

"Oh," said Father Thomas Edmund, "it certainly 'worked.' Marcus was quite dead."

"What happened then?"

Father Thomas Edmund sat for some time in silence before replying. Then slowly, softly he began. "Ten years ago, a man named Marcus de Lille, well-versed in occult practices, was turned upon by his twin children. For decades he had wielded untold wealth and power throughout Europe, a silent but undeniable force. The twins, gifted and wounded, were at his side. Then, as I say, they turned upon him. They conspired with gypsies to entrap their father as he traveled from one great city to another, to kill him, and ritually to disfigure and dismember his corpse according to the unsavory laws of folklore—all an effort to destroy the power he had wielded in life and prevent him from drawing upon it in death. In that goal, they failed. He was killed, but the source of his power has resurrected him to demand vengeance and further destruction.

"We found the twins, Sir Simon and I. They had fled from the gypsies, who had assisted in that bloody deed and were terrified of the consequences. They had passed through Germany and France and made their way into England. Jean-Claude was becoming more erratic. Isabel could no longer restrain him when the full moon was upon them.

"I was there on other business, returning to a nearby monastery in the company of Sir Simon, and we happened to see them. It was on such a night, when the beast was fully awake in him, that he roved, maddened among the Yorkshire fields, thirsty for the blood of any stray creature he might find. He was standing high upon a hill. Such a dreadful, beautiful, mysterious sight, sharply outlined against the moon. Sir Simon raised his rifle and carefully aimed it at the heart of the beast."

Father Thomas Edmund paused.

"Well?" I demanded.

"Isabel walked between Jean-Claude and us, staying Sir Simon's hand. Then she called to Jean-Claude by name, and for a moment, the moon-madness too was stayed. He collapsed, half-restored to himself. We bound him, took him away, and handed him over to those who could assist. For a long time he was restored to health and lived in safety. Then the darkness returned, and, in his terror or newly aroused appetites, he fell."

"What of Jean-Claude? How did he come to be what he is? What is the process? What causes it, what doesn't cause it? All that is so muddled. And the theories thrown around by Baring-Gould and others are inconsistent and dissatisfying. Witchcraft? A magical girdle? Poison?"

"There are two answers," said young Brother Ephrem. "One is that some force breaks or manipulates these laws. The other is that God himself intervenes."

"Doesn't that mean basically the same thing?"

"It's a question of origin," he explained. "A created being acting upon another created being prompts this seeming breaking of the law. The Prime Mover, on the other hand, does not break the law, for it is his law to begin with. He acts upon wounded creation to redeem. Petty manipulation is beneath the all-powerful God. It is unnecessary for him."

I was silent for a moment. Then, almost against my will, I said, "This is interesting but…"

As I trailed off, Father Thomas Edmund Gilroy began to chuckle. "But, says this daughter of the skeptical academic, I fail to see the practical application in our current enterprise. No, dear

Brother, do not be downcast or affronted. You expressed it well. Very well. Now, Miss Howard, think of all created things, spiritual and physical, as beautiful, conceived by the all-good God. Now envision rebellion—the rebellion of those ministering spirits. Their work now is the perpetuation of disharmony. All of creation suffers, broken by that disharmony, and preyed upon by the vengeance of the rebels."

"You are speaking of demons now," I said.

"Yes. Of demons and their pawns. Think of the werewolf as an as-yet living pawn. A man reduced to the beast—wounded in his nature but rendered more fully subject to that woundedness by circumstance and his own vice. The werewolf is merely one category of the *energumens*, those influenced by the demonic. The particular charism of that influence manifests in the lycan form—the wolf."

"So, they are born werewolves?"

"Born with a strong predisposition to the lycanthropic vices."

"Which are?"

"Bloodlust, blood frenzy, ungoverned appetites."

"Not every man who is ungoverned turns into a werewolf," I argued.

"That is true."

"And there are other sins."

"That is also true." He smiled. "And you have them well organized in your notes."

My cheeks warmed, though I tried to look unembarrassed. "Scientific organization of facts is an asset in one's research." I hoped I did not sound too prim.

"Indeed, my dear. The compliment was quite sincere."

I muttered my thanks then pressed on. "Men have appetites. All men. What circumstances cause the werewolf transformation?"

Father Thomas Edmund began ticking off points in the air with his finger. "Vicious practices of violence or licentiousness that place such a man under the sway of a stronger being—particularly the demon who exerts influence through the astral forces of the moon. Deliberate subjugation of that man to a more particular occult force or person. A man who falls victim to the lust of a werewolf is not himself killed, but the poison lures him into those self-same practices."

"Practices," I repeated. "You mean rape and cannibalism."

Sir Simon dropped his fork with a clatter and looked at me in horror.

"According to Baring-Gould," I added, my cheeks warm again. "But"—I recalled the scene of my dream—"Jean-Claude was born a werewolf, wasn't he?"

"Often it is the case that the violence or occult entanglements of the father are passed on to the son. In the case of Jean-Claude, we may say that he was born with the propensities of the wolf already flourishing within him. Isabel has told us that, for him, the torment of metamorphosis came frequently through his childhood. When he was on the verge of manhood, his outbreaks became more intense and more dangerous."

"And what precisely do you do to—or for—werewolves?"

"Well," he said, as if administering a gentle corrective, "my authority is properly speaking focused upon the undead, though in practical experience the categories are often intertwined."

"As now?" I asked.

"As now," he agreed. "The personal aspect is clear and simple. Strip it of its dramatic trappings and we have the questions of power and of revenge. The father wishes to absorb to himself—and to his master—his children. He would seek to use the unrestrained brutal force of Jean-Claude and the singular abilities of Isabel. At the same time, there is a vicious delight for him in the destruction—the consumption—of those children. They have sought to be free of him by the means he showed them."

"Is there no way to be free of him?"

"Of course there is. That is where our business commences."

"And Isabel…" I pressed. "What precisely is this gift of hers?"

"A colleague of mine suggests that, before the wounding of man through sin, our thoughts were as open to each other as words may be now. There was no need to conceal the inner workings of the mind of man. If this were indeed so and is so no more, would that not be yet another mercy on the part of Providence to spare us the machinations, torments, and petty expressions of such minds as we possess?"

"So the thoughts of men were open to each other?"

"Perhaps so."

"Is Isabel then some sort of primitive specimen of cognition?"

"A broken, wounded specimen that looks back upon the harmony and beauty in God's creation before sin entered the world. As, indeed, are we all."

"That's rather beyond my ken, Father."

He smiled. "Are you still searching on your father's behalf for the key to all mythologies? You will not find it in your modern theories, my dear."

Brother Vincent, who not yet spoken a word, suddenly looked up at Father Thomas Edmund. "But does it aid us in our scholarship or in this enterprise, Father, to remain so dismissive of those modern theories?"

Father Thomas Edmund merely looked at the young man.

"Perhaps your father, Miss Howard, has more to offer than we would give him credit for. And we could say the same for many a thinker today."

Still Father Thomas Edmund did not reply.

Brother Vincent looked steadily back at the older friar before rising. "Good day, Miss Howard." With that, he stalked from the room.

The words were nearly upon my lips to inquire further about this strange young man. I wondered if interest in my father's work were a sufficient basis for excommunication. I recalled various points about the Spanish Inquisition, without any clear remembrance of the source of this knowledge. Did they still burn people at the stake or torture them into submission to authority? This last question had some personal importance behind it too. Was I in danger of punishment at the hands of the Inquisition? Did the Inquisition even still exist, and would these white-robed priests take a hand in its operations?

I looked at Father Thomas Edmund, feeling foolish. The thought of that round-faced little man, with his spectacles and his smiles, burning anyone at the stake, was absurd. I dismissed the Inquisition and Brother Vincent and returned to the subject at hand. "Is their father dead? Or undead? Or neither? Is he a vampire?" This last seemed to me to be unlikely. I had not studied that particular topic in depth, but I did not associate white moustaches with sinister blood-drinkers.

Father Thomas Edmund paused for a moment, as if meditating before replying. "He seems to fall into the category of demonic reincarnation. He was indeed dead and was not preserved in an undead existence. I have found no evidence of vampiric activity on his part—not now and not ten years ago when first this family came to my attention. As I have told you, he has been restored to life through the power of some other being."

"Not a drinker of blood," remarked Sir Simon grimly, "but a high priest to one who is."

"And who would that be?" I asked.

The priest tilted his head, like a friendly, thoughtful, round-faced robin. "Can you not deduce that, my dear? I am sure you can. We have a creature greedy for blood, associated with moon-maddened lycans. The ranks of demons operate in their own hierarchies, as I said, and attach themselves accordingly—attach themselves to persons, places, or inanimate objects. Thus, the gods of the ancients held nations in their sway."

I was startled. "One moment. Are you suggesting that the old legends—the myths of Artemis or Diana or whatever name we choose for her—are derived from these demons of yours?"

"They are not demons of *mine*, my dear. In fact, those of my acquaintance have indicated a strong personal dislike for me and others in my way of life."

"Do you mean friars or exorcists?"

"Both. The minor rank of exorcist involves particular work, and the classification as a *duellator contra lamiis* refers to the even more precise category of combatting the blood-sucking undead."

"So not the father but the goddess could, properly speaking, be under your authority?"

"Yes."

"So...why don't you..."

"Imagine this in terms of an invitation. Just as a demon cannot enter without invitation, I cannot exorcise that demon without due authority—itself often dependent upon an invitation."

"What if she imposes herself on property or persons belonging to you?"

"Then—pardon me, my dear"—the little man removed his spectacles to blink away an invisible irritant from his right eye— "then we would dispatch her in short order."

I mentally examined all I had learned. Werewolves under the sway of some occult power, itself ruled by the vicious, arbitrary manipulations of a demon whom I could not help imagining dressed in Greek robes and carrying a bow and arrow. It all seemed to return to a single point. "So, you can't do anything about this?"

"Oh yes," he said brightly, "indeed I can. In fact, this power to dismiss demons is granted to all the baptized."

"Oh!" I cried, delighted with a new thought. "I could do it too?"

"Dismiss demons in the name of Jesus Christ, and they must obey. You must not, however, rashly attempt anything beyond your strength. That would be foolish, my dear, and dangerous."

I grinned. "The goddess of wisdom should not take up arms against the goddess of the moon."

A light shadow of concern crossed his face, and I hurriedly assured him, "Oh, Father, I promise. I won't do anything rash. I wouldn't know what to do, in any case." Even as I made the promise, a small voice queried in my mind: *But you will not always have an exorcist on hand, Athene Howard. What will you do when you are all alone and a fresh attack comes?*

I had no ready answer, so I tried to smile and looked away from the all-too-perceptive eyes of the priest.

Chapter 16

I'll burn my books—ah, Mephastophilis!

— Christopher Marlowe, *Doctor Faustus*

It was late when the sad and troubled day came to its end. A little cart, drawn by an ancient dappled nag and driven by Brother William, conveyed Isabel and me to our respective dwellings. I had hoped Sir Simon would accompany us, but he had excused himself from the company after we dined with the mysterious pronouncement that, "There are things to which I must attend." It was the sort of thing I expected from my father, and I resented it from Sir Simon.

Isabel was silent for the entire ride—had been so since she reappeared from her sojourn in the chapel. When she arrived at her own temporary residence, she descended and passed into the house without looking back.

As we rambled and bumped home in the chilly twilight, I thought over the events of the day. What a strange business it was, illuminated yet more mysterious with the revelation of that villainous figure we had met. He was such an odd mixture of infirm nobility and menace. I could not fathom it.

What would we do? What could we do? Could Isabel rouse herself from this new, despairing mood? How could we battle a man so powerful as they all believed him to be? And what of the missing brother—I had almost forgotten him, to my embarrassment. The others had been contented enough in their long period of waiting. Now it was all over, disrupted and destroyed by that strange old man with his scar and his threats of vengeance. I thought of his words to me and shivered.

Then too I thought of the progress of my research. There was something missing. I could not place it. Some element that would elevate my scholarly labors into practical effectiveness. I had not yet found it. Just that morning, in the sudden rain, before the arrival of the priest and that odd, lanky young man—whose name still escaped me now that I had more fascinating elements to consider—I had exuded scholarly confidence. Tired and disheartened, I wondered if I were doomed to endless, fruitless study. What had these silly books to do with anything? I had nothing to offer that noble band facing so powerful, so dramatic, so wonderfully interesting a threat.

I looked up with a sinking feeling in my stomach. We were on the street where my father and I lodged. I thought of snakes and wished we could ride further.

Brother William was resistant to mental influence; he brought the cart to a standstill and did not suggest that we ride on forever.

"Good night," said Brother William. "God keep you."

"Good night," I replied.

Still unwilling to venture into the serpent's den, I stood there watching his shock of alarmingly red hair dwindle away into the darkness. Then, with a start, I realized I had left my bag behind that little chair in the parlor of the lodgings of Isabel and Sister Agatha. My bicycle leaned, abandoned, against a tree beside their house. It was a good thing that my noble steed was inanimate or I would have been forced to condemn myself for inhumanity. As it was, the loss of bicycle and bag was the least of my worries.

On the doorstep I shook myself and tried to embrace a more cheerful outlook. "Come now, Athene, everything always looks brighter in the morning."

With a nod for emphasis, I tripped lightly over the threshold, softly closing the front door behind me so as not to disturb the household.

The hall was completely dark. My father had been in Brussels for three full days. I assumed Madame Deshalle and her ghoulish son were abed. It was odd, though, to see no light anywhere in the house. Yet there *was* a light—a dim light coming from one of the rooms down the hall. I was on my way to investigate when a slight sound behind me, like the scuffle one associates with the furtive movement of a rat, made the hair on the back of my neck stand up straight and my skin erupt into waves of prickles.

"Athene? Athene?" The hiss of my father's voice made me start and look around. To my astonishment, he crept out of the shadows in a corner of the hall and grabbed my arm, hoarsely whispering: "Girl? Is that you?"

"Who else would it be?" I demanded in my usual voice. "What on earth are you about, Father? Have you been hiding in the broom closet? When did you return? I did not expect you back for... Father, why are you locking the door?"

As I thus questioned him, he hushed me and, grabbing me by the arm, propelled me into the small room that served as his temporary study, closing the door behind us, turning the key in the lock, and throwing the bolt. He stood, his back against it, as if he would block any attempt at entrance or egress.

I had seen my father in many emotional states and knew them well. This man who stood before me, his white hair standing on end as if pulled by frantic hands, his eyes wide, with dilated pupils darting about the room like a rabid squirrel, and his limbs trembling—this picture of abject terror was a stranger to me.

"What on earth is the matter? Are you unwell?" My eyes fell upon the furniture and books which he had, in his usual manner, built into a veritable fortress of disorganization. "Father! What has happened to this room?"

This was not an everyday scene of distracted scholarship. Here was a scene of deliberate, though frenzied, destruction. At least one hundred books, their pages torn to shreds, lay in tormented disarray over every conceivable surface in the room. The two chairs were so covered in scraps that I could not see the fabric beneath the white shreds. The room was ablaze with light, but not by the electric utility. A veritable mountain range of lighted candelabra stood atop the paper piles all over the room, as so many crowning, fiery pinnacles in the disaster. A strange smell pervaded. Aged hair musk? Rotten eggs? What was that unpleasant odor?

"What on earth—"

"On earth!" My father groaned and grabbed the hair upon his head in both fists so that it stood up in the most alarming manner. "On earth! Girl, be quiet! Do be quiet! Sit down! No, don't sit down there! There!"

He ushered me into an overstuffed chair, rousing a snowstorm of dusty paper from it so that we were both momentarily overcome with a fit of coughing.

"What is it?" I demanded once the fit had passed.

"It's all wrong, Athene. All wrong! It's not what you think. How could you think it! Oh, but I must tell you. How can I do it? How can I make you understand? It isn't at all what you think."

"It…it isn't?"

"Girl! Don't argue with me!"

The suppressed violence in his voice unnerved me even further. I tried to look the picture of nonargumentative attention and began calculating how long it would take me to reach the door, unlock it, and escape. He had clearly lost his mind. How long would it be before he turned on me? Perhaps he had taken some drug. I had never suspected him of it before, but I thought it distinctly possible now. Yes, I thought. It must be insanity or opium. But didn't opium calm the addict? Would it provoke this degree of frenzied activity in one so pedantic and sedentary?

He was scattering papers right and left and waxing ever more desperate with each passing moment. "It must be here… Where is it? How can it have disappeared? It was here! My glasses are here. Then where is it? I wrote it down… I know I wrote it down…."

"Can I help?"

"No one can help!" moaned Father. "We are out of time! We are out of time!" He collapsed into his chair and again pulled at his overstrained hair. "Money and theories and power. Golden rain—like Danae. Danae. All power and dreams and visions, bringing us to one single point—destruction. My work—those endless years of work. All tending to destruction. He was right, he was right, always he was right."

Pity flooded over me, drowning even my concern. I rose from my chair, walked to him, and touched his arm. "Father…"

He looked up at me, such a strange, silent, anguished look.

"If there is something, could we send for someone? Perhaps Father Thomas Edmund?"

He shook his head. "No, it's too late. Girl, it is too late. Too late for me. But for you—Athene, listen to me. Listen carefully." He leaned forward and grabbed my hand, holding it with painful pressure. "You're…you're a good girl, Athene. You have sense. Use it. You know—you will see. You may see more clearly than I could. I didn't—I didn't want to see! I never wanted to see!" He groaned again. "God! She was sorry for me. That was it. Her own airy daydream of salvation."

"Who?" I asked timidly.

"Who what?"

"Who is *she*?"

"Agatha. Don't be stupid again, girl! Of course it was pity. That was the enticement. A doomed, empty, naïve dream. A remnant of her youth. She ought to be more sensible."

"Why did you want to go? Because…"

"I forgot, Athene. I had forgotten. All these years, buried in the dust. I've dismissed those dangers. And then Agatha…"

"Did you…" I paused. Then the edge of curiosity cut so finely into the barriers of prudence that, biting my dry lips, I blurted out the rest of the question. "Did you love her?"

He looked startled. "Love her? What are you talking about? Are you really as stupid as I always feared, girl?"

"I...I didn't know. But I don't understand. What *were* you to her?"

"To her? I was her priest. I ministered to all the novices. Then... well...but that's nothing to the point, Athene. Nothing. That is all gone. Done with. Long ended. Do you not see? There is a power so great, a being so vicious. Athene, have you no concept? No concern? There is no time! You must—you *must* see!"

"But how am I to see anything when you tell me nothing?" I broke out. "I can't see and understand if you talk in riddles! Tell me plainly. What *is* it that I am to fear? How am I to see it?"

From beneath the pile he tore forth and brandished something above his head—a book. A single, small book, undestroyed in that carnage.

He tossed it into my lap. I picked it up and gazed at it, perplexed. It was dimly familiar, but the title gave me no assistance: *The Ancient Feasts and Festivals of the Gods of Greece and Rome.* Hoping to find further inspiration, I opened the book. Upon the first page, I saw an inscription in red: "Until she lusts for tribute—Marcellus Solomon."

"Who is Marcellus Solomon?" I asked, even more bewildered.

"A great thinker—a teacher. He opened the door for me. And then—" He gasped hysterically, "But I didn't want to see or to couple with goddesses! I didn't want any of it! I said it was nonsense! I say it is nonsense!"

"What happened to Marcellus Solomon?"

"Death. Only death." He groaned. "His body—they said it was footpads, but I knew—no, I tried not to know. I didn't see. I refused to see! The three wishes, Athene!" As my father's desperation intensified, he waxed even less coherent. "There are always three wishes! The three wishes. That's the poison. I didn't know. I didn't know, Athene. Girl, I didn't. Truly, I didn't. The woman, the work...I don't remember the third...the work...always the work... It is always three promises! I don't know which it is! Laurentalia? The Nemoralia? Not a mere observance of the Nones. The gods! The feasts of the gods! She won't wait any longer. Not a phantasm, girl, do you hear me? Not a phantasm!"

I searched the store of knowledge in my brain. "I don't understand…" The world began to swim around me.

"The promise is a curse. Beware of the lies that seem truth. Pteria! The oracles! The promises of all mythic creatures! She will demand tribute! She will always demand tribute! And the tribute is blood! The blood that reclaims! The blood that possesses! She will take back. Remember, Athene. Always three…always three…"

His voice trailed off—or perhaps my mind was slowly lapsing into incoherence. Was I falling asleep? Sleep or not, I was falling indeed.

"Falling, falling," said the ponderous voice of Father Pierre.

Forever falling. Like Alice and the feathers. No, that was Icarus. Deeper than did ever plummet sound…right into the bowels of the lost library of Alexandria.

"A feast day, a festival day, a day of celebration." Was that Isabel giggling these words? Horrific thought, Isabel giggling!

I wondered I was not frightened. Such a strange sensation. Surely I ought to fear, when the world was tumbling about my ears.

"No!" I laughingly chided myself—and the laugh seemed to echo about me in the maelstrom of falling, tumbling reality. Why fear the inevitable?

"Honour thy father so that you may live…" Whose voice was that?

A shower of shining gold coins rained down upon us and all around us. "Forty days and forty nights…" declared Father Pierre.

Miss Howard! Miss Howard, are you there?

"Remember…" tolled the voice of my father.

"Falling, falling, falling…" chanted Father Pierre, adopting the sing-song tones of a nursery rhyme. "Down, down, down you go… into the fires of hell."

Dear God, how hot it was!

"Always be dutiful, Miss Howard… Miss Howard?"

Wake up, Miss Howard!

Memory, that fickle muse, turned her face.

There I am, "The Interruption." A small child, correct in my little gray dress and pinafore, standing faithfully at the door of my father's study. Leaning first on one foot then the other—a childish practice of shifting my weight, as if testing to see if one foot could bear the exercise better than the other—the sort of little characteristic twitch that incited my elders to rebuke me. Even a rebuke would be a sign of notice. Better than being forgotten, as I so often was.

Don't play with your mousy brown hair, Athene. Such uninteresting tresses, but frizzled braids will earn a scolding from the nurse, who smells so strongly of strange liquors.

Perhaps today he will look at me. Perhaps today he will see me. That little hopeful lift of the stomach—how sickeningly familiar.

Give up, Athene! Even if he does come, you know that it will be the same. That surprised, weary look in his eyes.

The tears sting my eyes. God, how can this still hurt?

There is the door—closed, as it always is and always has been. No, there is a crack, a faint opening. Wisps, like ghostly fingers, beckon around it, calling me toward it. I walk forward like one in a dream and reach out to touch the edge of the door. A strange noise—a hiss and crackle, as if from an open fire. My fingers feel the heat and reflexively draw back.

A gust of wind or a billow of smoke or I know not what throws the door open in my face. Now the room is before me, illuminated in a lurid shade of orange, as if the unseen power who decrees the drama of my life has turned a garish stage light upon it. Such an odd scene. A terrible play to haunt my dreams.

Silly that such immovable, overdrawn stock figures should be so distressing. There is my father, sitting so still, staring down at me without speaking. And there—is that?—surely that is my own body collapsed upon the floor?

"Someone should shake her and wake her up," I say to no one in particular. "It's much too hot to sleep here."

"Falling, falling, falling…"

"Remember…" tolls the voice of my father.

Athene! Wake up! Wake up!

"Athene!"

The unholy shriek of my father's voice shattered the illusion. With a wrench, I obeyed, tearing myself back into consciousness to find a reality more dazzling and terrifying than that listless, wandering dream. I sat up, coughing and choking in the smoke, every inch of my body in agony from the heat. My eyes burned and rushed with reflexive tears.

My senses were tangled and bizarrely constrained. I could not see through the chaos and flames. My throat was clogged with smoke so thick it seemed to have been bitten off and swallowed, and my nose—I shuddered and turned sick. Burning dust, burning wood, burning hair, and burning, roasting flesh. There before my painful, blurry gaze, one object—a burning stump of something that once was human—contracted and became hellishly clear.

The blazing body of my father, upright in his chair, death writ large on his sizzling countenance. As I watched, his skin melted away, and his skeletal remains, for an instant, quickened anew with a blazing life that flashed out toward me through an open jaw, like a silent, deafened scream from the flaming bowels of hell itself.

I opened my mouth to shriek, but the smoke and heat stifled the noise in my throat. In the next moment, I lunged toward what had been my father. Behind me, heralded by the tumult of splintering wood, something crashed into the room. Before I could turn to see the new arrival, heavy, wet fabric crushed my head and face, blacking out the cruel sight of my incinerated father, and powerful arms encircled me to drag me from the inferno.

I struggled against the suffocating, soggy folds, as I was carried, like a sack, to someplace I could not see. The blood rushed in my brain. Phantasms of fire danced before my eyes in the darkness—mocking, fiery faces, hovering and leering, the spirit of vengeance and despair. I was on the verge of fainting when I found myself deposited unceremoniously on the ground, and a hand pulled the wet blanket from my face. Looking up, my eyes streaming and my senses swimming, I beheld Sir Simon's well-singed features.

I struck at him with both my hands balled into ineffectual fists. "He—he—my—father!" I coughed out the words in waxing hysteria. "My—father! My—father!"

Sir Simon stood there, silently withstanding the assault. Then he took me in his arms and hushed me like I was a child.

"Stand back! Stand back!" bellowed a man in Dutch, pressing against the crowd. Sir Simon led—and partly dragged—me even further from the fire.

"My father...my father..." I kept whispering over and over, dazed and sick, watching the conflagration consume its prey. The last of the curtains burned out in a frantic wave of blackening white, displaced by roaring flames and black clouds.

As the fire and the smoke wrestled in the darkness, a small, distant flash of white declared an approaching figure. Father Thomas Edmund Gilroy was running up the street, holding his hat against his head so it would not fall off in his speed, his white robes flowing beneath his black cape.

He came to a stop before Sir Simon and me. After looking at us both without speaking and, for once in my experience, not smiling, he looked beyond us, scanning the crowd of onlookers and busy, eager men with their faces blackened from the smoke and smeared with sweat, tears, and perhaps blood. Finally, his eyes turned to the furious, flaming building. As we watched, a miserable groan of timber and overstrained brick welled up from the depths of the house.

One of the men cried out a warning, but it was drowned in the tumult as the entire building collapsed in upon itself, sending billowing, blinding, suffocating smoke out into the street and toward us. Sir Simon turned in the last minute, flinging his cloak around his head and shoulders and encompassing me once again in the stifling, protective muffler.

The suffocating moments passed. Slowly, cautiously, Sir Simon lowered his cloak. The air was heavy with smoke. Laboring men stumbled about in the hazy light of the smoldering ruins, strangely animate creatures in the midst of decay, like clumsy corpses granted an undead existence.

Father Thomas Edmund, his white habit now a dingy, unsightly gray, walked forward and gazed into the smoldering remains of the house.

The sun rose dully, as if it had been roused too quickly from a deep, drunken sleep, and looked sourly down on the men as they cleaned the debris. Father Thomas Edmund stood without moving, silent and watchful.

One of the men cried out over a new discovery in the rubble. A few minutes later, the bustle announced the departure of the charred corpse of my father from the black hole that had been a house. The misshapen remains were decently draped, seeming through that gesture to have been rendered more human than the fire had left them. One man stumbled in the procession that bore the weight of the stretcher and a charred hand swung down into view. My stomach turned, and I choked back a new, exhausted sob.

At the side of the small, useless ambulance summoned to aid where no aid could be given, Father Thomas Edmund Gilroy knelt beside the stretcher and bent over the draped, hideous form.

When he arose, he appeared older than I had imagined, and his eyes were red—though whether from smoke or weeping I could not have said.

"Come, Miss Howard," he said. "You must rest."

CHAPTER 17

16 JUNE–2 JULY 1906: TOURNAI, WITH A FEW TRIPS TO PARIS

Everyone can master a grief but he that has it.

— William Shakespeare, *Much Ado About Nothing*

THE DAYS THAT FOLLOWED MIGHT HAVE STRETCHED INTO WEEKS. Even in memory they come back in dreamlike confusion, at one moment seeming to be spread across years and at another coming upon each other in unlikely rapidity. I could not have rushed in a single day from the graveside to the office of a Parisian lawyer and thence back to Tournai to suffer endless questioning from the local police investigating the circumstances of the fire that had consumed that house on the Rue Saint-Georges—the house and all its contents.

"Madame Deshalle and her son were not found in the house. There is no evidence that they remained there. They have searched"—the inspector held out his hands in an inclusive gesture—"everywhere. There was only one body."

One body. My father's body. I felt disgust rising in my stomach and rifled through my little purse to retrieve a small hard piece of peppermint from Hortense. Prudent, sweet, kindly Hortense. I held the peppermint in my mouth and focused on not letting it clack audibly against my front teeth.

The inspector looked at me over his glasses and made an appreciative, consoling noise. He was a thin man with even thinner moustaches and an air of weariness that indicated his nerves had attained an even more surpassing thinness. Then he returned to his papers.

"When did they leave?" He had asked this question at least a dozen times, and I knew he had no expectation of my answering it. "They did not die here. They must have fled. But where?" Once again, that gesture, this time to gather in a world of possibilities.

The peppermint clicked.

He looked at me over his glasses again and sighed.

Shortly after this unhelpful impasse, I returned to my temporary lodgings in a hotel in the Rue de Bas Chemin.

The hotel was cramped, uncomfortable, and, I feared, expensive. The proprietor's plump daughter, Marguerite, wore an abundance of scarlet ribbons—the least obnoxious mark of her obsequious affectation. She constantly sought to express her sympathy—even weeping over me in the most alarming manner—but was desperate to find out scandalous details of "the tragedy" so she could share them among her friends and acquaintances. I had never been the subject of gossip before and found myself roused to bitter resentment. One sight of flowing crimson was enough to make me frantic. I spent most of my day, when not occupied in the tedious, bewildering details of business, trying to sneak to and from the hotel without encountering the oh-so-sympathetic Marguerite.

When I returned, to my surprise I found a rotund Frenchman waiting for me, with sweat standing in unnatural abundance on his bald pate and beading on the thin streaks of hair he attempted to use to conceal the baldness.

"Monsieur LePont!" I cried. "You are here?"

Only three days earlier I had quitted my father's lawyer in Paris, with his assurance that all would be well and there was nothing for me to worry about. Yet here he was, puffing and sweating and looking a picture of agonized concern.

"Come inside. Can I send for some refreshment?" I made the offer uncertainly. It would require communication with Marguerite, whom I had perceived, well-bedecked in her accustomed ribbonry, peeking at us through gauzy white curtains in the front parlor. Then again, if the man were not refreshed, he might expire in the front hall, subjecting me to further intense questioning on the part of the police.

Puffing and fretting, he doffed his hat and accepted the invitation.

The front door opened and there was the robust form of Marguerite, ready to bathe us in obsequious concern.

I steeled myself and forestalled her. "We will go into the little parlor. Please send in some sherry. And we do not wish to be disturbed."

I hoped my tone sounded firm. To my own ears it sounded shrill and desperate. Nevertheless, it had its due effect. Marguerite flounced off, a tray with sherry and two glasses duly appeared, and we were left in privacy.

By this time, Monsieur LePont had regained his breath and, by frantic administration of his hat in the form of a fan, had somewhat slowed the flow of his perspiration. He sipped appreciatively at the proffered beverage and sighed. "*Quelle folie!*"

I waited with patient detachment for him to begin.

"Mademoiselle, you are, I think, surprised to see me?"

"Yes."

"Very surprised to see me."

"I am surprised," I agreed, compromising. "I hope all is well?"

This made him sigh even more deeply, almost to the point of groaning. "It is a catastrophe, my dear mademoiselle! A catastrophe! A little more wine, I think, perhaps?"

As I poured the requested wine into the glass that he held out, it crossed my mind that if Monsieur LePont were metamorphized, he would hardly be fit to be a werewolf. He cast back his glass and drank the wine, smacking his lips in the most appalling manner. To keep from hurling the decanter at his round head, I began imagining all the creatures into which a vengeful goddess might transform him. An elephant perhaps? Not with such a nose as that. Some sort of ape seemed more likely, and I racked my brain to determine what species might best apply…

I realized that his blinking eyes were fixed upon me. He was awaiting my response.

"I am sorry," I said, slightly mortified. "I do not understand. Would you please explain that point to me again?" I tried to look tragic and pathetic so he would not feel the full force of the insult of my inattention.

He shook his head. "Indeed, mademoiselle, it is quite appalling. Horrifying. Unexpected. The house, the books, all that your father invested in the banks…every last sou!"

"Every last sou…"

"All given in trust!"

"In trust to whom?"

"To the university! To continue his work!"

"I don't understand," I said dully.

"It is, as it were, a sort of entailment. The money, it was all for the work. Now—pfft!" He made a dismissive gesture to match the sound. "Nothing!"

"Wait." A startling thought emerged. "That sounds as if I am entirely without funds."

"Indeed. You are quite without funds, mademoiselle."

Without funds. I thought of Marguerite and was relieved at the thought that I could, at least, no longer afford to be tormented by her curiosity.

"I shall leave at once!" I cried.

Monsieur LePont blinked at me.

"The hotel. It is far beyond my means. Also…" Another thought dawned. "This sherry is quite unpleasant."

"My poor young lady, you have no means whatsoever!"

"There must be *something*," I argued. "Some remnant."

"Nothing whatsoever."

"What of the house?"

"Pah! Quite gone."

"What of his books?"

"Pah! Quite gone too!"

"What of…"

"Mademoiselle Howard, the pain to me is quite dreadful! There is nothing. Your father, he trusted me and gave to me all his business. Yet he left everything disposed in this will."

"What will?"

"This new—this last—this unknown will. All is given in trust to the university to commemorate your father's work and legacy."

There it was. My livelihood, swallowed up in the jaws of the Université de Paris.

"Ah, well," I said cheerfully, "I suppose that is that then! Let us have some more of this dreadful sherry before you go on your way, monsieur."

Monsieur LePont, who seemed to believe I was out of my wits and was perhaps a little perturbed that his long journey not been repaid by at least a scene of hysterics, finished the sherry. When I rose to my feet, he rose as well. I accompanied him to the door. Then, struck with a spontaneous urge to escape the house to which I had only just returned, I retrieved my hat and stepped with him out into the street.

We were barely in time to escape the approach of the scarlet ribbons. *That's for you, my girl,* I thought. *You can wonder until I return for supper.*

This brought to mind the fact that I could ill afford to pay for supper.

"How much have I in the world?" I asked.

Monsieur LePont shrugged his plump shoulders at me and sighed. "How much?"

"How much money have you in the world? How much money have you with you at this time?"

"About thirty francs," I said after a rapid calculation.

"Then," said the lawyer, "that is precisely how much money you have in the world." And with that he bowed his head, bade me adieu, and left.

I walked on. It was a beneficent gesture on the part of Fate to have inspired me to leave my large case behind in the parlor at the home of Sister Agatha and Isabel. Had I not done so, I should be even more entirely without means. I had already depleted my little fortune in selecting a few modest pieces of clothing. I could not live in those scorched rags, and everything else had gone up in flames.

Even the snakes, I thought. And my father.

The shivering and the sick feeling in the pit of my stomach returned. I produced another peppermint and continued walking.

No money and no means of support. I must seek employment. Perhaps the friends of my father would assist. I was soon lost in an imaginative world of drudgery, honorable incomes, and endless scholarly labors. If nothing else, I told myself, my shorthand was respectable.

As I thought and walked, I made my way unconsciously until I looked up and realized that I stood in the Rue Sainte-Georges before the shell of our destroyed lodgings. It was early afternoon. The sky was overcast but granted enough cold sunlight to present an ungarnished picture, a vision devoid of the histrionic intensity brought on by the night. I gazed at the gutted corpse of a house. In that moment, something reached into my heart and, as one might put out the flame of a candle, extinguished my ability to feel emotion. Even the thought of my father prompted nothing. Only empty, clinical rationalism. I wondered if this was what Isabel felt like all the time. Mine, I was sure, was a symptom of exhausted grief or an oppressive deficit of sleep. I assumed—I expected—my emotions would reassert themselves in due time.

Death was such a strange, bewildering business. I had known people who had died. Elderly, distant sorts of people. Or young people whose deaths were sighed over as premature and tragic then largely swallowed up in the passage of everyday things. This death was real—so real. The image of my father's face as the fire consumed it flashed before my eyes again. This time I needed no peppermint. These things do happen, as someone trite once said.

With these thoughts—and with a purely academic question in my mind about whether proceeding were safe—I stepped into the black, ashen hole that had been the house.

Standing in the midst of the destroyed library, I surveyed a scene that appeared to be made up of undifferentiated carbon. Black, gray, empty, and hideous.

"If there is a hell," I said aloud, "I wonder if it looks like this."

If there is a hell, my mind replied, *I wonder if Father is there.*

A cold breeze brushed against the back of my neck, but I did not shiver. My fingers were oddly cramped with cold despite the thickness of my gloves. I flexed and stretched my hands, painfully reawakening the blood in them. With the pain came a slow, steady trembling. Still I stood there, listening and waiting, though I knew not for what I waited.

Something stirred. A rat, most likely. I was strangely unconcerned. Rats were vile but unlikely to approach me. I thought of childhood tales and all the complexities of folklore. Perhaps the rats were forerunners of a vengeful spirit. Or perhaps my father was right that they were merely vermin, searching the rubble for anything edible. Anything salvageable.

When I first saw her in the darkness, it seemed that she had been standing there all along, watching me as I stood there. My eyes contracted, and my gaze shifted to rest upon her. Slowly, with the gradual clarity one finds in adjusting the settings of a spyglass, she came into focus.

My heart tripped over itself, hesitated, then resumed its beat with quickened pace.

She stepped out from the darkness and stood before me—a woman in a long, pure robe and a light, lacy blue veil upon her head and face.

A gentle gust of wind—whence it came I could not say—brushed back the pale blue veil from her face, disclosing a rare, terrible beauty. A white face. The long, graceful arch of the nose. Wide almond eyes. Eyebrows painted on by Aphrodite herself. Her hair, soft and long, glimpsed beneath the veil of improbable starlight, shone so glorious and so glossy that I knew it to be unreal. *The face that launched a thousand ships and burnt the topless towers of Ilium.* I

211

wondered how I could ever have imagined the dark features of Isabel lovely. I wondered if my mother had been half so beautiful.

"Do not be afraid, Athene…"

"I am not afraid," I said truthfully.

She looked down on me, a picture of purity, and fixed that gaze of great tenderness upon me. I thought I smelled the clean, clear beauty of fresh water and with it a sweet odor I could not place. My mind was full of delicate blooms on thin-leafed shrubs, the sort that cluster about the banks of the Mediterranean, and I thought of Leander swimming the Hellespont. Poor, doomed young man.

"I don't believe," I heard myself say.

"Do you not?" the lady replied serenely. "Your mind is as clear as crystal water, Athene, and your heart as pure. You have suffered much, and I come to bear you consolation."

This was promising, but still, beyond the false testimony of my awakened senses, I felt nothing. I heard a strange echo in the distance. It distracted me as if it were something I ought to recognize. Meanwhile, the world seemed to be slipping away. There were no sounds of the street, though I knew it to have been well occupied a moment before. The rats too had ceased their scratching. There were no living creatures on earth save me and this strange, wondrous lady. Yet that other noise intruded, and my heart remained cold.

"What do you wish?" asked the lady. "I shall grant your desires, for I know them to be noble. You have no care for riches, child. Do you desire…to see?"

The strange noise rose in volume—an echoing voice, reverberating against the gutted walls of the house and the unfeeling walls of my brain. The voice of my father but speaking words I had never heard from his lips.

Do you desire… Do you desire…to see? To see… To see… Athene… Athene… Have you eyes to see?

"I must think," I said.

The apparition paused, looking at me, probing my innermost thoughts.

"I shall grant you three wishes, Athene."

My heart lurched. I opened my mouth to scream. Then a rat ran across my foot, and I squealed instead.

"Miss Howard! Miss Howard!" The voice of Father Thomas Edmund Gilroy restored the strident sanity of reality. The streets were bustling, the rats were feral and widespread in the wreckage, and I was exhausted, hungry, beset by hallucinations, and standing in the middle of a singularly unstable structure.

I scurried out of the gutted hull of the house and met the priest upon the pavement where a wizened workman was carting away wheelbarrows full of char and dust.

"Mademoiselle! It is not safe! Do not go in! You see the signs?" The workman pointed to an impressive array of warnings, cautions, and official threats to enforce strict obedience in nosey passersby.

"She is with me, my friend," said the priest. "We will go now and leave you to your labors. Here is something for your trouble."

The coin or the cloth appeased the man. He touched his cap, spoke casual words of blessing, and walked off whistling with his heavy, dirty charge.

"Dear child!" said Father Thomas Edmund Gilroy. "Come! Do not stay in such a place. Sister Agatha and Isabel have been waiting for you."

He offered me his arm and led me away from the darkness and rats. "When you did not come today, they became quite concerned. I told them I was sure you were well but perhaps overwhelmed. There is much upon you now. Had I not come, Hortense would have ventured out by herself!" He chuckled. "She would have laden me with little packages for you, but for my promise to bring *la bonne femme* to *les bonbons!*"

I laughed softly. "It is good of you. I think I am tired, Father. I shall begin to see things soon if I am not careful."

He nodded without comment, as if allowing me to speak further, but I could not describe to him what I had seen in the house. It was a foolish fancy, and for all I felt he would be sympathetic and kind,

I could not yet speak of it, even to him. How could I say that I was imagining visions of beautiful ladies? It would probably come off as a blasphemous slur against the Virgin Mary or a sign of my own unbridled paganism. I could not bear the thought of provoking even the gentlest of rebukes from the priest. I clung too fiercely to his kindness to risk it.

"Do you suppose," I said, turning to a thought that always lingered beneath the upper reaches of my consciousness, "that my father is… Would he be in anywhere…anywhere uncomfortable?" Before Father Thomas Edmund could reply, I rattled out, "Because he wasn't a nice man, and I suppose he did things that were wrong— quite a few things, in fact—and he wasn't really fond of me, and he was rather a wretched sort of father all things considered, but…but he *was* my father. I shouldn't like him to be…uncomfortable."

"I pray not," said the priest. "I trust in God's mercy as I do in His justice."

"That is not much consolation."

The priest merely smiled.

We walked on together and did not speak again until we were at the steps of the house. Hortense met us at the door. Her manner was such that she might have been carrying little, delicate cookies in hand to coax an ill child into good humor.

"Mademoiselle! Come in! Come in! You are starved! You are cold! Come, come!" And she made all the wordless scolding noises one associates with domesticated fowl. Hortense was a small, bustling sort of woman, with short gray curls and rough red hands, and with these she robbed me of my coat, gloves, and hat, and ushered me down through corridors to a staircase at the back of the house, down which I had never before ventured, and into the kitchen. "Go, go! You will sit! Ah, there is the bell. I must go see Madame. You will go and sit. Isabel will prepare the English tea."

The kitchen was spacious, with a vast stove adorned with a red kettle beginning to hum and whistle, pots, pans, and other accoutrements arrayed about the walls and shelves in perfect order, and a large, sturdy table at the center of the room, well-laden with fresh macaroons and speculoos.

To my astonishment, Isabel was at the stove, wrapped in a thick white apron and tending to the kettle with an experienced hand.

"Good day, my dear," said Father Thomas Edmund. "You see I have brought her."

The back door opened, and an even more startling sight met my eyes. There was Sister Agatha, the sleeves of her habit rolled back, an apron spread over her skirts, and her arms full of clippings of herbs from the back garden. She bowed a graceful greeting to the priest. "Sit down, Father, and drink your tea. Here is your cup, Miss Howard. Sit."

I scurried down the steps into the kitchen and, perching on a high stool beside the table, obeyed. Isabel silently commenced other labors by the sink, picking through the herbs Sister Agatha had produced.

"Now, child," said that noble religious, "what is it?"

"My father's will," I said in rapid obedience. No one could withstand the authority of that austere brow. "I have no money. Not much, anyway. I never really thought about it. I mean, I was involved in the organization of his scholarship, and I knew his work. I knew some of the business of the running of the house or preparations for travel. But I had no idea that he would leave his money to the university. I...I know I must determine a means of support. I think I shall return to Paris and seek the assistance of my father's friends. They may be able to recommend me. Perhaps as a secretary. I could assist at a library, even..."

Sister Agatha looked long and hard at me. The mark on her face flushed, and I thought that I might have offended her. In the next moment, I knew I had misinterpreted her emotion.

"Athene," she said quietly, "for the time being I wish you to remain here. There will be plenty of time for you to determine the proper course. For now, you will remain with us."

I stared at her. "My father's friends..."

"Your father's friends are here. And you will remain with us."

I buried my face in my hands and loosed a torrent of hysterical tears. If Sister Agatha had given me the slightest encouragement, I would have thrown my arms around her proud neck and sobbed my heart out all over her noble Breton face.

"Why?" I asked. "Why would you care for the daughter of a man who abandoned your faith? The child of a false priest?"

Sister Agatha handed me a large, manly handkerchief. "Dry your eyes, Athene. Drink your tea."

"I am sorry, Sister." I gasped through my tears. "I promise I am not usually like this." Eager to redeem myself, I declared, "I shall have to pay my way. And...and I shall help. I do not know much about kitchen work..."

"Well then, it will be good for you to begin now." Sister Agatha produced, as if by magic, a pile of potatoes and a little sharp knife. "Scrub these, peel them, and begin to dice them."

I accepted the task and began to battle the large, ungainly vegetables. Just when I feared I would lose a finger in this unexpected new challenge, Isabel came to my side and demonstrated how best to wield my weapon.

I looked my thanks. "Do you do this often?"

"As often as the need arises," she replied. "I am well-versed in all domestic duties, Athene. I can prepare food and perform such tasks in the convent, in the world, and in the woods. I have vast experience, you see."

"You surpass me there," I said. "I am utterly unschooled. My father—"

"Was a determined iconoclast," said Sister Agatha sternly. "And if you continue to swing that knife around in that reckless manner, Athene, you will be removed from the kitchen and placed in confinement as befits a lunatic."

I accepted the rebuke and set even more diligently to work upon the potatoes.

CHAPTER 18

20 JULY 1906: TOURNAI

What strange creatures brothers are!

—Jane Austen, *Mansfield Park*

SOMEONE WAS SHAKING ME AWAKE.

I sat up into complete darkness and reached out to switch on the small light at my bedside. An unsteady electric glow illuminated the room. It appeared to be empty.

My other senses slowly came to life. I could hear the steady throb of dull rain upon the roof and window. A glance at my watch told me the time. Half past two. Always in time for the witching hour! I looked back into the dusky reaches of memory to discern where I had picked up that pleasant piece of knowledge that could thus tyrannize my sleep and rouse me at so unfortunate an hour so many times. Whatever the source, I consigned it to the darkest corner of perdition.

Blinking away the remnants of sleep, I steeled myself against the still-strong conviction that rough hands had shaken me. First, I endeavored to recall my dreams, to learn from them the source of my sudden wakefulness. No memories came, only the black emptiness of dreamlessness. Then I thought of snakes, sudden fires, demons, the impish face of the son of that missing madame, and the incinerated corpse of my dead father.

That was enough to inspire me to spring from the bed and commence a ritualistic search of the entire room. My nightly routine had waxed into an elaborate affair, beyond all sane constraints. Before I could convince myself that the place was safe and put my head upon the pillow with a reasonable assurance that I would not *immediately* suffer some dark violence, my nerves compelled me to this careful examination of every nook and cranny. Sometimes I looked in places three or four times to prove to myself that my search had been complete.

On the wall was a large spiritual print depicting a seedy-looking antiquated person in the act of being expulsed from the yawning jaws of an enormous fish. This image of Jonah resurrected from oceanic bowels was faded into a dim gray and brought no consolation until I removed it and verified that no flattened demons lurked there.

I had not yet reached the point of turning in a circle three times, kissing a talisman, and whispering an incantation. But, I told myself somewhat censoriously, I would be that far gone soon enough. What *would* my father have thought?

The mere thought of my father forced me to begin the process anew, this time determined to focus upon the minute logistics of the task and to whisper my findings in as emphatic a tone as I dared.

"Nothing under the bed. Nothing under the mattress. Nothing under the bedsheet. Nothing under the quilt. Nothing under the pillow or inside its case. Nothing in the far corner wedged against the wall behind the bed—not on this side and…not on that. Now for the chest of drawers…"

A wordless feeling of thanks rose from my heart—thanks that the room was so simply furnished. The small closet took me some time because I removed each and every article within it. After twenty minutes, I stood in the middle of the well-searched room chilly and frustrated, exhausted and paradoxically stark awake, embarrassed at my own childishness. It was a mercy that I had not been forced to share a room, though the presence of another person might also have been a fitting check on my unraveled nerves.

"And now, Athene," I told myself firmly, "you will crawl back into your cold bed and go to sleep."

Sleep was a worthy aim but doomed. I knew full well that I would lie awake, eyes straining and peering into the disquieting darkness, my mind racing with bizarre, unspoken terrors until the sun rose and I was forced from my bed raw and miserable. Nevertheless, I was determined to discipline my unruly spirit and curb the hysteria of my imagination. What sorts of evil creatures would venture out in so much rain anyway?

I switched off the light and was in the act of leaping back into the bed (to evade goblin arms, which might suddenly materialize from beneath the bed) when I heard the telltale sound of a creak in the hall. One particular floorboard perpetrated this disruptive sound. I had identified it within a few hours of habitation and learned to step to the side and avoid it.

Tonight, when I seemed to be the single person awake in the entire house, someone trod upon that precise point. That sound, at least, was undeniable.

I crossed the room in an instant and, as noiselessly as I could, opened the door the tiniest, tiniest crack.

The door, ill-suited for such clandestine doings, protested in little jerking squeaks.

Cursing the noise, I endeavored to peek through the crack. I could see nothing. I pulled the door open even further and cautiously poked out my head.

At the far end of the hall, at the top of the stairs, illuminated by rain-streaked light from a streetlamp outside, I saw the retreating form of a woman in a nightdress, overladen with a dark, simple robe. From her height and her gait, rather than any clear personal details, I identified her as Isabel.

My curiosity was aroused to a fevered pitch. What on earth could draw her from her warm bed and cheerless dreams to venture out into a cold, dark house in the middle of the night? Isabel was not remotely carnal in her appetites, so I assumed this was no romantic tryst—though that particular thought and the person of Sir Simon leapt to mind and roused a flush. I did not want to subject that response to introspection, so I shook it off and went on. One way or other, her disappearance had something to do with her brother.

I reached for my own thin robe, considered then dismissed my bedroom slippers (which had a clackity heel attached to them), and sneaked out into the hall in silent pursuit.

After avoiding the creaking plank, I found myself frustrated by the uncooperative staircase. It bore carpeting, which should have proved my ally, but the construction seemed to have internalized all the unspoken complaints of the elderly mistress of the house. She would suffer the pangs and discomforts of old age in virtuous silence; the staircase would not. Every step I took seemed to announce to the entire household—and perhaps to anyone passing in the street— my careful descent. I considered briefly if it might be more rapid or more silent to lean against the well-polished banister and slide down. I dismissed this possibility almost immediately. The banister had probably never borne the weight of anything beyond an elderly hand and, if it did not collapse under me and bring down the entire house about my ears, it was far too likely that my graceful descent would end in an inelegant collapse at the bottom. I pressed on, determined not to lose my quarry.

That Isabel did not move more quickly was odd, I thought. She did not behave as if she knew she was perceived. She had made her way down the stairs and was slowly passing through the downstairs hall, pausing to look side to side into each of the rooms as she passed. I could see her more clearly in these moments if a helpful window coincided with the streetlamp at that particular angle. She was indeed in a dark robe and wore silent bedroom slippers. Her long hair lay in a thick black plait, unadorned by ribbons or cap.

She was not dressed to go out. I wondered what on earth she was about. If this were merely an ill-timed search for a cup of water, I would feel even more foolish than before.

Isabel stopped and turned back.

I ducked into a doorway and stood as still as I could, my heart pounding in my ears.

After a few uneventful moments, I peeked out again. Isabel had continued blithely on her way.

On we went, winding silently into the deepest recesses of the house, which Hortense inhabited in daylight. We neared the kitchen. I breathed a silent prayer that this would indeed prove to be our destination. If that were so, I already had the perfect hiding spot chosen.

To my glee, the wish proved father to the thought. Isabel continued on her way down the little, turning stair into the darkened kitchen and lit a large ornamental lamp that sat upon the table. She sat down upon a small stool and looked down into the heart of the lamp as if reading some secret message in its fiery depths.

Meanwhile, I hid myself in the little nook at the top of the stairs. There, among the brooms and mops, I drew the heavy baize curtain back around me, leaving a thin peephole so I could continue my surveillance. My little, green-ensconced haven smelled strongly of vinegar and perhaps a splash of stale lemons, but it was snug and admirably suited to my present task. I wished Isabel had been inspired to light a fire and warm the kitchen. As she had not, I was relieved to have my robe to wrap about me. The temperature was oddly cold for July, but perhaps that was a consequence of this nocturnal sneaking. There were large, thick rubber boots in my little enclosure too. At first they served as a seat cushion for me, but then I found that if I sat upon the dry mop and stuck my feet into the boots, my chilly toes were kept from frostbite.

I had just settled myself for the duration when the uninteresting beat of the rain was interrupted. The ticking of the little cuckoo clock suddenly worked itself into a fevered pitch and erupted into an elaborate chime to proclaim the hour. A maniacal-looking bird popped out and shrieked one…two…three times. Three o'clock. All evil things held sway. I found I was trembling—though whether with fear or excitement I could not have said. Isabel maintained her place, silent, watchful, and still.

I was just wondering how well a broom would serve as a weapon against preternatural threats when the imperfectly lighted room darkened. I looked, albeit unwillingly, toward the source of the new darkness. There, against the windowpane of the outside door, stood a tall, thick shadow like a man wrapped in oil-soaked coat, such as sailors wear to withstand the water, and wearing an unfashionably wide-brimmed hat.

Isabel raised her eyes.

The door opened. For a moment the rain sounded thunderously loud, falling against the folds of his coat and that outlandish hat. Then the visitor ambled into the kitchen, closing the door behind him and cutting off the deafening percussion of the downpour.

My chosen place of concealment granted me a clear view, but at first I could discern little in the figure beyond marked height and breadth of shoulders. Then he swept off the large hat and disclosed vast clouds of curling dark hair, a thick, bristling, unbridled beard, and wide dark eyes set beneath thick, bushy eyebrows. It was not an unhandsome face but was most remarkable in its simultaneous capturing of two warring natures. It was as if the wolf and the man were both frozen mid-metamorphosis.

"What a night!" he said in a deep growl of a voice and, peeling off his drenched coat, tossed it, along with his dripping hat, upon a small pile of the discarded, soiled linen of the household. I expected him to be dressed in a brown robe like his erstwhile brethren, but instead he wore a nondescript suit of dark gray. He stepped forward to lean upon the table in a poised, nonchalant stance, which I immediately suspected was a pose for the benefit of his audience. I saw, or perhaps imagined, a small, ill-concealed tremor in his hand as he reached out to lay it upon the table.

"Well, Jean-Claude, you have been imprudent, haven't you?" Isabel said it as if observing something obvious and not of marked importance.

The man burst into a guttural laugh, well matched to his deep voice. "Ah, the greeting I could have predicted. After ten years, gushing tears, the frantic embrace and passionate rebuke of a loving sister. Such depth of feeling. Such poignant humanity. My God, Belle!"

"Your God?" Her voice was dry. She folded her arms over her chest, eying him as a severe schoolteacher, armed with an invisible pair of pince-nez, might eye a recalcitrant pupil.

"*Mea culpa!*" He held up his hands. "If I confess to all, will you have done, Isabel? I have not come to trade rebukes. I have come to speak to you."

For a moment, she did not reply. In the silence, still interrupted by the ticking of the cuckoo clock, I saw him as if looking through her eyes. Now I could discern the marks—the ravages of savage living. The muscles, taut and primed like a bow with arrow nocked and ready for sudden, deadly flight. Irritated marks, almost like rashes, peeped out from beneath the harsh, wiry hair about his face. There were lines too deeply drawn and a strange puffiness about the eyes. The eyes too—such large, round, dark, piercing eyes. The sort of eyes that would melt the spine of an unguarded woman. I would not venture to look too deeply into them. I understood the loyalty of his brown-robed brethren. A dangerous man to know, I thought, and deadly to love. And his hand was, indeed, trembling.

"You look dreadful," said Isabel. "Worse than you used to."

"You look wretched yourself. Thin and eerie and unloving. Ten years in your convent haven't taught you tenderness, have they? Gwynne was well spared, I think, for all he mopes after you now."

"He stood friend to you."

He stopped, looking both sulky and engaging. "Yes. Yes, he did. And he has. But you *are* maddening, Isabel."

"I suppose I am."

Once again, they paused.

"Were you so unhappy?" she asked.

"No, not at first. You know what occurred."

"You could not withstand him?"

He laughed bitterly. "What a question, Isabel. Withstand him? Who can hold back the force of the tide? There is no real, no lasting hope while he is in existence."

"You must have been weakened. You must have become embroiled in other sins. You must—"

"You are not my confessor, Isabel. Imagine all the gross entanglements and guilt you wish."

Neither of them spoke again for some time.

"No moon tonight."

"I do not need the moon." His voice was strident now. "I can still be before you in this man's form."

"Yes, but your eye wanders. It is furtive, anxious. The pretense will not last for long, I think, Jean-Claude. Then it will all fall away, and you will decline into despair, destruction, and death." Only Isabel could imbue these words with such a tone of matter-of-factness.

"And you wouldn't spare me a tear, would you, Isabel?"

"I do not think I am the crying sort."

"You always were cleverer than I." He picked up an apple from a bowl on the table in front of him then threw it back into its place.

"The fruit will bruise," his sister commented.

"Belle, I know I am in the wrong. Always in the wrong. But you have never appreciated what I suffered. If you were any sort of sister or had any affection for anyone, you'd help me."

"And how am I to help you? What is it you want me to do?"

"I don't know! Don't you see I'm in anguish? Even my peace is gone—no peace. No joy. This endless, horrifying hunger. Don't you see? There's only one way out. He will destroy us both. You must kill me, Isabel. Kill me now when the evil I have done is not complete and I can still call my soul my own! If you love me, you will spare me! Put me out of his power."

"What am I to do?"

"Didn't I just say it? *You're* the clever one! Kill me! Kill him! Join him! You're the one he wants! You always were. I'm only a pawn between you two in your twisted game. You may as well kill me now and be done with it." His voice caught with a sob, and he whispered the final rebuke: "You're just like him."

She did not move, but as if she had, he changed in an instant. "Oh, Belle!" he cried, every mark of penitence in his voice. "Oh, Belle! Forgive me! I didn't mean it! It's just that… Oh, Belle, you know I didn't mean it."

Was it my imagination or had a coaxing note sneaked into his voice?

"You wouldn't have said it if you were yourself," she replied.

They paused.

"What was it, Jean-Claude?" she asked. "A woman?"

"Blast it," he growled. "Don't play games. As if you didn't know."

"I don't. You know that."

"I don't know anything. Didn't you hear me? I said it, didn't I? You're the clever one. Do you want me to talk about love to you, Isabel? Or loneliness? Or shall we talk about gross animal appetites? Frustration? Shame? Desire? Do you want to know of lust and carnage? The desires of the flesh? You won't understand any of it on your lofty pedestal. Not a word of it."

"Why did you walk away, Jean-Claude?" she persisted. "You knew! You knew what would happen."

"Did I?" He shrugged. "Perhaps I did. But what is knowing, Isabel? I'm not like you. I never was. I cannot just…know."

"Did he send you?"

He turned his head and gave no reply.

"This is pointless." She turned her back to him.

"Isabel!" For several long seconds, the desolate cry lingered. Isabel made no response. With a low growl, Jean-Claude grabbed his hat and coat and roughly drew them on, still damp though they must be. Then he paused.

The hat and coat sat oddly on his form—a trick of the damp, perhaps.

A half-formed, terrifying thought burst in my mind, and a cry of alarm—of warning—rose to my lips. Jean-Claude whipped back around, a new canine gleam in his eye, and seemed on the point of springing transformed into that creature with its murderous teeth, claws, and vicious hunger raging from every pore.

Then Isabel moved to face him, tearing from concealment beneath her garments a long, narrow, deadly blade. She stood, tense and waiting, like a fencer primed for parry and heartless riposte.

For a long, interminable moment, they stood there, frozen, staring at each other.

"Oh, God, Belle." His body relaxed, limp with despair. "Not you. Never you."

She made no response and did not lower her guard or her eyes.

"You really are. You really are just like him." His words ended in a growl, and I saw, with a rapidity I had never witnessed, an eruption of fur from his face, signaling an almost instantaneous transformation.

With a poignant howl he bounded off, crashing through the door into the pouring rain of the moonless night and into the deeper darkness of his lycan form.

Silence descended, but still Isabel stood there, blade in hand, staring at the spot where her brother had stood. Finally, she straightened herself, lowered her weapon, and walked to the door. She closed it, locked it, and turned those strange, deep-seeing eyes upon me.

I stepped timidly from my hiding place. "Is he really gone?"

"Yes."

I waited for her to say more, but when she did not, I blurted out the question that weighed upon my mind. "Why...why did you let me witness that?"

Isabel looked at me without speaking. The lines of exhaustion stood out on her face, and I thought perhaps she was older than I had ever supposed.

Then she gazed down at the hand that held the blade, and I saw a trickle of blood across her palm. She tested the wound, and, looking about the weapon for a cause, disclosed a thin, jagged point upon the hilt.

She retrieved a clean white rag from the cupboard, tore it into strips, and began binding her bleeding hand.

"Why did you let me see it?" I persisted.

She replied without looking up from her task. "Shall we call it a tether upon my conscience?"

I considered this, frowning.

Her bandage finished, Isabel extinguished the lamp. "It is late. We must return to bed."

We walked back upstairs. All the while my mind was racing, processing all that I had seen and heard.

"Good night, Athene," said Isabel, on the verge of crossing the threshold into her own room.

"Wait," I said, overwhelmed by a clarifying thought. "Was that a temptation, Isabel? Which sin was it? Was it..."

"Go to sleep, Athene. Just go to sleep." She stepped into her own room and closed the door.

I had every intention of disobeying Isabel and staying up, wide-eyed, to think this business through to some conclusion. My determination, however, was overcome by exhaustion. As soon I settled back into my bed, convinced that nothing on earth could compel me to rest again that night, I fell deeply asleep.

From that sleep, I rose to the level of half-waking, half-dreaming.

I was in cold, clammy water, murky darkness. A large, angular shape was before me. I reached out and clasped it—the wood at the end of a pier. I pulled myself partially from the water and gazed down the long pier.

My eyes cleared. At the far end, illuminated by moonlight, a figure stood.

As I watched, the figure began to walk toward me. I recognized his gait before I could clearly discern any feature.

Athene... Athene...

He did not shimmer. This seemed inappropriate. The least a phantom could do to provide a respectable atmosphere was to shimmer. There I was, suspended in a deep, dark pool of dreams, and he hadn't even bothered to acquire the proper trappings for the job.

"You aren't even a good ghost. It isn't fair," I heard myself say.

Think, Athene. You do have brains after all.

"You can't really be my father," I insisted. "My father is intolerably rude."

As I stood there awaiting some response or ghostly message—something to justify this preternatural disruption—the vision before me began to change. The water receded and the paralysis of dream was full upon me. Frozen in painful fascination, but with inchoate dread rising in the pit of my stomach, I watched as his neck expanded out into wide, white froths of fabric, and strange, stiff, beautifully detailed clothes extending beneath that ruff. A sharply pointed beard emerged, darkly defined, framing his eerily familiar face, even as his hair began to grow, long and lanky, intensifying into silky brown locks. I blinked. Then I blinked again. His form multiplied into three, all gazing at me with a glassy stare. Cowed by the intensity of this trifold observation, I tried to sputter some protest, but my efforts produced only curling white swirls of smoke from my mouth. Synchronized sadness entered the six eyes, and, with a ghostly sigh that struck some hidden mechanism as one might find in the bowels of a clock, the two flanking figures began to turn inward, so that for a time they gazed not at me but at each other. The central figure, my father yet not my father, continued to look at me, ever at me, with deepening sadness, perhaps with a touch of exasperated boredom that was all too familiar.

Turn, turn, turn, went the dance. Turn, turn, turn went the men.

Then another voice came—a bright, chipper voice, disembodied but unmistakable.

"*Sed contra*," chuckled Father Thomas Edmund Gilroy.

"Hum," sighed the ghostly, turning three.

"*Respondeo!*" declared Father Thomas Edmund.

"Hum," said the ghostly, turning three.

"Oh, my dear friend!" laughed Father Thomas Edmund.

The dance stopped, and all three figures gazed at me with wide, frantic eyes. The voice of my father came forth from those three sets of transformed lips, pronounced with slow, ponderous, reverberating tones, "As Charles I said…*remember!*"

"Remember what?" My sleepy voice rose in despair.

I sat up in bed, harsh bright daylight streaming over me, and with no answer.

CHAPTER 19

21 JULY 1906: TOURNAI

To a father growing old nothing is dearer than a daughter.

— Euripides

I HAD SLEPT MUCH LATER THAN WAS MY WONT AND WAS PUNISHED for it. Prey to a host of indistinct anxieties, I tried to think of pleasant memories of my father. A kind word. An affectionate look. There were none. Yet there had been something. Something that had made him want to warn me. To spare me. Even…perhaps…to protect me.

At this unlikely thought, I snorted with unladylike derision and forced myself out of bed.

I dressed myself—a simple enough business now that my worldly belongings were so reduced—fetched my treasured notebook, and went in search of Isabel. At the door I stopped and glanced into my notebook to the chart of sins I had assembled some time before. With the stub of a pencil retrieved from my pocket, I made a dark star beside the word "idolatry." Then I continued on my way.

I did not know precisely what I feared, but I had a sense of foreboding and rebuked myself inwardly for having slept so docilely after that strange scene I had witnessed. A tether on her conscience, indeed! I was ill-suited to that office if I went about sleeping when existential crises were afoot.

A door in the front hall was open. I paused there, though I did not expect it to contain the person I sought. This was the private boudoir of Madame Landreau, the elderly owner of the house. The frilly, pink sort of room had once (so Hortense told me) served as the library of her even-more-aged father-in-law. Long ago, illness and antiquity had taken him off to his fathers. Soon after, her husband had succumbed to some internal complaint. As she aged, and as more of her loved ones preceded her in death, she became more cheerful, more simple, more pious, and more infirm. Now she was a wizened, tiny mass of smiling wrinkles, consigned to her bed or to her chair and attired in an endless series of ruffle-necked, pure white gowns— or virtually identical ruffle-necked, pure white nightgowns.

"Ah!" she cried when she saw me and commenced her usual campaign of sweet nods and smiles. "Ah!"

I dropped a curtsey, as a little girl might. "I hope you slept well, madame."

She beamed and nodded and smiled. "Ah! Ah! Oui, oui, Anna. Sweet, sweet Anna. Oui, oui!"

Anna was her granddaughter, long dead. I now shared the name of Anna with Isabel and also with the little yellow canary in the ornate, pagoda birdcage hanging in the window. The bird exuded a special illusion of immortality. A long, lean, lazy cat slept in the windowsill. He too was now dubbed Anna, though sometimes Madame's mind wandered, and she would call him Leon.

"Ah, Anna. Sweet, sweet Anna." She was now speaking to the cat. "Come, puss, puss! Sweet Anna."

Hortense appeared in the doorway, carrying a tray laden with doilies and little, delicate offerings for her beloved mistress. "Madame, madame! Sit back. Here, your pillow has fallen. Ah! There is your blanket too. Oh, madame! Naughty puss. Go catch a mouse!"

The cat eyed her sideways as if exhausted by the confusion of his name before relaxing into an even more languid position and drifting into blissful, deliberate unconsciousness.

Hortense smiled at me. "I have something hot for you, child! Go to the kitchen. I will come to you."

Curtseying again to the mistress of the house, I scurried away. When I stepped into the kitchen, I happened upon a bizarre scene—a lightened recreation of that which I had witnessed in the middle of the night.

A tall, broad man was entering by the kitchen door, and a tall woman stood at the stove looking at him. But here the man was a stalwart, open-featured blond and the woman a noble figure robed in white. Sir Simon and Sister Agatha. Of Isabel there was no sign.

"Athene," said Sister Agatha. "Sit. You must eat. You are rested?"

She looked at me critically. I did not know what to say, for I could not lie under such an eye, but I was not yet certain if I would say anything about what I had seen. Luckily, she appeared to be too busy appraising my health to bother about the secrets nestled in my conflicted bosom.

"Is Isabel still abed?" I feigned casualness as I settled myself to eat the food the august sister set before me.

"She certainly is not. She has been up for several hours."

Sister Agatha did not offer additional information and, as I sipped too soon on scalding coffee and nearly choked on it, I could not inquire further.

"I see you have returned," I said to Sir Simon as soon as I had finished sputtering.

He collapsed comfortably into a chair beside me. "Yes, I have returned." His uninterested tone changed to a concerned one. "How are you, Athene?"

"I am well." His immediate use of my given name delighted me. "I mean, as well as I can be, but, you know…life and death are part of…life and death…" I broke off, feeling gauche.

"You are comfortable here?"

"Oh yes. Very comfortable. Where…where were you?"

"What's this?"

I had dropped my satchel and notebook onto the table without thinking. The notebook was folded open, and Sir Simon was examining the exposed page. Blushing, I hurried forward to close the book, but his hand forestalled me, raising it to look more closely at the detailed diagram sketched across the page.

"It's nothing. Well, if you must know, I find such measures instructive. I organized all of these sins of yours in the form of a chart, connecting each offense with the corresponding prohibition."

"I am not at all pleased to have them attributed to me *en masse*, Athene," he remarked dryly. He clicked his tongue, and after a moment he set the book back down and closed it. "It's comprehensive. I hope you produced a corresponding one for the virtues."

"My scholarship is always thorough," I assured him.

"I am sure it is. That is precisely how I described you to my mother. 'Miss Howard is an exemplary scholar,' I said."

"Your mother?" I said, astonished and flattered at the thought of such a conversation, though I wondered if he were merely teasing me. "Do you have a mother?"

"Of course I have a mother," Sir Simon replied in a tone of deep offense. "Why wouldn't I have a mother? Your manners are absolutely appalling, Miss Howard."

"You have a father too? I mean, is he alive?"

"Why shouldn't he be alive?"

"I don't know, I just wondered. Is he…what sort of man is he?"

"As a matter of fact, my father died some years ago. He was a good, noble, and kind man!"

"You don't need to be so offended. I merely asked a question. My father…" My stomach began to rise, and I quickly dismissed that thought. "What did he do?"

"Do?"

"Your father."

"He tended to his property and cared for his family."

"Did he engage in this sort of enterprise?"

Sir Simon's face turned a rich shade of copper. "My father was a respectable man and staunch in his allegiance to Rome—as all have been in our family for centuries."

"How reliable of you. Have you had representatives in all of the appropriate uprisings?"

"Of course."

"And you are the most recent rebel?"

"Hardly. I too am well-respected throughout the county, as staunch and unromantic a baronet as any could desire."

"You're a baronet?" I repeated, disappointed. "I thought you were a knight!"

Sir Simon began to laugh. "For what sort of feats of service to king and country would I receive such an honor?"

"Battling lycanthropes and other preternatural pests?"

"I do not think such concerns rate highly in the mind of His Majesty."

"Defense of your church?"

He chuckled. "I'm positive *that* concern does not."

The outside door opened, and I looked up, half expecting to see Jean-Claude, exhausted from his nocturnal lupine endeavors, come to beg for eggs and kippers. Instead I saw Isabel looking absent, unconcerned, and as if she had enjoyed a full allotment of sleep.

"Good morning, Isabel," I squeaked.

"Good morning, Athene." She turned to Sister Agatha. "Father Pierre Jarvais requests a meeting with us this morning. He will be here at eleven."

That was more than enough encouragement for me. I practically bolted the remains of my food. "I will—I have—I am sure I would be in the way," I said and flew out of the room. A meeting with Father Pierre was something I would avoid if I possibly could. He certainly would not invite me to his confidence.

"Mademoiselle!"

I turned in the hall, surprised. "Yes, Hortense?"

She was hurrying toward me, holding something. "This has just arrived for you, mademoiselle."

"For me? Here?" I took it, half expecting to see something from Monsieur LePont or at least from his office. Some legal document, perhaps?

Instead, what I saw made my blood run cold. The small, thin brown parcel had been carefully wrapped for mailing, and the address, written clearly, was in a hand I knew as intimately as I knew my own.

The writing was my father's.

Shaking, the old sickness returning to claim its sovereignty in the pit of my stomach, I took the parcel, mumbled something, and hurried away.

Behind the locked door of my little borrowed bedroom, I set the parcel down upon the dresser, clasped my hands behind my back, and commenced to examine the thing from a discreet distance. After several minutes, I ventured beyond this unproductive procedure and timidly stepped forward to handle this missive from the dead.

First, I examined the postmark. It was dated the day of my father's death—that was reassuring. At least I was not required to imagine his scorched corpse collecting paper and pen to prepare this package with a flourish of bloody ink. It was directed to me at our Paris address. A small counter address in the corner explained the delay in its arrival; Monsieur LePont had redirected the parcel to me here. Of course, I scolded myself. And how perfectly reasonable it was, after all! If I were not careful, I would begin seeing ghosts and goblins in every petty thing.

Thus reassured, I took up the parcel and opened it with a bold but tremulous hand. A short note had been stuffed in at one end, confirming my deductions.

MADEMOISELLE HOWARD,

In the organization of your father's effects, I have come across this parcel and hereby convey it to your present address.

With my compliments,
M. VIVIAN LEPONT

Inside was a small leather notebook, the sort my father often employed in his work. I had habitually collected them, organized them with a system of notation in the margin, and filed them, assembling a vast array of concordant notebooks so that he could return to his scattered, scribbled notes and find particular points when he needed them. This book bore none of my characteristic marks—that was the first thing I noticed. A secret book, I determined. Given his strange behavior before his death, dismissed by me as sulkiness but indicative of that frantic terror that had consumed him even before the fire, a secret notebook was hardly surprising.

I brushed away a tear. Drowning him in cheap sentiment would be unpardonably cruel to his memory.

The next thing I noticed was enough to dry every tear. I stared at the page, wide-eyed. This book was beyond anything my father had ever written. He was usually scattered and often haphazard. This was a bizarre, disastrous mess of observations and half-developed ideas, all around a complex system of financial figures. Conspiracies, concerns, and even otherworldly terrors I had been prepared to find; long columns of financial accounting I had not.

Someone walking along the passage knocked against the wall. I jumped up from the bed and concealed the book behind my back.

"Who is it?" I demanded.

No one responded.

After a moment's consideration, I strode to the door, unlocked it, and stuck out my head to confront any lurking dangers with at least the appearance of fearlessness.

No one was there.

I returned to the room and almost immediately stuck out my head again, as if I might catch an evil, prescient shadow.

Still no one was there.

I closed and locked the door and checked it three times to be sure. Then, once again, I gazed down at the gift sent from beyond the grave.

I was eager to plumb the depths of this book, to dive into the wonderous mystery enclosed therein, and to have consort in some small way with my dead father. Even so, a serious complication had risen in my mind. In battling this preternatural threat, it was unclear to what degree my thoughts and actions were exposed to the knowledge of some evil person. I still did not understand how Isabel's mind operated and imagined that her father's was even more mysteriously powerful. Could they see what I was doing? Could they read my thoughts? Could they see the book through my eyes?

I considered it for a few minutes, wondering if I could risk waiting to find Father Thomas Edmund to ask him how to proceed. My desire to read the book, however, made such prudent restraint seem impossible.

I decided to take a midway course, seeking, to the best of my abilities, a place of safety and security in which to begin my reading.

I grabbed my hat and coat, made my way down the hall and the stairs, and—having ascertained no one was about to witness my departure—left by way of the front door. Safe in the street, I walked with deliberate step to the nearby Church of Saint-Brice— another beautiful Romanesque specimen, whose simple nobility had impressed me. I crept in at the door and found for myself a seat in a pew illuminated by a colorful ray from the sun. If there were anywhere that would serve as a sort of mental bank vault, unassailable by the powers of evil, it would probably be such a bright, spiritually ornamented spot as this.

I opened my father's notebook and began to read the first entry.

Three times three

Then came the first, long series of figures and dates, riddled with emendations, question marks, and strange commentary.

<u>1881</u>
The Poetics of Myth
F10,000
£43,800
F68,000—benefactor or moneylender?

Marcellus Solomon—15 August 1882

<u>1883</u>
£34,000
F52,000

The dates spanned back twenty-five years. I had, however, reviewed various papers and notes from my father from a similar date. Since that time, he had acquired an even more robust hand, with sweeping lines and trailing (often misplaced) accents. This script was clearly of a more recent vintage. The entire book appeared to be a sort of retrospective financial log. Something a man might write when endeavoring to reconstruct the past.

Still puzzled, I turned another page.

<u>1885</u>
£100,450
F38,000—Marcellus Solomon (legacy & library)
Foundation for studies of comparative religion
Lauritz Aldebrand
Honors received 15 August

<u>1889</u>
Frazier—*Comparative Religion & Myth*
F180,000
£15,255
Wolves
Extraction of the Philosopher's Stone

<u>1892</u>
Sorbonne
Myth and the Mind of Man
£62,000—how trebled?
F183,000—Marcellus Solomon

I did not know. I did not know. I could not see. How many,
like me, have been lured in by the promise of wealth or
power or desires fulfilled or perhaps the illusion that it is
something one does because others do it too? How many
initiates have no idea what—or the awful who—her—they
are embracing?

I flipped several pages to glance at a more recent tally and found:

<u>1905</u>
The abstraction of the pure soul of the chosen one.
To overcome that which is and transform.
Not overcome—to reduce to its core. The reduction to
pure power.
£152,000
Loisy
A Dogmatics of Dream
F200,000
WHEN THE DEBT IS CALLED IN…
Tribute. Who is the tribute?
Gilroy: Whose is the money? Sorbonne and now St.
Thomas
The Laurentalia? The Nemoralia?
~~Marcellus Solomon—Lauritz Aldebrand~~—*Marcus de Lille*

The name was there. Sharp. Undeniable. There among the
figures. A name that made me sick with terror. Shivering rattled
through me. I wished I had a peppermint to steady my stomach,
which was once again rising in rebellion.

A gnarled hand touched my right shoulder.

Like a compressed spring that suddenly breaks free of constraint,
I leapt from my seat to perch with unladylike balance upon the back
of the pew, one hand outstretched to batten off any attack and the
other with notebook drawn back as a weapon.

Then I clasped it to my breast to be defended at all costs.

Then I wheeled it back again to be able to project it as a missile while I surveyed my assailant.

A little elderly woman with aged, mannish features, button-like eyes that popped out of her head at my unexpected and inexplicable behavior, and a thin, threadbare white lace veil across her stringy hair, began choking her alarm and withdrew her extended hand to clutch at her chest. In a minute I had her reclined upon the pew, whispering incoherent apologies as I worked to calm her frantic nerves and slow the beating of her overtaxed heart.

"Pardon me, mother," I said. "Oh, poor mother, I am so dreadfully sorry! I was startled. Are you well now? Can I fetch you some water?"

"No, no," she wheezed, closing her eyes and trembling as she lay before me. "I am well. I am well."

A young priest with a pronounced jawline hurried over toward us, cassock rustling and a look of irritation and suspicion in his eyes. I renewed my apologies, stuffed the notebook back into my pocket, and made my way out of the church again.

Nowhere was safe, alas. Not even churches.

I walked through the streets, meditating on what I had read. It was not much. In fact, it was very little. I wondered if the rest of the book had anything weightier to offer.

Nevertheless, it was enough. My father had been considering his career. I could recognize various references to his own work, to the work of his fellows. The money was now gone. I knew that all too well. A wellspring of scholarly support had dried up—or, more likely, receded.

And Marcus de Lille or Marcus Zoran or whatever the man's name might be was at the bottom of it. It seemed to me to be absolute nonsense—but dangerous nonsense. A mess of masks and mirrors, smoke and sleight of hand, but with a deadly core.

I recalled little phrases, little comments. Money, money, money. Did it all come down to money after all? Father Thomas

Edmund had spoken of the financial brilliance of the father of Isabel and Jean-Claude.

"The bankers had their say and the bankers hold sway," I muttered. "Who was it who said that?"

"Miss—Miss—what—what was it?"

I looked up, startled. I was standing in the street before my temporary home. An inordinately tall and thin young man stood there. He was attired for the outdoors—I could not have put my finger upon any precise problem with his appearance—but for some reason I wondered if the man were drunk or under the influence of a drug. Such bright eyes, such fitful movements of the hand.

"Mr. Cantor, isn't it? Are you well?"

He began shivering violently. "Is he here?"

"Is who here?"

"Gilroy." His teeth rattled. "I want to see Gilroy."

"I do not know." The percussive rapidity of his front teeth fascinated me. Wouldn't they wear down to dust at any moment? "I am only just returned myself. I don't know when he will come, but I believe Father Pierre Jarvais is here. Perhaps—"

"No." He shook his head rhythmically—and not in time with his teeth, a grating discordance. "No, I wanted Gilroy. But…but it doesn't matter. It doesn't matter in the least. The bankers will have their way. And hold sway." He barked out a bitter laugh, turned on his heel, clattered down the front steps, and hurried down the street.

After a moment's hesitation, I went into the house, all the while rebuking myself for failing to give some magical reassurance to the disturbed young man. As I stepped in, the parlor door opened, and Isabel looked out. She gestured for me to enter and, still removing my hat and gloves, I obeyed.

CHAPTER 20

21 JULY 1906: TOURNAI

The end of life cancels all bands.

— William Shakespeare, *Henry IV, Part 1*

IN THE LITTLE PARLOR, I FOUND A COUNCIL OF WAR WELL UNDERWAY.
Several opposing camps ranged about the room.

Sir Simon stood at the center with powerful arms akimbo
and legs apart, looking rather like King Henry VIII posing for his
portrait. A Viking Hal, without the sanguine, carnal jollity.
Father Pierre Jarvais sat upright at the edge of one of the chairs.
Sister Agatha, ranged opposite him, achieved an even more
rigid posture. Isabel settled herself back into a chair in the corner
behind Father Thomas Edmund, and I sat down beside her.
Two others, silent and still, sat in chairs just inside the door: the
dour, brooding Brother Vincent and, in well-worn brown,
Brother Leopold, from the Franciscan monastery in Zagreb. A
council of war indeed.

"We cannot simply assault this person," Father Pierre was saying
with laborious patience.

"I am not saying that we should assault him," was Sir Simon's
exasperated response, "though the argument could be made. Can
you not pursue some sort of exorcism?"

"Calm yourself, Simon," said Father Thomas Edmund placidly.
"Father Pierre is correct. These things have certain rules, you know.
We must...er...*exercise* discretion."

Father Pierre looked exasperated then too. Father Thomas
Edmund, untroubled by such disapproval, smiled at me, but I was
for once too distracted to appreciate his wit.

"I did not know you were here," I whispered, frowning. "That man, Mr. Cantor. He was here and asked for you but would not stay. He hurried away. He seemed quite distressed."

Father Thomas Edmund frowned and nodded his head in acknowledgement. Then he looked back toward the two combatants.

"We are bound in obedience," Father Pierre was saying in a voice that probably terrified young novices. "We are recalled to Rome, and Father Thomas Edmund will accompany us."

"What can possibly be more pressing than this issue at hand?" demanded Sir Simon.

Father Pierre looked at him for a moment. In a voice that might have been calculated to be kind but succeeded only in sounding patronizing, at least to my defensive ears, he said, "You forget, Sir Simon, the primary object of our order. It is not to grapple with these revenants and wounded creatures. It is the preaching of truth and the dispelling of error."

"Are not these revenants and these 'wounded creatures,' as you call them, the embodiment of error?"

"An embodiment of the consequence of human frailty and sin, yes. But at the moment there is a more grievous and widespread danger—"

"More grievous than consummate evil? You have the power to stop him—to destroy him!"

"We are mendicant priests, not assassins, Sir Simon."

"And have you no responsibility here? Who else assisted in the retrieval of Jean-Claude and Isabel? Who else has failed in healing one and protecting the other?"

I looked at Brother Leopold, but he was gazing with steady, untroubled eyes, at the window.

"But," Sir Simon continued, "instead of helping—instead of doing what conscience demands—you will waste yourself in empty pontificating and debate about petty points."

"You forget yourself, my son," replied Father Pierre sternly. "And you are mistaken. Error is not an impersonal, inoffensive force.

It brings disruption and destruction in its wake. I do not speak merely of the destruction of theories or academic traditions. I am speaking of the destruction of souls."

"As am I," was Simon's mutinous response.

"Further," continued the prior in a voice to quench all insubordination (except that of Sir Simon), "in our obedience to the master of the order and to our Holy Father, we do not neglect the pastoral care of those under our protection. Isabel and Sister Agatha will travel with us."

"And Jean-Claude?"

"At the moment, our greatest assistance to that fallen brother is prayer. Prayer—and vigilant, strict response to the deep, poisonous, abiding threat that is in our midst."

I thought Brother Leopold nodded, but, if so, it was so subtle a movement that I could not be sure.

"We stand on the edge of a precipice." I had never witnessed Father Pierre in the act of preaching and found the display powerful, though I was tempted to deride him for pomposity. "The threat to the Church lies not only without; the threat comes within. Poisonous doctrines make their way into the teaching and preaching of the Church herself. Our own priestly class, seduced by novelty and by sophistry, begin to wield the language and the weapons of our enemies. Progress and science, and a new philosophy—scarcely deserving of such a name—attack the tree of Tradition with vicious, iconoclastic fervor. They strike at the heart of the Deposit of Faith, at the heart of philosophy and theology, and bring duplicity, confusion, and destruction in their wake. With the reduction of the supernatural to merely natural propositions, they work to achieve the complete dismissal of the divine reality. Reduce Him to a mere man and what hope can there be for any man reduced to a vicious, slathering beast!"

I wondered if such a display sprang from pride or nobility. That impressive profile was well deployed in this spontaneous sermon. I glanced around the room and wondered if anyone else was gripped, as he thus declared himself. Sister Agatha looked passionately engaged,

Brother Leopold respectful, Father Thomas Edmund thoughtful, Isabel absent, and Sir Simon furious.

"It is for this reason," said Father Pierre, "that the master of our order and the Holy Father recall us to Rome, to consider the influence of this poisonous, dangerous heresy upon our own universities and houses of formation. Thus, Father Thomas Edmund and I go to examine the Pontifical University of St. Thomas and to review with special care a large bequest made to the university by the Lauritz Aldebrand Estate—Miss Howard!"

The involuntary shriek of astonishment I had emitted startled Father Pierre into sudden silence and caused all eyes in the room to turn to me. I leapt to my feet, clasping the notebook from my father in my hand. "I will come with you."

For a moment, they all continued to stare until Father Pierre regained his poise. "Thank you, Miss Howard," he said. "We appreciate your generous offer. However, this is the business of our order for us to address as we see fit. I think it prudent that you remain here."

"It may be prudent," I said, assuming an air of firmness that ill-concealed my terror at standing up to so formidable, so courteous a man. "I *shall* be coming with you. And I shall be of assistance to you. You see—" I held out my new treasure. "This is my offering to you. What it contains will be vital to your success. I shall happily lend it to this enterprise. I shall *not* give it up into any hands."

Silence reigned for several moments after I finished this bold speech. All others in the room looked from Father Pierre to me then back again.

"What is this offering?" inquired Father Pierre.

"It is the notebook my father sent to me. It contains information vital to the success of your work."

Father Pierre extended his hand. "May I see it?"

Since I had just said I would not give up the book, I thought this ungenerous of him. If I could have thought of an excuse, I would have used it, but I could not. I obediently handed it to him.

He looked through the pages without comment.

I could hear the clock ticking and Sir Simon's annoyed breathing. No one spoke.

"How," said Father Pierre with careful emphasis, "will this serve our work?"

"I don't know," I admitted. "But it *will!* I don't fully understand it yet, but there *is* some connection. There must be."

This was not the sort of evidence that would aid one in achieving a decisive victory in parliamentary debate or elevate a theory to the level of scientific proof—and well I knew it. I endeavored to look full of guileless faith and hoped the impact would be as persuasive as my argument was not.

"If I may, Father Prior," began Father Thomas Edmund. "Miss Howard would indeed be a valuable companion for Isabel and Sister Agatha. And it would suit our purposes well to have everyone remain together. As you and I have already discussed, we do not wish the urgency of the situation in Rome to outweigh this more local concern."

To my astonishment, Father Pierre nodded. "You have a kind advocate, Miss Howard." He looked at Isabel. "Yes. I see the wisdom in this. I shall grant your request, Miss Howard, but"—he fixed me with as stern a look as I ever wish to receive in my life—"only on condition of absolute obedience. I will not have recklessness or rebelliousness. If you are in my charge, you are fully in my charge. As the responsibility is mine, so is the authority."

"Yes, Father," I said with every atom of obedient fervor I could muster.

He looked at me again then, long and hard. I thought I could see a strange twitch on one side of his upper lip, which in an ordinary person would indicate a sudden desire to laugh but in Father Pierre must mean something more austere.

"We will depart tomorrow. Father Thomas Edmund and I will make the arrangements. Sister Agatha, I would speak with you."

The tall Breton nun, whose moon-shaped birthmark was in docile abeyance, bowed her head and rose to follow him from the room. As the door closed behind them, Sir Simon burst into deep, good-humored laughter. "Of all the meddlesome creatures in the world," he said when breath was available to him, "there is no other quite like you, Athene!"

"I don't think I'm that unique," I said with saintly humility.

"You're a nuisance."

"And you're rude, but I don't mind it so much."

He chuckled.

"I suppose you'll be foisting yourself upon the company too."

"Not at all. I have other business to attend to."

"Oh."

I must have looked the disappointment I felt, for he chuckled once again. "Never fear, Miss Howard. I shall return ere long to rescue you from whatever trouble into which you entangle yourself." Before I could think of a suitable retort, he stepped forward to the priest. "I leave you, Father. You know my errand."

Father Thomas Edmund raised his hand in benediction toward the massive form of the baronet. "God speed you, my son. *Christus lux nostra…*"

"*Et clypeus.*" Smiling, Sir Simon bowed to me one last time and departed.

Brother Leopold rose from his seat and stepped forward. "Miss Howard," he said gently, "I was sorry to hear of the death of your father. We remember him in prayer. May his soul rest in peace."

That thought sobered me. My tears rose, but I suppressed them quickly and thanked him.

"I shall go and prepare the others," he said to Father Thomas Edmund. Then he left us.

Isabel too rose. "I am glad you will be with us, Athene," she said and walked from the room.

"Well, well," said Father Thomas Edmund. "Now we go to Rome. And this book of your father's—Athene, may I see it?"

I handed it to him willingly enough.

Brother Vincent, who had continued to sit silently, moved in his chair as if he might join the priest in his reading, but appeared to change his mind and settled back into that same deep, gloomy meditation.

As Father Thomas Edmund read, I looked to the other as a source of conversation. For some time, I looked in vain. Finally, he looked up, having pursued his thoughts to some thoroughly unsatisfactory end, to judge from his face.

"Do you go to Rome too?" I asked by way of forcing him to speak.

"Oh yes," he said.

"Have you been to Rome before?"

"Oh yes."

"Do you battle evil errors or vampires or werewolves or none of them?"

Brother Vincent laughed. "None of them. I am yet a student."

"And will be a priest?"

"Through God's grace, I hope to be."

What might have been modesty in another man seemed oddly like sullen prevarication in him. If he would be so infuriatingly uncommunicative, I would retaliate by persistent inquiry. "What do you study?"

"What I am instructed to study."

I began to dislike Brother Vincent intensely. "Are you familiar with my father's work? You spoke of it once before."

"I know of it, yes." He paused. "He was an interesting man, I think."

"What parts of his work interested you particularly?"

"I have not pursued his work in depth. It is not…not work approved among our community."

I thought I discerned a hint of apology in Brother Vincent's voice, but it was wasted on me. "My father styled himself a master of heterodoxy. Does heterodoxy interest you?"

"Certainly not."

"I mean—does it interest you the better to combat it? You must cast all such wicked notions from you. Dismiss them, battle them, proclaim them anathema—is that not so?" I was becoming positively uncivil to the man. Inwardly, I rebuked myself for such rudeness and sought for the provocation. What in this odd Frenchman with his dark, unruly curls, his soft, round jawline, and his brooding self-pity aggravated me so? I didn't even know the man!

I was about to apologize outright when I realized that my words had finally instigated a response.

"Yes, of course," Brother Vincent said in a dull tone. "We will simply turn away from every new idea, every new proposition, rejecting them wholesale out of fear." He looked at Father Edmund. "What if these are the turning point of dialogue? A new means for preaching? For fulfillment of the great commission? Are we simply to turn from them in terror? To condemn them? To flee? Or to confront them? Engage with them? Find in them what we may be able to value and turn them to serve the Church. St. Paul spoke to the people of Corinth through their conception of the unnamed god and showed to them the reality of the true God. Could we not do the same through these new philosophies, these new scholars? Are we always to be restricted behind siege walls?"

For a moment, Father Thomas Edmund did not reply. Then he said, "Brother, we will not debate. You know that I believe them dangerous, and, moreover, that I trust the authority and guidance of Mother Church. Your enthusiasm and your expanded, capable mind feels trapped by that guidance, but that is not truly the case. Trust. And be patient."

"And if I may never pursue these ideas?"

"If so…God is still Good."

I looked toward Brother Vincent. Some strong emotion registered in his face. I looked away, embarrassed to have witnessed it, but at the same time endeavoring to imagine what that dark flush and sudden depth in the Frenchman's eyes could connote.

"I must go and prepare," he said shortly. "Good day, Miss Howard." And with that, Brother Vincent departed.

"I do beg your pardon, Father," I said in sincere penitence. "I don't know why I pestered him like that."

"Don't you?" he replied with a half-smile. "I assumed it was because he reminded you of your father."

"My father?" I was astonished. "Is he like my father?"

"He is like your father was more than twenty years ago."

"Brooding and melancholic?"

Father Thomas Edmund's smile grew. "Perhaps with less of a touch of melancholia. Your father was passionate and gifted."

"And what happened?"

"He became deeply engaged in his work. Slowly he moved away. Finally, he could not—or would not—turn back."

"Because of his work or because of my mother? Or...because of me? I've read Milton," I pressed on. "The thrilling bits were delicious, but I was disgusted and offended by his treatment of my myth. According to his theology, Sin was a daughter conceived in the mind of Lucifer. She sprang forth from his head, like Athene from the head of Zeus. Sin coupled incestuously with her father and brought forth Death."

"Milton," replied Father Thomas Edmund Gilroy, "though undeniably possessed of poetic genius, had some rather silly ideas."

I giggled in spite of myself and wiped away a few stray tears.

"Oh, my dear Athene. My poor child." He did not venture into the realm of overdone consolation, and I was grateful for it. How could he answer my unanswerable questions? Who can say what first drives a man into such lasting separation from his chosen way of life? What first—and what last?

"Why?" The word stuck painfully in my throat. "Why? Such a horrible death. Why?"

"I do not know." He shook his head. "My dear, it is a hard thing. A very hard thing for you to suffer."

"What did he do? Was he a pawn? Or a victim? Or is this unrelated? It could be unrelated. An accident. A senseless, stupid accident? Nothing to do with anyone? Just dead, dead, dead…" My words broke into sudden, wrenching sobs.

Father Thomas Edmund sat silently across from me, waiting, with his eyes contracted in concern. After a few moments, I choked back hysteria and wiped away the tears, pushing roughly against my swollen red eyes. "I'm sorry," I gulped. "I'm sorry. I'll be collected again in a moment."

"My dear child. You would be an unnatural creature indeed were you not shocked and grieved by this. Death is a dreadful, cruel thing."

"It seems so. More like the ancient gods than the one you worship."

"My dear, in the beginning it was not so. We are not meant for death. Death is an aberration, a brokenness."

"But God permits it. Like werewolves."

"God permits it. He desires to unite with us in love. Love is an act of free will. Just as we can choose to embrace love—to embrace redemption—we can choose not to do so."

"Like my father."

"You do not know the state of your father's soul at death. That is knowledge permitted only to God, and, through him, his blessed ones. Pray for your father, child. It is the truest service and the most proper honor you can give to him."

I considered this in silence before sullenness settled upon me. "I didn't eat the rotten apple."

He beamed at me. "Sonship brings blessings and crosses as its inheritance."

"Do you suppose it is something to do with apples after all? I mean, they don't seem to do well in mythology one way or the other."

"In Genesis, I believe the most accurate translation is 'fruit.'"

I sighed. "Oh well. Life and death. I suppose everyone is lonely."

"Loneliness is part of that inheritance."

"Father Thomas Edmund…"

"Yes, Athene?"

"All of those dreadful things you see—how is it that you are always so cheerful?"

"Does it bother you, my dear?"

"Oh no! It's pleasant. It just doesn't seem natural."

He chuckled. "Your choice of words always delights, Athene."

"Please," I begged, leaning forward in a sudden, desperate wave of eagerness. "Please, Father. Let me help. I don't know if it is all connected. I think it is, but even if not, I do not know what to do with myself. I am quite alone, you know. Let me be of some service in this business if I may. Please. I promise to find my way when it is finished. I do promise!"

"My dear child, you are welcome to come with us. I spoke in all sincerity to Father Pierre—you would be a consolation and a companion for Isabel. As to the relation between your father's death and this affair of Jean-Claude, I cannot say what that relation might be. Yet…"

"Yet?" I asked hopefully.

He gazed out the window. "Child, there is no way of knowing what occurred. We know that your father suffered a loss of faith and undoubted success in his profession. We know that he stumbled upon some dangerous knowledge. We know that he died in that fire, and we know that he made some effort in response to that dangerous knowledge—some protective effort. I don't know that he thought it through clearly or beyond the instinctive response, but…"

"But was it…" I almost blurted it out but stopped abruptly as, to my own disgust and mortification, tears once again rose to my eyes. "Was any part of it for me?"

Father Thomas Edmund looked at me, and his voice, though still gentle, had a surprising firmness. "Yes. He did wish to protect you. Of that I am certain."

A few more stray tears escaped down my cheeks, and I brushed them away. I cleared the gruffness from my throat. "We won't know—we can't know what happened. But maybe he was an innocent bystander or an unknowing victim. Maybe it was all an accident. Maybe it has nothing to do with him or me."

"No!" Father Thomas Edmund's exclamation made me jump. "No. That I do *not* believe. Your father was no hero and no martyr, but he was also not a casual, unconnected victim—though there are thousands such. The guidance of Providence is clear in one respect—we shall go to Rome, and there we shall find what next we are to do. All will be well, Athene. All will be well. Now, I must go. I hope to see Mr. Cantor before we leave. I shall send word when all arrangements are made so that we may gather again for our departure. Good night, my dear, and God bless you."

I stood at the window and watched until his Homberg hat, white robes, and black cape turned the corner and were lost to me.

"There goes a good man," I said to myself with a sigh, "if there really are such things."

CHAPTER 21

22 AND 23 JULY 1906: ON THE WAY TO ROME

Receive, and commit to memory, and possess the power of imposing hands on energumens, whether baptized or catechumens.

— Rite of Ordination for an Exorcist

A FEW SHORT HOURS OF PACKING COMMENCED. MY BELONGINGS were scanty enough, but Hortense brought little bags of peppermint to stuff into every crevice so that, when fully packed, my bag was surprisingly heavy.

We were to depart early. We ate in the kitchen with Hortense, paid our final respects to our hostess, for we would leave before she woke, and each went to our beds to obtain what sleep we might.

I was restless and fretful, sick at heart as only an early morning departure can make one. Every time I closed my eyes, my mind returned in a whirling mixture of Brother Vincent's face, my father's face, the fiery room collapsing about our heads, my father's notebook scattered in a shower of pages—

I buried my head beneath my pillow to stifle thought, only to emerge nearly suffocated and waxing frantic over my sleeplessness.

Resisting the urge to look at my watch for the twentieth time, I endeavored to recollect myself. If I could but identify the immediate cause of my disquiet, perhaps I could dispel it. It was the notebook, of course, but what of it? Its contents? Its existence?

Its accessibility.

I sat up at that thought. It was all very well for Isabel to say that she could not read my mind. Had Father Thomas Edmund not also said that demons could read or witness one's behavior? That seemed to me to be a loose point, and one I was not prepared to suffer lightly.

I rose from my bed, switched on the light, and, fetching my notebook and writing materials, commenced recording the contents of my father's book in shorthand. Three hours later, my hand ached from the effort, and a cramp in my index finger made the completion of my task excruciating. Nevertheless, I persisted until I could sit back and admire my work.

The next part would take special courage. I rose and marched over to the small fireplace in the corner of the room.

Since I began residing in this house, I had refused to have a fire in my room. I could not look at a blazing log without nausea and a mounting terror that I might see my father's face there. The summer warmth had protected me from the cold, and I had hoped to avoid facing this particular demon for many months to come.

I would not, however, be cowed by such fears. I settled down beside the cold grate and began methodically pulling out the pages of my father's notebook. My stomach churned over the task, but I tore each page into tiny fragments, all the while building a little mountain out of the torn pieces.

The cover was in my hands. I looked at it for several moments, handling it to feel its thickness and to assess its combustibility. Then I moved aside all the paper, placed the cover at its base, and rebuilt my mountain. Fetching matches, I lit one with a trembling hand and ignited the heap in five or six places.

As the tiny blaze caught hold, I scavenged in my belongings for one sacred piece of peppermint and sat, sucking away, watching the paper light up in a burst of blue flame, then glow white, then curl into black char. A few stray tears fell when I glimpsed a disembodied "A" in my father's hand, just before it vanished into blackness, but no deluge followed.

When the paper was burnt away, I set to it with a poker until I had reduced it all to dull ashes.

In the middle of the night, when I was finally falling asleep, enlightenment forced me into raw, dreadful wakefulness. I remembered the look in Brother Vincent's eyes, and, as if I had experienced the emotion myself, could interpret it. His was a look of wounded academic pride.

After that, I of course overslept. Sister Agatha was driven even to call to me from the staircase. I dressed with such rapidity that it was a wonder I was not missing some critical part of a decent young lady's wardrobe. I was crawling about on the floor, futilely endeavoring to discover the secret location of my second glove, when Isabel appeared at the door, fully dressed and with her hat already upon her head.

"Athene," she said with irritating calm, "your missing glove is caught in the fold of your skirt, which is turned up at the back. You have forgotten your handkerchief—it is there on the shelf. Hand me your bag. Very well, you may carry it yourself. There is a cab at the door. Sister Agatha is ready. The train will not wait for us."

I gasped out inadequate apologies, thrust my own hat upon my head so violently that it rebelled and fell off, and hurried after her.

Despite my tardiness and the additional complexities of travel brought about by my bicycle, we arrived at the station in time. Ironically, though many more persons were involved in this departure, the process seemed simplified in comparison with the luggage-laden progress we had made across Europe some months before.

"You may wait here," said Sister Agatha. "I shall obtain our tickets from Father Pierre."

Thus dismissed, Isabel and I settled upon a bench, my precious bag leaning against my ankles. My mind wandered, taking in the bustle and noise of the station. The periodic whistling and rushing of trains here and there and everywhere. The wafting conversation of passersby. The shouts of preoccupied porters as they ran to and fro behind overburdened trollies. A dowager in long furs, cooing in the face of a yipping brown dog the size of a large rat. He wanted to do battle with the lanky, lifeless head of the fox across her shoulder, but his mistress forestalled him with the little treats she carried in her beaded black purse.

I remembered I had not eaten breakfast. Procuring a peppermint and offering one to Isabel, who declined, I looked out again into the crowd.

A group had gathered beside a departing train. Slowly, achingly, the long train had begun to move away. Puff-chug. Puff-chug. A groaning of stiff wheels. Life quickened along the track. Revitalized, the train began to pick up speed and, in a few moments, had hurried away, leaving an expanse of empty track behind.

A second train came and took its place. As it settled, I saw reflected in the window the face of a young, tired-looking girl with wide gray eyes, shockingly unkempt hair, and a forlorn expression. With one hand, she clasped at the handle of an aged bag as if it contained all she possessed in the world, as indeed it did. With the other hand, she held one of the handles of an unwieldy bicycle. What a child she looked. A child in need of grooming and tending.

A porter ran between me and my reflection, shaking my concentration and breaking the enchantment of this mortifying picture. In the next moment, we were surrounded by a crowd of white habits and black capes.

"We are ready to board," said Father Pierre. "Sister Agatha, you and the young ladies will sit together, accompanied by me."

My heart sank.

"The other friars will sit together. We have several changes to make. Here is our travel schedule. I have made you an agenda to follow. Now, come with me."

Like little ducklings, we filed behind him. Father Pierre Jarvais and Sister Agatha, an austere pairing. Father Thomas Edmund Gilroy, pleasant and prompt, with the brooding face of Brother Vincent beside him. Then Isabel and I, a study in contrasts. Behind us walked Brother Leopold, his brown robes a disruptive accent against the others' white, and with him Brother William, whose hair appeared somehow redder than ever. Behind them was Brother Philip, wearing his outlandish, wide-brimmed hat, and his familiar, unwieldy tamburica case strapped upon his back. I had not seen him since that day near Blaguša. When he arrived, he had whispered a polite greeting and, "I was so sorry to hear of your father's death, Miss Howard," before graciously relieving me of my bicycle. Now he followed along in the wake of Father Pierre. A few people stared at our religious procession, but most were concerned with their own business and did not attend to us at all.

Father Pierre saw us to the carriage then left to arrange his brethren next door.

After a moment, Brother Philip's head (shorn of his ridiculous hat) popped in. "Pardon me, Sister Agatha. I nearly forgot. Brother Vincent and I prepared food for you all. The journey will be long."

Sister Agatha bowed her thanks and nodded for me to rise and take the parcel he held out to us. I obeyed with alacrity and deep gratitude.

Duly fortified by cheese, bread, and an apple, I settled back to gaze out the window. Our slow departure had quickened almost immediately, so we were by then barreling peacefully through the untroubled, gray countryside. It was not a picturesque day. Rain came and went dully and without drama. The train, oblivious to the unpromising atmospherics, continued on its mechanized way, a perfect specimen of heartless locomotion.

Father Pierre did not appear. I assumed he was occupied with business along with his brethren—either that or the merciful intervention of some benign power spared us that uncomfortable traveling companion. My eyes began to mist over. The rattling of the train passed away. Exhausted from so many disrupted nights, I fell slowly into the dark, comfortable depths of unconsciousness. Dreams eluded me, wisps of thoughts that refused to materialize and instead drifted away like the smoke from the engine of the steady, complacent train, bound for the Eternal City and little caring what petty stops necessity required it to make along the way.

I awoke from that deep sleep to sudden eerie consciousness.

I was not on the train at all. I was in that house—the burned house. The dead house.

I was in the room invaded by the snake. The room that had been mine but was no more.

Sitting bolt upright in bed, I gazed at a beautifully crafted gold chair in the corner of the room, illuminated by a brace of red, dripping candles. In the chair sat Marcus Zoran, who had once been Marcus de Lille, juggling three round green balls. His sleek white hair and long white moustaches were in perfect order. The scar across the front of his face stood out like a crack on the glass before a picture of exquisite respectability.

"Good evening, Miss Howard," he said sweetly. "I do apologize for interrupting such virtuous rest."

I closed my eyes and repeated the formula, "Get thee behind me, Satan," three times for special emphasis before I timidly opened one eye.

He was still there, wrapped in an opulent black cloak, with his well-groomed hair and strong scent, continuing to play with the green balls.

I pinched my left leg under the bedclothes and barely refrained from squealing at the sudden pain. As I blinked back the tears that rushed to my eyes, the man in the chair sighed and shook his head at me in a gentle, almost indulgent rebuke. "I am quite real, my dear, and you are quite certainly awake."

I had one more test. Beneath the bedclothes, I grasped my handkerchief, balled it in my fist, flung out my arm, and hurled the little missile across the room. It hit him squarely on the shoulder, fluttered open harmlessly, and drifted down to the floor.

Marcus Zoran caught his three balls in one hand and arched his eyebrow.

I squeaked and pulled the blankets over my head. Some breathless moments passed as I awaited the violent onslaught, the full range of his fury and power.

Nothing happened. Finally, I lowered the bedclothes.

He was sitting in the chair, still watching me, and looking bored. The juggling balls had disappeared. "Have you finished with this childishness, Athene?"

I stared back at him.

"Ah, good." He shifted his position, resettling himself in the chair and crossing one leg over the other. His fingers drummed a well-tailored knee so that the jewels on his fingers flashed and danced in the candlelight. "Now, let us have a little chat, my dear."

"I'm not your dear." My rattling teeth undermined my attempt at confidence. "I am not your...your dear...and if you do not leave this room and this house this instant, I will scream until help comes."

"Ah." He waved an airy finger at me. "Well-performed, my dear, but I promise! I have no lustful intentions. On my honor!" He held up both hands as if playacting nobility and virtue. "And, my dear Miss Howard, if you scream, you will never know what I have come to say to you."

This truth should not have dismayed me, but it did. I found that the instinctive desire for security was closely seconded by a desperate curiosity to hear and understand why so strange a visitor had come. What message could he have that would bring him not to one of my more worthy compatriots but to me?

I realized my mouth was open in mute confession of this fact and quickly closed it.

The man in the chair chuckled. "Shall we chat?"

"You would not come if Isabel were here."

"Is she not beside you? Well, well. If she is not here with us, it is a delight for both of us that she is gone, *n'est-ce pas?* I know her absence must give you hope in other quarters as well. Is that not so, my dear? Ah, do not blush, Athene. Your secret is safe with me!"

"I don't have any secrets!"

He clicked his tongue. "Do you not, my dear?"

"You killed my father," I stammered, but I lacked conviction.

"Calumny. You have that on your little chart, do you not?"

"You killed my father," I whispered, terrified at this knowledge of my notes.

"Ah, how is it that he knows? Can it be that he really *can* read minds?" He laughed and held up my little book. "Never fear, Miss Howard. I have not the mystic arts requisite to decrypt your little code. You may imagine me baffled! I commend your enterprise. How much labor it must have cost you!"

"You killed my father," I whispered again.

"What a foolish assertion. Do I look like a murderer, my dear?"

"Isabel says—"

"Oh! Well. If you are going to take the word of my hysterical and unworthy offspring, there's nothing more to be said. They are undutiful children, Miss Howard, and I do confess to disappointment in them. Yes, I believe I can honestly admit it to you—one who has always been such a worthy and dutiful daughter, despite undeniable provocations—they *do* disappoint me. Would that my own motherless daughter, whom I reared and raised and cultivated in so many gifts and arts—would that she had possessed half of your filial piety. No, Miss Howard. I will not allow you to judge me by the testimony of that wayward girl and her undisciplined, reckless brother, who conspired with low creatures to destroy the father who loved and protected them. You will say they suffered. Perhaps so. Who is not wounded or burdened in this life? I sought to teach them strength in their weakness. Power in the things that crippled them in life. And what was my reward? Betrayal. Violence. Blood. Bah!" He waved his hand in dismissal. "They did not even do the thing properly. No, they would not—could not—appreciate all that I had to offer to them."

"Then why come to me?"

He leaned forward. "I am coming to you, Miss Howard, because you are named for the goddess of wisdom. You, my dear—you may even surpass the power and knowledge of Isabel."

In spite of myself, I felt a rush of pleasure at this flattering suggestion. "You are trying to trap me. Why?"

"Bah! That is your suspicious mind again. You are suspicious in all the wrong places, dear Miss Howard. Your mind runs on those silly priests and their childish creed, does it not? Tell me this, Athene—have they told you anything?"

"They have told me as much as it is safe for me to know."

"How magnanimous of them. Is it as much as you desire to know?"

"That is immaterial."

"Has it not yet occurred to you—you with your gifts—that they have told you as much as it is safe for *them* for you to know?"

I fought away the thought and clung to any other fancy that passed into my aching head. "Why do you hate them? Are they your sworn enemies? What made you the monster you are?"

He settled back in his chair, playing with his rings, a picture of aged indolence and irony. "Ah, yes. The little storyteller. Eager for meaning. Would you cast me as the picaresque, young hero thrust upon a corrupt world and forced to live by his wits? Battling against the tyranny of Rome? Foiled by the machinations of a smiling, bustling, round-faced priest with his idiotic eyes shining benevolence?"

"He is a better man than you could ever be!"

"Fools often are."

"You're evil."

He laughed outright. "Oh, what words you have learned to use, my dear Miss Howard! And you deploy them with such childish enthusiasm! All the while searching for that illusive 'meaning' to all you say and do and see. Meaning in life, meaning in death. It is not to be found, Miss Howard. Everywhere, every day, men die, and their deaths mean nothing. The man crushed by the hooves of a runaway horse. The man drowned in a sudden flood. The man whose brain bursts. The man killed by his brother over a worthless whore. All meaningless. They were merely men. And they merely died."

My heart, thudding into my stomach, called out for peppermint and found only indigestion.

"This meaning, this purpose you seek—I tell you it is to be found. It is to be grasped. But you must grasp it. May I give you a different story, Miss Howard? A story of strange, secret delights available only to a few? Shrug your shoulders at the ecstasy of power. That is because you have not tasted it. Have you eyes to see? Have you ears to hear? Listen how the words of their petty God mock their pretense. Hypocrites and cowards. Fitting companions for my errant offspring."

"I don't believe you," I whispered.

He laughed. "What is it to *know*, Athene? What is it to *see*? I could show you such things…and perhaps it would be a fitting recompense. Here am I, the dishonored father of such undutiful children. Here are you, the most dutiful daughter who ever lived, uncherished by an ungrateful father. *Quelle tragédie!*"

I tried to dismiss him, but I could not recall the words.

"You must think on it, my dear. We will speak again another time. Whatever you do, resist the urge to feel pointless guilt for this little interview. Guilt is one of the tools used upon the simple-minded. For now…" He smiled, a mouth full of delicate, almost womanly white teeth. "For now, dear, sweet Athene Howard, you must sleep."

In a flash, I found myself blinking away sandy tears, half reclined and uncomfortably cramped against the corner of the train carriage. I scrambled into a seated position and looked around. Sister Agatha was fully upright but with head bowed—in prayer or sleep. And Isabel—Isabel by the window—had the full force of her alarming eyes upon me.

My cheeks warmed. I looked away like a child caught in the act of munching a stolen piece of gingerbread. I immediately regretted the involuntary movement, which so savored of guilt, and looked back, ready to confess, to pour out my aching heart and confused mind and demand her counsel. She was, after all, well placed to serve as a counselor when battling the machinations of her own father.

She had turned away and was looking out the window. I could not recall her attention with my eyes, and words failed me. I sank back on the cushions, caught up in the scattered thoughts left by that strange visitor.

The slow braking of the train combined with my poor posture almost threw me from my seat. I scrambled up into a steadier position as we pulled to a stop along the platform. We were tracing the coast—past Marseilles, I thought.

"We will need to change trains," declared Brother Philip at the door. "And we shall have time for tea. Father Pierre sends his apologies. We have been engaged in conversation. He bade me conduct you into the station."

We followed obediently. The friars joined us on the platform. Brother Vincent looked gloomier than ever, and the color on Father Pierre's marble cheekbones had heightened.

"Come, come," said Father Thomas Edmund, "let us have our tea. Athene? Come along, dear."

I hurried after him, still unquiet in my mind and less certain of delight in that cup of tea than I might have been a few hours earlier.

CHAPTER 22

23 JULY–11 AUGUST 1906: ROME

Rome is the city of echoes, the city of illusions, and
the city of yearning.

— Giotto di Bondone

AFTER TEA, WHICH IN MY CASE WAS POISONED WITH AN INTENSE BUT
indefinite feeling of guilt, the remainder of our journey was tiring
and uninteresting. My companions were occupied with their own
thoughts—or perhaps were lost in prayer. Eventually Father Pierre
joined us as he had threatened. That made further conversation
impossible. Whether it had been a dream or some dark reality, I was
too alarmed by that strange encounter with Marcus Zoran to risk
sleep again. I sat staring out the window with fixed attention yet
without seeing any of the landscape that passed.

We arrived in Rome late. We were met by carriages, driven by
more men in white robes and black capes who greeted us, loaded us,
and carried us off through the city, negotiating potentially terrifying
encounters with other vehicles and their aggressive drivers, and
winding our way up Aventine Hill.

"The guest quarters at Santa Sabina are prepared for you," said
Father Pierre Jarvais to Sister Agatha and thus indirectly to Isabel
and to me. "We shall consider if a more suitable arrangement can be
made, but as our own business here in Rome will involve a great deal
of consultation with the Curia…"

"I understand," she said, "and I thank you, Father Pierre."

He bowed, a noble indication that he knew his duty and would
perform it to the utmost.

Our arrival at Santa Sabina was uneventful. The night was moonless and overcast, so I saw little of our surroundings beyond the ghostly impression of white walls, darkened here and there by trees and bushes. The shadowy, indistinct form of the building seemed enormous and even monstrous in the darkness. My companions, however, were untroubled.

"Athene!" called Sister Agatha. "Come, girl!"

I hurried after her, carrying my bag.

"Ah! *Signorina!*" A large hand with prickly black hair across its back reached out of the darkness and grasped the bag.

My hand tightened around the handle. But then the white robe of a friar materialized beside me, and I loosened my grip. "*Grazie.*"

With his free hand, he gestured for me to follow Sister Agatha. I stumbled through a large doorway, and once inside, I walked behind them as we wound our way through dimly lit corridors.

Isabel appeared in a doorway. "We are to sleep here, Athene." She took my bag from my conductor with a nod of thanks.

He raised his hand as if in benediction and murmured something I could not quite understand.

"*Qui fecit cælum et terram,*" replied Isabel. "*Bona nocte.*"

He pattered off and disappeared.

One candle was lit on a little stand between two beds. Beside the candle stood a tall, thin, long-nosed Madonna who looked bemused about the pale-faced infant glaring out from upon her bosom.

"Good night, Athene." Isabel divested herself of traveling clothes and climbed into the opposite bed.

I imitated her, though more from a feeling that such behavior was expected than from any desire to sleep. I crawled, shivering, into my small but not uncomfortable bed, anticipating a night harassed by unpleasant dreams or horrid visitations. Instead, I found dreamlessness and soft rest.

So began a week of peace and comfort. Isabel spent her time in prayer, almost without ceasing. She joined me for meals but ate little, whereas I ate everything with enthusiasm. Brother Giorgio, the dark-haired friar who had greeted us the night before, seemed to have adopted me as his own special charge. The moment my face appeared in the door of the small dining room, he would hurry forth from the kitchen, eager to set before me a veritable smorgasbord. I wondered if he waited there for me to appear or if he had other duties and merely possessed a special sense of when I felt hungry. Brother Giorgio bustled about as I ate, smiling with childlike delight, replenishing my plate even when I demurred. I wondered if he and Hortense shared some primitive ancestor or if I were simply the sort of person who cries out for such ministrations. It was a blessing for both of us, I thought, that my appetite could almost match his ambition. If the trials of recent months had reduced me to a near-skeletal existence, I felt sure I would match even my hosts in rotundity ere long.

At first, I endeavored to sit with Isabel. On the first day, I was determined to remain with her, thus proving my value as a companion. After two minutes in the silent chapel, however, I escaped in search of a more congenial occupation.

"How can you be content to sit there for so many long hours doing nothing?" I asked her later.

"Doing nothing?"

"Well, you know what I mean. Can you hear him—your God, I mean?"

"I hear only silence."

"Don't you...don't you find the silence...maddening sometimes?"

"Oh, Athene." Isabel sighed, though not in exasperation. "It is the only place and the only time when I have relief."

The next day, I endeavored again to join her, with hardened resolve. After what seemed like a century of uneventful stillness and silence, I permitted myself a covert glance at my watch—and discovered only four minutes had passed.

After a quarter of an hour, I thought I might go mad.

I held fast for three quarters of an hour. Finally, fretting and fidgeting, I quietly excused myself and escaped outside. The life of the vestal virgin must require some training, I thought, or a special disposition I lacked. Since Isabel was to be thus unchangingly occupied, I and my bicycle ventured out among the streets, monuments, and churches.

I had visited Rome many times in company with my father. It was not my favorite city. I found it ill-kept, rambling, and too crowded for comfort. Many classical sites were well known to me, and in prior visits, Rome's ancient history had been my only interest. Now I saw a new city, and I delighted in my freedom for exploration.

I was indeed free enough. We saw little of the friars except in passing or from a distance. The guest quarters were outside the cloister, which was forbidden to us. I saw priests or brothers now and then as I passed through the permitted corridors. Other times I would see them at prayer and would listen to their voices chanting together in slow, laborious tones. My patience was better disposed toward such moments than the silent stillness so completely embraced by Isabel. The unity of male voices was beautiful, and in it I could see a true aesthetic appeal in this strange religion. I wondered if the silence became endurable after years of careful training. The serenity of Father Thomas Edmund's countenance seemed proof that happiness was possible in such a life.

One morning I met Brother Vincent in the hall. He looked tired, yet to my surprise, his face brightened when he saw me. "You are well, Miss Howard, I hope?"

"Very well," I said. "And comfortable here. It was good of Father Pierre to permit me to come."

A shadow passed over his face. Raising one hand, he pushed back an errant black curl from his forehead, as if, by that gesture, he might wipe away that which overshadowed his brow. "He is very good," he said, more to himself than to me.

"He seems so."

Brother Vincent did not reply but stared dully at the ground. I restrained myself from shifting my weight from one foot to the other to disperse the growing feeling of awkwardness.

Finally, he sighed and looked up. "Ambition is a hard sin, Miss Howard. A very hard sin."

"Is it?"

Father Thomas Edmund had likened this man to my father. A strong desire rose in me to warn him, to stop him—and, as quickly as it came to life, the desire died. What could I say? "Don't be like my father or you'll die in a fire?" "Don't abjure your faith and your vows or you'll become entangled with werewolves and occultists?"

"Your father's work—" In the distance, a bell began to toll. "Ah! I shall be late. Apologies, Miss Howard. I hope you enjoy your walk."

I left Santa Sabina with a heavy heart.

It was a warm, sunny Friday morning. My path was roundabout and doubled back upon itself. By midday I had wandered beyond the Field of Mars in the *rione* Sant'Angelo, past the dirty remnants of the Roman Ghetto, and across the ancient Ponte Fabricio toward Tiber Island, the Insula Inter-Duos-Pontes—the tiny, strange island between two bridges. What an etymological mixture the nomenclature of Rome displayed. Antiquity, Christianity, and literal-minded functionality.

I paused at the crest of the bridge to gaze down into the muddy-banked Tiber. In the water I could see the reflection of two wide arches, of the breadth of the bridge, and of myself, a small, blurry spot of color centered at the top.

Such a testament to the stolidity of volcanic ash, travertine, and bricks. What scenes had this most ancient of bridges beheld? I imagined young Roman maidens tripping lightly across the bridge—perhaps to offer sacrifice to the god Aesculapius, or some other hungry deity. Passing over the Tiber, that flowing white water, rippling with legend and mythological significance. Tiberinus, drowned in the River Albula, elevated by divine edict to serve as Volturnus, guardian of stormy waters. Here too were Romulus and

Remus to be drowned. Here were convicts to be executed. Here was…water and mud.

The mud caught my attention, and the rudder of my mind turned to navigate into a new stream: the success of engineers in battling the dangers of flood. Floods sounded rather romantic—the two ancient springs that fed the Tiber, swelling to burst the banks of the city, threatening property and life, and the city withstanding the onslaught and rising, renewed from the soggy assault. Mud was lacking in narrative interest.

Then again, I reminded myself, I had never been caught in a flood. It was probably a horrifying ordeal.

Rousing myself with this practical consideration, I continued on my way. I rode the short distance across the island, making my way to the far tip to contemplate the legacy of the temple of Asclepius.

Here, said legend, they had cast the body of the tyrant Tarquin. As dirt and silt gathered about his rotting corpse, the island had formed. Now it stood, vast, with two bridges, like the outstretched arms of the tyrant, holding fast to the opposing banks of the Tiber. In later centuries, workers had spread travertine across the banks so that the boat-shaped island now had an almost artificial feel to it.

What a strange, isolated place it was, nestled there in the middle of the river that flowed through the city and quickened it into life ever ancient yet ever new. It had its own special stillness. I could imagine a government endeavoring to contain disease and contagion here, but Rome, that eternally revitalizing city, would transform an island of corruption and death into a place of healing. How much was there in common between the ancient temple to Asclepius and its grandchild, the Fatebenefratelli Hospital?

That ever-succeeding, ever-changing quality was part of Rome, where ancient arches and Roman columns stood behind a Baroque façade, even as painted ceilings and geometric designs in marble marked the Christian reformation of a land once dedicated to a host of gods and goddesses. I wandered into the Basilica of St. Bartholomew to admire its interior and wondered if the gods minded the appropriation. The sunlight danced through high windows, illuminating the detailed and colorful walls, ceiling, and floors. Gold and white majesty. Antiquity and Christian scenes dancing together. As I walked out of the Basilica, the sun was high in the sky.

Settling myself upon a small stone at the far corner of the *piazzetta*, I prepared to enjoy my little picnic of bread and cheese. Brother Giorgio had prepared it for me despite my urging that he not bother himself. He had also packed olives, fruit, and some light, sugared cookies in a little napkin.

And a benediction in every granule, I thought to myself.

A few people sat nearby—sojourners enjoying the drowsy warmth of the day. A few passed into the church. A pair of lovers, arm in arm, meandered together along one bridge, across the island, and back along the opposite bridge, all the while gazing into each other's eyes. I wondered if they ever saw their surroundings or if they even knew they had thus crossed the river, the island, and the river again. I imagined them suddenly finding themselves in an unexpected place, an entirely different region of the city. Would they laugh together at their unconsciousness? Or would they fret because of the likely rebuke of the girl's stern, doting mother? I thought of Sir Simon and wondered if, after this business ended, he would finally marry Isabel. I wondered if the ties of the convent were incomplete enough for her to be free. I hoped not. I didn't think she would be a good wife.

Depressed, I walked to the bridge and threw the crust of my bread into the Tiber, frightening a small brown bird that flew away from its perch above the central arch. I gazed after it for some time.

I could look at my shorthand copy of my father's notebook again, I supposed, but to what avail? Every time I looked into it, which was many times a day, I found no new insights, no key to synthesis and understanding. How could I fare better on such a warm day?

I yawned again, struggling against the impulse to close my eyes, to resist the harsh glare of the sun. At least it was warm. Perhaps a nap upon the grass. Surely I was safe here?

A strong scent wafted by. I looked about to find the flower that might have produced such a smell, but no flowers were in sight. It was familiar, but I could not place it. Where had I smelled that overpowering, unpleasant scent before?

Then I recognized it. Panic rose in my throat, but it was too late. I had succumbed. Sleep was well and fully upon me. With a feeling of inescapable doom descending, I cried out wordlessly for aid.

There I was, once again, in the candle-lit bedroom of that lost house, bedbound and blinking before the amused countenance of Marcus Zoran.

"I do wish you would leave me alone!" I wailed.

"I am sure you do," he said with mock sympathy as he toyed with the corner of that opulent black cloak of his. "Poor Miss Howard! Plagued by demons, beset by unfulfilled dreams, and deprived of her beauty rest. Did not your father tell you, my dear? Beauty is far less valuable than intellect. Be consoled that you have the latter and do not yearn for the former. Now, shall we have our little chat?"

"No." I crossed my arms in the manner of a sullen child. "We shan't. Go away."

I glared at the dazzling rings dancing upon his fingers, and I hoped that his nauseating cologne would suffocate him someday. He must bathe in it. Perhaps the cologne was necessary. Perhaps being undead or reincarnated or whatever he was brought with it disgusting odors. My stomach began to churn. I wished I had thought to bring peppermint with me into this wretched dream.

"Did you bring a little bottle of holy water this time, I wonder?"

"I wish I had one. I'd throw it all at you."

"And what do you suppose that would achieve, Athene?"

"I don't know, but I hope it would do *something*."

"Very well." He lounged back in his chair with that insouciant and discordantly youthful posture. The chair creaked a feeble protest. "Kill me. Destroy me. The roots of my work entwine so deeply into the earth beneath every nation—my will must triumph. I tell you, Miss Howard, centuries of destruction will follow, whether your little, stupid priests march through their silly rituals or no. There is a power greater than any they can muster against me."

"I don't know that. But Isabel may be spared."

"Oh," he said, unconcerned. "My children I shall certainly destroy. That is not at all in question."

"And the priests?"

"They destroy themselves every day. Do you not see the cracks, the strain? The disruption and disagreement? The growing mutiny? Their internal collapse needs little encouragement from me."

"But you do encourage it."

Marcus Zoran shrugged. "There is a piquant delight in such things. My dear Athene, what do you know of Hungarian mythology?"

His question startled and confused me. "Not much," I admitted. Curiosity twitched. "Why? What does that have to do with anything?"

He yawned. "Oh, just my concern to appease your yearning for coherence. The shape-shifting demon Ürdüng spends his well-earned eternity in the depths of the underworld stirring a cauldron filled with the souls of sinful men." He held up his long, thin, ringed hand. "No cloven hooves for your critical inspection yet conceive of me in like manner. I am come to gather spices for my pot, for I delight in this brew, just as you delight in that noxious black coffee Brother Giorgio pours for you each morning. Shall we wager on the likelihood of my success? What would you pledge, I wonder?"

"Why won't you leave me in peace?"

"How repetitive you are today, Athene."

"You're the one who keeps repeating my name," I retorted. "What of Madame and her son?"

"Who?"

"Madame Deshalle. In Tournai."

He shrugged. "What of them?"

"Are they dead?"

"Does it matter?"

"I imagine it matters a great deal to them." I added, with less certainty, "And maybe to God too."

Marcus laughed. "What a creature you are, Athene! How well you parrot! Your father would be horrified! And he deserves it. He never appreciated your loyalty."

"Why, why, why?" I demanded. "What on earth can you gain?"

"You are slow of mind today, Miss Howard, and horribly scattered. Do you suppose to bewilder me by this? How absurd. I have told you of ecstasy. The ecstasy of power. The ecstasy of destruction. When first these powers came to me—oh, that delicious, that thrilling embrace—that sensuous, vitalizing force…"

He ran thin fingers through his white hair so that the gems glistened in the aged tresses, and he closed his eyes as if relishing the remembrance. I thought he even smacked his lips, so keenly did he savor this perverse memory.

My stomach was in full rebellion now. Even when I had matter-of-factly accepted the carnal needs of my father (which he fulfilled in a perfunctory manner outside the home) I had not dwelt upon the particulars. With this strange, almost grotesque old man, fantasizing about his strange relations with demon goddesses—

"Ah, you blush, Miss Howard. Your virgin innocence is shocked."

I endeavored to restrain myself from fidgeting. "No man cavorts with goddesses and survives. Ritual dismemberment or incineration or some other wretched conclusion always comes. Or you'll become a grasshopper."

He responded by yawning, raising one bejeweled hand in imperfect concealment of that breach of etiquette, and once again began to play with his rings. "Shall I tell you the story of my errant youth, Miss Howard? How dull for both of us. Once upon a time"—the derision in his tone was palpable—"there was a great man with a perfect goal—the reduction to and abstraction of the philosopher's stone. Gold, Miss Howard. Gold. Well, our great man determined gold was his path to power, and he turned to the gods to obtain his gold. And the gods looked kindly upon him. The gods embraced him. The gods made him one of their own. He was granted the power to build nations—to build them or to destroy them. All through gold."

"I don't understand the interplay of international politics. The cries of newspapermen and politicians are incoherent to me."

"You mean they do not interest you," he prompted with an indulgent smile.

I flushed.

"Do not be embarrassed, Miss Howard. It is the sign of a lofty, superior mind not to be brought down by the petty concerns of mere men and their inconsequential national struggles."

"Then whom do you seek to aid?" I demanded. "What cause are you championing?"

"Oh, Miss Howard!" He broke out into laughter. "You are quite incorrigible! Russia, Austria-Hungary, France, England—take any of the great powers. Take them all. They are nothing. The greater their conflict, the greater the profit. And the wider destruction."

"If all you want is chaos, why care about gold?"

"It is my chosen weapon. A weapon no man, no nation can resist. A brilliant, alluring, scintillating weapon of fire, the weapon of supremacy."

"Why attack my father? What do you care about scholarship?"

"Ah! But are not ideas a form of currency? Ideas, Miss Howard, come from gold and go to gold, and he who wields the gold commands the ideas. He can bring down nations, mountains, the entire world!"

"It sounds like a lot of nonsense," I said, "but then, I didn't believe men could be turned into wolves."

He stopped playing with his rings and turned to face me. It took every ounce of my willpower to keep from throwing the white, fluffy bedclothes over my head to escape that satirical, cruel scrutiny. "Power, Athene. Power and destruction. That is the meaning you seek. What is it you desire? Truly? Is it not a form of power? The power of knowledge? Knowledge beyond your father's? Knowledge beyond those priestly clowns? The power to satisfy every yearning—

every lonely, tragic longing of your little soul? What would you give to have Isabel removed from your path, and to have your secret romantic desires fulfilled? Desires you refuse even to admit to yourself. To have…"

I closed my eyes and placed my balled-up fists over my ears, pressing until the drum of my ear rang with pain. I shouted at a deafening pitch to drown the sound of his mocking laughter: "I WANT TO WAKE UP! I WANT TO WAKE UP!"

Louder and louder rose the laughter, and my voice rose to a shriek. "I WANT TO WAKE UP! FATHER! I WANT TO WAKE UP!"

A raucous cry rang out beside me, startling me awake. I was sitting upon the grass, confronted by an enormous black crow cawing in my face. I squealed and scurried out of its way. The ominous bird flapped its wings and flew away in dismissive disgust.

I looked around, cold, frightened, and disoriented. I was alone.

I gathered up my few belongings, grabbed the handles of my bicycle, and rode through the little island and across the Ponte Cestio. At the base of the hill, before I could make my weary way up toward Santa Sabina, a sudden, startling apparition materialized. A carriage, elegant but aged, a large, noble crest upon its door, had come to the bottom of the hill. At the window I saw two faces looking out at me—one of them amused, the other catatonically alarmed.

The first was Marcus Zoran. The second was William Cantor.

I leapt from my bicycle, leaving it to clatter onto the side of the street. I was on the verge of shrieking at them when Marcus Zoran bowed to me and raised his stick to tap the roof of the carriage. "Ride on," he commanded with a yawn, settling back into his seat.

I gaped at the coach until it had disappeared. Then I grasped my abandoned bicycle to run to the monastery.

CHAPTER 23

11–12 AUGUST 1906: ROME

...when I found him whom my soul loves.
I held him and would not let him go.

— Song of Songs 3:4

THE CLIMB TO SANTA SABINA IS NOT ONE TO BE ATTEMPTED LIGHTLY, and the weight of my bicycle intensified as I ran. I was breathless and inclined to be sick when I reached the top. I meant to continue to our guest house, but as I passed the large, carved wooden doors of the church, someone pushed the righthand door open. I stopped and stepped back to let the owner of the hand step out into the sunlight.

Several moments passed. Beginning to feel as if courtesy had descended into absurdity, I ducked my head around the door to understand the delay. My forehead almost collided with that of a rotund, elderly Italian man.

"Signorina! Signorina!" he hissed and gestured for me to enter.

"Grazie, *Signore*," I said, "*Per favore...*"

"Signorina! You come!"

"No, grazie, per favore..."

"Signorina!"

There was no questioning that tone. I dropped my bike and scurried into the church, where Mass was underway. I hurried into the back and settled into a dark corner, shaking with cold and fear.

Several moments passed before I became fully conscious of my surroundings. This was not the first of their liturgies I had witnessed, though I had never endured one through to the end. I could see Isabel far ahead of me and Sister Agatha with her.

Then I recognized the voice of the preacher—Father Thomas Edmund. His Latin was excellent and his Italian, though strongly anglicized, quite passable. I began to listen. It was the first time it had occurred to me to consider him in that role. I could well imagine Father Pierre, like Obadiah Slope, holding forth and dispensing hellfire and damnation from a pulpit, though with a velvet-like gentleness that fictional clergyman would have scorned.

Father Thomas Edmund was speaking with earnestness about some precise point regarding the Old Testament. There was a great deal of knowledge behind that pleasant face, I realized—and not merely knowledge regarding the realm of the preternatural. I had listened to academic lectures from my cradle and flattered myself that I could discern a crank scholar within thirty seconds.

His chosen text (or perhaps the one prescribed for him by the Church—I was not entirely clear on the logistical arrangement of such matters) was familiar to me. The sacrifice of Isaac. I knew the tale primarily through the writings of Søren Kierkegaard. Once, as a form of discipline for some supposed infraction—the precise nature of which is as bewildering in memory as it was in the moment itself— my father instructed me to read a German translation of *Frygt og Bæven* and to produce my own translations of the text in English and French. What my father intended through this, aside from obtaining well-executed translations for his personal use, I could not say. My conclusion from the exercise was that Abraham was a maniacal zealot and Isaac a brainless pawn.

Here I was called upon to consider something different—a language of covenant and sacrifice. "As we know, there is no deceit in God," said Father Thomas Edmund Gilroy stoutly.

I thought this a debatable point but permitted it for the nonce.

He spoke of Isaac, peppering his paragraphs with the recurring phrase, "his only son…his only son…" Then he turned from the Old Testament to the New, and I found he was speaking instead of another Son. "The sacrifice of Isaac is a type of the sacrifice of Jesus Christ. Just as Isaac bore the wood to the top of the mount of the Lord, Jesus Christ bore the wood of his cross to Calvary." He spoke directly of the crucifixion, one of the earliest surviving depictions of which was to be found on the wooden doors of this very church. From this, he commenced a long meditation on the beauty and intimacy of divine mercy. His final point was a strange, a remarkable paradox—that of redemptive suffering: "And he waits with longing, arms outstretched upon the wood of the cross, to clasp us in the divine embrace. Here at this altar, joined in his blood, purified through suffering, we are being made ready to share in the eternity of that embrace, foretold through his promise: 'Behold, I make all things new.'"

I wondered if my father had ever preached and if his preaching was at all like his academic discoursing. How overwrought it had become. A fantastic, overworded battlement against his adversaries, dismantling one mythology to build another.

Yet he had died in a fire, a blazing mess of incoherence.

I closed my eyes tightly, as if I might squeeze the thought away. Then, blinking rapidly, I reopened them, eager to find some more promising focus for thought.

The architecture echoed the template of San Bartolomea all'Isola, but here color was exchanged for white and gold. The columns were, I knew, remnants from the Temple of Juno, one of many ancient gods who had been worshipped here upon this hill.

I looked up at the central fresco behind the sanctuary. It was not visible from this vantage point, blocked by a large ciborium over the altar, but I had looked closely a few days earlier and recalled it now. The fresco depicted Christ the Teacher wearing flowing, colorful clothing and speaking before eager crowds, while lambs drank from a stream flowing down to the bottom center of the apse semidome. Here was a figure as unlike the ancient gods as I could conceptualize. Taking on humanity, not as Jupiter would to seduce a comely maiden (or non-maiden, if that were more to his taste), but for an even more intimate and lasting embrace. The embrace of the gods always ended in destruction. What would the end be for the coming of this man-god? Would there not be destruction in his wake too? In my mind the voice of Father Thomas Edmund echoed: *Behold, I make all things new.*

The chime of bells recalled my attention. I looked down from lofty pondering to see that the ritual had progressed to the altar. All knees were bent and all heads were bowed. I felt none of their pious impulse, but for courtesy's sake I settled onto my knees. From that distance, I could see little of the particulars of their practices, but noted the regular, almost terpsichorean rhythm of it. This role, like that of the preacher, had not occurred to my mind in connection with Father Thomas Edmund, yet I supposed it must have been more properly his work than any other. The priest performing a sacrifice to his God—in this case, according to their teaching, a sacrifice of his God to his God. Such a strange, outrageous notion.

To my surprise, I found myself more willing to consider this on its merits than I would have been had a mighty voice called out to me from that altar. I thought of Isabel and the peace she found in the silence. I thought too of the unsavory, unpleasant scenes I had witnessed. Marcus Zoran had no power here.

The Mass concluded and most of the attendees quietly departed from the church. A few old women remained, rattling beads and murmuring over candles. Then Father Thomas Edmund emerged from far at the back of the church. He moved briskly through the sacred precinct of the sanctuary. Yet there was an unwavering reverence, even affection in his movements, in the genuflection, in the bow—or was it a filial nod?—toward the Madonna in the shadows.

As he bustled down the nave, I rose from my place.

He stopped and looked at me. "Good day, Athene."

I wanted so desperately to say something, to ask something, but I could not gather my scattered thoughts. I simply looked back at him and waited.

"Come, child," he said. "We shall have a cup of tea. Come."

I followed him, still silent but with a rising feeling of hopefulness that the little round-faced priest always inspired. We settled into one of the public parlors over a tray of tea.

Father Thomas Edmund poured out a generous, steaming cup. "Tell me about it, Athene."

I toyed with my teacup, uncertain how to begin.

"Child, there is something on your mind. Something weighing upon you. Come. Let me help you bear it." He smiled that kindly, ordinary sort of smile that was such a beam of quiet gladness. A light to dispel the darkness and to laugh in its face.

I began my tale. I began with that first, real meeting with Marcus Zoran and Isabel—a meeting about which he already knew. In my mind, however, it was the forerunner of those later meetings. I described the dreams that had tormented me, and that most recent and most real encounter at the base of the Aventine Hill. All of this he received in silent consideration, prompting me here and there with a gentle question.

I forced myself to speak too about the fire in the house and the peculiar thoughts and visions that rushed together in my recollection of it. Thence I passed to the bizarre vision of the woman in the burned-out house—that hideous fantasy or illusion or apparition or whatever it was. A visionary moment or the result of exhaustion and trauma—I did not care. I wanted it out of my brain. I wanted freedom from the memory.

"Could you see her feet?" asked Father Thomas Edmund.

"Her what?" I replied, startled.

"Her feet."

I considered the point. "I don't know. I didn't see. I wasn't paying such close attention. It was a vision, you see. I don't know!" Embarrassed at this apparent lapse in observation, I cried out, "I wasn't looking at her feet."

Then I thought again. The woman slowly materialized, conjured in my memory. I could see her veil, her pure dress, the features of her face—

"No. I could not see her feet."

He nodded thoughtfully.

"Does it matter?"

"It's one of the signs."

"Signs of what?"

"The demonic. What was it that gave you pause, Athene?"

My answer this time was ready enough. "The three wishes. My father spoke of it that night—the night of the fire. The three wishes. She was offering me three wishes. And that, according to my father, is the mark of a trick."

"The particulars of mythology or folklore here are properly your father's province," he agreed. "It is one of the marks of the demonic to be loquaciously generous, promising worldly goods and spiritual delights."

"And real visions?" I asked. "Offering to let me see?"

Father Thomas Edmund smiled. "Had you been visited by our Blessed Mother, you would likely have received a command to pray and do penance, not flattering remarks about your undoubtable talents. Her perfect humility and sweetness is incapable of such petty sycophancy."

"Yes," I said, assuming a casual air that belied how self-important this knowledge made me feel. "Aquinas attributes vanity, like pride, to the devil."

"Aquinas identifies pride as Satan's sin. John Duns Scotus suggested that it was a form of spiritual lust, but I am inclined to think that a theological splitting of hairs." He considered this point for a few seconds then continued. "Some have conjectured that this rebellion was a matter of a moment. Spiritual beings such as angels apprehend reality immediately upon perceiving it. The Evil One perceived the mystery of the Incarnation—that God would be born in the Virgin's womb and share in our humanity. That most beautiful and glorious of angels, Lucifer, rebelled at the thought of that outrageous act of love."

"The Virgin's womb," I said. "And this other woman. You think she is the goddess Diana."

Once again, Father Thomas Edmund paused to consider the point. "Yes. The woman is, from your description of her, an all-too familiar creature. She has borne many names—Artemis, Diana, Hecate, Cynthia, Mene, Selene. The more ancient myths you know—their names and their legends echo down in various forms to these Greek and Roman tales. A goddess who drives her moon chariot across the night sky. A huntress. A virgin. A lover. All manifestations of the same being, the same demon. A mistress of witchcraft, of moon-madness, of lycanthropy. Consuming the souls of her prey and feasting upon their blood."

I blinked. "Well, that's positively terrifying. That is who you think came to me in the burnt-out house?"

"Over time, she has developed demonic relationships with many. Some know her for what she is, but others do not. For some, she comes in the guise of a muse or a patron, perhaps without any direct vision or encounter. For others, as Marcus Zoran implied, it is a real and personal form of seduction." He shook his head. "It is far, far better to be a dupe drawn in through weakness or ignorance."

"Why?" I demanded, thinking of my father. "How is it any better to be tricked into servitude to such a creature?"

"The evil person, habituated to vice, does not will any differently. He chooses evil. This makes him an object of blame. The wanton person has been habituated to vice as well but to the extent that his will has become irrelevant. Second order desires have no effect. He is compelled in the continuation of his vicious habits. That makes him an object of pity."

"So we stake vampires and seek to rehabilitate werewolves?"

He smiled. "We dispatch demonic beings and seek to save their victims and, if still living, their minions."

"Is this not also a form of theological hair splitting?"

"It is a complex business," he acknowledged. "Scholastic precision and pastoral judgment are of vital importance."

"Otherwise, you might burn an innocent old crone as a witch or stake the wrong body as a vampire. Like the Spanish Inquisition."

Father Thomas Edmund shook his head and sighed. "Someday, Miss Howard, we shall have a talk about the true history behind that highly favored myth. For today, my dear, we have done very well. Very well indeed. I am going to pray over you."

"What sort of prayer?"

"Minor exorcism."

"You think I am possessed by a demon?"

"Let us say, I fear you are oppressed. It is a different thing. May I do so?"

I was rather thrilled at the prospect and settled myself to be amazed. Father Thomas Edmund, without a hint of a pun or a chuckle, produced a small bottle of water, which I presumed to be blessed, and a small leather book from his pocket. Opening both the bottle and the book, he commenced a lengthy and detailed pronouncement in Latin, complete with multifarious crossings with his hand over me, and some sprinkling of the water about my head.

Overall, though it lasted nearly a quarter of an hour, I had to confess that the experience was disappointing. The language deployed possessed various exciting points, but I witnessed no special phenomena and felt nothing remarkable during or after Father Thomas Edmund concluded. It all seemed pedantic and decidedly lacking in atmospherics. It reminded me of my scholarly endeavors with Aquinas. I stifled a sigh and tried to raise a cheerful, untroubled countenance to the friar.

Father Thomas Edmund Gilroy's eyes twinkled at me. "I am sorry to disappoint, my dear."

"Oh, I am not disappointed." I considered whether this lie was a sin and where it would fall in my chart.

"The behavior of demons is only theatrical inasmuch as it can terrify or deceive the credulous sinner. It really isn't exciting at all. The real, exquisite beauty and wonder is to be found in contemplation of divine simplicity, which often prompts no consolation or feeling at all."

I doubted him but tried not to show it. "I suppose so."

"You do not see it, nor do you feel it. Valuable though those two points may be, they do not have any sway upon what is or is not in fact reality. Emotion and experience can be assets. They can also mislead. Your ability to discern—your pragmatism—is one of your strongest attributes. Do not underestimate it."

"Thank you." Gratitude was not the appropriate response, but I had no other idea what to say.

"Well, well," he said, still smiling. "For now, perhaps it suffices to say, do not go about fraternizing with strange women in burnt-out houses anymore, and when your dreams are tormented by Marcus Zoran or anyone else, come and speak to me at once."

"Perhaps…" I took a deep breath and said, with more desperate speed than coherence, "Perhaps I could be one of them too—a nun I mean. I could live with them and learn and be like them and not…" I was going to say "be left alone," but the words stuck in my throat.

Father Thomas Edmund looked at me appraisingly. "Do you desire to become a nun?"

"Well…" Truth seemed inescapable on such a point. "Not terribly. Do nuns usually want to be nuns?"

"Usually."

"I suppose that's that then!"

Part of me was relieved—after all, would not that life have required me to spend more time in prayer and silence like Isabel? Yet I was hurt at the lack of a special calling to this separate life. My own father hadn't wanted me, I thought with maudlin self-pity. Why should I assume this Papist God would?

I laughed, affecting lightness. "It was only a notion that came into my head. I am sure something will come up soon enough. Some post, I mean. I have not begun to search yet, but I am sure—"

Father Thomas Edmund was still smiling. "I don't think you will be left in desolation and want, Athene Howard."

"I hope not," I retorted. "Although that would probably mean I was due to be one of your saints. Your Church seems fondest of the unhappiest people."

He chuckled. "What outlandish notions you have, Miss Howard. Now come. Brother Giorgio will be anxious that he has not seen you since breakfast."

This was not the first time that Father Thomas Edmund or others had joined me in the small dining room of the guest house. That day, as we supped, a most alarming companion presented himself: Father Pierre. He settled himself opposite Father Thomas Edmund and began slicing an orange with exquisite precision. I watched, fascinated, as the man preserved even the tiniest bit of pulp. I wondered if even a drop of juice would be lost under his cautious eye.

Another friar entered then. He was a tall, youthful fellow with an English face and manner, but he wore a world-weary expression that seemed in conflict with his appearance. Father Thomas Edmund introduced him to me as Father James.

"Well, James, I believe we have reached a resolution," Father Thomas Edmund said cheerfully.

Father Pierre glanced once at me, then at Father Thomas Edmund, before returning his attention to his orange.

"Yes," said Father James. "It took some untangling, but your concerns were justified."

"Your father's notebook," Father Thomas Edmund continued confidingly to me. "It confirmed many concerns raised among those who oversee our universities. 'Whose is the money?' That was the question your father asked. As you know, questions of influence of a more philosophical nature have concerned our order of late, even prompting the meetings between Father Pierre, the master general of the order, and the Holy Father. We called in Father James here to assist."

"Are you involved in finance?" I asked.

"Alas, yes," replied Father James. He looked as if he might have said it was a weighty, dull business and aging him with perverse swiftness.

Father Thomas Edmund repressed a smile and went on. "He's done all the requisite digging and has found some problematic connections, now dutifully removed."

"Tentacles of evil even in your midst!" I cried. "So, my father's notebook *has* been of use!"

Father Pierre finished his ritual dismemberment of the orange, tidied the remains, and rose. "Indeed."

He turned and left us. With extraordinary strength of will, I refrained from making a face at his departing back. Then I caught Father Thomas Edmund's discerning eye and blushed.

"Your father was insightful about money in this instance, even if he was not as prudent—usury-ly."

For a moment, the weight of the world vanished from Father James' face, and he looked like a mischievous schoolboy. "One more rotten pun out of you, Thomas Edmund, and we will ex-*change* you for a Jesuit."

I interrupted their chuckling, "But why is he—Marcus, I mean—here?"

Father Thomas Edmund frowned and nodded. "It is not unexpected, of course. He is here for Isabel, certainly, but for what else…"

"The money is everywhere," said Father James. "When we begin to pull upon that thread, we find snares all over—government, the universities, organizations, properties—even land upon this hill."

"And can you not stop it?" I cried.

"We can only address that which is in our proper province."

"You did see William Cantor," noted Father Thomas Edmund. "That at least is within my purview, and I mean to look into it." He smiled. "But here is good Brother Giorgio, and I believe he has— why yes! It *is* panna cotta!"

That night, even with these pressing questions still unanswered, I once again slept the sleep of the just, untroubled by dreams and sustained by the mysterious workings of whatever powers cooperated with the pastoral efforts of Father Thomas Edmund—and perhaps with the soothing influence of the substantial dessert provided by Brother Giorgio.

The next day dawned bright, clear, and strange. It was a festive day, and I was generously invited to join. The daughter of a loyal patron to the house at Santa Sabina was to be married.

We went along as a merry throng to witness the marriage ceremony. At least twenty white-robed friars were in attendance, including Father Pierre, Brother Philip, and Father Thomas Edmund, as well as Brother Leopold in brown. Sister Agatha, plagued with a headache, remained behind, but Isabel was present too.

My untroubled night had renewed me, and I viewed the scene with decided satisfaction. The nuptial Mass, performed with pomp and solemnity, took place in a tiny church on the outskirts of the city, where the countryside rolled out in stolid contentment all around. I wondered why it had not taken place in one of the major basilicas, and one of the elderly matrons endeavored to explain the familial significance of the location. But then the ceremony began and, with many unintelligible whispers and gestures, she mercifully abandoned me.

Afterward, we ventured forth to commence what promised to be many days of celebration. As we approached the place prepared for us, I heard music and laughter, smelled the aromas of wondrous foods, and felt the rush of earthy, reassuringly human fellowship. Marcus Zoran seemed a perverse, an impossible dream. There could be no viciousness in a world with such honest pleasures.

Someone behind me clicked his tongue in satisfaction. Brother Philip was there, weaving his way past me to the group of musicians. He spoke something into the ear of the leader, who listened, laughed, slapped the young friar upon the back, handed him an instrument, and pointed to a bench. In the next moment, Brother Philip had joined in their merry music making.

A young Italian with indecently beautiful eyes invited me to dance. Without any pretense toward grace, I threw myself into the country dance. Breathless, laughing, and exuberant, I weaved in and out with the rest of them, delighted in this feeling of freedom and exhilaration, as a child might when freed from petty chores and infant cares. As I danced, the thought of Father Pierre's satirical eye flashed into my mind, and I glanced in his direction. I could just see him in the distance, entering the rectory with the local priest whose nose looked like a porous red sponge.

Relieved, I laughed in the cordial embrace of a farmer who smelled strongly of olives, then passed into the arms of his neighbor who smelled of cheese, and continued down the line of delightful strangers.

The moon, waning, seemed in a benign mood, not begrudging the illuminative efforts of thousands of candles and twinkling strung lights wound about the rafters of a timber loggia that might have been constructed merely for this wedding feast.

Feast, indeed, it was. Round Italian matrons served more food than even Brother Giorgio could have managed—pastas and breads, wines and red sauces, carbonara and artichokes, spicy greens and smooth cheeses. I devoured it all with enthusiasm that would have looked debauched in any other setting.

Meanwhile, Isabel helped in the kitchen, not speaking, not minded by anyone, and Brother Philip continued to play with that merry band with an ease and immediacy that seemed almost magical.

For some time, Father Thomas Edmund walked apart with a pale, pimpled young man who stood wringing his cap in his hands, whispering something no one else could hear.

The marriage itself, though often lost in the bustle, came to me in little glimpses. More than once I saw the little bride beaming and blushing on the arm of her groom, his eyes brightened by wine and anticipation—acknowledged, approved lovers shyly clinging to each other. The company, with no shyness whatsoever, commended them and even offered impertinent personal suggestions. One weeping matron was embracing the bride while Father Pierre and the local priest, who had emerged with an even redder nose than before, were both raising their hands in benediction when a sudden new noise intruded, rending the peace and the joy of the night with one ruthless blow. A rushing, miasmic discordance that spoiled the beauty and brought back terror.

It was the howl of a wolf.

All heads turned, craning to see.

He stood on the crest of a naked hill—a monstrously large animal, his head thrown back in reckless abandon as he sang his bloody paeon to the waning moon. Sleek, curling fur and sinewy muscles, a massive, monstrous, magnificent creature.

"Jean-Claude!" Isabel's voice broke from the silence.

The legends of folklore were suddenly fresh and clear in my memory: the lycanthrope, recognized in wolf form, freed of the chains of moon madness and restored to himself.

No such miracle would there be that night. The wolf looked down at us—looked long and hard and straight at Isabel. Then he howled again so loudly that my ears rang with pain.

The next moment, he leapt from the far rock and disappeared from our view.

Before anyone could move, Isabel broke from the company and leapt upon one of the horses tethered alongside the road. Six men jumped forward to stop her, but she thundered past them. In a moment she would be gone—she would, she must be upon the wolf, no matter how quickly he sped through the hills. We raced after her, the men now bearing rifles, and a rush of robed figures, brown and white, among the hunters.

Then we saw a second creature, contorted and canine, in the middle of vicious transformation, loping up a side street from the west, in desperate pursuit and blood lust. A voice shrieked—I recognized it, as if in a dream, as mine. "Isabel! Isabel, look out!"

The feral wolfman sprang from the shadows. The next moment, his savage teeth and claws latched deep into the side of the screaming, terrified horse. Locked together like some horrifying hybrid of folklore and myth, the wolf and his victim hurtled around the small square, with Isabel fixed in her saddle like some maniacal carnival entertainer. Men raced to assist and were thrown back in the rush of claws and teeth and shying hooves. One man—the farmer with whom I had danced—lost his balance and would have been trampled before our eyes had his fellows not dived in and pulled him to safety.

The tormented horse shrieked and tossed to escape the teeth. Three times I saw men raise guns then lower them in despair of a clear shot.

The hooves nearly caught me in the teeth. Brother Philip, his instrument abandoned, grabbed me by the arm and threw me toward one of the screaming matrons. She gathered me up and, no matter how I struggled, dragged me away from the scene. Over the matron's round arm, stained with red sauce, I saw Isabel turn. With a lurch that had the force of her entire body behind it, she drove down the horse on top of her assailant. Teeth, claws, fur, black dress, and writhing flesh merged in a contorted crash upon the ground.

The dust of the melee settled, and Isabel rose to her feet. Her face was white and her breath came in sharp, quick little gasps.

The horse whinnied and flailed upon the ground, lying at such an unnatural angle that even I could see it was cruelly, wretchedly wounded. Wounded unto death. Isabel saw it too. Gazing down at the raging animal, she announced, "His legs are broken."

Before anyone else could move, she pulled a rifle from the hand of one of the men and fired into the head of the suffering creature.

The blood splattered against her dress. In one last kick of collapse, the struggle was ended. The horse lay dead. I looked away, sick at the brutal sight. The crowd stood, stunned into silence.

I heard, without fully understanding the noise, the low "Oooooo-huuuuu…" of an owl.

"He is gone," declared Isabel. "Pursuit is fruitless."

The distant prospect indeed held no lupine form. When I looked back, shrinking, Isabel was gazing down at the dead, crushed wolf. "Fool. Blind fool. I warned him." Then she glanced at the horse. "What a tragic waste."

Brother Leopold was at her side in a moment, kneeling beside the dead wolf, grief in his honest face.

"Are you all right, Miss Howard?" It was Brother Philip. "I hope I did not hurt you?"

"No, no," I whispered, still gazing transfixed at the two dead animals upon the stones. "Who was it?"

"His name is Luke," he whispered back.

"It—it can't be!" I gasped. "It mustn't be!" The Franciscan Brother Luke. The tormented friend of Jean-Claude, the first of the wolves I had ever seen, months earlier in Zagreb. Now he was dead upon the stones. Dead in the height of his madness. Dead a wolfman. Dead and, for all I knew, damned.

I looked up at Brother Philip with tears streaming down my face. "What…" I began. Then a new horror intervened and robbed me of speech.

"Murder!" a woman shrieked in the distance. "Murder and death!"

The crowd mobilized without a clear plan for battle. A young man, stumbling and covered in blood, appeared from the eastern road, calling out a garbled mess of hysteria and pleas for help. Behind him, three men came, echoing his cries, with a bundle in their arms.

"Look away, Miss Howard," Brother Philip ordered over his shoulder as he moved quickly to share in the weight of that limp, broken bundle. I did not obey and saw the little lifeless hand—a child's hand—tossed and bumped with their hurried steps.

From the murmuring, clucking whispers of the women behind me there rose such a moan of agony that I wondered the heavens did not shatter in testament to their grief. The mother, young but with streaks of gray in her thick black hair, broke from the restraining arms of her kin, stumbling forward to clasp the dead boy in her arms. She collapsed with him to the ground, his black curls mingling with her own as if offering a caress he would never again return. For a moment, I met her unseeing eyes, wide and staring, as she rocked and moaned and wailed to the unfeeling moon. The lanterns and candles danced about us, illuminating the scene in an uneven mosaic of dark red cobblestones, stained with blood and discarded rose petals.

I wept and wished I could be sick.

The crowd closed in around us, shielding the mourning mother from view.

"There are dozens dead!" cried the bloodied young man. "Dozens! A massacre! A massacre! The wolf was upon us—there was no hope! We fought but..." He broke off, tearing at his bloody hair.

A stout, bald man, his face red with rising rage, stalked over to the dead wolfman, uttered a curse upon him—half pagan and half Christian—and spat upon the dead body. Brother Leopold, still kneeling beside his fallen brother, bore his part of the spittle without flinching. Several other men came forward to urge the indignant man away. Two of the white-robed friars raised Brother Leopold to his feet then turned to assist in the removal of the dead body. I watched their movements as if in a dream—a horrible, waking nightmare.

"We are too late," said Isabel beside me.

I looked at her through my tears, uncomprehending.

She stood there, silent and still, so unlike the dramatic figure who had leapt upon a horse, crushed her assailant, and dispatched the suffering animal. Her eyes, as glassy as those of the grief-stricken mother, stared out—not toward the scene of tragedy before us but into the distance that had consumed the wolf form of her brother.

"We are too late," she repeated.

"Too late for what?" I sobbed. "For the boy?"

"That is Jean-Claude's work. Too late for the boy. Too late for his mother. Too late for that...the other. And too late for Jean-Claude." The wind caught a wisp of Isabel's hair, its dark color a contrast against her face, drained of all color. "Yes, we are too late. Now we do not hunt to save. We must hunt to kill."

"And how many times would you kill him?" I demanded, though without understanding my own words.

"As many times as it takes."

With that she walked away into the crowd and disappeared from my sight.

CHAPTER 24

13 AUGUST 1906: ROME

He who aims at making an entire and perfect oblation of
himself, in addition to his will, must offer his understanding,
which is a further and the highest degree of obedience.

— St. Ignatius, *On Perfect Obedience*

WHAT WAS LEFT OF THE NIGHT GRANTED ME LITTLE REST. AS SOON AS
we returned to the monastery at Santa Sabina, I collapsed into my
bed, my senses deadened into one exhausted, throbbing ache. It must
have been nearly dawn by the time I drifted off. I opened my eyes
and could not tell if I had actually slept.

Isabel was no longer in the room. She had been silent since our
return and I, for once, was eager to avoid further talk. I assumed she
had slept—or not slept—and risen early to return to her prayers and
the consoling silence of her God. I wondered how it was that I had
not heard her depart. I must, indeed, have been asleep.

As I dressed, I tried to rouse myself to some sort of enthusiasm
with the thought of Brother Giorgio and his unending store of
hot coffee. Raw and sick, my stomach rebelled even at the thought
of that all-too-necessary stimulant. The mere maintenance of life
seemed too heavy a burden.

With what must have been an allotment of supernatural strength,
I prepared myself adequately to leave the room. I was making my
way down to the dining room when I turned a corner and nearly
collided with Sister Agatha.

I started back, and my apology caught in my throat, never to
emerge. Sister Agatha was in hysterics, clutching the beads at her
waist and tripping on her white skirts in her haste. The moon-

shaped birthmark on her face stood out like a dark blemish against her horror-blanched skin. Even before she spoke, I knew all too well what she would say.

"She is gone. She is gone!"

"Isabel?" Father Pierre's sharp voice came from behind my head. I turned to see him approaching from the door that led to the church. Father Thomas Edmund walked beside him.

Sister Agatha was weeping now. She held out a piece of paper to the prior, and I craned my head to read the few words inscribed upon it.

Forgive me. Pray for me. — Magdalene

"Ten years!" wept Sister Agatha. "She seemed ready! She seemed so free! Then all of this!"

Father Pierre looked at her without speaking. Almost imperceptibly, a flush mounted his face.

"It is even more serious," said Father Thomas Edmund. "I spoke yesterday with a young man attached to the British ambassador. He is serving here in an advisory capacity regarding financial dealings. This morning—Father Pierre, I grieve to tell you, but Father James has just come and told me that William Cantor has taken his own life."

"No!" I cried. "Impossible!"

"Yes, and I fear—I am sure he was as deeply enmeshed in the dealings of Marcus Zoran as it was possible for him to be."

"We must hurry," I insisted. "All these things converge together! We can't lose her now!"

"But don't you see?" cried the Breton nun, her regal serenity shattered and her voice broke with suffering. "We can. They always can be lost!"

I stared at her. In a flash, I envisioned her life—envisioned in particular the loss she had suffered perhaps many, many times. The disappointment. The struggle against disillusionment and desolation.

The struggle to remain faithful, remain hopeful, in the midst of so much poignant loss. I thought of my father.

"Yes," I said. "They always can be lost...or saved."

Sister Agatha and Father Pierre looked at me—she with the tears still streaming down her cheeks and he with the mounting red slowly receding.

"She is right," said Father Thomas Edmund. "Whatever other games he has in play, the desire for vengeance is constant. He cannot get at her directly, for she has closed her mind to him. He attempted to reach her through Athene. When one door closes, he seeks another. A more subtle spiritual assault has failed, so now he is more direct. For months he has pursued her, taunted her, tempted her. Now he openly assails her with the sight of her brother in that form, and the sight of the bloody consequences of his descent. Isabel has extraordinary—almost inhuman—control of herself at all times. This was so sudden and sharp that she reacted when, under other circumstances, she would have remained cool and controlled. What does that mean?"

"That he has succeeded," Father Pierre replied.

"I do not know that," I interrupted. "I trust Isabel. The only thing that might weaken her resolve against him is a chance to save Jean-Claude, and I don't see one—not yet. Perhaps not at all. Also..."

"Yes?"

I moistened my lips and clenched my toes in my boots as a silent, invisible mark of determination. "Is he not also accountable to that other creature?"

Father Thomas Edmund once again came to my aid. "Yes, we must recollect the demon to whom he owes his own powers. She will demand tribute."

My father's voice echoed in my ears. *She seeks sacrifice. The scent of flesh and blood raised in tribute and the feeding of her hounds.*

"All demons seek death and destruction," Father Pierre began with mild impatience, "but..."

Father Thomas Edmund forestalled him. "Forgive me, Father Pierre. I believe Athene is right in this, even in her trust of Isabel. I do not know what she has done, but I do not believe it bodes well for the plans of Marcus Zoran. She is not wise to proceed thus, but we will help her in spite of her disappearance as best we can." His eyes were grieved, but he was smiling. "There is much to do, and we must hurry."

"Where do we begin?" I asked.

Father Pierre's voice broke in. "You, Miss Howard, will remain here."

"What?" I cried, aghast.

Father Pierre looked at me with all the cold, autocratic intensity of his entire being. "The work that must be done is neither safe nor appropriate for an undefended young woman, Miss Howard."

I balled my hands into fists and pressed my nails into the palms to keep from screaming my exasperation. "I keep telling you all, it is this sort of nonsense that has led to heroines being left in highly vulnerable and ill-informed positions and thus killed throughout literary history."

"As we are not engaged upon a question of literary history, this subject is not open for debate, Miss Howard," he replied with unendurable calm. "You will, however, be relieved to learn that you will not be left vulnerable. You will remain here in the monastery, as will I and Sister Agatha."

I could not quite say that I would rather be unprotected than imprisoned, but I thought it. I looked appealingly to Father Thomas Edmund and found, to my dismay, that he was meeting the gaze of the austere prior. Then he slowly nodded. "Athene, it is for the best. You are already known to Marcus. Who knows how he may strike at you—or at Isabel through you. And if Isabel should return—"

"This is one of the cruelest tricks ever played upon anyone, *ever!*" I declared with a tragic lack of eloquence. Stalking into one of the little parlors, I sat down, arms crossed, in as masterful an imitation of an infant sulking as might be seen.

They all ignored me. Preparations bustled all around me. The door was still slightly open, so I could watch. They were all intent upon their shared task and ignored me. I sat, a smoldering mass of resentments, finding fresh cause for annoyance in every person and thing that met my eye.

At least a quarter of an hour had passed when a brown-robed figure laden with strange objects entered the room. Brother Leopold walked forward, set down his burden upon the table, and after one glance in my direction, went about his work without interrupting my self-pitying interior monologue. After a few minutes—during which the injustices suffered by Athene Howard outweighed everything from the massacre of the Holy Innocents to the worst excesses of the French Revolution—his activity distracted me, and I began to attend to what he had in hand.

He was methodically folding a large collection of what appeared to be nets—the sort used in the capture of large animals. I reached to feel the strength of one of the nets and found it far surpassed my expectations. A creature caught in such a snare would be held fast for some time. Brother Leopold clearly expected good hunting—there were at least twenty such nets in his pile. Folding completed, he reattacked the pile, taking each net and rolling it tightly. One end he pulled free and used to bind up the rest. I noticed he used the same method with each net and wondered if, like the knots tied by sailors, his were designed to unfurl when wielded in the hands of an expert.

"I don't understand," I began, but then I hesitated, feeling that what I was about to say would prove a breach, if not of etiquette, of decency.

He looked up.

I took another approach to the question. "Seeking Isabel—I do understand. And, up to a point, I have understood the seeking of her brother. But after last night, after what Isabel said last night, why do you have such care in the recovery of such a creature? Even if he were restored to manhood, he does not seem to me to be a good man. Isn't Isabel right? Shouldn't you be hunting to kill?"

Brother Leopold returned his eyes to his preparations, finishing with the last of his nets and stowing them all in a large canvas bag.

"We seek to save wherever and whenever we can. And to offer the hope of redemption."

"But does it ever work?"

"Oh, yes," said Brother Leopold. "It can work. Some men do choose redemption when it is offered."

"How many?"

"Perhaps one in one hundred."

"The odds sound decidedly unpromising," I said. "What of the others?"

"That, Miss Howard, is the business of God's mercy. Now. These are ready."

"What happens if your ropes snap?"

"There is a greater fisherman and his net perdures. Also—" He pulled forward a large, flat, irregularly shaped briefcase and opened it. At first, I thought it contained a brace of pistols and wondered if he planned to challenge Jean-Claude to a duel. Then I realized there were four small guns with oddly large barrels.

"What are those?"

He produced another case of a similar size and, opening it, disclosed a dozen long medical syringes filled with a bright silver liquid.

"Folklore decrees the silver bullet for the dispatching of werewolves," Brother Leopold said, looking down upon this array of weaponry. "We prefer a recipe of our own. Hundreds of years ago, the English would have called it dwale—an herbal concoction for the soothing of suffering men and beasts. Vinegar, bryony roots, henbane, mulberry juice, hemlock, mandragora, opium…"

"And that will…"

"Rightly administered, it will render the beast unconscious."

"But wrongly administered?"

"We do not administer it wrongly," he said simply.

"Is this…this business a common occurrence?"

"There is evil," he agreed, "but in the cities it tends to be concealed or more publicly presentable than this particular malady permits.

Most of these poor creatures are driven out into the countryside. Reduced to scavenging. Sometimes we hear of them and attempt capture before a shepherd kills them. The creatures are not often organized as they may be now. That takes a more powerful mind than is usually left by the ravages of the madness."

Brother Leopold closed the case. I noted a large round medallion engraved upon it, about an inch in diameter and displaying a cross above a pair of keys. A swarm of bees, primed for battle, circled the front of the cross and keys.

"What is that?"

"It is the Clypeus Medal," he replied. "My great-great-grandfather received it from the hand of the Holy Father. It has passed down to me."

"But what is it for?"

"It was commissioned before the formal papal decree identified the spheres of revenant missionary work—the Dominicans committed to the undead and we Franciscans to the oppressed lycanthrope. This was an Ambrosian guild, comprised of lay men, laboring together and willing to sacrifice their own lives while working for a common purpose."

"The saving of souls?" I hazarded.

He bowed in agreement. "And the dispatching of evil revenants."

"*Christus lux nostro et clypeus*. Christ is our light and shield." Memory stirred. "Sir Simon is one of you."

He looked surprised.

"I heard him use that phrase in farewell once."

He nodded. "He is indeed an honored member of the guild, as was my great-great-grandfather. The guild is not widespread anymore, but there are pockets of activity rendered authoritative by cooperation with the mendicant orders."

I thought of Sir Simon and wished he had been there. He would almost certainly have agreed with the others in leaving me "safely" behind. Even so, it would have been a reassurance to have so strongly built a warrior among us. Brother Leopold, while not

301

precisely skeletal, appeared to have embraced poverty to the degree of pronounced leanness.

"I suppose all his business back and forth has involved the guild?" I inquired.

"He is diligent in his labors for the guild." Brother Leopold finished his packing, placing the two cases within his large canvas bag along with the nets, and rose to leave me.

"Do women ever receive the medal?" I asked.

He looked back at me. "Sometimes." He smiled, strapped his well-packed bag about him, and left.

I walked to the door and watched the retreating brown back with its wolfman kit.

Father Thomas Edmund came up behind me. "What are you thinking, my dear?"

"He seems committed to saving these lycans."

"He feels their plight deeply." His voice was quiet.

A thought struck me. "Is he one of them? One of the few?"

"Yes," he replied. "He is of their kind."

"But he's not a wolf now?"

"Not for nearly twenty years."

"Is it safe for him to be about this work? I mean…I suppose you'll be out in the moonlight and is that not…dangerous?"

"In many cases it is not prudent. Some, like Brother Leopold, are called to this work and find in it both resolution and preservation."

I considered the point then recalled myself. My cheeks warmed. "Father, I do beg your pardon for my ungracious behavior. Forgive me."

"Of course, my dear. It is a hard trial to be excluded from this now, I know. It is best, however, that you remain safe."

I sighed and tried to appear as if I were not still resentful. "How often do you deal with this sort of business?"

"Oh, once or twice a year. Not usually quite on this scale. This is a special case. The history and the complexity of the relationships make it so. My dear Athene, we must go. We will return soon. Pray for us."

Then he too left me.

The hours of waiting stretched on to eternity. I went listlessly to the dining room, and Brother Giorgio clucked and fretted over me like a mother hen over a recalcitrant chick. One might have thought I had skipped every meal for days rather than simply missing my breakfast. All his ministrations only reminded me that I had been left behind to be protected from all harm. I escaped from the kind old man as quickly as I could.

There was no sight of Sister Agatha. I assumed she was off somewhere and in prayer. Father Pierre appeared, like clockwork, upon the hour to find me in my wanderings. Every time, our exchange was the same.

"Are you well, Miss Howard?"

"Yes, Father Pierre. Thank you."

He would nod and say, "All will be well, Miss Howard." Then he would leave me for another hour. I tried to convince myself he was only concerned for my welfare, but I felt sure he was also checking on me to ensure I had not fled from this kindly prison.

I opened my shorthand notebook for nigh on the millionth time, endeavoring to make sense of my father's notes and to find there an absolute answer to the whole mysterious business. And, as I had every preceding time, I threw the book from me in unenlightened disappointment.

I paced my room, paced the doorway in front of the church, paced the gardens, and, when Brother Giorgio left the sacred precincts, paced the dining room.

Why had I obeyed? They had no real power over me. I could not, however, bring myself to flout the wishes of Father Thomas Edmund. I felt, moreover, that I could not openly rebel against Father Pierre. Much as I disliked the man and was sure he disliked me, I could not bring myself to disobey him. This conundrum was too much for my overtaxed brain to process.

Finally, through what seemed endless hours of walking, I burned out the fire of my resentment and felt reason and docility returning. I made my way down to the church, selected a spot at the furthest back of the nave, and for a long time thought of nothing whatsoever. I sat indecorously upon the ground, concealed by shadows, and leaned my back against a wall.

Whichever took possession of me then—meditation or sleep—it was violently disrupted when a browned hand with dirty fingernails reached out and grabbed me by the shoulder.

I jumped and stared into the face of a ragged peasant boy with wide black eyes and curly black hair which, by the odor, must have been rubbed with garlic.

"Signorina!" he hissed before thrusting into my hand a letter smeared with some dark brown stain.

"What is it?" I demanded. "Who are you?"

"Urgent! Urgent!"

He ran out of the church, slamming the doors behind him.

The echo was still upon us when I saw Father Pierre approaching from the far end of the nave, near the altar. He frowned at the door then looked to me.

"I don't know who he was," I said, "and he gave me this."

I handed the letter to him and watched as he opened it, still frowning. By the steady movement of his eyes, I could trace his progress in reading the page. When he reached its conclusion, he raised his eyes and began again. My impatience was reaching a fevered pitch by the time he finally handed it back to me. "It concerns us both, it seems."

The letter was brief:

PIERRE,

Isabel is found. We cannot return. I beg your patience and your assistance. Come to us at Santa Maria Sopra Minerva. I will explain further when we meet. Bring Miss Howard. She too is needed.

— TEG

"Father Thomas Edmund sends for us," said Father Pierre unnecessarily as I read it over a second time. "It appears urgent. We must go."

Now it was my turn to frown. "Are you sure it is safe? It contradicts all that was discussed this morning."

"Do you have any specific reason for suspicion of this letter?" Father Pierre tapped the paper with one long finger.

"No," I smiled wryly. "Nothing but the instincts derived from reading too many secular texts."

"Such instincts are not entirely out of place in such unconventional enterprises, Miss Howard." He considered the letter again. "I fear too much the dangers from delay. Sister Agatha will remain here. We will take every reasonable precaution and travel quickly. I shall have the porter summon us a cab."

Thus, within five minutes, I found myself opposite Father Pierre in a horse-drawn conveyance with a sturdy-looking Italian at the reins. The cab was black all over and provided with black curtains, black tassels along the edges of the seats, and even black ornaments along the ends of the windows—balls, and carved leaves, and what might have been an attempt at flowers. Odd that a vehicle could look so funereal when not operating under the authority of an undertaker.

I looked at Father Pierre and was shocked to see his face. He looked concerned—such a man could not be convicted of something so plebian as worry—and even tired. I was moved in spite of myself. I took a deep breath and rattled out my script as quickly as I could before anxious thought could interrupt. "Father Pierre, I must beg your pardon. I did desire to guard Isabel, but I failed. Please—please forgive me."

The priest turned an astonished face toward me. As I watched, another emotion succeeded the first. I could not discern what it was. "Miss Howard—" He stopped and turned his head, as a dog might when his ears prick at the sound of some strange, unknown approach. "Why have we stopped?"

Father Pierre leaned out of the carriage, and I peered from behind him. We were in a little wooded lane, oddly isolated this close to the city. A few stone buildings were visible amid the bushes, but I did not recognize the neighborhood.

I was about to ask Father Pierre where we were when a volley of shots rang out over our heads. I threw myself into the corner of the carriage. If I could have crammed myself into the seam of the aged upholstery, I would have done so.

"Father Pierre!" I hissed. "Do not...! Come inside! Come back inside!"

That regal profile was still recklessly extended through the window. "A man has fallen. He is down beside the horses, and he is badly hurt." He reached for the handle of the door as if he intended to step out of the carriage.

"No!" I cried. "Father, no! Leave him!"

He did not listen but swiftly left the carriage. I could hear the driver blustering and swearing and fighting his team of horses, which kicked and reared and whinnied. Peeking out the open door, I watched as Father Pierre hurried to the side of the fallen man who lay just outside the reach of the shying hooves.

It was then that the strange thing happened.

The man who appeared to be dead sat up so suddenly I thought it was the manifestation of his disembodied soul rising from his corpse. In the next instant, I saw him raise a pistol and turn the barrel so that, in perspective, it contracted into a single round point aimed directly at me.

I froze, and the world froze with me. I heard the report of the gun as if it had been fired from a great distance. Yet a movement of light came before it—a flash of white anticipating the flare of the vengeful bullet. Father Pierre stood with his back to me, a formidable barrier before the window.

For a moment, he stood so still that, even through the black of his cloak, I could see the gory, gaping hole in his back. Then he pitched forward on his face into the grass.

I wrenched open the carriage, careless of danger, and knelt beside him on the ground. With an effort, I turned over the body. Terrified and frantic, I marked the spreading red stain, like wine spilled across the rippling folds of white fabric across his front, and black, grotesque gore at its source.

The horses tore in their harness. The driver cried out, "Signorina! Run! English lady, go!"

"Please," I begged. "They will come at any moment! Please! Help me!"

"Signorina, run! Oh, lady!"

I heard the flurry of equine feet and wheels, and I turned to see the driver and his team fleeing around the corner, abandoning me and Father Pierre with his murderer.

I looked up, wild-eyed, at that villain. He was lean, with thick black curly hair and freckles—half a boy and not yet half a man. He looked at me with wide, alarmed eyes.

"Help!" I cried, not thinking how ludicrous it was to ask a murderer for help. "Please, help me!"

He shook his head. Then, as swift and lithe as a young gazelle, he dropped his gun, turned, and ran away into the forest.

"Is there no one?" I cried. "Father Pierre! Father Pierre! Please!"

I looked down at him as if he could save us both from this dire impasse.

Father Pierre was looking over my shoulder. The pain had vanished from his brow and a soft, childlike contentedness had taken its place. As I gazed down at him, tears spilling from my eyes to mingle with the seeping, dark blood, the merest smile crept upon his lips, and a gentle light appeared in his eyes. It was the sort of look one might see in the dawning comprehension of an infant who knows that he gazes up, not into strange, blurry uncertainty, but into a loving face.

His hand gripped mine over the wound, gripped it with more strength than I would have expected in a dying man.

"Please, sir," I begged, sobbing. "Someone will come soon. Please, Father."

He shook his head, still looking beyond me. That quiet smile pulled at his slackening mouth. "Look…look, child," he gasped. "My dear child, look!"

I turned my head to follow his gaze. I saw only the woods and the desolate, empty expanse of a tepid sky. When my eyes returned to his face, his jaw hung loose. His eyes, still and lifeless, stared into nothingness.

"Father Pierre?" As I whispered his name, horror crawled across my skin, sending shivers across my entire body so that my teeth rattled and my toes shook in my shoes. The fit was still upon me as my eyes, fixed upon the body of the dead priest, involuntarily focused anew on the leaves of trees that bordered the heath—a barrier of green that slowly parted. It released one, two, six—a dozen or two dozen tall, broad gypsy men, attired in their motley blend of rags and country dress. The murderer was with them, no longer wide-eyed but striding along with an assumed air, half of confidence and half of nonchalance at his new status as the murderer of priests.

The shortest of the men—a stout fellow in green with a face that looked as if a giant had sat on it—chewed upon the end of a soggy cigarette for several moments before spitting it out and barking some short command in a dialect I could not identify. A jeering, appreciative laugh broke out from a skinny tall man. The short, stout man silenced him with a glance. He ambled up to where I clung to the body of the dead priest.

Someone—something—approached. The men stepped aside to receive this new presence.

Small, wizened, and cruelly triumphant—such was the face of the gypsy queen we had seen in that little village outside Zagreb so many months before.

"You must send for a priest," I said through my tears. "You must."

The old crone cackled and coughed. She gave a shrill command. Someone struck me upon the head, and I fell to the ground unconscious.

CHAPTER 25

14 AUGUST 1906: ROME

So she departed, she and her companions, and
bewailed her virginity on the mountains. At the end
of two months, she returned to her father, who did
with her according to the vow he had made.

Judges 11:38-9

I AWOKE TO STRANGE SMELLS AND UNFAMILIAR CLOSENESS. OPENING
my eyes, I beheld an unknown space made of red, orange, and brown
objects that blurred in my bruised vision. My head ached from where
that ungentle hand had fallen. I turned it instinctively before pain
and disgust overcame me, waking me fully to the reality of the dirty
rag gagging my mouth. My hands too were bound. I could feel the
ropes tearing into the flesh of my bruised wrists. With every lurch of
the world about me, pain intensified.

After several throbbing moments, as the lurching continued and
was accompanied by the rattle of wheels, I realized we must be in
some small carriage or wagon. A filthy vehicle, from the smell of
it—I could now delineate a mixture of stale spices, strange herbs, and
uncleanliness. I wrinkled my nose in revulsion.

With consciousness, memory returned. The faces of my captors
flashed before me, and a new, sick terror flooded my brain. I was a
prisoner of the gypsies, dragged from the woods, bound, and subject
to torture or dishonor at their gross desire. My maiden flesh recoiled,
but I forced myself to gather my thoughts. In a moment I could
reassure myself. I had suffered no appalling violence. Not yet.

I moved my head again to try to clear my mind and evaluate
these unpalatable surroundings. I was leaning against something

cold, hard, and bound in taut fabric. My first thought—that it was some sort of carpet rolled up—I dismissed. It was too unevenly shaped to be a carpet.

The next moment, the answer came to me. It was not a carpet. It was not a blanket. It was not even a package. It was the body of Father Pierre Jarvais, bound up like a mummy in dirty burial rags, and rigor mortis was at its zenith.

This gruesome realization paradoxically brought comfort. I edged my trussed-up body closer to the dead priest and felt, somehow, that I was safer for it. I could not speak, but whispered frantic apologies in my mind, as if the clerical corpse could hear and as if the guilt were somehow mine.

We halted, and I rolled so that I was almost smothered against the body. Exerting my full strength to wrench my abdomen free and my face with it, I extracted myself and emerged even dizzier than before.

At the far end of the carriage—perhaps from the front, but I was too disoriented to tell which way was front and which was back—a curtain parted, and two figures stepped in. A fat man and a thin man, like something out of a vaudeville. I blinked to try to see my adversaries more clearly and thereby rendered them all the more like caricatures. The fat man was still chewing on a piece of straw, and the thin man was rubbing two bony hands together so vigorously that the dry, blotchy skin flaked off. The fat man leered and said something to his friend. They both laughed. I could not understand a word of it, but my heart thudded into my stomach, and I began to devise impossible means of self-defense against unknown, brutal horrors.

The stifled scream trapped in my throat emerged as a pathetic gurgle.

The men stepped forward.

A shrill rebuke and dismissal rang out.

At the opposite doorway, as if rising from a heap of discarded cloths, the bony, wrinkled face of the gypsy queen emerged. I recognized the grotesque, elderly creature. The memory of the most terrifying book of my childhood rushed to my mind. I had found it among a discarded pile and sneaked off to my room with my prize: *King Solomon's Mines*. The witch-finder Gagool of Rider Haggard's imagination. *Like a wicked antique monkey*, I thought. If I could have moved to hide my head under a blanket, I would have relapsed into childhood attempts at nighttime self-defense.

The men bowed submission to the woman—Tiena, whose name at least I could discern in so much incomprehensible mumbling— and left the wagon. My relief at not being the victim of base assault was soon undermined by even greater terror. If I were preserved, it was not for my own good. They had some darker plan in store.

Clapping her hands three times, Tiena called out a new command and, as if springing from the creases in the fabric walls, three women appeared to do her bidding. They favored me with more than one curious glance, but did not speak or question Tiena's orders. I was bathed, scrubbed with strange-smelling preparations and smeared with ointments and perfumes that made my head ache all the more and my stomach wrench with disgust. Dizziness came too, and I thought once again of suttee and the drugging of the widow before death.

This thought inspired me to a slight and momentary struggle. Three rough blows to the back of my head were my reward. I reeled. An arm was about my neck, while hands pulled my hair to force my head back. Someone pinched my nose, and I gasped. Tiena was before me, cackling as she poured some vile, suffocating mixture down my open throat. Thus pinioned and poisoned, I choked and gasped and lapsed into submissive half-consciousness.

My recollection of the ritual that followed comes like a hallucination, a vision deep underwater, or a dream from the life of another person. Paint upon my face, white fabric about my body, laughter and incantation ringing in my clogged ears. In my drugged mind's eye, I imagined myself as a highly painted doll or clown garbed in white—and white recalled something different yet oddly familiar. As familiar as my own lost face beneath this painted mask. Someone in white. I wanted someone in white.

As if from a great distance, I thought I saw a figure watching the proceedings—a trembling, dark-faced woman clinging with protective desperation to her wailing child. Then she disappeared, and the paint and incantation continued. A sudden blast of cold air stirred me awake. I struggled to clear my mind. The concerned face of Father Thomas Edmund was before me. I reached for him. "Father, help me!"

Someone thousands of miles away laughed and kicked me into silence.

Hours may have passed—or even days—before I opened my eyes. The weight of my eyelids was oppressive. The strength of Heracles, I thought without connection. Next came the stumbling, awkward, exhausting effort of walking. I *was* walking. In truth, someone was dragging me along. I shook my head to force away the clouds and blinked into the blackness of full-fledged night.

These were streets—the stones of the road jarred painfully, but the pain was helping to restore my dulled wits. I blinked and blinked again. I knew this place. I could hear water too. "The major tributaries of the Tiber River," said a guidebook in my head, "are the Chiascio, the Nestore, the Paglia, the Nera, the Aniene." Useless information, I thought, despairing. My head is full of useless information. Think, Athene, think!

We moved out of the shadowy streets. Suddenly, the full moon loosed her harsh shafts in blinding profusion, deepening the surrounding darkness. In that contrasting light, the shadowy bulk of Tiber Island rose before me, and I knew where I was.

Cloaked in darkness, the pack of gypsies moved with eerily silent footsteps across the Ponte Fabricio. I saw the piazzetta at the center of the island—cold, empty, and brutally illuminated with the moonlight—with a sense of clarified foreboding. Even in my distracted state, my mind sharpened with a sense of the awfulness of the approaching plan.

"Iphigenia," I whispered to myself. "Andromache." I preferred the latter. A hero had come to rescue Andromache. Iphigenia died, a sacrifice to appease the gods, to end the blood lust, and to ward off certain vengeance. The daughter sacrificed by her father's hand, that the ships of the Achaeans might venture forth and assault the walls of Troy. It was a poor analogy. The blood of Iphigenia only perpetuated the feud of the House of Atreus. Perhaps these gypsies had not read Aeschylus or Euripides. I was hardly in a position to recommend a course of study.

I stumbled and was dragged back up onto my bare feet and forced to continue on toward the monument at the center of the island. Was it to be the wolf, I wondered, or the demon herself? Either way, as we neared the place of sacrifice, I was determined to put up a fight once again. I would be no passive victim to this grotesque practice. I threw my full weight and struggled against the ropes that leashed me like a craven animal.

My determination was short-lived. The fat man in green leveled his open hand and boxed my ears, so that the blood rang in my brain and the world swam about me. How many blows could my head withstand before my brains were irretrievably addled? Perhaps I would not live to find out.

My attacker barked some command and another man—a lazy, vicious creature with a bulging stomach and a bowler hat—slung me over his shoulder for the last few yards. My head ached and the gag in my mouth bit painfully against the sides of my cheeks. When we reached the appointed place, he tumbled me to the stone-paved ground, shrugged his shoulders back into place, wiped the sweat from his brow, snatched a piece of long dry grass from a patch off to the side, and resumed his blank-faced bovine chewing.

A ferret-like man, giggling like a halfwit, took on the task of binding me with a chain across the front of the *guglia* in the piazzetta. I gazed piteously at the saints depicted above my head and wondered why they did not do something—some merciful, beneficent gesture to free or relieve me in this dreadful hour.

Meanwhile, the cackling gypsy queen approached in a rumbling cart chair drawn by three filthy, lanky little boys. They deposited their burden at the edge of the piazzetta and scurried off to the side to await further orders.

With the awkward gait of age, Tiena tottered forward to where I cowered, muzzled, bound, sick, and hopeless. With one long black fingernail, she lifted my face and leered down at it. Then she pulled her hand away, leaving a long, deep scratch upon my chin, so that I choked down a wordless cry of pain.

"The blood price," she hissed. "The blood price."

Father Pierre's young murderer, whose casual manner seemed studied, froze and looked at his compatriots with suspicion.

"Yes!" The queen closed her eyes as if in ecstasy. "Yes! The blood price. Blood for blood. Death for death. All must be appeased!"

The young man's eyes flashed resistance, but his look vanished into sullen submission as four tall men stepped toward him. They bruised him and bound him but did not mock him. Then they dragged him to the other side of the guglia and chained him there. They would take no chances. The priest was dead, and the priest-killer must die if the people were to escape the curse without commencing a new one.

"Come," cried Tiena, her hand upraised in command. "Leave this place! The beast will come to claim his prey." Her next words were spoken in their strange dialect. They roused the crowd of gypsies to chant and cheer with enthusiasm. They moved together across the Ponte Fabricio, and not a face turned back to look upon the young man or me.

No one had stopped to think about my place in this whole network of blood feuds. The girl without father, mother, country, or creed was expendable. It was all very well for the gypsies to be so eager to protect themselves. I might have had more sympathy had they not been so reckless in the disposal of my person. Perhaps they would have been better preserved from such situations if they did not go about chaining innocent people to Christian monuments to be torn apart by wolves.

I was lost in such bitter meditations when two strange noises dragged me from my thoughts and back into the present. The first was the long, low hoot of an owl. The second was the gentle clank of the chain opposite. I turned to look toward the companion of my fate.

He was not looking at me. Nor was he any longer staring with dull resignation into the dirt, as if contemplating his own mortality. He was squinting into the moonlight.

I heard a third, unmistakable sound: the familiar mechanical clicking of a well-oiled bicycle coming toward us.

My heart began beating with frenzied haste. I squinted toward the sound. A figure was riding toward us from the Ponte Cestio. Even in the moonlight, his form was unclear. A dark, undefined figure perched above spinning wheels, with the sharp, unmistakable form of a rifle strapped upon his back.

He was within a few feet of us when I recognized him.

"Princess," said Mihai, "I have come."

This was undeniable—no other creature on earth could boast such wiry limbs and raucous curls. I made muffled noises encouraging him to hurry and unbind me.

"I shall free your mouth. But, princess, you must be silent!"

For several seconds after he removed the gag, I could be nothing *but* silent. I worked my jaw to relieve the stiffness and gulped down air to soothe my parched throat and tongue.

"Water," I whispered.

Mihai nodded and held his finger to his lips once again to enjoin silence. Producing a small, corked bottle from his pocket, he opened it and lifted it to my lips.

The sting of some intemperate drink, which was *not* water and not any beverage known in civilized circles, nearly annihilated me for a moment. Then the impact lessened, and I found the pain had been scorched away. I glared at Mihai and whispered a half-sincere, "Thank you."

He nodded.

"Now, my wrists!"

But Mihai walked to the other side of the pole and stood over my unwilling companion.

The boy looked up at him, resigned and mutely appealing. He had not been gagged but did not speak. Instead, he raised himself up onto his knees and bowed his head in submission.

"Slayer of priests," said Mihai. "I am not the knife of Tiena. I have hidden *her* far from the vengeful claws of the gypsy witch. Now I come to rescue this princess. Will you take charity and fight along with us?"

At this singular invitation, the young man looked up and responded with an eagerness that could not have been feigned. "Yes, Master. I will serve."

"I am no master." Mihai leaned down and cut away the cords that bound the young man's wrists. "But here is your weapon. If you turn on us, I shall kill you. Now, come and take your place."

Thus armed and united, the two young men turned to range themselves on opposite sides of the guglia.

"Mihai!" I hissed. "Cut me free and I shall help!"

"We will protect you, princess," he said. "I have protected *her*, and I will protect you."

"What?" I cried in horror, forgetting all caution.

"You must remain. The beasts must have their prey. You will draw them. We will meet them. We will triumph, or we will die."

"That is a wretched idea. Mihai! This is ludicrous! Mihai!" I struggled against the ropes and tried to kick him. "Cut me free!"

Instead of obeying my desperate command, he bent, rifled through his large sack, and produced a handful of something sharply pointed—stakes, I thought. More suited to vampires. Perhaps he had come equipped for all possibilities.

I soon realized my mistake. Planting the objects in the ground in a circle around us, Mihai retraced his steps along his freshly sown path, lighting each one. A revelatory series of rockets fired, exploding in the air as a deafening, colorful display of fireworks. Red, yellow, green, orange, and blue assailed the white light of the moon.

"Are you mad?" I shrieked.

"Be silent, be still," Mihai whispered. "The beasts approach."

I continued to protest but our new ally turned, shook his head, and gestured to indicate that he would gag me if I did not obey. I sat down miserably on the stones and tried to look as invisible as I could in a bright white gown, surrounded by lunatic gypsies with bizarre notions of allegiance and idiotic ideas about female security, illuminated by moonlight and fireworks, and bound to a pole in the middle of the piazzetta, exposed to the merciless hunger of a pack of demon-bidden wolfmen.

"Saints and angels and perhaps the Virgin too," I muttered, "if you have any concern in this, I'd be obliged if you would do something."

There was no howl. My first awareness of the creatures came from a low, rhythmic panting that grew in volume and seemed to come from all sides of the island. Then—there! Slowly moving out of the darkness and into the open embrace of sterile moonlight, the pack made its approach. I watched in dreadful fascination, futilely endeavoring to count them—once, twice, three times. Sometimes it seemed there were fifteen. Then sometimes twenty. Over and over I began the count again, and all the while they made their slathering, heartless approach, drawn as if lulled by waves of moon-mad melody to devour the flesh of this sacrifice. It was exquisite and absolutely sickening. I wrenched my eyes from the sight and continued to pull at the ropes that bound me.

"Dear God," I whispered, tears of desperation beginning to drop from my eyes, "Dear God. Holy Mary. Someone. Help me."

Something small and white caught my attention—something moving about the periphery of the piazzetta. I stopped in my struggle and stared. There was nothing to see. I blinked—there it was again. And there again. Someone else was here—someone else steadily approaching on all sides.

A lean, brown, limping, maimed creature was nearly upon me, licking his lips over broken teeth, his red eyes twitching in greedy, canine delight.

"Father, Son, and Holy Ghost!" crowed Mihai at the top of his lungs. "The alloy! The alloy!"

Suddenly, with a roar, Sir Simon's massive form erupted across the Ponte Fabricio, wheeling an enormous quarterstaff about his head, racing like a battering ram into the midst of the beasts. The wolves drew back. Three of them seemed bent on repelling the assault, but the quarterstaff was upon them in an instant, and they lay dazed and tangled in a heap, leveled by one mighty stroke.

At his heels, a stream of figures in white, with black cloaks billowing, flowed with unnatural energy into the piazzetta. Brother Philip reached the pole first. In a swift, deft moment, he removed his cloak and threw it over my shoulders. Then he bent to untie me.

A snarling beast leapt upon him and threw him to the ground. I shrieked and struggled futilely to assist him.

"Stop struggling!" cried one of the friars at my elbows. He had raced in, a brown-robed blur from the opposite side, and bent with cold, dry hands, to the task of untying me.

"Help him!" I screamed.

The sound of a muffled gun interrupted me. The beast collapsed, groaning, an emptied syringe still sticking from between his shoulders.

"Brother John!" Brother Leopold, a tranquilizer gun in each hand, threw one to the Franciscan at my side then swung free one of his nets. Thus poised, he faced his quarry.

Sir Simon reappeared from the melee of fur and furious, feral assault. "Finally!" he said under his breath. Then he set to with his quarterstaff again.

"Not that one!" cried Brother John. "*That* one! The legs! Not the head!"

"Stand down!" roared Sir Simon. He flung pell-mell back among the beasts, swinging his staff with ferocity and scattering furry adversaries in every direction. Brother Philip and Brother William leapt after him, the former gracefully and the latter less so, assisting the Franciscans in lassoing necks and binding legs before the stunned, moon-crazed creatures could recover themselves.

Three or four man-wolves howled in craven dismay and scampered off, escaping from the island into the city beyond. As the dust settled and the men and their torches finally surveyed the battlefield, the moon, drifting across the sky like a sulky goddess, glanced back at us and, as if permitting the tips of the train of her blue-white gown to pass over the scene, displayed before us six trussed, salivating, mewling, miserable creatures, helpless from blows and well-wielded snares.

Sir Simon was breathless, staff still in hand, and seemed to be gathering himself to deliver a thundering rebuke to his brown-robed companions.

Before he could speak, Father Thomas Edmund ambled amiably into the piazzetta. "The process of scholastic discernment does not operate well on a battlefield," he remarked with the merest twinkle in his eye.

"Cursed…confounded…foolishness," began Sir Simon. "If you are not going to…to fight…keep out of my way."

"You can't go about braining every poor creature in your path," Brother John rebuked him.

"I can and will if it saves you from being torn to shreds," he snapped. Then he groaned. "Blast it…"

I gasped. "Did they hurt you?"

"No, only a scratch. One of those creatures you wanted me to spare, Brother. He fair near took a bite of me."

"That's him over there." Brother Leopold seemed unconcerned at the tacit accusation. "He will go with us and perhaps have a chance."

A howl echoed in the distance. I shivered despite the woolen folds of the black cloak. "What I want to know," I said through chattering teeth, "is why on earth you are all are out here on a moonlit night. Can't you consult a farmers' manual or something to determine the days you ought to stay safely at home?"

"That is precisely what we do," said Father Thomas Edmund. "How else can we find what we are looking for?"

"You were looking for wolves?"

"Looking for wolves and for our stray lamb." He smiled. "And this is not a moonlit night."

I pointed upward. "It most certainly is."

"Nevertheless, I tell you, this is the night of the new moon. There is a dark unreality at play."

My trembling intensified.

"Father—Father Pierre—" The words caught in my throat.

"I know, child," said Father Thomas Edmund. "I know. Your driver was not a brave man but nor was he indecent. He brought word to Santa Sabina and thence to us."

"You did not send for us. The letter was false. But how were we to know?"

He patted my shoulder. "You could not, my dear. You did as well as you could."

"How did you find me? Have you found Isabel? What brought you here?"

"One question at a time, my dear. We have not succeeded in our efforts."

"Someone's been leading us a wild goose chase all over the countryside," supplied Brother Philip.

Father Thomas Edmund nodded. "We returned to find you and Father Pierre were gone. Sir Simon had returned and was raging about the place like an angry bear."

"He accused us of managing to lose all the womenfolk in his absence," put in Brother Philip. "Then the driver of the carriage appeared, but—"

"But," continued Father Thomas Edmund, "before we could do anything, Mihai strolled into our midst, hooting and offering to bring us straight to you. He has been following the gypsies for months and knew all from the moment of your capture."

"Obliging of him," I replied tartly. "I have much to address on that point with our 'Mihai ex machina...'"

Sir Simon materialized again at my side. "Miss Howard, did they—" He stumbled with uncharacteristic awkwardness. "Are you..."

"Oh, no," I reassured him. "Honestly, if it hadn't been so dire in its probable consequences for me, tonight's events would have been fascinating. I was frightened, but they couldn't—they didn't harm me. Not in the way you fear. You see, they really couldn't. The chosen victim must be unstained. Unspoiled."

"The less said of that, perhaps the better—" began Father Thomas Edmund.

"The sacrifice," I interrupted him. "It was a virgin sacrifice. To appease the wolf. Can't spoil the sacrifice before she is devoured or it might not work."

"Unnatural girl!" Sir Simon cried. "Where on earth did you learn—"

"*The Golden Bough*. Or, if you prefer an older source, Ovid."

For a moment, Sir Simon struggled to regain his composure. "Athene, you really are the most..."

"I am sorry," I said. "I think I must faint now."

And with that I collapsed in a heap at Sir Simon's feet.

CHAPTER 26

14 AUGUST 1906 AND INTO THE FOLLOWING MORNING:
AVENTINE HILL, ROME

It is the season when the most scorching region of the heavens
takes over the land and the keen dog-star Sirius, so often
struck by Hyperion's sun, burns the gasping fields. Now is
the day when Trivia's Arician grove, convenient for fugitive
kings, grows smoky, and the lake, having guilty knowledge of
Hippolytus, glitters with the reflection of a multitude of torches;
Diana herself garlands the deserving hunting dogs and polishes
the arrowheads and allows the wild animals to go in safety, and
at virtuous hearths all Italy celebrates the Hecatean Ides.

—Statius

I praise you because I am fearfully and wonderfully made.

— Psalm 139:14

"DID I FAINT?" I ASKED WHEN I AWOKE. I FELT COMFORTABLE AND
safe, which was odd because I recalled a great deal of trauma and
violence. Shaking my head to dispel grogginess, I registered the fact
that I was on the grass on the side of the piazzetta and held tightly in
Sir Simon's arms.

"Yes, you fainted. And before you ask, it was not at all graceful.
Your eyes rolled back into your head and you collapsed into a
gurgling heap."

"Are you well, Athene?" said Father Thomas Edmund. "This has
been too much for you."

I struggled into an upright position, reluctantly removing the
supporting arms of Sir Simon. "I am well. Death by being torn apart
by werewolves would have been too much for me."

"Yes. If they had torn you to pieces, there would have been far too much of you—and all over the place too."

I laughed. Then I groaned and held my hand to my head. "This whole business is not conducive to health, is it?"

As my fingers brushed against my forehead, I thought of that familiar image of Athene leaping from the head of her father Zeus. Then my father's face flashed into my mind. *Remember*, he'd said, and the voice echoed in my brain. *Remember*. In a fit, as if of brain fever, I saw the swirling, dancing images in new clarity. *Tricks for the bemusement of fools*—that was Marcus Zoran. Green balls juggled in the air, balls with gypsy faces carved on them. The unearthly white skin and intense eyes of the woman in the shell of our residence in Tournai. Father James speaking of land upon Aventine Hill. And my own voice, "I wonder what happens when the gods want their feasts back…"

"What is today?" I cried.

"It's nearly midnight," answered Father Thomas Edmund.

"But of what day?"

"We are on the brink of the fifteenth of August."

"That is it! The Nemoralia! My father said it. That's what this has all been about. The money. The possession and torment. The killing of Father Pierre. Even this silly business with the gypsies. It all paved the way for the Nemoralia!"

"Lie back down." Sir Simon would have forced me to obey his command, but I pushed his hand away.

"I'm quite all right—let me finish! The Nemoralia is a festival in honor of the goddess Diana. The virgin goddess of the moon. The huntress. Her festival culminated on the fifteenth of August—it is culminating now! And how should she reclaim it? Through bloody, vicious sacrifice. The feeding of her hounds. This is not the altar. This is a cheap, grotesque distraction. A trick for the bemusement of fools—and we are the fools. Don't you see? She wants it back!"

"Wants what back?" demanded Sir Simon.

"That!" I pointed desperately to where the Aventine Hill loomed far above us. "This is Rome! Rome! Why are there no men shouting at us from the windows, demanding silence? Why are the streets not teeming with outraged citizens annoyed at our noise? Why is there a brazenly full moon when there ought not to be one? It is not yet finished. There is a darker act being played—concealed behind some mysterious curtain that separates us from the eyes of the world even in the middle of this city—and we must be swift to arrive in time!"

Father Thomas Edmund had stood still through my speech. For a prolonged, excruciating moment he remained silent, looking up toward the crest of that long-sacred hill. A gentle wind caught his robes so they fluttered ever so slightly. I thought of what I had read months earlier in the writings of Aquinas, describing the movement of the Spirit.

Slowly, he lifted his arm and pointed toward the hill.

We all followed the direction of his finger, peering up toward a far distant point—not as far as Santa Sabina but hovering beside it. A faint but undeniable glow.

As if inspired by our awareness, the fire intensified so that, even at that distance, we could see it was a wide circle of torches. "A midnight ritual," I murmured. "The Nemoralia."

Father Thomas Edmund's voice broke in with crisp authority. "Brother John, attend to these poor creatures. Brother Philip, Brother Leopold, come. Brother Vincent..." He turned to face the young Frenchman.

I had not even noticed him in the frantic battle, but there he was, on the far side of the piazzetta, kneeling on the ground, gazing down at some huddled mass in the grass—the bound-up body of Father Pierre.

Brother Vincent looked up slowly and met the eyes of the priest. "I shall see him brought home with dignity."

Father Thomas Edmund nodded. "I shall send you assistance." Then he turned and called, "You will come with us, Brother William."

There were two more yet to join our ranks. Mihai bowed low to Father Thomas Edmund then pointed in the direction of his newly pledged slave. The murderer of Father Pierre Jarvais fell on his face at the feet of Father Thomas Edmund. He said nothing.

"Come," said Father Thomas Edmund quietly. "Come, boy. We have work to do. Run ahead of us to the doors of Santa Sabina. Ring the bell without ceasing until they come. Tell them Father Thomas Edmund requires immediate help. Bid them ring the bells. And bring me my other bag. Go! Run."

The gypsy boy set off at a sprint across the bridge and up toward the silent church. Mihai, abandoning my bike beside Brother Vincent, took his place at the front, and we set off.

The climb up the Aventine Hill was like a procession, lit by electric torches borne in the hands of monks. Processions ought not to proceed at such a rapid pace, perhaps, but there was a rhythm, half militant and half ritualistic, to the ascent. Even at this speed it would take at least ten minutes to reach the top—ten precious minutes that brought us closer to midnight.

The others did not seem weary at all. Sir Simon strode ahead beside Father Thomas Edmund, with Mihai persisting alongside them. I spared a moment to note, with relief, that Sir Simon was intent enough on the pressing business at hand to be distracted from his protective instincts. Otherwise, he would have sent me back to be locked up in safety, and I would have had to battle against him.

Brother Leopold, his eyes closed in prayerfulness, walked beside me without mistaking a single step. A swath of that false moonlight overspread his face for a fraction of a second, showing the strong potential for transformation still lurking within him. It was gone in the next instant. The friar, unchanged, walked quickly. I said nothing, afraid to rouse him from that prayerfulness in case it might be a sort of armor protecting him from lunar influence.

Brother Philip hurried on the other side of me. Even without his wide-rimmed, outlandish hat I could have identified him by the instrument strapped to his back.

"Do you bring it everywhere?" I whispered.

I saw the ghost of a grin in the missish moonlight. "You never know when music will be useful," he whispered back.

"To lull the beasts?"

"That depends on their taste in music, I suppose." His chuckle was a youthful echo of Father Thomas Edmund's. The lines of exhaustion stood out unnaturally on the brother's face, emphasizing the early gray of his hair, but when he smiled, the weariness melted away. "Bring the wolves. The hounds are ready for them."

We continued in silence, onward and upward along the side of the hill. *Up, up, up to face the fire-breathing monster Cacus.* The words resounded in my mind. Here the monster had hidden in ages long past, lurking over the Tiber river. No Heracles to crush him now. Had ancient inhabitants seen mist or fog about the hill and attributed it to the monster? Innocuous natural occurrences, translated by the imagination into something of sinister, preternatural import. Perhaps even rainclouds, gathering as they were even now.

I stopped, startled, and stared.

"What is it, Miss Howard?" Brother Philip turned to me then followed my gaze back up to the hill. The sky, hitherto cloudless, now displayed a single, long, condensed stream of white, circling down from around the moon and moving at a rapid pace toward the crest of the hill above us.

"The curtain!" I whispered. "And the goddess!"

Brother Leopold froze and gazed upward, as a dog might when about to sniff the air and discern the scent of danger. "Run!" he cried and set off at a loping pace up the hill to where the road, not yet consumed by the clouds, stretched before us.

We obeyed. The billowing clouds continued to rush with unnatural speed, as if they were drawn down by hand to wreathe the top of the hill, isolating it from the rest of the city below. We were nearly at the top, and the clouds nearly upon us, when Brother William stumbled. Brother Philip and Father Thomas Edmund dropped the wide black bags they carried and turned to assist him, but the clouds descended upon them and cut them off from view. I moved to help, but Sir Simon grabbed the discarded bags with one hand and with the other pulled me forward, far from the wall of cloud now sealed between us and our lost friends.

Brother Leopold, Sir Simon, and I stood there, gazing back down the hill. The false face of the full moon, in a sky once again cloudless and cold, stared down on us with icy complacency. The barrier of impenetrable cloud cut us off from the rest of the world—from our lost brethren. Three seconds later we would have been trapped, like them, below the drama on Aventine Hill.

No one spoke. Brother Leopold closed his eyes. His lips moved again in prayer.

My heart sank into my stomach. I was on the verge of tears when I saw something move in the midst of the fog—something or some *things*.

Father Thomas Edmund and Brother Philip, bearing the limp body of Brother William between them.

Brother Leopold opened his eyes and moved quickly forward. So did Sir Simon, and together the men bore the deadweight of the young friar.

"Is he dead?" I whispered.

Father Thomas Edmund shook his head, coughing and endeavoring to inhale the fresh air.

I leaned over the prone figure and smelled a strong fragrance of poppies, as if his habit had been saturated in perfume, and heard the reassuring snore of deep, contented sleep.

"No, no." When it finally came, Father Thomas Edmund's voice was hoarse and halting. "He will be well enough."

"He's drugged," said Sir Simon. "And we will be too if we don't hasten."

I shook my head. "I don't think so. Look. It has stopped. It would have cut us off from the hill. But instead we are inside it, cut off from the rest of the world." I looked up. "But why does Marcus want separation at all?"

"For someone's glorious triumph, no doubt," replied Father Thomas Edmund wryly.

Sir Simon slung the sleeping Brother William over his broad shoulder, and we continued up the hill. I felt, rather than saw, the ruins of the imperial palace of the Palatine far below. It was as if we climbed some sacred mountain—Olympus or Sinai, Etna or Kailash, Athos or Ida—far above the petty world of men. We were entering the realm of the gods, and the gods were displeased.

I glanced at Father Thomas Edmund, who bustled along with untroubled step, and recalled Santa Sabina at the top. For this sweet, bespectacled friar, though he once again carried his bag of revenant-battling weaponry, we were merely walking on the path toward a house of prayer.

The circle of torches was not far ahead now. I would have slowed my pace and approached with caution, but the men marched on. Even bearing the weight of Brother William, whose red hair bounced and danced with each jarring step, Sir Simon's stride did not slacken.

At the edge of the circles we halted. Fifteen torches, in clusters of threes, had been spread at regular intervals in a wide circle. At the far side sat Marcus Zoran. His coiffured white hair, released from its usual slick confinement, danced in a breeze I could not feel. He held a pomegranate in one hand and wielded a sharp, thin dagger in the other. With delicate, precise movements he extracted bright, juicy avrils from the core of the fruit, one shining jewel at a time, licking each one from the tip of the knife.

Without looking up, he called, "Did you enjoy your first act, Athene? I could not have deprived you of your moment to take a central role in the stirring drama! You are welcome, dear Miss Howard. Such wonderful fruit." Thus signifying his return to more important matters, he continued munching contentedly.

Father Thomas Edmund Gilroy stepped into the circle and set down his large bag. Sir Simon, after rolling Brother William with care onto the grass, marched forward and stood beside the priest.

"Ah, me," sighed Marcus Zoran. "So few delights in life." He stabbed the stump beside him so that the blade vibrated, flashing in the moonlight. Next, he dusted the discarded flesh of the fruit onto the ground, rose, and pulled a red silk handkerchief from his breast pocket, with which he removed the juice from his delicate fingers. This purification accomplished, he produced his cane as if from the air and leaned on it as he turned to look at us.

"You have been quite a bother, all of you. Quite tiresome. Now, shall we play?"

He sauntered our way, swinging the cane at his side and tapping it rhythmically upon the ground. He was within a few yards of us when, lifting the cane into the air, he raised it as a conductor might wield a baton to swell the song of an invisible orchestra.

From the bowels of the earth, a rumbling, creaking noise rose all around us. Long, clawed hands, part skeletal and part canine, emerged, like the ruthless, tearing hands of the maenads of Euripides or the pitiless, crooked claws of the harpies of Virgil.

A translation echoed in my brain. *You should have seen one ripping a fat, young, lowing calf apart—others tearing cows in pieces with their hands...hung up in branches dripping blood and gore...*

The words faded quickly in the face of this new, appalling reality. A host of mangy, hideous, half-decomposed lycanthropes stood before us, assembling to themselves undead flesh and wiry fur imperfectly patched. I counted twenty-one before I abandoned the sum in despair. Snarling and writhing, they advanced. The howl of a wolf sounded low and long in the distance.

In an instant, Brother Leopold stood between me and the undead creatures, pistols in each hand. Brother Philip threw his hat to ground, peeled off his cloak, and stood beside him, producing matching weaponry. The tamburica strapped to his back twanged anxiously.

One of the snarling, hideous creatures advanced. He retained enough of the form of a man, even in this bestial, half-rotten transformation, to bear the power of speech.

"Traitor," hissed the creature through his snarling teeth.

The others growled their agreement and continued forward toward Brother Leopold.

Marcus Zoran laughed. "Midnight comes! What a delicious moment! Shall we declare its approach together? Ten seconds... eight seconds...six...four..."

As a perceptive theater critic might see through the trappings and glean the heart of the drama, Father Thomas Edmund did not appear impressed by the performance. I could not imagine him lapsing into such a discourteous action as to roll his eyes, but he turned his head toward the darkened mass of the Dominican church beyond and, illuminated by the false moonlight, I saw his eyebrows dryly elevated.

"Three...two..." crowed Marcus Zoran.

The crystal peal of the alarum, rung from the bells of Santa Sabina, interrupted him, shattering the rhythm and distracting wolves and men. A harsh, adolescent snort broke from Brother William.

A group of white figures were hurrying out to us, led by Mihai and the murderer of Father Pierre. I picked out the faces of Father James, Brother Ephrem, and Sister Agatha.

Father James, carrying a second large black bag, stood beside Father Thomas Edmund. Father Thomas Edmund gestured toward the bag at his feet, and Father James knelt and began rifling through both.

Meanwhile, Brother Ephrem pulled up Brother William from the ground.

The red-headed friar yawned and rubbed his eyes. "Have I missed Prime?"

Sister Agatha, her veil fluttering behind her, hastened to me. Her hands were upon my shoulders. "Athene," she breathed into my ear, "child, are you all right?"

I nodded.

No further speech was possible. Marcus Zoran, perhaps annoyed that our attention had been drawn away from his own performance, reinserted himself. "She comes!" he cried, his eyes wide and shining. "She comes!"

As if on cue, a gust of wind sped about the circle, extinguishing the torches and whipping up the white hair of the occult master into a wolf-like coiffure. A flash arched down from the moon and nearly blinded me. Blinking away the shocked whiteness from my eyes, I beheld in the center of the circle a sleek, veiled figure standing majestic and tall—the woman of my vision in the burned house. Her cold, white face looked sternly down upon us. Without speaking, she extended a graceful, strangely lengthened white arm, with long fingers and sharp nails pointing—not at us but off to a darkened edge of the circle.

From this shadow, a figure in black walked forth with deliberate step.

"Make an end!" cried Isabel. "I am here."

Sir Simon muttered something in an exasperated breath. Sister Agatha moaned, and my own despairing cry caught in my throat. Father Thomas Edmund said nothing. Mihai, looking completely unperturbed, bowed toward her.

"Come!" cried Marcus Zoran, almost dancing, a grotesque picture of unholy delight. "Come, Isabel! Come and beg! Come, girl!"

"What would you ask of me?" The dulcet tones of the woman in white rang metallic and unnatural to my ears. I wondered, as one wonders in a dream, what language she was speaking.

"Vengeance!" cried Marcus. "Vengeance!"

A shaft of light shot from the moon, like a flaming arrow, to the center of the circle and the feet of the woman in white. The torches reignited all at once. The woman's voice grew harsh with desperate yearning—vicious, all-consuming hunger. "The blood. There must be blood."

"Yes, yes," said Marcus with a touch of impatience. "There will be blood. Plenty of blood. Always blood. Blood and despair and destruction. Won't there be, Isabel? Oh! Were you ready to kneel?

Are you ready for punishment, Isabel? Will you go on your knees? On your knees!"

She continued to approach until she stood only a few feet from him. He shot out one hand and slapped her face so violently that the force threw her to the ground.

In an instant, the circle erupted into ferocious conflict.

The wolves broke free of some invisible restraint and attacked. Five were upon Sir Simon in an instant. He tossed them off and beat them with the quarterstaff, a massive bear grappling with a fierce pack.

Four more advanced upon Father Thomas Edmund, who met them with a steady eye. They came within a few feet before a large net, thrown by Father James, gathered them up together, a tangled, enraged mess of fur and bloodlust. Brother William, still half asleep, lent his weight alongside Brother Ephrem to pull the net, binding the creatures. From beneath his cloak, Father Thomas Edmund produced a large, hooked stake, which he thrust at the center of the heap, driving it deep into the ground to clamp down his quarry.

The leader of the lycans leapt and pinned Brother Leopold, wrenching the guns from his grasp so they flew far from the friar's reach. One fell in the bushes, and the other landed painfully on my right foot. As the brother in brown struggled to keep the snapping teeth from ripping off his face, I scrambled to pick up the gun, steadied myself, and fired repeatedly into the creature's back. Three needles poked from it but did not abate its fierceness.

"The—the other one!" gasped Brother Leopold.

Before I could make any further attempt, another creature knocked me to the side as it leapt to set upon Sister Agatha, choking her with the beads at her waist. I turned to her aid, while Sir Simon charged in with his quarterstaff to beat off Brother Leopold's assailant. For once, no Franciscan voice cried mercy. I tore at the greasy, wiry fur of the beast, struggling to evade the savage teeth but desperate to free the shrieking nun. Brother Philip was upon us in a moment, raising his tamburica in one well-aimed blow upon the head of the wolfman.

Amid the sickening sound of the crushing of bone and wood, the heroic swan song of the strained strings swelled and burst, whipping forth to lacerate the stunned face of the beast. The creature collapsed upon the ground, whimpering. Brother Philip struck him a second time, and there was silence.

As I unwound the rosary from Sister Agatha's throat, Brother Philip threw the destroyed tamburica, pulled free the snapped strings of the instrument, and used them to bind the limbs of the unconscious beast. "It won't hold for long."

"Can't you kill it?" I demanded.

He did not respond but retrieved his own guns and fired three shots into the back of the largest of the wolves. The creature convulsed and howled and collapsed. The stilled body passed through rapid stages of decay, a counter-metamorphosis into destruction, until the creature was reduced to a heap of rotten, indistinct matter.

Brother Leopold rose, leapt, and rolled to evade two more creatures, kicking at them as he passed. Scrambling, he retrieved his gun from the bush to fire at the creatures, which immediately decayed into dust.

Brother Philip, gasping for breath, held his arm, and I saw blood staining his white robe. Yet he did not pause but hurried to assist Brother Ephrem, who was beset by three other beasts.

Sir Simon ran forward, quarterstaff raised, bellowing fury, straight in the direction of Marcus Zoran.

With an answering howl, the massive form of the wolf Jean-Claude bounded through the fire and into the circle, capturing the left shoulder of Sir Simon in his jaws so fiercely that I heard splintering bone and tearing flesh. Through his teeth, a stifled roar burst from the wounded hero, and he fell upon his knees. Marcus Zoran, laughing, turned from Isabel long enough to kick Sir Simon, sending his body hurtling toward us, knocking down Brothers Ephrem and Philip as he rolled.

I ran to his side, gasping, "Oh! Oh! Are you killed?"

To this unhelpful response, he commanded through still-clenched teeth: "Isabel!"

I obeyed, turning toward the hill where Isabel lay upon the ground, unmoving. As I watched, she raised her head and gazed down at me.

The calm voice of Father Thomas Edmund, now in an uncontestable tone of command, cried out a name in Latin and again in Greek—the name of the demon goddess. The awful, pale beauty of the infernal woman exploded into the sky, expanding into the massive form of storm—a storm where the face of the goddess flashed in white and purple, a vengeful harpy or a blood-crazed gorgon. Shrieking, she bent to attack her prey and fell back, collapsing into herself so that the wind and waves of water reverberated outward into the empty air.

Father Thomas Edmund strode forward into the midst of the storm. He held forth a crucifix in one hand and a small silver wand-shaped instrument in the other, with which he sprinkled the face of the enraged hell-creature, and continued to challenge the roused demon.

"*In nomini Jesu Christi…*" chanted Father Thomas Edmund.

Brother William stumbled at his side, stifling a yawn and carrying a small bucket of water that sloshed and spilled every time Father Thomas Edmund dunked his weapon and renewed his rite of sprinkling. Father James followed in their wake, struggling with a large apparatus.

They proceeded unchecked by the force of the wind, yet it drove me back so that I had to fight to keep my balance. I could not obey Sir Simon's command to go to Isabel's side. A piteous cry broke from me but was lost in the cacophony of battle. All the while, the little, round-faced, bespectacled priest continued his ritual against the furious, hideous beauty of the goddess. I could hear his pleasant voice still chanting commands in Latin. The moon, contorted in fury, rolled and spun and flashed against his measured approach.

Marcus saw it too and hastened his own efforts. "Submit, Isabel!"

The wolf Jean-Claude advanced upon his sister, the blood of Sir Simon dripping from his fangs. His eyes blazed red in lust and fury.

Isabel had risen to her feet, but suddenly froze. Now she turned her back on the prancing figure of her father and the snarling wolf form of her brother. She knelt upon the ground toward Santa Sabina and bowed her head in prayer.

"Kill!" shrieked the goddess. She licked her ghostly lips and extended long, dry, bony hands, as a frantic, starved animal might strain for food. "Destroy! Tear her to pieces!"

Once more Marcus Zoran raised his hand and beckoned—a terse, wordless command, the command of execution.

The wolf Jean-Claude leapt upon his sister with a roar, claws outstretched, piercing her body with vengeful violence. Isabel went limp, and her face, contracted in pain, gazed up into the dripping fangs of the man reduced to a monster. In this final moment, as the werewolf prepared to rend his victim into fragments, Isabel whispered something to her brother. Then she closed her eyes and bowed her head in submission.

Father James cried a warning and Father Thomas Edmund Gilroy stepped aside. Father James fired from his weapon a cluster of rockets that twisted and spun until they exploded into myriad blinding white stars, raining down shining, crystalline salt upon our heads, lighting up the hill so that, by some wondrous influence, the moonlit world was transformed.

The power of the false moon wavered in the promise of the pale, damp yellow of dawn. An aging sky, bearing the trauma of the night, looked bravely down upon us. The clouds parted, and the wraith turned her colorless face away, pained at the advent of cleansing light. Then it was as if the world and all its tormented contortions paused. It seemed that all creation, animate and inanimate, turned to witness the final consummation of Marcus Zoran's vengeance upon his children.

"*Misericordes oculos*," whispered Brother Leopold, his face bloody and his habit torn. He fell on his knees and whispered again: "*Misericordes oculos.*"

The creature who was Jean-Claude froze, holding to himself the unresisting form of his sister, as the hailstorm of blessed salt fell about them. As we watched, the red light faded from his eyes. Suddenly, with a wrenching howl, the huge wolf flung the bloodied woman away from him. Isabel flew and rolled dozens of yards, landing beneath the branches of a small, shivering bush.

Sister Agatha and I rushed toward the fallen young woman, but astonishment arrested our progress. With a single, canine bound, the beast Jean-Claude crossed the blood-soaked grass and, in a movement that seemed more that of a man than of a beast, leapt to stand upon his back paws, flinging his front legs forward to grasp his astonished father. What looked like a moment of ravenous brutality lacked its commencement; the wolfman, his father trapped in that iron grip, rocked back and forth, as a weeping Madonna might rock the dead body of her son.

"Jean-Claude!" shrieked the enraged Marcus. "Jean-Claude! You stupid beast! Obey, you craven creature!" He struck the beast in the face with those jewel-encrusted hands so violently that the gems tore out bloody tufts of fur and skin.

The creature repaid no blow with violence. He did not snarl but rather moaned, as a dog in grief might lament the deepest agonies of an irrational soul.

Isabel raised her head and gazed up at the tormented lycan.

Marcus Zoran's eyes widened in alarm. "Stupid boy! Stupid! Do you think you can stop me? You cannot kill one who is already dead! Do you not see the power I wield? Do you not see her? You fool! You base, low, vicious thing. You beast! You slave! You gross, ignorant…"

Isabel, regaining her strength, crawled toward the two figures, panting in desperation.

"No!" cried Sister Agatha. "Isabel! No!"

No longer impeded by the storm, the nun and I ran toward her. Tripping over our torn, wet skirts, we scrambled up the slope to stop Jean-Claude's twin.

Mihai was well before me, with the nameless murderer of Father Pierre upon his heels. The boys raced up the side of the hill and pushed Isabel aside, each of them holding pistols from which they fired a shower of silver bullets while hallooing out that strange battle cry. "Death and freedom! Father, Son, Holy Ghost! Father, Son, Holy Ghost! The alloy! The alloy!"

Shots thundered around us, bringing on the illusion of a dance as the wolf and his prey, so closely held that they might have been a single figure, spun together in the ricocheting assault. Meanwhile the massive, retching, wheeling form of the goddess, cast down from the pinnacle of the hill, reached out with talons of air and moonlight, snatching futilely at the two struggling creatures. Shrieking and straining, whirling in a mess of teeth and torment, she plunged into the Tiber River, conjuring a pillar of suffocating water.

In the strange respite, I grasped Isabel's wrist and pulled her toward Sister Agatha with all my might.

"Let me go!" she shrieked. "Athene! Let me go! Jean-Claude! No!"

In the midst of the maelstrom, the wolf stopped and turned his large eyes, relieved of the red of madness, to stare one last time at Isabel, who now struggled like a wildcat to go to his aid. The talons of the goddess stretched one last, desperate time and clasped her prey. With a mournful howl, the wolf Jean-Claude, fighting against the demon's grasp, leapt with his struggling father locked in his arms from the height of Aventine Hill. A vast leap—an impossible one. Long before they could have reached the opposite bank and safety, the wolf and his victim fell through the dispersing cloud to be devoured in the gluttonous, watery jaws of the swirling Tiber.

As we stared, horrified, into the maddened waves, a shudder passed through the natural world, as if the burden of fever had lifted from a trembling body. Calm descended. Sir Simon stood close beside me and might even have spoken my name, but for once, I hardly marked him. Isabel ceased to struggle in our arms. Her eyes fixed upon the Tiber, after her lost brother. The moon regained a serene, impersonal countenance then shrank and faded into the western sky. The rich skirts of approaching dawn swept away the long train of her gown, sewn of cobwebs and moonbeams.

WE SEARCHED FOR THREE DAYS ALONG THE EDGES OF THE RIVER. Neither Sir Simon nor Isabel could be persuaded to remain home and recover from their wounds. The days were endless, persistent endeavors, with our company ill-rested and sick at heart. Through the nights, electric torches danced along the riverbank, over tangled, thorny brush complicated by the interjection of logs and tree branches thrown up by the wild tumult of the waters. Searching, fearing, and wondering.

On the third day, a boat piloted by Carabinieri dragged the river and produced a bulky, waterlogged mass. Their shout of discovery brought us all together on the riverbank—Sir Simon, the friars, Isabel, Sister Agatha, and me, along with many of the strangers who had come to our aid.

I could see nothing clearly as the boat and its unwholesome catch approached, but in a flash Isabel was in the water and Father Thomas Edmund stood beside her, fighting against the entangled carnage of flotsam to free that dreadful thing from the ruthless grasp of the waters. The others soon followed. There we were, a struggling, sodden crew, pulling with frantic desperation at that cold, grotesque thing in the rippling water.

It broke free from its invisible restraints, causing several of us to lose our balance and fall over. I went under water completely and was pulled out, choking and coughing, by Sir Simon. Sopping wet and chilled to the bone, I sat shivering on the riverbank, even less effective in helping the others than I had been before. Sir Simon wrapped me in his coat, and I looked the thanks I could not speak.

It took several men to draw the two bodies, still locked together, onto the shore. When Father Thomas Edmund touched the tangled corpses, they fell apart. Isabel knelt beside one form, while many hands dragged aside the other.

The men surrounded the second body, shielding it from my view, but for the merest instant, the robed friars parted, and I glimpsed the face of the older man. His mouth gaped widely, the rictus of a petrified scream captured in those bared teeth while his eyes stood open in a look that mingled skeletal fury and animal terror. As I watched, the long scar upon his face swelled and expanded. A sickening, wet sound followed, and the pieces of that splintered body, no longer held together by the influence of the goddess, collapsed into grotesque, dismembered fragments. The two halves of the head broke free of the neck and rolled unevenly upon the ground.

Once again, a form in white stood before me, blocking my view. Father Thomas Edmund met my horrified gaze.

"Athene," he said gently, "you do not need to see more."

"Yes, Father," I whispered, and looked away.

The head of the creature who had been Jean-Claude was cradled in Isabel's lap. With one pale hand, she smoothed back the straggly black hair and revealed the bearded, bloated face of a man with red and blue splotches on his skin from his long submersion in the water. The eyelids were closed, but I felt sure they could have revealed empty echoes of Isabel's own dark eyes. Across the face ran scarlet lines, such as would have been made by scratching fingernails.

I looked to Isabel. She sighed as if marking the unexpected peace that even I could discern on the dead man's face. Then she raised her eyes to mine, and I saw the stream of tears.

"Come," said Father Thomas Edmund quietly, "we shall bring our brother home."

Chapter 27

1–6 September 1906: Rome and thence to Calais

There is a sacredness in tears. They are not the mark of weakness, but of power. They speak more eloquently than ten thousand tongues. They are the messengers of overwhelming grief, of deep contrition, and of unspeakable love.

—Washington Irving

Three weeks passed, weeks of quiet and mourning. Weeks of tidying and convalescence too. Sir Simon, in defiance of the doctors and the Dominicans, had insisted on aiding in the recovery of the bodies. In doing so, he developed a fever and required nursing. This task Brother Giorgio and I undertook together.

"I have never been so fussed and fretted over in my entire existence," complained the Viking-Celt champion from his bed on the third day.

I handed him his dinner tray. "Nor so well fed."

"I could waste away into nothing," he complained even as he set to devouring his steaming bowl of soup packed with meatballs and greens and an enormous chunk of freshly baked peasant bread.

I perched myself on the windowsill of his room, the door left open for the sake of decorum, and gazed out the window to watch a long procession of worshippers approaching Santa Sabina for evening Vespers.

Sir Simon was still eating when I gave in to a strong impulse, pushed myself to standing, and pulled off the apron I had donned in assumption of my role as nurse. "I'll return after Vespers."

Astonished, he lowered his spoon. I scurried out of the room before he could speak.

In the church, I sat at the back, following the movements and degrees of the rite, silently speaking my own words of gratitude.

There was much for which to be grateful. The friars had dealt with the logistics of the crisis quickly and in an orderly manner. The morning after the discovery of the bodies, Mihai and Father Pierre's murderer left before dawn without speaking to any officials. Mihai bowed before Isabel, bending to kiss the air above her foot. "Farewell, princess. We will go to serve. We have much to atone."

The gypsy boy beside him nodded agreement.

"Does he have a name?" I asked.

Mihai shrugged. "If he did, he will have a new one. And a better one." They grinned at me and walked away from the church.

"What will happen to them?" I asked Father Thomas Edmund, who had come to give his blessing before their departure.

"They go on pilgrimage," he said. "I rather expect they will come to rest in some remote place, among some hard-working brethren. Perhaps Cistercian."

The body of Father Pierre Jarvais, returned to the priory of Le Saulchoir, was duly laid to rest among the remains of his brethren. I wondered if someday miracles would occur at the site. I had little experience of saints. Perhaps he was one. If so, I thought, saints were not always pleasant people.

One day I asked Father Thomas Edmund about Father Pierre and miracles over tea in one of the parlors. He merely smiled.

"But was he a holy man?" I insisted.

"I believe he was," said the friar. "And a good man."

"Does that mean he was a saint?"

"My child, I would not have you deny Father Pierre your prayers any more than I would have you deprive your father of them. Or me."

"Oh, Father Thomas Edmund!" My heart swelled. "I hope you may live forever!"

"Thank you, Athene." His voice was grave, but his eyes twinkled. "Of course, given my line of work, I would have to consider that eventuality somewhat problematic."

My laughter rang through the parlor, but no one seemed to mind.

We carried the body of Jean-Claude with a solemn, quiet rite and laid him to rest in the Convent of Saint Bonaventure on Palatine Hill. There was no pomp and a great deal of peace in that quiet ceremony. Isabel stood by the grave for a long time afterward, with Brother Leopold beside her, his eyes closed and his lips moving in prayer.

I never asked about the disposal of the remains of Marcus Zoran. My questions were of a different nature.

"Why did he come to me?" I asked Father Thomas Edmund. "I know he thought me of little consequence, another pawn in his plan, but why bother?"

"He was striving to draw Isabel to him," he explained, "to the place and time of the sacrifice. To do that, he had to work to remove her from safety, a safety of which you were increasingly a part. Perhaps he thought he could tempt you. I do not know. He has tried to manipulate the world to bring about his goals. In the end, he was baffled by the one thing he had not counted on."

"What was that?"

The priest smiled. "The goodness and common sense of Athene Howard."

My cheeks warmed with pleasure at the compliment. I mumbled my thanks. "I don't know that I made that much of a difference, really."

"Well, Athene, let us consider the point. If you had been, as planned, a victim in the fire that killed your father, or murdered by gypsies, or devoured by werewolves, what would have been the fate of Isabel upon the Aventine Hill?"

I shivered. "Do you suppose he will come back again?"

"My father?" asked Isabel. I had not noticed that she had entered the room. "No, he will not."

I looked to Father Thomas Edmund. He shook his head.

"But how can you be sure?"

"It is my business to be sure about such things," he said.

"But will it make any difference? He said we could not undo the things he had done. He said that nothing we did would spare the world from the destruction he has wrought. Is that true? Is there not evil everywhere?"

"The world is fallen," Father Thomas Edmund smiled, "and death has been vanquished through the Cross."

I spent more time in the church, however, beseeching God and all the saints, principally the Blessed Virgin Mary, to ensure that this time, death would retain its hold on that particular soul.

We also had to attend to the business of those outside the cloister walls. A formal complaint was made to the Carabinieri, and I was subjected to a few interviews regarding the actions of gypsies formerly encamped amidst the Roman Ghetto. Tiena and her followers had not remained to chance the ire of Marcus Zoran.

"Will they be sought?" I asked the inspector as he prepared to depart.

The inspector held his wide bicorne in his hands and shrugged. Though he did not say it, his attitude conveyed the Ministry of the Interior's indifference to the activities of gypsies who had already fled the country. The murder of Father Pierre was troubling, but it too would pass without official comment or, more likely, be so drowned in paperwork as to be forgotten.

The day before Isabel and Sister Agatha were to leave for Calais and return home across the Atlantic, the three of us joined the friars for Vespers. Sir Simon also joined us, flouting every caution and command, with his bandaged arm still in its sling.

Before the prayer began, a single figure walked slowly forward. Brother Vincent threw himself to the ground. "Mea culpa. *Peccavi*," he cried. *"Domine miserere mei!"*

The community seemed untroubled and continued with the psalms. Brother Vincent remained there, facedown upon the floor. At the end of prayers, the prior of the house, a kind and possibly addled old friar named Father Lawrence, came up and spoke to the prostrate figure. Brother Vincent rose at his bidding, and Father Lawrence clasped the Frenchman in his arms.

"What will happen to him?" I whispered to Father Thomas Edmund when we were outside again.

"God's will."

"But will his studies continue?"

"No, he means to abandon them."

"Isn't that unfortunate?"

"I suppose that depends upon what you consider fortunate, Athene."

I frowned. "It seems a severe penance."

"Sometimes that is the principal mark of the living reality of the Spirit."

"What is?"

"Denial."

I could not follow him but feared to ask anything further.

Now the farewells came in rapid succession. Father James, restored to his persona as a grave-faced, administrative keeper of the books, bade us all Godspeed. Only when he parted from Father Thomas Edmund did the hint of mischief return to his eyes. "Send for me anytime you need me. I'm always happy to help with your theatrics, Thomas Edmund."

"You are, as always, an asset, James," replied Father Thomas Edmund with an answering twinkle.

As the white-robed figure made his way down from Santa Sabina, we saw two visitors approaching: an elderly man with long gray hair, a thick white beard, and a cane, and a little boy, perhaps four years of age, with a halo of black curls about his head. The little boy was torn between the support of one elderly hand and careful bearing of a precious burden upon his back. Their progress was slow and wove back and forth across the road, but they appeared untroubled by their lack of speed—pilgrims for whom there is nothing so imperative as each slow step toward their goal.

They came and stood before us at the door of the church, both making a low obeisance toward Father Thomas Edmund. Without speaking, they looked beyond to where Brother Philip stood, his arms folded behind the scapular of his habit.

Noting their attention, he stepped forward. "Can I be of service, Signore?"

The old man tapped his ears and shrugged. Then he tapped the boy on the shoulder. The boy scrambled out of the straps of his burden and held it out wordlessly to the young friar—the hard, black case of a musical instrument. "*Il mandolino*," bellowed the old man, as if we and not he were deaf.

Brother Philip, his eyes shining, spoke his thanks in broken but eager Italian.

The old man merely nodded and gestured toward the case. "Play! Play!"

Settling himself upon the steps of the church, Brother Philip produced his new instrument, a beautiful piece of wood and string, and began plucking to learn its mysteries. As I returned to my guest room in the monastery, I could hear the echo of his minstrel voice singing of the vengeful, flesh-eating undead, to the delight of his audience.

It was at this much-belated moment that I began to wonder what would happen to me. Where would I finally come to rest? I had not entertained the thought for some time. Now it rushed back upon me with renewed force. Everything was being quietly, methodically handled. Who would take care of Athene Howard, without country, without family, and without funds? I endeavored to thrust the idea away, for I clung to the vague expectation of "work" emerging for me so I could earn my keep, but the question lingered on the fringes of my mind and brought a new, almost constant sickness in the pit of my stomach.

Finally the day came when I gathered my few belongings and departed by train with Sister Agatha, Isabel, Father Thomas Edmund, and Sir Simon, retracing our steps to the French coast.

Memories flooded upon me as we went. Memories of my father. Zagreb. Paris. Tournai. The fire. The gypsies. As I stared out the window of the train at the disappearing countryside, my reflection stared back. A distant and lost memory stirred—the young woman, Athene Howard, who had stumbled her way into this adventure, among this strange, wondrous band.

I turned and considered them. Isabel's eyes were closed, but her fingers were moving on the beads at her waist. Sister Agatha, still regal despite the stark lines of exhaustion on her face, looked as if she had aged several decades in our adventures. She gazed off into the middle distance, though her hand too moved along her own set of beads.

Father Thomas Edmund, distracted by a bit of soot that had intruded behind his spectacles, failed to give me the reassuring smile I had come to expect from him. But Sir Simon, sans bandages but his arm still retained in a sling, was looking at me. He bestowed a wry grimace, which was sufficient.

Settling back into my seat, I closed my eyes and endeavored to remove all thought from my mind. Sleep was too elusive, but I could imitate the women beside me. Stumbling even in my mind, I began the measured repetition of *Aves*.

The miles passed more rapidly than I wished. All too soon, we found ourselves standing amid the bustle and noise of the dock, beside the ship that would restore Isabel and Sister Agatha to their proper home.

"Will you not be lonely?" I asked. "Or bored?"

Isabel smiled—such a gentle, sweet, serene smile. The smile of one who has passed through the long, harsh illness and sees the relief of final rest approaching. I wondered how perilously close she had been to damnation. I wondered how easily she could have brought destruction down upon all our heads. Was the religious life her form of penance? Like Mihai, would she sacrifice her life to atone for past sins?

"Oh, Athene, I shall miss you." She clasped my hands in hers—the closest thing to a caress of which she seemed capable. She curtsied farewell to Sir Simon then turned to Father Thomas Edmund and bowed her head to receive his blessing.

"God bless you, child." Sister Agatha bent and kissed my cheek. She had taken a few steps away when she stopped, hesitated, then stalked stiffly back. "Your father was a good man. A dear friend. I always mourned his loss. Do not fear that I shall forget to pray for him—or for you." Then she kissed me again and rejoined Isabel.

We watched them walk across the gangway and onto the ship. The two women turned in a final farewell and waved. I saw them standing, silhouetted against the skyline, just as I had first seen Isabel in the company of Sir Simon so many long months before. Then they were gone.

We walked slowly back to the carriage together.

"When will you return to England?" I asked the priest.

"When I am finished with the library," he replied. "When I am in London again, you must come and see me."

I nodded but wondered if such a thing were likely. Why would I go to England? I had no one and nothing to draw me there. My heart returned to its new place in the pit of my stomach. I wished I had an apple. Or some peppermint.

As Sir Simon helped me into my seat, Father Thomas Edmund said, "Oh dear! I seem to have mislaid my umbrella! How thoughtless! Wait for me for a moment, my dears."

As we waited, I glanced uncertainly at Sir Simon. He was looking off through the window after the ship, a small smile upon his face.

"I suppose you will return to your home now," I said.

"Yes," he agreed. "I suppose I shall."

"I wonder what will become of me."

"That *is* a question," he acknowledged without exhibiting much concern—the beast.

"I suppose I could go as a secretary to a scholar. There might be some of my father's colleagues who would be willing to recommend me."

"Likely so." Sir Simon smiled. "You would be valuable to any scholar."

"I really am quite knowledgeable about many things." This awkward echo of commendations my father had received in his professional career rang flat upon my own ear.

"You have been exposed to a great deal," he agreed.

Hateful, horrid, unfeeling man. "I was helpful to all of you."

"When you weren't being an absolute bother, you were sometimes remotely of assistance."

"I think I would make a wonderful secretary."

"I don't have experience of secretaries, so I am not a good authority on such things."

"My shorthand is excellent."

"I am sure it is. Your father's friends would be well served."

"Or I could be a governess." I warmed to my tragic theme. "Or even a housekeeper. I'm not good at housekeeping—well, I haven't had much opportunity to practice—but I did try to keep my father's things in order. And Sister Agatha let me help in the kitchen for a time."

"Perhaps becoming a secretary is a better idea."

"Life…can have meaning," I insisted, "even for those who are alone."

"Father Thomas Edmund says that the years from thirty to eighty can be long and desolate for the childless."

My heart sank even deeper into the pit of my stomach, and I envisioned a bleak, lonely life of no adventures, no happiness, no hope.

"Of course," said Sir Simon, "there is one other possibility." He folded me into an enthusiastic, one-armed embrace and soundly kissed me.

When I could breathe, I called him a heartless brute.

He laughed and called me a foolish darling.

"You are always lamenting my unmaidenlike frankness, but when it comes to lovemaking, you're dreadfully uncooperative."

"I think I'm cooperating with manly prowess, considering my incapacitated arm." He kissed me again. This time I was prepared. After what I thought sufficient encouragement, I moved to push him away. He groaned and felt his wounded shoulder.

"Did I hurt you?" I cried.

"Desperately." He moved his free arm to encircle my waist. "This notion of a secretary is timely. I shall need assistance in that quarter until my arm is healed."

"You do not write with that hand, do you?"

"Don't bother me with unimportant details."

"Perhaps I could write. I know one fascinating story at least—"

"My wife will not waste her time writing Gothic nonsense."

"Your wife will do what she pleases," I replied. "And you haven't asked me. All you've done is say rude things and offer presumptuous embraces. I think I would write it all very well—"

"I have no choice but to marry you, unless I am prepared to face the full fury of the offended Church on your behalf. It's either you or excommunication."

I was about to make a spirited retort to this unloverlike comment when a shadow appeared at the door of the carriage.

Father Thomas Edmund Gilroy beamed at us. "Well, that's settled. Bless you, my children. May I come into the carriage now? I promise to be the most gracious and sleepy of chaperones."

And, sweet man, he was, as usual, true to his promise.

FINIS.

Acknowledgments

Many thanks to all who assisted in research and all early readers, including Jean-Michel Potin, OP, Archivist of the Dominican Province of France; Eamonn Gaines, former lecturer at Queen's University of Belfast; innumerable Dominican friars; and, of course, the incomparable editorial team of Karen Ullo and Rhonda Ortiz, who entered into the spirit of the novel with glorious enthusiasm.

About the Author

In addition to scholarly pursuits, Eleanor Bourg Nicholson occasionally strays into fiction, including her epistolary novella, *The Letters of Magdalen Montague* (Kauffmann Publishing, 2011; Chrism Press, 2021), and her Gothic novels, *A Bloody Habit* (Ignatius Press, 2018) and *Brother Wolf* (Chrism Press, 2021). A former assistant executive editor for *Dappled Things*, she is assistant editor for the *Saint Austin Review* (StAR) as well as the editor of several Ignatius Critical Editions of the classics. Her writing has appeared in the *National Catholic Register, Touchstone, First Things, The Catholic Thing, The Imaginative Conservative,* and elsewhere.

By day, Eleanor is the resident Victorian literature instructor at Homeschool Connections and with her husband homeschools their five children. By night, she reads the Victorians, writes Gothic novels, and cares for feral offspring.

Made in United States
North Haven, CT
22 December 2022

29952468R00212